For anyone who is struggling to find the person they are meant to be:

Keep searching, you'll find them.

"And into the forest I go,
to lose my mind and find my soul."

– *John Muir*

Theme Song:

Power Over Me — Dermot Kennedy

Playlist:

Afterall — Beartooth
The Enemy — I Prevail
Crazy — From Ashes to New
See Through — The Band CAMINO
Rescue Me — A Day To Remember, Marshmello
Why Am I Like This? — The Word Alive
Tapping Out — Issues
You Found Me — The Fray
Hard Feelings — Palisades
Heavier — Slaves
Talking Body — Five Hundredth Year
Loverboy — You Me At Six
in the dark — Bring Me The Horizon
Broken Heart — Escape the Fate
Contagious Chemistry — You Me At Six
Part Of Me — American Wolves
Popular Monster — Falling In Reverse
Like a Nightmare — Deadset Society
If Our Love Is Wrong — Calum Scott
Pavement — SayWeCanFly
Hated — Beartooth
Right Here — Ashes Remain
Iris — Goo Goo Dolls

Listen to the playlist on Spotify

Preface

I'd like to start by thanking you from the bottom of my heart for picking this book up in the first place and being willing to give it a shot. It means the world to me that readers are interested in the world I've created and the words I've written.

However, the first thing I have to state is this book will not be for everyone. This book is a work of fiction, but that does not mean that there aren't very realistic incidents that could be triggering to some readers.

Consider this a blanket trigger warning.

This book is meant to go in *blind*. I've purposely written the blurb to reveal absolutely nothing about the overall plot of this book. I recommend not to read spoilers, if only for you to receive the full impact of the book in both a plot and emotional aspect.

This being said, if you have any triggers, **any at all,** I would suggest reaching out to me or someone you know to ask if you will be okay reading this book, or visit my website to see the list of potential triggers. Or maybe giving this book a pass altogether.

Only you know what your limitations are. Please proceed with caution.

www.authorcericci.com/content-warnings/

Follow the River contains content intended for mature adults 18+ years of age. Some of the content will be triggering for readers.

PROLOGUE

His breaths come out in fast pants as he tosses a duffle bag on the bed. Throwing open the closet doors and yanking the drawers out of his dresser, he fills the duffle in record time. He doesn't stop in the bathroom for the rest of his stuff, knowing he can buy what he needs when he gets where he's going.

Panic tries to flood his veins, but he tamps it down. This isn't the time for hysteria.

Slamming his apartment door behind him, he rushes down the stairwell, car keys in hand. Before long, he's situated behind the steering wheel, ready to disappear into the night.

Hopefully, without a trace.

He's counting on no one noticing he's gone, but deep down he knows his prayers will go unanswered.

His God, if he even exists, doesn't answer the prayers of sinners.

And a sinner, he is.

Driving through the silence of the night, he heads to the airport. His foot presses onto the gas with more force than it should, the car accelerating to dangerous speeds.

But he doesn't care.

Time is of the essence, and if he doesn't leave now, it might be too late.

The world as he knows it is on the line.

He *has* to leave.

In less time than should be possible, he throws his car into park on the tarmac. It's the only way anyone will be able to track him, but at this point, he doesn't have any other options.

His pilot, one he keeps on standby, is already in the cockpit when he comes rushing up the stairs.

"Are we ready to take off?"

"Yes, sir. Just waiting for the okay from air traffic controls. Please take a seat. If luck is on our side, we'll be in the air in less than five minutes."

Luck.

Sending up a silent plea, he begs for luck to be on his side tonight.

For tomorrow, or however long he needs it.

Because he knows the harsh reality of this situation—and it's life or death.

ONE
Rain

FIVE MONTHS EARLIER

"*In other breaking news, Pennsylvania Senator — Theodore Anders — has been brought into police custody for interrogation involving an alleged rape and molestation of a minor,*" the newscaster drones from the television in the waiting room.

"*Two weeks ago, voice recordings surfaced of a minor, disclosing information on the senator, accounting for the incidents in which Ted Anders forced the child into sexual acts against his or her will. The Federal Bureau of Investigation is looking into these recordings and is in search of the child in question. The identity of said minor is remaining confidential until more information is gathered to support these claims.*"

My shaking leg halts as my eyes snap up at the monitor, seeing a photo of the man they're speaking about.

A fucking senator, for Christ's sake. Someone in charge of making decisions for the welfare of our country.

A fucking rapist and child molester.

I turn my attention back to my phone, doing my best to drown out the sounds of the news and all the bullshit they spew. One way or another, news stations are always biased, which is why I can't stand watching.

Our country is constantly in a state of turmoil. School shootings. Sex trafficking scandals. Terrorism, either domestic or foreign. Police brutality. People with power, abusing children. Sexually or otherwise.

I don't need the news to tell me the world we live in has gone to shit. It's present on every form of social media, where people will post whatever they feel like, without bothering with things like research or fact checking. But why would they bother attempting to educate themselves when they can simply post whatever they want, hidden behind a phone or computer screen, without fear of any backlash unless it comes from a comment thread.

"Ciaráin, are you ready?" the receptionist calls my name, pulling me from my thoughts.

As ready as I'll fucking ever be.

Pocketing my phone, I follow her through a door and down a hall to an office, where she stops. She motions me to enter with a smile before retreating back the way she came.

Twisting the knob, I push open the door, spotting a woman who appears to be in her early forties sitting in a lounge chair, notepad and file folder in hand, scribbling away. I take a moment to observe her before she notices me. Dressed in a pencil skirt, blue blouse, and pumps, she fits the cliché of a female therapist, just *looking to help.* A Birkin bag sits on her desk across the room, and when she uncrosses and resituates her long tan legs, I notice the familiar red soles of her shoes.

Rich bitch.

Her blonde hair, hanging loose around her shoulders, sways as her head pops up at the sound of the door closing behind me. Her eyes, bluer than any I've ever seen, lock onto mine, and she smiles.

It does nothing to permeate my scowl.

"You must be Ciaráin. I'm Doctor Erica Fulton," she says before standing, reaching out to shake my hand.

Ignoring her, I stride over to the couch opposite her chair and take a seat.

Let the games begin.

To her credit, she doesn't seem perturbed about my brush off, just sits back down in her seat. She's probably dealt with worse, being a therapist and all.

Fucking *therapy.*

"Well, Ciaráin, are you ready to get started?" she asks, flipping her notepad to a clean sheet. She glances up when I don't respond. Taking my silence as permission to speak, she continues, "All right, then. Usually, I start my first session going over some basic information with you. The topics you would normally talk about with your previous therapist, that kind of thing. Get a little more comfortable talking with each other before we dive into the heavier issues."

I remain silent, staring at her, a mask of indifference on my face.

Actually, scratch that. That's just my face.

"Let's start with the big, ominous question. What brings you in today?"

I have to force my eyes not to roll as I lean back in the seat with my fingers resting against my temple.

I was forced by my cunt of a mother. She decided, out of the blue, she wanted to be a decent human being. For fuck's sake, I had to take it upon myself to ask Nana to schedule a therapy appointment when I was a kid, since Mom was too busy self-medicating to notice I was drowning. But now, she has an interest in my mental health? My fucking happiness?

Blink.

"According to your file and the notes from your previous therapist, you've been in therapy for about nine years, starting at the age of twelve. You were diagnosed with depression and PTSD, and have been on and off a wide range of antidepressants for seven of those years, correct?"

Yes, yes, and fucking yes. Except, you missed the anxiety. Fear of abandonment. The fact that I never took a single one of those pills because I don't need some chemical trying to turn me into someone I'm not.

Blink.

"Your file also states you've had suicidal ideations, but have never made any attempts. Is that still correct?"

Hearing those words, *suicidal ideations,* brings the night rushing back to me.

The empty bottle of Jameson. The mirror, dirty with white powder residue left behind from the cocaine.

The barrel of a gun pressed into my temple.

My finger on the trigger.

I bury the thoughts inside my mind, breathing deeply through my nose.

Nope, Doc. Can't say that's correct.

Blink.

"Tell me about your childhood."

I snort involuntarily.

Is this bitch serious? What fucking childhood? You have my file right in front of you. You know, while I might have come from money, my childhood was stripped away from me by the people who were supposed to be in charge of protecting my innocence.

She lets out a subtle sigh, flipping her notepad closed. I'll give her credit, she lasted longer than I figured she would. Most would've given up when I refused to shake their hand.

"Look, Ciaráin, I'm here to help you. I can't do that if you don't talk to me. Yes, we can sit in silence if that's what you need, but that isn't the point of therapy." She leans forward in her chair, her blue eyes softening around the edges. "I know you're going through a lot right now — "

"You don't know shit," I snap. "No one knows shit. And I'm so fucking sorry my last piece of shit, incompetent therapist somehow led you to believe you have any fucking clue about who I am or what I'm dealing with."

Dr. Fulton leans back in her chair, absorbing my outburst. "I apologize, I didn't mean to insinuate. All I want is to do my job, to help you. Will you let me do that?" Her words, her question, it comes out like a command.

I meet her eyes. She's got balls of steel, this one.

Briefly, I nod, allowing her to continue.

"All right, let's try another approach. Why don't we talk about your relationship with your family? No siblings, just a mother and father?"

"I have no father," I grind. "He died when I was a kid. I have my mother, if you can call her that, and the man she calls a husband." I meet her eyes with a hard stare, daring her to push me.

She accepts the challenge.

"Tell me about your stepfather."

"If you want to talk about him, you should set up a meeting with him. God knows the asshole needs a shrink way more than I do." I smirk, leaning forward in my seat. "After all, adding another client to your list can help you afford a matching wallet for that purse."

"I'm sorry, Ciaráin, but I don't believe that for one second. You might *want me* to believe it, but we both know there is so much more to you and your story with your parents than is in that tiny folder." She raises a brow. "So why don't you stop deflecting and start talking?"

My jaw ticks. "I'm not talking about him. Nor my mother."

"Okay," she concedes, shutting the folder. "Then what brings you to Colorado?"

"College," I reply, my annoyance easing.

"How is that going? I read in your file that you played football at Clemson for the past two years. Will you be playing for the Buffaloes this season?"

My brow furrows. "You really want to talk about football? No offense, but you don't seem like the type of woman to know a touchdown from a homerun." I make a point to let my eyes travel the length of her body, starting at her goddamn Louboutins and not meeting her eyes again, until after I make it a point to stare at her rack.

The way her nostrils flare tells me I'm right.

Flipping open the file again, she glances around the sheet. "Then tell me about Roman."

My blood freezes in my veins. "Off-fucking-limits."

She inhales deeply through her nose. "Enlighten me. What *are* we allowed to talk about in our sessions? The weather?"

I quirk a brow. Balls of steel and feisty too.

I'd be willing to bet my left nut she's a firecracker in bed. Not that I'm interested. I'm not a fan of being challenged.

Rising from my seat, I stare down at her. "I don't think we have anything to talk about, Dr. Fulton. I'd say I'm sorry for wasting your time, but we both know I don't actually give a shit."

I take my leave, heading back into the waiting room. My hand is already grabbing the door handle, ready to get the hell out of here when I hear Dr. Fulton behind me, calling my name.

"Ciaráin," I pause for a moment, my back to her. "You can't just walk out when you don't want to talk about the hard stuff."

"Fucking watch me," I challenge, turning sideways to catch her gaze. "Besides, I have practice in an hour. I only came to this appointment to appease my poor excuse of a mother. But please, do us both a favor and forget I ever came here." Nodding to the folder in her hand, I add, "Oh, and make sure you shred that damn file and set the pieces on fire the minute I'm gone."

Just as I'm turning back to the exit, my eye catches the television again, Senator Theodore Anders' image still taking up the prime time news spot.

I slam the door behind me in haste as I exit.

Fuckers like that man deserve to die.

TWO

River

"Lennox, get your ass over here!" Coach Scott barks at me through his megaphone from the opposite end of the field, cutting off my conversation with my backup quarterback, a redshirt freshman from Idaho by the name of Garrett. I let him know I'll be back shortly and start jogging over to Coach.

It's the first day of practice, and it's a scorcher here in Boulder for the first week of August. If I'm being honest, it's always hot as hell this time of year in Colorado, something I'm used to, being a native to the state. The temperature is reaching nearly one hundred degrees and the sun is blistering on my shoulders. Smoke still lingers in the air from the recent forest fires, but at least I can breathe outside without feeling as if I'm drowning in ash like a few weeks ago.

The fires every summer. They paint our clear blue sky with smoke and debris, clouding the view of the mountains almost entirely. Sometimes for months, like this past summer.

Instead of spending my weekends out in Crested Butte mountain biking or rock climbing in Estes Park, I was forced to stay inside, keeping my lungs safe from the toxins in the air.

So, the fact that I'm outside playing football right now? God, I'm thrilled. I was beginning to go damn near stir crazy being locked up in my apartment while the fires made it unsafe to be outside for extended periods of time. The only interaction I was having with my friends or family was coming from FaceTime and playing video games, and for an extrovert like myself, it was a nightmare.

I snap out of my reverie once I reach Coach Scott. He's a recently retired NFL running back from the Denver Broncos, now turned college-level coach right here at CU. He started coaching a couple years before my freshman year, a good chunk of the reason I decided to stay local for college, even when I was scouted and recruited by some of the best teams in the SEC and BIG-10.

He also happens to be a man I know extremely well, almost like a second father, seeing as he has known me since I was in diapers.

"Hey Coach," I say, pulling to a stop beside him. His eyes are hidden behind a pair of aviators, a ballcap on his head sporting the University's logo. He looks every bit the intimidating man the world sees him as. Ruthless, both on and off the field, never taking his eye off the ball.

Something he ingrained in not only his son, and my best friend, Taylor, from a young age, but in myself as well.

Don't lose focus, and the world is yours for the taking.

"River," Coach replies in a way of greeting. His eyes are still locked on the field where different players are practicing various drills.

"You have a new receiver."

My brows shoot up. This is news to me.

We've been trying to recruit another high caliber wide receiver since my freshman year, when Taylor decided to follow his gut and play baseball at University of Michigan instead of football here. He had options, since he's talented in both, but he decided to step from under his father's shadow and forge his own path, playing the game that called to his heart more. And while I miss playing with him, I respect the hell outta him for doing it.

Still, a new wide receiver is exciting. Andrew Benson has been one of my receivers for not only my time at CU, but also in high school. By now, we have pretty good on-field chemistry, especially since we've been great friends since childhood. But I can't always count on Drew; that's too predictable and unrealistic to rely on a single wide receiver all the time. I need someone else I can trust to go long and catch whatever I throw at them.

"Who is it?" I ask, my eyes searching the field for an unfamiliar form, number, anything. But the issue is we have plenty of new faces and practice uniforms on the field right now, since we lost quite a few players last year to either graduation or the NFL draft.

"Transfer from Clemson. Junior." Coach finally tosses me a glance. "He tossed up some very impressive yards last season. Could be our ticket to a bowl game this year if the two of you mesh on the same level you and Drew do."

I wrack my brain, trying to think of receivers from Clemson, but I come up blank. Keeping track of stats for other teams isn't high on my list of priorities, but *especially* if it's a team we never face during the season.

I roll my eyes at Coach before whipping my gaze over to where the wide receivers are running through single ladder drills with the running backs. I notice a couple new numbers in the mix, but none stand out. "You act as if I should just *know* who you're talking about. Again, I ask. Who?"

Instead of answering, Coach raises his megaphone to his lips. Covering my ears just in time, I hear a muffled, "*Grady, over here!*" shouted to who I'm assuming is my new wide receiver.

Grady? Doesn't ring any bells.

I watch as all the heads in the group snap up to look at us, except the one player running the ladder drill. No one moves to come our way, so that leaves one option on who must be Grady.

Number eighty-three.

His head is down, dark hair wet with sweat as he keeps his attention on his feet. He's laser-focused, moving with a profound amount of agility back and forth through the ladder. The ease in which he maneuvers his frame screams athleticism, and my heart pounds in my chest as I continue watching him stay zoned into his task.

Immediately, my brain latches onto the fact that he has every component to make the kind of receiver I prefer to work with. Not only because he is clearly built for this sport and is dedicated to honing his abilities, but there's *also* the fact that he will put his training as a higher priority than listening to the order to come over here while he was in the midst of a drill.

I even catch Drew nodding his approval at Grady disobeying Coach to finish out his drill.

This defiance for the sake of growth, it's something only Drew and his twin brother, Elliott, and I know will gain the highest respect from Coach. It's a secret we keep from the rest of the team, hoping they learn it for themselves and earn that level of reverence from an NFL great like Graham Scott.

But this little trick is something we only learned by being raised with Coach Scott in our lives. If Taylor wasn't part of our friend group or our team back at Summit Academy, I don't think we would have been smart enough to figure it out.

But Grady somehow managed to do just that on his first damn day.

My eyes stay trained on number eighty-three as he works through the rest of the drill, not stopping until he hits his mark, and the offensive coach stops the time on his watch. The second he steps out of the ladder, his eyes snap up to look in our direction.

I'm unable to tell the color of his irises from here, but what I do know is whatever they are, they carry a lot of heat with them. I can feel them burning into me from fifty yards away as he bends to grab his helmet from the ground, only growing in intensity as he jogs closer to us.

Crossing my arms to watch him approach, I take in his tall, lean form. He might only be about an inch taller than my six-two, but his presence is loud, large, and dominating in itself, even at a distance. He's not built like a brick shithouse, seeing as he is made to run, but the skin of his arms and legs that are visible under his practice uniform are well defined and toned. Veins pop in his forearm from his grip on his helmet, bulging out from beneath his skin like a roadmap. At least, that's true on the skin that isn't completely covered in ink. Which is only the lower part of his left bicep.

When he pulls to a stop in front of me, I blow out a breath, because I do know who he is. I don't know how I didn't put the pieces together earlier when Coach mentioned his last name.

Because Ciaráin Grady has been throwing up astronomical stats the past two years at Clemson, being in the running for the Heisman both years.

And now, he's here at a college that isn't exactly known for its football.

Which begs the question...*Why?*

His attention is focused on Coach, not even giving me a second glance, when he says, "Coach?"

That one single word, sliding over me like a smooth, rich whiskey, has my stomach doing somersaults and backflips and every other gymnastic move in the book on an instant.

Coach grunts before nodding to me. "Grady, I'd like you to meet your QB. My hopes are you'll be able to mesh well together. Even despite the fact that you haven't played together the previous two years."

For the first time since he's stopped in front of us, his eyes leave our coach and zero in on my own. They're two deep pools of honey whiskey, the most distinct amber I've ever seen on a human. Seems fitting they match his voice.

"River Lennox," I tell him, ensnared by his gaze as I extend my hand to him. "The guys call me lots of shit besides that, though.

QB, Riv, Len. Whatever works."

Those golden eyes stay on mine as his own arm reaches out to shake my hand. But the second our palms touch, fingers wrapped around each other's hand, fire licks at my skin.

Actually, fire is putting it mildly. It's more like a bolt of lightning, zapping each and every nerve ending in my hand, sending shockwaves of electricity and heat coursing through every inch of my body. All from a simple handshake.

From the flare in his eyes before he quickly looks down at our joined hand, he feels it too. That is, before he drops my hand like it literally burned him, and his gaze returns to mine.

"Ciaráin Grady." He speaks his name slow and fluidly, sounding like *keer-en*.

When he doesn't say anything else, I quirk a brow. "Do you just go by Ciaráin?"

He smirks slightly. "I guess my old team used to call me G or Grady, so that would be fine too. You're welcome to come up with something else, so long as it's more creative than asshole or dickhead."

"Not asshole or dickhead. Duly noted." I nod in all seriousness. "Well, Garrett over there" — I point to my backup QB on the other side of the field — "goes by G, so for clarity's sake, I think I'll stick with Grady." I give him a wry smile before continuing, "But welcome to the team, man. I have to say, you transferring might be a gift from God. I've needed another stellar wide receiver for two years now."

"I aim to please, Len," he retorts. The way my nickname slips off his lips sends a shiver through me. I want to hear it again just so I can watch the way his lips form the letters as he says it.

My brain latches onto the single syllable like my life depends on it, and replays over in my mind on a loop in the span of only a second. As irrational as it is and no matter how much I don't understand it, I crave it. My name on his lips.

"Did you need anything else, Coach? Otherwise, I'm going to get back to it," Ciaráin asks him, flicking his gaze back to our coach.

"Not at all. Go finish up the drill," he replies, dismissing Ciaráin before tossing his chin at me. "And River, go get Garrett. Once they're done, I want to run some routes. Get you two used to each other as quickly as possible."

And that's where we are ten minutes later, running easy routes, easily getting the feel for each other's speed and playstyle. He's quick, very light on his feet, giving me the freedom to throw faster and for more yards than I normally would with another wide receiver. Hell, even Drew.

Simply put, our chemistry is off the fucking charts and it's got me all kinds of jacked up.

The next time it's his turn for a route, I give him a wicked grin before giving him the universal *go long* signal with my hand. I catch his smirk and subtle nod before stepping back into position. And then back further and further, until he's far enough away that I'm ready to let it fly.

And fly, it does. Sails down the field through the air, landing safely in Ciaráin's arms over halfway down the field.

I let out a holler, never feeling so high in my life. Ciaráin returns my excitement with a *whoop* from his spot down the field. And yeah, we both completely ignore Coach's glares from the sidelines. Though, if I know Coach Scott, he's secretly jumping up and down like a kid in a candy store on the inside.

Adrenaline is coursing through me and my hopes are through the roof for the season if this is the kind of shit we can do together on day one of practice. There's definitely no false hype around this guy's ability when it comes to football.

I could get used to this.

Ciaráin comes running up to me, panting slightly before tossing the ball into my hands from a few feet away. "Nice one, Len. Though, you think you could send it further next time? If I can break into the record books for receiving yard, there's no way I'm not getting the fucking Heisman this year." He gives me another smirk, one I'm noticing seems to be his signature. And before he turns to head back to the end of the line, he bites his lip and...winks at me.

And my heart drops to my stomach and out my ass.

Wait, what? Was he just...flirting with me?

I blink after him a couple times, and for the first time today, I let myself take a *good* look at him. The kind of look that, if this was a hundred years ago—hell, even *fifty* years ago—I could be beaten to death and strung up in the town square.

Okay, I might be slightly overdramatic, but I'm not far off.

But still, I stare at him, taking in his muscular thighs encased in his pants, the pads doing *everything* to make his ass look like a goddamn peach I'd give my left nut to take a bite into.

The way I'm studying him, it portrays...interest.

And interested, I fucking am.

Despite the rules I've put in place for myself regarding my

teammates, which are only two—don't look, and *definitely* don't touch—and despite the fact that I try to limit my hook-ups with the male population at CU…I'm fucking interested.

Really fucking interested.

My eyes take in his form again while he bullshits in line with Drew, letting Garrett have his run through with the receivers. His helmet is dangling from his fingertips, the pad of his thumb toying with the strap absently while he talks.

But even from ten yards away, I see his eyes dance with the same excitement that was taking hold of me not more than two minutes ago.

A thousand questions run through my head.

Is that glimmer there from the high of the game? Is this chemistry between us just from being two players in sync? Or is it something more than that? Does he feel this physical attraction too?

Is he also…into guys?

Fuck me.

This is the hardest part about being bisexual. Girls are *never* this hard to figure out, contrary to what straight men might think. All I have to do is flash my dimples and a heated smolder, and poof…their panties are gone. It's practically magic.

But with dudes, it's like trying to teach a monkey advanced statistics. In Spanish.

Case in point, I'm standing here gawking at this sexy as fuck wide receiver when I should be, I don't know, paying attention to the drills that we are running or talking to coaches or going over the playbook or literally *anything other than gawking at this sexy as fuck wide receiver.*

And for the entire practice, that's what I keep catching myself doing.

Watching. Sneaking glances. Flat out creeping on the guy to see if I can catch anything that will alert my gaydar if he might be down for a roll in the sheets.

And I don't need to be thinking with my dick on the field.

But those thoughts are only taken further the minute practice is over and he pulls his pads and practice jersey over his head in one fell swoop, revealing a glorious, sweaty chest, and a set of abs Ryan Gosling would be jealous of.

He's tanned and trim, ink covering his entire right arm in what looks to be some sort of Celtic design. The left forearm has a wing of maybe an eagle, two thick black bands circling about halfway up with a date in Roman numerals above them. He even has some words scripted on one side of his hips, running on the diagonal of his perfect cut V that tapers into his padded pants.

In short, he was crafted to be the downfall of any bisexual man, and *Jesus Christ,* I might be drooling.

No, seriously. I actually checked to be sure I wasn't.

And the second he lifts his arms — *how the* fuck *did I not notice those arms?* — to wipe the sweat from his forehead, his biceps *glowing* under the sun, I become insanely grateful these pants make it damn near impossible to pop a boner.

Yeahhhh...I'd definitely fuck the shit out of him.

"Good first practice, yeah?"

I jump at Coach's voice beside me, not realizing he had stepped up from behind me.

"Yeah, definitely." I cough, doing my best to remove my eyes that are currently superglued to Ciaráin's body. Which I cannot do. They are firmly cemented in place, memorizing the way every muscle twitches and flexes as he starts stretching himself out next to Drew.

Coach catches the direction of my gaze and lets out a laugh. "He's something, ain't he? We fell into some serious luck when he decided to transfer out here."

That he is, Coach. And hell yes we did.

But I just nod, keeping my eyes on Ciaráin.

"He's going to be one helluv an asset to this team. You two keep up the good work. Maybe get to know him on a personal level off the field."

How about biblically, Coach? Sound like something you'd be okay with?

"Absolutely," I respond instead, because yeah, Coach might know I bat for both teams, but it's not like we shoot the shit about that kind of thing.

Talk about awkward.

Coach pats me on the back in the way he has always done since I was playing peewee football with Taylor, Drew, and Elliott. "Hit the showers, kid. I'll see you in the morning." I glance at him as he walks away for a moment before my eyes find their way back to Ciaráin, who is rising to his feet and grabbing his pads to head into the locker room.

"Coach Scott doesn't mess around, even on the first day," he says as I head over to him, my feet carrying me closer to the object of my newest obsession.

"Nah, but would you expect anything less from someone with five rings?"

He shakes his head, half a smile peeking out, and I get my

first glimpse of his perfect, white teeth. "I suppose I shouldn't."

"You get used to it," I say, attempting to remove my eyes from his mouth. Shockingly enough, I'm able to, only for them to be caught by his eyes once again. "He's a tough nut to crack, but he's the definition of a teddy bear."

Ciaráin licks his lips and nods. "I can see that. But of course, we'll only be grateful for it down the road when we make it rain and bring the thunder on game day."

"Hell yeah we are, man." I add a laugh, but it feels forced. *Why am I nervous?* "Making it fucking rain."

My thoughts snag on that phrase.

Make it rain.

And for some reason…it reminds me of his name. I think I've seen it spelled before when they announced him for his Heisman nominations the past couple years.

Yeah, his name literally spells *rain*. With that weird little accent bullshit over the *a*, but still.

We start walking to the tunnel when the idea hits me. "Hey, why don't I call you Rain?"

His shoulders go rigid as soon as the last word leaves my mouth and those amber eyes flash up to mine. That fire is back in them again, except this time it burns with something like anger, causing me to freeze in place.

"Nah, man," he grinds out, shaking his head adamantly. "Not that one. Ciaráin is fine."

Then he walks off the field and through the tunnel without a backward glance, leaving me wondering what the hell I said wrong.

THREE

Rain

The door of the locker room closes behind me with a soft click as I make my way over to my cubby to start getting dressed for the game. First game of the season, to be exact.

The state of the art locker room is seemingly empty, which I'm glad for. Whenever it was a home game while I played for Clemson, and even in prep school, I always tried to be the first one in to suit up, giving myself a little bit of extra time to get into the right headspace.

I also prefer to dress without an audience of eighty other men, even though it's not like they *watch*.

But as I round the corner, I find River Lennox, our QB, sitting on the bench inside his cubby about halfway down the wall. The guy is pretty cool, and a damn good quarterback too. Almost making this transfer worthwhile.

I have to admit, we've been fire on the field together in practice.

Nearly unstoppable, even if we've only been playing together for three short weeks. All that does is give me hope for a successful season, though.

At least that's hope for *something,* seeing as football is just about the only damn thing getting me out of bed in the morning.

I pull to a stop and watch River, dressed only in a pair of running shorts, leaning forward with his elbows on his knees. His arms are crossed over his legs, and I watch as he taps his left hand absently on his right knee in a sporadic rhythm, the arm flexing with the movement, causing the few tattoos there to ripple.

He's not wearing headphones, at least not that I can tell from here, so I call out to him, "If you're trying to keep a steady beat, practicing to become a drummer or some shit, I hate to break it to you, man, but you're in for a world of disappointment."

River's head immediately snaps up at the sound of my voice, as if startled to find himself no longer alone. He recovers quickly, just like on the field, and lets out a laugh.

"Definitely not looking to join a band. I prefer to march to the beat of my own drum, anyway." He grins before standing up and turning back to his cubby, pulling out his padded pants.

"Then what were you doing? Having a damn seizure?" I hold my hand to my chest and gasp. "You don't have like some... nerve disorder, do you? Because dude, I am aiming for a damn ring this year and we can't get one when our quarterback has a twitchy hand."

He lets out another throaty laugh before grabbing a ball out of his locker and tossing it at me. Which I, of course, catch with ease.

"Fuck off, Grady. I was mentally playing a song, okay?"

I throw the ball back into his waiting hands, my brows furrowing. "*Mentally* playing a song? As opposed to actually listening to it?"

He spins the ball in his palms, comfortable as hell with the damn thing in his large hands, and smiles as if I caught him with his hands in the cookie jar. "I do it a lot when I'm nervous. Anxious. Or, I mean, just in general sometimes. I dunno. I think of my favorite song of the day or week, the one I can't stop listening to or thinking about, and tap my hand to the words. Somehow, it calms me. Like a coping mechanism or whatever." He shrugs, as if it's the most normal thing in the world.

I nod, thinking about it. We all have our ways of dealing with stress. Life. Whatever works for him to get his head in the game, I guess.

"What one is it today, if you don't mind me asking?"

A wide grin spreads over his face. "'Afterall' by Beartooth, though that's usually my theme song before every game. The chorus, hell, the whole thing, it kind of hits deep. Makes me remember I've got it good. Even if I screw up on the field, it's a small problem to have in comparison to the shit people deal with on the daily." He shakes his head, realizing his small tangent. "Sorry, I can go on about them all day since they're kind of my favorite band in general."

Pulling out my phone, I bring up my Spotify app and type in the song. "You mind?" I ask before hitting play. He shakes his head and turns back to his cubby, pulling on his socks, then trading his shorts for the pants.

I start getting dressed myself, letting the sound of the song play out into the silence of the locker room. It's really good too. The beat and the sound, both are phenomenal for getting pumped before a game or work out or something.

But the lyrics, the meaning behind the words, laced with understanding of what it's like to live with mental illness…it sets me on edge.

All because of one fucking line.

Head on the ground and my thoughts on the ceiling.

A cold chill runs down my spine and my knuckles blanch from gripping the wooden shelf of my cubby. Instantly, I'm taken back to that night.

The sweat running down my face.

The cool barrel of the gun.

My finger twitching on the fucking trigger.

"I'm gonna have it stuck in my head on the field now." He laughs, tossing on a cut-off tee and sitting back in his cubby, leaning against the wood frame. His words effectively pull me from my memories before the demons have a chance to sink their claws in too deep for me to climb back out.

Clearing my throat, I quickly exit the app and toss my phone down to my side. "I'd happily turn on something else for you," I give him a half smirk, attempting to cover my unease. "Perhaps 'Baby Shark' would be a better choice?"

River groans before laughing again, the sound echoing out into the still empty locker room. "Hell no, that shit lived in my brain on repeat for months."

"'Barbie Girl', then?"

His grin is huge, and I have to admit, it's a good look on him. Especially the dimples that pop in his cheeks I'm sure the girls have wet dreams about. "You always such a fucking dick?"

"Only on the days ending in *y*," I reply dryly.

He shakes his head, but he's still smiling. "Well, if you decide you aren't going to be such a douchewaffle, let me know. There's an after-party, post-game. We aren't really *supposed* to go, but it's still early enough in the season that we can get away with it. You should come, get to know the guys a little more off the field." He gives a nonchalant shrug. "Or not. It's your call."

I nod, thinking over his offer. It would be nice, spending time with the team. Making some actual connections with the guys instead of sitting at home in my apartment, always painting or drawing or doing homework.

I don't think I've had actual *friends* since… high school. When I had Siena and Roman, the fraternal twins I grew up with from the age of eight. But the day they both left to move on with their lives after graduating, leaving me behind for another year at Foxcroft Hall, I was officially on my own.

And I've been that way ever since, never allowing anyone to get close enough.

It's time to change that, though. I'm sick of living my life without any semblance of human connection deeper than a one-night stand or a teammate I only connect with on the football field. And River is a cool enough guy from what I can tell. Always happy and smiling, and he seems genuinely nice.

"I'm in," I tell him, just as the door to the locker room opens and a few guys start pouring in.

It'll be nice to have River as a friend after years of being so fucking alone.

"I know you seem like an introvert, man. But I promise you, these Tri Delta after-parties are the ones you don't want to miss," River tells me as we pass through the threshold of one of the sorority's off-campus party houses. As soon as we enter, I'm overwhelmed by the pounding base of A Day to Remember and Marshmello's "Rescue Me," which is surprising because I would never expect these sorority types to be down with ADTR.

River claps his hand on my shoulder, immediately causing me to stiffen at the contact, but it quickly subsides. He nods at a few people as he leads me over to the keg in the middle of the living room. The girl manning the keg, a thin little blonde with a rack most guys would die for, hands River a solo cup filled to the brim with the foamy liquid.

"Don't you normally have to buy in for a cup at parties like this?" I shout in his ear after the girl hands me my own cup of beer.

He goes to respond, but the music is actually shaking the entire house, so I can't hear him.

"I can't hear you," I motion with my hands by tapping my ear.

He smiles—the fucker is always smiling—leaning into my space in order for me to catch what he says this time. "Football perks," he yells, his lips practically brushing my ear, causing me to shudder.

I pull away quickly, taking a sip of my beer to hide my unease and simply nod as I swallow it down.

Honestly, it's lukewarm and tastes like shit. And the music is already starting to cause my brain to throb behind my eyes.

Why did I come here again?

Oh, that's right. I decided to make *friends* this year.

Sigh.

I'm already starting to regret my decision.

River leans over again and yells, "I'll be back," before crossing the living room, weaving his way through the throng of dancing bodies and into the open kitchen where he wraps an arm around a pretty brunette. Curvy in all the places a woman should be.

I make my way away from the commotion, toward the stairs leading to the second floor, and find a spot to people-watch against the wall.

I'm not one for large crowds and lots of noise, so this is pretty much a goddamn nightmare, but at least I can watch a bunch of drunken idiots be…well, drunken idiots.

After a few minutes, one of our cornerbacks, Elliott Benson, slides up beside me. He's got his own cup in hand and a brooding expression on his face as he leans back against the wall beside me.

Well. Wait.

If he's brooding, it might be his twin brother, Drew. You'd think I'd be able to tell them apart, seeing as I practice and work out with Drew every single day as the two starting wide receivers for the team.

But alas…

"Hey, man," I say, and I'm grateful as hell the music has somehow toned down a bit. Either that or I've gained super-hearing.

Elliott slash Drew gives me a *sup* nod, taking a drink of his beer, his eyes searching the dance floor, as if he was looking for someone, which doesn't help narrow down who is next to me.

He looks at me, his blue eyes piercing me, and he smirks. "You have no damn idea who I am, do you?"

I huff out a laugh. "That fucking obvious?"

He shakes his head and rubs the back of his neck. "It's a blessing and a curse, that's for sure. Caused plenty of issues between me and Drew, though. We aren't exactly on speaking terms currently because of it."

Ah, so it is Elliott.

I suppose the VANS on his feet could have given him away, since Drew is always talking about his damn Adidas Ultra Boosts like they are God's gift to the planet.

"You're brothers, you'll always figure it out," I tell him, even though I have no damn clue if that's the truth. You have to actually *have* a family in order to know shit about how they work.

The only twins I know are Siena and Roman, and they were always at each other's throats, but somehow, they always made up. They were exact opposites, but still consistently remained half of a greater whole, and they knew that. Time after time, they would throw shade at each other, but then turn around and defend their sibling against anyone who dared to cross the other.

From what I've seen, the twin bond is the strongest thing in the damn world. I swear, they could feel each other's physical and mental pain as if it was their own. I've witnessed it. So, if Si and Ro fought so bad they weren't speaking?

Shit. It would be like tearing their souls in half and expecting them to figure out how to survive.

I can't imagine it would be much different for Elliott and Drew.

"I do know one thing, even if Drew would never say it aloud, much less to me these days, but he's jealous as fuck you're here."

His words cause my brows to furrow in confusion. That doesn't make sense. Drew and I both play at the same time, so it's not like I took his starting position or anything.

Elliott must read my face because he laughs. "You just have such a good in with our QB," he says, motioning toward River across the room. He's got his arm slung around the shoulders of the little brunette from earlier, and she's got hers curled around his waist. "Though it looks like you have some competition with Abbi over there."

Competition?

I frown so hard, I swear my face might get stuck in this position. "What are you talking about?"

"Aren't you and Riv..." He trails off, glancing between me and the quarterback in question. "...like, together or whatever?"

If I was drinking my nasty beer, this would be a good moment for a spit take.

I gape at him. "W-what?" I stutter, horrified.

"Dude, it's no big deal. Love is love and all that. Or in this case, fucking is fucking, maybe? As long as it doesn't negatively impact our season, Coach isn't going to say anything. But the way you two connect on the field? I mean, shit. We're going to dominate this season. Whatever it is you two are doing together, keep it up."

My teeth clench together and I'm almost positive they are going to wind up as finely ground powder. "We're not doing *anything* together besides playing football. I'm not gay and clearly—" I point over to River, who just kissed the top of Abbi's head, "—he isn't, either."

Elliott laughs and gives me another smirk, delight dancing in his eyes. "You really don't know?"

"Know what, Elliott? Jesus Christ, stop being fucking cryptic," I snap.

"Lennox bats for both teams, Grady. Everyone knows that."

Bats for both teams?

I must say the words out loud because Elliott lets out yet another loud, irritating laugh. "I know you're a football player, but please tell me you got the idiom. He's *bisexual,* dude."

Ice freezes everything inside of me as my eyes whip back to focus on River. He's still wrapped up with Abbi, looking cozy as hell. As if sensing my gaze, his eyes rise and meet mine. A grin crosses his face, exposing a set of dimples deep enough to see from across the room.

No, there's no way.

Keeping my eyes locked on his teal ones, I grind out, "Are you sure?"

"As sure as I am that the sky is blue. I've known the guy since we were like eight, seeing as we went to prep school at Summit Academy together. It's never been much of a secret after he came out his freshman year."

As Elliott speaks, River gives me a curious look, his head cocking slightly and mouths "What?" to me from across the room, to which I shake my head, and turn my attention back to Elliott.

"I'm not... we're not... fuck, *no,*" I stumble through the

words, not sure where the hell I'm trying to go with them or if they're even meant for Elliott or more for myself.

Bisexual? What?

"That might be true, man. I promise, I do believe you. But the way he's looking at you right now?" Elliott says as he glances up to River, then shakes his head. "It's somewhere between eye-fucking and a predator ready to devour its next meal."

My eyes immediately flick back to River, and I'm horrified to find Elliott is right. I catch River's eyes making a full sweep of my body, taking their time rising back to my face after pausing over any part of my body he would most likely love to see naked.

And when the guy finally realizes I've caught him blatantly checking me out? He doesn't blush or show any signs of embarrassment.

No, he just tosses his head back in a laugh, only to aim his dimpled grin and penetrating gaze back to me to fucking *wink...* before returning his attention to the girl beside him.

Like it never *fucking* happened.

As if him literally eye-fucking me isn't infuriating enough, my blood practically begins boiling when I realize...I'm *jealous* of the girl who seems to be taking his time.

Which makes no sense in the slightest because, uh, *I'm not into dudes.*

The headache that was starting to form behind my eyes earlier is only building in pressure with this new revelation. Rubbing my neck, I take a deep breath as I do my best not to completely lose my shit.

River is bi. He just checked me out. He's been nothing but friendly

to me since we've met, but never hinting he was into me. I've never felt
so welcomed onto a team, thanks to him, but is it because of attraction?
Or because he actually gives a shit about the team meshing well?

Fuck me.

My thoughts are blazing through my brain at a million miles per hour, and I can't seem to wrap my mind around how I got myself into this kind of situation.

But then I realize something.

I should have known better than to be willing to attempt friendship with anyone at this place, or even in general, ever again. I've never been a good friend, even back in high school when I had the twins.

Thinking of them brings a tightness to my chest. Siena and Roman were everything to me; they'll never be replaced. I still frequently talk to Siena, even if it's only through text messaging a couple times a month. I know she's busy going to school at University of Michigan. But that doesn't mean I don't love her, miss her, or think about her on almost a daily basis.

Or even Roman, regardless of the state I left our friendship in on the night before he left for college. The night he made a move I never saw coming, and it led our friendship to a turning point we wouldn't be able to come back from.

The night he bent us, but I made sure we broke.

A knot lodges itself in my throat, but I manage to speak to Elliott around it. "I'm gonna head out, man. This isn't really my scene."

He chuckles. "Yeah, not mine either. I'll see you at practice. Want me to let Riv know you're heading out?"

My eyes slip back to River, but he's completely engrossed in conversation with a couple guys from the team, sipping his beer without a care in the world. With his arm still slung over Abbi's shoulder.

Even after he just gave *me* the universal signal he's DTF.

And there's that goddamn twang of jealousy, rearing its ugly head once more.

"Yeah, whatever," I answer noncommittally, shuffling past him and the crowd gathered near the door, breaking into the freedom of the night.

I catch an Uber easily since it's a Saturday night in a college town. But on the ride back to my apartment, I'm only able to latch onto one thought running rampant in my brain.

How the hell did this happen…again?

FOUR
River

August has flown by in what seems like a split second, and with it the first few games of the season. Thankfully, due to the talent of yours truly, all those games were also huge W's as well.

Okay, well, I'll admit, it's not just *my* talent making this season look like we could possibly go undefeated.

A huge portion of that comes in the form of CU's newest wide receiver.

The guy is a beast on the field during the game, laser-focused on the ball, and the ball alone. I don't think I've seen anything like it. Or felt anything like this when it comes to playing with someone this new to the team. *Meshing* doesn't seem to be the right word.

We're damn near unstoppable.

But with that, also comes a small issue.

He's quickly turning into the object of my latest obsession.

This chemistry we have, it's screwing with my head. It's distracting to say the very least because it's all I can do not to watch and try to evaluate every goddamn move, and word, and glance he makes.

Which is difficult because he's been pretty distant since the party I took him to a couple weeks ago after our first game.

No, that's putting it mildly. Ciaráin has been *avoiding* me anywhere that isn't the football field. We don't talk in the locker room while getting dressed like we did that first game day, and any time I see him somewhere on campus, he turns the other way like he didn't see me toss him a friendly wave.

Why? I don't have a clue.

I guess the only thing I can be grateful of is whatever is going on with him doesn't seem to be messing with the vibe we have while we are on the field.

Small miracles, it seems.

But part of me, the part of me that's ever the hopeful optimist, can't help but wonder.

Does the on-field chemistry we have translate into something other than football? And more importantly…would he want it to?

I'd have to be blind and possibly stupid to not notice how good-looking the guy is. He's a walking bad-boy sex doll, what with his sharp jaw and inked arms and *I don't give a fuck* attitude. Add in that he is a top-tier athlete and has the body of a god?

I'm done for.

He's every deadly sin wrapped in a single heartbreaking package.

But even if that single look on the first day of practice is the only one I'll receive, I still want to be his damn friend because he seems like the kind of guy that, once you're in, you're in for life.

Doesn't mean I don't *want* to stem his rose.

But my guess to either option, seeing as we've barely spoken since the party two weeks ago, is a resounding no to all the above.

Which, let's be honest, is probably for the best.

The last thing I need is to fall into bed with my teammate and cause a huge stir-up with the dynamic we have flowing as an entire unit. It's why I created my set of rules in the first place; everyone is happiest when I follow them.

Then again, I've never *wanted* to make a move on a teammate before.

Well, maybe Jensen Holmes back at the beginning of my freshman year in high school, when my dick decided he liked the idea of guys. Specifically in the middle of the locker room when I saw Jensen in nothing but his briefs. But that's a story for another time.

Or *never*, seeing as I've never been more mortified in my life.

Before I can completely shake the traumatic thoughts from my brain, I slam face-first into someone else in the hallway of a lecture hall.

Glancing up at the person, I'm met with the copper eyes belonging to the very object of my thoughts.

No, not Jensen. The other one.

Ciaráin.

He looks as startled as I feel, doing a double take after gaining his bearings. The second he realizes it's me, though…he frowns.

Clearing my throat, I roll my shoulders and give him a smirk. "Hey man, sorry about that. Wasn't paying attention."

Ciaráin lets out a cough and rubs the back of his neck, something like anxiety, and not just my own, mixing in the air between us. "Len. Hey. Uh, it's fine. No big deal, already forgotten."

Is it though? Because you're acting like I have the plague and it's all you can do to stay away from me.

Honestly, what the fuck is going on with him? Anxious or nervous is not a look I would *ever* put on him, but that's exactly what it is. More than that, he's…uncomfortable.

Before I can say much else, he's slipping past me and heading out the front door toward what I'm assuming is his next class.

"Ciaráin?" I call out, but he keeps walking. I know he's close enough to have heard me, he's just choosing to act like he didn't.

Yeah, fuck that shit.

Making the decision to be pushy, I jog after him, catching up quickly as he was only maybe twenty yards ahead of me.

"Hey, man, do you have a minute to talk?" I ask, pulling up beside him.

He shakes his head, glancing at me as we walk side by side. "I have to get to class."

My hand snags the pocket of his hoodie, keeping him in place. "I promise, it's only gonna take a second."

His eyes roam over my face briefly before he lets out a sigh and nods in concession. "You have two minutes. I really do have to get going."

"We can walk and talk, c'mon," I tell him, gesturing for him to lead the way.

Rubbing the back of his neck, he starts moving toward his class with me behind him. The silence between us is awkward and stressful, setting me on edge. My hand taps against my leg haphazardly as I try to figure out the best way to figure out what the hell is going on with him.

"Did I do something to piss you off?" I blurt, stopping in my tracks.

He stops walking and turns to face me, his brow furrowed. "No, River. You didn't do anything to piss me off."

The deliberate way he repeats my words has my mind reeling.

"But I did do *something*? Upset you or whatever?"

Ciaráin shakes his head. "What? Why does it matter?"

Raising my arms out to my side, I shrug. "I don't know, dude. Maybe because you're my teammate and I want to make sure whatever is making you avoid me isn't going to transfer onto the field during a game?"

He clears his throat, rubbing his neck more, but he doesn't say anything.

"Seriously, what is going on? C'mon, Rain. You—"

"I thought I told you not to call me that?" he snaps suddenly, cutting me off.

My brows furrow, replaying what I said in my head. "Seriously? *That* is what you're picking up on? Me calling you by a damn nickname instead of the actual issue at hand?"

"The only *issue* is you don't seem to have boundaries," he grits, his fingers curling into fists at his sides.

Boundaries?

"What are you talking about?"

Ciaráin shakes his head and releases a huff of air. "Let's use this as an example. I've asked you not to call me Rain, yet you did it anyway. Who's to say you won't completely ignore any other requests I make just to screw with me?"

I can't help it; I laugh at this ridiculousness. "Okay…I'll bite. What other requests might there be?"

He rolls his eyes and looks up at the sky, as if asking it for an answer. "Off the top of my head? If I were to catch you checking me out and asked you to stop?"

Hold. The. Phone.

Has he caught me checking him out and is only now saying something?

I mean, other than that night…

"I'm sorry?" I ask slowly, my hand itching to start tapping to calm my erratic heartbeat.

"I fucking know, River. I found out about your *preferences* at the Tri Delta party." He lets out a grunt of frustration, running his hand through his hair. "Elliott made some jackass level comment about me hooking up with you in order to gain favor. But the thing is, he was actually serious. He thought we *were* hooking up."

Fucking Elliott. Goddamnit.

"Okay, so I'm sure you set him straight. No harm, no foul, right?"

He grinds his teeth and shakes his head. "That's not the point."

"Enlighten me then, Ciaráin. What *is* the point?"

Seriously, because I'm starting to get really annoyed with this lack of communication happening right now.

Ciaráin scoffs and pins me with a hard glare. "You really don't get it, do you?"

When I lift my brow, not answering, he shakes his head. "Fine, you want to know what it is? You have this habit of doing whatever you want. We might not know each other well or for long, but I've picked up on it," he says, tapping his chest with his index finger twice. "You've had everything handed to you on a silver fucking platter and have this obscene sense of entitlement that only comes from being a damn trust fund brat." He crosses his arms and rolls his shoulders. "Fuck, everyone knows that you and Coach's son are best buds. Is that how you got your starting position as a true freshman? Through your connections?"

My nostrils flare as his insinuation washes over me.

This jackass.

Yeah, I might be best friends with Taylor, but I earned my spot, just like Elliott and Drew did. My ties to the Scott family have absolutely nothing to do with it.

And the entire team, Ciaráin included, knows this. I've more than proven my talent and worth at this point.

Not to mention everything else he's said? Not true. At-fucking-all.

"You know that's bullshit," I snap, my temper rising quickly.

"Yeah, that might be true. But it had to suck, right? To have someone think you didn't *earn* what you have? That you've been given *special treatment* because you've got some sort of *connection?*" His brow lifts, daring me to challenge him.

Ah. Now I see his point.

But the only issue is, none of this is my fault. I didn't *do* anything. Not really.

I didn't ask to be bisexual, just wake up one day and decide *I think I like dick as much as I like pussy* and now the rest is history. This is *who I am* to my very core, and I can't change that.

It isn't on me if he can't deal with it, it's his own damn problem.

And okay, sure I've been checking him out a lot but from the sounds of it, he isn't really aware of it besides that one time.

At least, I hope.

Letting out a sigh of frustration, I give him a pleading glance. "Look, man. I'm really sorry Elliott said shit to you. But everyone on this team can see what kind of athlete you are by the way you perform on the field. You've more than earned every ounce of trust I have in you to do what you came here to do."

And it's true. I mean, we clearly aren't sleeping together or whatever Elliott thought. But also it's true that I trust him. I don't know why, but from the first day, it's like it was as simple as breathing.

Don't have a place to put the ball? Give it to Grady.

Heavy defenders? About to get sacked? Give it to Grady.

Fourth and long? Give it to Grady.

It just…makes sense to me, so I never thought to question it. And I can't exactly be mad at the results coming from following my gut instinct.

Ciaráin frowns. "*I know* I have. But I don't want this kind of bullshit dragging me down and messing with my game."

"What are you saying? You don't want to fuck around with me? Okay, dude. I got it. You're not into dicks."

Unfortunate turn of events for me, but I've survived this long without boning a teammate. I think I'll make it through this too.

He licks his lips before settling them in a thin line, taking his time to measure his response. "I'm saying I think it might be best if we kept our interactions strictly professional. Football related.

Other than that, we have no reason to be seen together, talking to each other."

I laugh. "What the hell is this, Ciaráin? Are you trying to make me some dirty fucking secret? That makes no sense at all. Why can't people see us together? We're *teammates*."

"*Because* if one person already thought I was giving you a nice dicking after like two weeks..." He glances around the open area at the passersby paying no attention to us before fixing me with his stare. "I'm not about to be subjected to these kinds of bullshit theories just because my quarterback enjoys cock."

"So what? That means you have to act like we're teammates and teammates alone?"

"We *are* just teammates. We're nothing more, never will be."

Ouch. All right then.

Don't get me wrong, I wasn't expecting some sort of declaration of love or whatever. But shit, that was a tad harsh even by my *I refuse to filter myself* standard.

"I thought..." I start, letting out a humorless laugh, "I thought me inviting you to that party was me trying to be your *friend*. Sure, I might be bisexual, but I don't make it a habit of fucking around with my teammates."

Not to say I'd be opposed to fucking around with you specifically...

Shaking my head in an attempt to dislodge those thoughts, I sigh. "Look, Ciaráin, I'm sorry. I don't know what else there is to say. I don't think Elliott meant anything by it, not really. The guy is a dickhead sometimes, but he's good people."

He nods a couple times, his eyes flashing between mine. "I appreciate it, man, but it doesn't matter." He shrugs. "I'm not doing this with you."

"Doing *what*? Having a goddamn friendship?" My voice is rising as I try to contain my outrage. Because honestly, this is...it's stupid. No other word for it. "Plenty of straight dudes are friends with guys who are gay or bi. It's the twenty-first century."

Ciaráin gives me a warning look before lowering his voice to a deadly level. "Let it fucking go, River."

He's right, I should let it go. I know this.

I'm not one of those people who needs everyone to like me; I never have been. My bluntness and my pervy jokes are off-putting to some people, but I couldn't care less most of the time.

So why do I care that he wants nothing to do with me?

Because I should cut my losses, duck, and run to lick my wounds and focus on making sure the two of us are still meshing on the field. That's the most important thing when it comes to the two of us anyway.

I *should* let it go. Because that's the smart, rational thing to do.

But, spoiler alert, I don't let it go.

No, instead I step up in his space, close enough he has to look me in the eye and give it to me straight. "Why should I? You haven't given me a real answer, let alone a good enough reason."

His teeth gnaw at his bottom lip and I glance down to watch his fists clench over and over again, like he's attempting to hold himself back from doing something stupid. Like hitting me.

When he finally does speak a minute later, his voice is laced with venom, deadly as it licks over my skin. "Then let this be it. I don't associate myself with fucking faggots. Now get the fuck out of my face before I deck you in yours."

My jaw drops when my brain finally catches up enough to register what he just said to me. What he just *called* me.

I'm no stranger to the word faggot. Ever since I came out in high school, I've dealt with various levels of homophobia, even in a place as chill and accepting as Boulder. It's rare, but it does happen.

But shit, I never thought it could cut this deep from someone I barely even know. Someone who, for some damn reason, I have this insane draw toward. Like a moth to a flame.

And by doing that? He drew a line in the sand, each of us standing on opposite sides.

Because I can't respect someone who would say shit like that to me.

Ciaráin doesn't wait for me to respond, just turns on his heel and continues down the path toward whatever building his next class is in, like he didn't drop a bomb on me, easily causing a rift between the two of us from this point onward.

I stare after him, his form retreating up the stairs and into the building, finally beginning to understand why it seems like every interaction we have ends with him walking away from me.

FIVE
Rain

"Keep going, man. You're right there," Drew tells me as he focuses on the stopwatch in his hand.

The muscles in my legs are burning as I continue to work my ladder drills with my favorite of the Benson twins cheering me on. Not that I really have anything against Elliott, per se. It's just after the *enlightening* conversation we had at the party of Sorority Row back on the night of our first game, I would prefer to steer clear of him. I'm not in the mood to answer any of his questions, or God forbid, have to remind him *I'm not fucking gay,* nor am I fucking the quarterback—or blowing or whatever else—to get any favors.

No. The ball ends up in my hands on game day because I'm a damn good player, and everyone on this team knows it. I've more than proven myself to them at this point.

Except today, it doesn't feel like I am.

What it *does* feel like is that my feet might fall off or even be burned down to nubs on the rubber floor of the gym with how fast my legs are moving. But it's not enough.

I know without looking at the stopwatch in Drew's hands I'm slower than normal. Despite how hard I'm working, I know I'm not hitting the mark today.

That tends to happen when your head isn't in the game.

The thing is, my head is never *not* in the game. At least not when I'm on the field or the weight room. Those are the two places where I can let loose, work out my aggression and rage in a conducive environment.

My sanctuary.

Except this garden of Eden is tainted with a slippery snake who goes by the name of River Lennox.

He's everywhere I am. Always. Like he seeks me out and watches me just to make me uncomfortable.

Sure, I know that isn't necessarily true. We're teammates, we have to see each other on the field and in the weight room or whatever. But seeing him on campus randomly, in a lecture hall, or the team cafeteria?

At the fucking grocery store on a Sunday night?

Yeah, all that, I could do without.

Glancing over to where he's currently doing leg presses with Garrett, I feel a growl work its way out of my throat, a low rumble from deep within my chest as I continue to pound my legs into the floor.

Yet if I'm being honest with myself, a majority of my irritation is with myself, not River.

Because I don't know why I had to go off on him the other day. It's not a damn crime to be bisexual, I'm not some sort of ignorant asshole. Hell, Roman was bisexual and I never felt weird around him.

Until he decided to kiss you the night before he left for college, leaving you not only with a broken friendship, but behind in hell, my brain reminds me.

Not that I'm one to hold grudges or anything.

Okay, that's a bold-faced lie, but not necessarily when it comes to Roman. I'd like to believe we somehow would have gotten past it, after an awkward phase, and by now we would be able to drunkenly laugh about it whenever we got together like *hey, remember the one time you kissed me, but I'm not into dudes?*

But him kissing me and then just...leaving? Leaving when my life was spiraling down into the darkest pit of hell with no cord to pull to save me from impact?

Not to mention him confusing the hell out of me.

It was like a final nail in the coffin of what was a friendship, *a brotherhood,* from the time we met at eight and nine years old.

That is what makes me hold grudges.

So why is it a big deal River is bi, but not Roman?

I pull up and step out of the ladder at the end of my reps, waving Drew off before he can tell me my time. I already know it's terrible, but I don't need to know *how* terrible.

Instead of forcing myself into the proper headspace, my eyes zero in on River once again, taking in the way the muscles in his legs flex with each press he makes on the machine.

Even I can admit the guy is good-looking, what with those

eyes I swear change from blue to green on the hour, his brown hair cut in a neat high fade, and two dimples popping in his cheeks. And on top of that, he also has to be charming and funny and nicer than easily eighty-percent of the people I've ever met.

He's the poster child for every parents' golden boy and every girl's perfect man.

Except he isn't just into girls…

Goddamnit, I don't know why my brain keeps latching onto that. I don't know *why* I felt the need to tell him to basically go fuck off because he is more fluid sexually. That's not any of my business, anyway. But it was the same feeling that hit my stomach the night of the party, when I first found out.

It was like fight or flight, in a sense. Self-preservation.

And for the life of me, I don't *get it*. I wish I did.

Because, truth be told, I enjoyed getting to know River a bit the few times we talked. I don't know *much* other than he's originally from Colorado and went to school with Elliott and Andrew, as well as Coach Scott's son. That, in addition to his pretty decent taste in music, sums up every piece of information I know about the guy.

As I watch him hop off the leg press and playfully shove Garrett into the seat, I start to see it though. Why my gut is telling me to get the hell away from him.

He's…so much like Roman.

Yeah, they have the same hair color, but that's where the similarities in looks end. Ocean eyes versus dark hazel. Built for highly skilled contact athletics versus lean and limber, like a runner or swimmer. Preference of shorts and a tank top over a three-piece tailored suit.

And don't even get me started on the fact that Roman would never in his life get a tattoo, where River has multiple.

On the outside, they're nothing alike.

But right now, the way River is laughing and joking and is so damn happy even though we're working our asses off in the middle of practice? That has *Roman* written all over it.

Fun, carefree, outgoing. So likeable it's sickening to see.

Shit, I'm sure the guy would give the damn shirt off his back, just the same as Roman would. Making this all the more confusing.

I never truly dealt with my fallout with my best friend for over half my life. In fact, I've been holding onto it in the most unhealthy way possible; shoving it to the back of my mind and pretending it doesn't exist.

So, is it the fact that they're so similar that rubs me the wrong way? Or is it because of this overwhelming sense of...maybe kinship I feel with him?

I honestly don't know how to describe it, only whatever it is, it's a double-edged sword. Easily the greatest thing to happen to me, at least when it comes to my football game, but also lethal to it if today is any indication.

It's moronic to think this, but sometimes I wish we didn't have any on-field chemistry. That the two of us didn't make such a great team when it comes to the game.

Not entirely true.

I love winning and the high I get from a great pass or a touchdown will never lessen with time. And if I didn't have a quarterback I could mesh with on a decent level, that would never happen.

I just wish we couldn't read each other to the point it seems like our brains and bodies are a single unit. Our minds have blended together into one, and I don't even have to look at him to know where the ball is going and how fast I need to run to make sure it ends up safely in my arms. And from some of the insane passes he's been throwing at me this season, he feels this connection too. There's no way he'd trust me to nab some of the bombs he's been lobbing toward the end zone otherwise.

That's the part that frustrates me, as much as it shouldn't.

It's unlike playing with any other quarterback. And still, as much as it might infuriate me on a personal level, it's fucking exhilarating.

"Is it my turn yet?" Drew mumbles loud enough for me to hear. I do, and it snaps me from my thoughts long enough to look over at him

I shake my head and motion for him to get ready to start the timer again.

I need to get my crap together and make this practice worthwhile. Which means I need to take my mind off River fucking Lennox.

"Let's go," I say, not waiting for his response before setting a grueling pace in the ladder once again.

And just like the last time, I know I'm not up to par. My entire body feels like it's moving slower than a turtle stuck in tar, and my brain continues to wander on thoughts of Roman and River, only increasing my frustration from a simmer to a damn boil.

The muscles in my back tense when I hear his laugh from across the gym, deep and husky, the sound like rich scotch sliding over my body.

God fucking damn it.

Stepping from the ladder again, Drew lets out a low whistle when he looks at the stopwatch, and gives me a wide-eyed look.

"Yeah, I know I'm off my grind today," I tell him, grabbing my water bottle from the bench a few feet away to take a swig.

"Um, man, I hate to break it to you, but you're—" Drew cuts himself off when the sound of River's laughter floats over to us, snatching both of our attention.

He and Garrett are acting like idiots, clearly done with their reps because they're not actually working out anymore. A glance at the clock tells me we're close to the end of practice and my heart sinks.

I didn't get jack shit out of today's lifting session. Unless reaching an obscene level of irritation is considered an accomplishment.

And all because of one annoying as hell quarterback who happens to be causing a damn ruckus with Garrett. Like right now, they're shoving each other until River grabs him from behind, his arm wrapped around Garrett's neck in a headlock.

When I catch myself watching him yet again, the tattoos on his arm rippling with the movement, I inwardly wince.

Why do I care what he's doing anyway?

Whipping my shirt over my head, I use it to wipe the sweat from my forehead before tossing it to the ground beside Drew.

"Again," I growl, motioning to the stopwatch in his hand.

Drew sighs, clearly thinking I need to catch a break. Or wanting to get another run in before our time is up. But he's a good teammate and friend, just nodding and hitting the button on the stopwatch in his hand, giving me the go to start my drill again.

He might think I need to tone it down, get my head on straight, and he'd be right. What I need is a fucking distraction from my already distracting as fuck distraction. And since I'm not allowed to box or do anything that might damage my hands and I can't exactly go paint or sketch when I'm supposed to be training, this will have to do.

Tonight, though? You can bet your ass my hands will be busy with a brush in hand.

My heart pounds as I move my legs as fast as humanly possible, lifting my knees, pumping my arms, breathing in steady breaths like my life depends on it.

And while it doesn't, in this moment, I swear my sanity *does.*

Because even now, as my body is damn near being pushed to the breaking point, I still sense it. His eyes on me, watching my every move.

I can practically feel him caress each inch of my exposed skin with his gaze; it's *that* penetrating. Powerful.

Gritting my teeth, I grind through the rest of the drill with what little energy I have left, my stamina completely drained at this point.

I'm left a panting mess of sweat and burned energy when my foot makes its last step through the ladder. Drew stops the watch instantly and I glance down at him with my hands behind my head, attempting to slow my breathing and heart rate.

"Well?" I ask impatiently.

"Dude," he shakes his head. "That was your best time of the day."

Letting out a cough, I take another gulp or water. "Meaning what? I've been shit all day."

Drew laughs humorlessly and tosses the stopwatch to me, which I catch with ease. "If you call beating any time you've ever had while here, then yeah, man, you were absolute trash today."

I glance down at the time on the display screen. It takes a minute for my brain to register the digital numbers shown and realize he's right. This is the best time I've put up since I've been at CU. Hell, maybe even ever.

How is that even possible?

Suddenly I hear a slow clap from across the gym and without turning to look, I know who it is.

But when I do turn to face him and give him a sour look, I'm not prepared for what I find.

Which is him *blatantly* checking me out.

Just like I asked him not to.

His eyes travel down my bare chest and torso to the waistband of my shorts as he claps, scorching every inch of my exposed skin. His gaze settles on the tattoo I have on my hip, narrowing in on the words that I know are too small to read from this distance, before making their way leisurely back up to my face.

And then the asshole stops clapping and *smiles.*

I bite into my cheek, needing to ground myself before I go over there and fucking kill him for looking at me like that.

That's one thing Roman never did. Act this forward with me in a sexual manner. The good friend he is, if there was any attraction he felt, he kept it to himself, thinking it would make me uncomfortable.

Until that night.

River on the other hand? He's got no qualms about letting me know, see, and feel *exactly* what he wants from me, and *that* is wrong on so many levels.

We're teammates. We have to rely on each other to come in

clutch when needed. To hone in on the chemistry flowing between us, whether I want it or not.

But how the hell can I trust him if he's constantly making me feel weird and itchy around him?

How can I know he has my back on the field when he's now decided to go out of his way to be completely obvious about his attraction toward me?

The answer is simple...*I can't.*

River walks over, his teeth gnawing at his lower lip in a way... fuck, it ensnares my damn attention. My eyes are glued to his mouth, his lips, a cocky smirk forming on them as he approaches me.

And when I finally detach myself from the trance to meet his eyes, the gleam in them lets me know I've been caught red-handed.

Shit.

Bile rises from my stomach, coating the back of my throat when he stops in front of me, only a foot away. His cocksure attitude is radiating off him in waves, causing my stomach to churn even more.

Nodding his head before cocking it slightly, he gives me a crooked grin. "You're looking good. Really damn good."

I try not to take it as some form of double entendre. I swear, I do. But I'm standing here half-naked before him and for the life of me, I can't unsee the way his eyes ate me alive only moments before he spoke. It was a literal eye-fucking to the third degree.

More like eye-*raping* because I *most definitely did not want it.*

"Whatever," I mumble, turning away from him to grab the towel I'd set on the rack of dumbbells, wiping myself off and quickly slipping my shirt back over my head.

The last thing I need to do is be shirtless around the guy. He'll probably take it as some sort of invitation.

Without a glance his way, I head over to grab the rest of my shit, ready to make a break for it.

Please, just go back to ignoring me and all will be right in the world again.

"Whatever?" He laughs, following me. "That's all you have to say?"

I glance at him before looking at the door, begging to escape and get home. Pursing my lips and pretending to think about it because uh, yeah, that's all I've got for him right now, I nod. "Pretty much. Hence me walking away, Lenny. You know, 'cause that usually signifies the end of conversation?"

To further prove my point, I start walking to the door. And of course, because the universe has some sort of plot to make me eternally miserable, River is right on my heels. Even as I exit the gym and start walking down the deserted hallway, I hear him behind me.

"What the hell is the issue here with us?" he hisses, grabbing my arm and tugging. It forces me to spin to face him and see the fury in his eyes, one I've never seen on him before. "Because the way I see it, my sexuality has nothing to do with my ability to perform on the field. And that's the only thing I can think of at this point for why you've decided to continuously ice me out for no goddamn reason."

I scoff and roll my eyes, waving my hand at him. "Did you not listen the other day? You're clearly the issue. Not your sexuality, just you in general. So do me a favor by getting out of my face."

River laughs in annoyance. "Because having a simple *conversation* with you, telling you that you looked good running a drill is getting in your face?"

"It is when you use the phrase as a come-on," I snap, closing in on him in barely contained rage.

"You really need a damn reality check if you think everything I say has some sort of hidden meaning behind it, a hint I'm trying to get in your pants."

A sneer works its way over my face as I glare at him in disdain because *fuck him*. I know the game he's playing, I see right through it. He's the kind of guy that'll take any challenge head-on, and fight tooth and nail to overcome it, beat it, whatever it might be.

And that is all he sees me as. A challenge. A game to play and win.

Yeah, not fucking happening.

"Go fuck yourself, Lennox."

He smirks, crossing his arms over his chest. "Why don't you do it yourself, Grady?"

My jaw practically pops out of its socket in an attempt to keep my damn mouth shut, to keep my cool and not let him get to me, no matter how much it goes against my nature.

"Feisigh do thoin fein," I growl under my breath in Gaelic. Because yeah, I'm a mature twenty-one-year-old guy who just told him to fuck his own ass in a language there isn't a chance in hell he speaks.

I turn again to head down the hall, but his hand snaps out and latches onto my wrist.

"Oh, no you don't, dickhead. You want to toss out insults? Do it in a language I understand. That way, I at least know *why* I have to fight my instinct to deck you in the face."

My eyes are glued to his hand on my arm, where his skin touches mine.

It's only the second time we've touched skin-to-skin for more than a brief moment and just like the first, there is liquid ice melting my flesh where the connection is. White hot and molten.

And it *enrages* me that he somehow manages to make me feel... whatever the hell this is. I don't think I could put a label on it if I tried.

"Get your... Fucking... Hand... *Off me.*"

"Or *what?*" he challenges, stepping into my space, his jaw hardened. "You gonna call me a faggot again? A queer? A fucking *twink?* Well, say it all, baby. Give me everything you've got. Because there is nothing you can say to me I haven't heard a hundred times over." His smile is menacing, filled with venom that doesn't fit the shiny persona he wears each and every day.

Because that's what it is. A goddamn mask.

He's nowhere near the perfect golden boy he makes himself out to be. Because this shithead, he's got a mean streak. A part of himself clearly craving hostility and malice. He might contain it for the rest of the world, but right now, I see right through it.

"Stay out of my goddamn way like I said, and we won't have to find out," I bite, yanking my wrist from his hold. I try not to notice the cool feeling washing over my skin where his hand used to be, already missing the contact.

No. Not fucking missing. *What the hell is wrong with me?*

I start walking down the hall again, away from him, and thank God I don't hear his footfalls behind me. But his voice, low and deep, cuts through the stagnant air even at this distance.

"How do you suppose I do that, huh, Ciaráin? We're *teammates.* We see each other *every damn day.* There is no possible way for me to stay away from you because whether we like it or not, we're stuck together for the next few months until the season ends."

Believe me, I'm counting down the days.

"You don't think I know that?" I grind, spinning to face him. "I think I know better than *anyone.* Just keep to yourself except when we have to interact, and we won't have an issue."

"Because that's working out *so well* for us now," he mumbles, shaking his head before running his hand through his hair. "I never asked to be your enemy. I don't *have* to be. You *made it this way.*"

He's not wrong. This is a majority of my own doing, and I know it.

It's me not being able to own my own shit, deal with my own past. It's not on him, and I know it.

But for the life of me, I can't seem to let it go.

"Well, maybe if you weren't intent on pulling shit like you did today, blatantly eye-fucking me in front of *our teammates.* Jesus Christ, I told you Elliott insinuated we were screwing around because you show me *preference* on the field, yet you did it anyway. But it's not that. You and I both know our chemistry on the field is because of this freaky telepathic shit we've got going on, and nothing else." I lick my lips and glance away, letting out a clipped exhale, wishing I kept the last bit out.

I watch his brow furrow. "You feel it too, don't you?"

Fuck.

Grimacing, I bark out my reply, "Doesn't matter. Just let me be. You play your game, I'll play mine. End of."

"It's not the end of *anything, Rain.* This, whatever the fuck is happening here, is only just the beginning. And we both know it."

Unfortunately, you're all too right about that one. "I thought I told you already, don't call me that."

He shrugs his shoulders in mock innocence. "Oops. I must've forgotten," he says, like he could possibly get away with bullshitting a bullshitter.

I watch him, my contempt lighting up within me. "You don't want to get on my bad side, Lenny."

The warning, because that's what it is, comes out low and lethal, like a gun aimed and ready to fire if he takes a single misstep.

And I won't fucking hesitate to take him down if he does.

He bites his lip and smirks, those dimples popping out to taunt me. "And what if I told you I'm only interested in getting *in* your *backside?*"

Oh, Jesus fucking Christ.

I'm on him in an instant, like white on rice, pinning him against the wall of the hallway with my forearm across his throat. His Adam's apple grinds beneath the bones in my arm, and I press tighter, smiling at the little gasp escaping him.

Seems the only way to get the asshole to shut up is to not let him breathe.

Putting a pin in that one. File it under "Ways to Take River Lennox Down a Notch."

Except...from the mischief dancing in his eyes, I just screwed myself big time.

He wanted to know what buttons to push. Where they were located. How hard he had to try and what would rile me up enough to force a reaction.

He was looking for a weakness, a chink in my armor that's been impenetrable for *years*.

And now he's found it.

Godmotherfuckingdamnit.

My nostrils flare as my eyes flash between his, the blue orbs with green flecks around the center you'd only notice this close. Shit, I try *not* to notice.

"Listen to me, River, because I'm only going to say this once. It's not fucking happening. We're not doing this, playing this little game I see you're plotting in your head right now." The words come out with such ferocity, such animosity, anyone who heard them would have to take them at face value. They'd turn and cut their losses before *I* cut *them.*

But I can tell he doesn't. Because he's not afraid of me like I want him to be.

Because deep down…we both know my words, each and every one, is a goddamn lie.

SIX
River

Fuck Mondays.

Seriously, fuck 'em, and whoever decided to invent them because they are the worst day of the week *bar none*.

And on top of that, fuck whoever decided to create seven-thirty lectures. I might be an early riser, sure, but it doesn't mean I'm fully functional at this hour.

Closing the door to the lecture hall as quietly as I can because I'm already fifteen minutes late as it is, I spin to look for a seat, finding one at the back of the class on an aisle.

Perfect. Thank God for being left-handed. No one ever wants those aisle spots.

After easing my frame into the chair, I grab my notebook and a pen from my backpack before sliding it out of the way.

Honestly, I shouldn't be bitching about this class. I should just be grateful Coach Scott was able to pull some strings to get me in the section, even though it was at max capacity because I was *drowning* in my old section. The time of day just didn't work with my schedule for practice, especially when we have two-a-days.

And while nepotism didn't get me my starting position on the field as a freshman, I'll gladly use it in this circumstance.

Flicking open the notebook, I'm about to start taking notes, my pen paused over the paper, when I feel it.

Him.

How? I couldn't say. I just know it's him. Just like I know he will catch whatever I throw his way on the field. Like an instinct. A second skin.

The other half of a whole.

"You've got to be fucking kidding me," a voice mumbles to my right, low, deep, and absolutely belonging to Ciaráin.

I glance up at him, finding him in a pair of black sweats and a long sleeve shirt with *Colorado Football* emblazoned on the front. His dark hair is covered by a gold and black snapback sitting backward on his head.

And when I look at his eyes, I'm not surprised to find palpable amounts of rage simmering in them. Especially after the "talk" we had last week in the hall outside the weight room. If you could call it that.

Biting my lip, I stifle a laugh the best I can because, *really, universe? What the fuck did I do to you on this fine Monday morning for you to hand me a spoon when I need a damn shovel to help bury myself in this damn hole I'm digging when it comes to this guy.*

Giving Ciaráin my full attention, I cock my head and answer with a cheery tone, one a little too loud for a dead silent lecture hall while our professor is going through his lecture notes.

"Morning to you too, Grady. Fancy seeing you in here," I tell him with a smile I don't quite feel, earning me a glare and a hissed *shush* from the girl in front of me.

Shooting her a look, I turn back to look at Ciaráin, finding him watching me closely under thick black lashes so long they almost graze his skin when he blinks.

"It was a fine morning until you walked in and sat down," he hisses, his voice lowered much further than mine. "What are you even doing here? You aren't in this class."

"I am now," I tell him, sliding down in my seat, and abandoning my pen and notebook on the desktop. "Just got switched in this morning."

"Fucking brilliant." He sighs, rubbing his temple with his index and middle fingers. "Well, obviously you didn't realize I'm in this class. But I am. So after today, make sure you are seated on the opposite side of the damn hall from me, yeah?"

I scoff, crossing my arms over my chest and settling in for what is sure to be a possibly riveting conversation. "You actually think you have some sort of power over me? Enough to tell me where I can and can't *sit in class*? How dense are you, dude?"

"I just want you to leave me the hell alone," he growls, his voice rising enough to catch the glances of a few people around us. His heated glare is enough to quickly make their curiosity wane though, before his attention is focused back on me. "So it seems I should be asking are *you* so dense you can't seem to grasp that?"

"Literally picked the first open seat I saw. And I'll continue to pick whatever seat is available," I tell him, my tone sharp.

"You should know by now I'm not one to take orders from condescending pricks."

His eyebrows shoot to his hairline before his glare hardens even more. "You want to talk about pricks? Go squat in a cactus patch, Lennox."

I smirk, not having heard something so colorful from him before. "Clever as ever, Grady."

He shrugs, turning his attention back to the front of class. As if he's actually paying attention with me right beside him, because we both know it's damn near impossible to think when the other is around. "I thought so. I know they have 'em here. Those weird-looking ones. Prickly pears, right?"

I raise my brow, curious as to where the hell he's going with this one. Taking the bait is stupid, but no one ever accused me of being smart.

Not when it comes to this guy, at least.

"Does it fucking matter?"

His eyes snap back to mine and I know instantly I screwed up from the sickening gleam in them. He licks his lips and gives me a wry smile, one showing his perfect teeth, and *fuck him* for being this attractive even when he's being a cockhead. "Not particularly. Although, the shape of those bad boys ought to add some real kink to your next round of anal play."

My jaw clenches, and I swear to God I feel a molar crack under the pressure. "Good looking out, babydoll. Want to try it out with me? You know, since you're awfully curious about what goes in my ass." The words come out through gritted teeth as I do my best to keep my temper in check.

A temper I never knew I had until I met Ciaráin Grady.

But I can't exactly lose my shit in a lecture hall filled with over two hundred students in the middle of class. No matter how much I want to drag him out of here by the collar of his shirt and scream in his face for being such an asshole. Or bend him over and fuck him for the entire class to watch.

You know, whichever would help him learn I won't back down faster.

Ciaráin grumbles something under his breath, in Irish from the sounds of it, and I lose my damn mind.

My hand lashes out and snatches the front of his shirt, reeling him into me so my mouth is practically on his ear when I hiss the words out, "What did I say about that shit? You got something to say to me, say it. Don't hide behind another language like a goddamn pussy."

Releasing him with a shove, I shift to face the front of the class, finding many, *many* sets of eyes on us. Including those belonging to our professor.

"Do we have a problem, Mr. Lennox?" Professor Johnston asks curtly. "Mr. Grady?"

Rolling my teeth over my bottom lip, I internally curse Ciaráin for getting us into this bullshit. And all because he can't handle me sitting next to him for *an hour* lecture.

"We're fine, sir. Just arguing over a play from this past weekend. Won't let it happen again."

My eyes land on Ciaráin, letting him know he better go along with this shit before we both get our asses reamed out by Johnston. Or worse, Coach.

It takes a minute, but I see his concession, so I look away to catch my breath.

"Sorry, Professor," Ciaráin grinds out. I can feel his eyes burning a hole in the side of my face, but I don't look, just keep my eyes locked on the front of the room. "We can continue it later. We didn't mean to interrupt the class."

Johnston nods. "See it doesn't happen again."

When the good ole professor turns his back and starts writing on the board again, I snap my gaze back to Ciaráin.

"Díul mó bhad," he hisses under his breath before rolling his eyes, turning his attention back to class.

"What the *fuck* does that mean?"

He smirks, not looking at me still. "Suck my dick. Though it's probably a poor choice of words on my part seeing as that's most likely *exactly* what you're wanting to do with my cock." He pauses, eyes meeting mine in contempt. "And then some."

That's fucking it.

Slipping my shit into my bag, I toss it over my shoulder and grab him by the arm. I yank him out of his seat, creating a ruckus sure to piss Johnston off and get me sent back into my old class I'll probably end up flunking.

But I don't care. I'm over it.

Ciaráin looks at me like I'm insane, and let's be real, right now, I feel it. I don't give him a second to protest or sit down though; I just grab his bag with my free hand and pull him out of the lecture hall, the door slamming closed behind us.

Dragging Ciaráin with me, I glance through the window of a classroom down the hall to find it empty and quickly move us in there. Away from prying eyes and ears.

"What the shit, River?" he roars, wasting no time to lay into me the second the door closes. I toss his bag on a desk and cross my arms over my chest, leaning against the door providing his only means of escape.

We're having this shit out, here and now. I don't care how long it takes.

"You told me to suck your dick. I got us a private place to make it happen." I shrug, baiting him. "Go ahead, baby. Whip it out for me. I'd love to see how many inches I've got to work with."

His nostrils flare as a look of disgust crosses his face. "What the hell is wrong with you?"

"Aw, don't be shy, *Rain*." I give him a patronizing smile, catching the way his jaw ticks when I use the nickname he hates. For what reason, I couldn't care less.

Whatever. It's only more ammunition at the end of the day.

"I don't care if you're small," I continue, tapping my fingers against my bicep. "I get that you could be self-conscious and all. Despite what the girls might say, having a small dick is a big deal. But not in this case, baby. It just means less for me to take deep into my throat."

I watch in pure satisfaction as the vein near his temple throbs in rage at the shit I'm spewing, knowing it's more than likely a bunch of bullshit. And when I glance down at his cock to drive my point home, I'm stunned, giddy even, to find he's sporting something of a semi behind those black sweats.

I've never been happier to be wrong in my life in regards to his...*size*.

I raise my brow. "I stand corrected. Looks like you've got quite a bit packing. Even better."

He scoffs. "Really, River? Which one is it? Dick size matters or it doesn't? You'd think as some sort of fucking faggot that you'd care how big a cock is while it's filling your ass."

There it is again. That damn word.

Faggot.

It doesn't matter how many times I hear it, it doesn't make it any easier to allow it to slide off my shoulders.

"Whoever said I'm the one getting fucked?" I quirk a brow in challenge.

"There's no way you haven't, seeing as you're a goddamn queer. And they tend to take it up the ass."

I roll my eyes and shake my head, so fed up with this shit. We're getting absolutely nowhere, only running around in circles, throwing punches and insults at each other like we're in a goddamn boxing ring.

Giving myself a second to breath, I sigh. "You do realize I'm *bisexual*, right?"

He lifts a brow in amusement, an arrogant smirk decorating his face. "Your point?"

My jaw ticks in irritation. "*Meaning* that labeling me as *queer* and *faggot* is not only derogatory, but also incorrect. *Bisexual* doesn't even define me. I don't do labels. I fuck whoever I want to fuck, whenever and when it suits me, *wherever* I want. Guys and *girls too*."

Ciaráin nods a few times. "Ah, well, that might be true in technicality. But, Lenny, my man, let me ask you this. Flat out, give me an honest answer. *Do* you take dick in your ass?"

"I don't see how my topping or bottoming is any of your business," I snap, evading the question because *it is none of his damn business.*

He has no right to know the answer to his question is yes. It's rare, seeing as I prefer to top my partner, regardless of gender. But every once in a while, I willingly seek out getting fucked.

Sue me.

But then my brows furrow momentarily as I continue to process his question. And realization dawns on me.

The question isn't if I do it or not...it's why he wants to know.

A slow grin slides over my mouth. The opening is there, and you can bet your ass—pun most definitely intended—I'm going to take it. "Though, seeing as you asked, yes, Grady. I take it as well as I give it when it comes to dick. And I wasn't kidding when I offered to let you take the merchandise for a spin." I'm in his face before I can stop myself, looking him up and down. I want to devour him in every sense of the word. "I have to say, you aren't my usual type. But at least if you fuck me from behind, I won't have to look at your face."

His hand shoots out, clamping around my throat as he forces me to step back until I hit the wall.

"The *fuck* you just say to me?" he snarls, squeezing my windpipe.

I suck in as deep of a breath as his hand will allow, knowing my sudden loss of oxygen isn't only from his vice grip on my trachea. It's him touching me.

It's electric. Especially when we're like this.

Volatile and angry.

It's a shock of adrenaline straight into my blood, like fucking heroin.

I grip his wrist with my hand, eating up the way the skin feels beneath my palm, and tug enough to be able to speak. "You heard me."

Ciaráin sneers before spitting his words out. "You need to learn how to shut your mouth before I break your damn jaw so it has to be *wired shut.*"

"Now why would I do that when I know how much you hate it when I don't listen?"

His body crowds me, pressing tighter against my throat until I can barely make the tiniest gasp. I can barely make a conscious thought, except *he might actually kill me* when it happens.

I feel *it.*

Him.

Hard against my leg. Waiting for me to drop to my knees and take him in my mouth.

My free hand moves of its own accord, coming between us to lightly trail a single finger down the length of his erection. The action causes him to freeze, loosening his grip around my throat to practically nonexistent.

I gulp down oxygen, taking a moment to look at him and the fury in his eyes tells me he had no intention of stopping until I just made him.

But still, the asshole I am, I pop those dimples with a smile and add a second finger to my caress of his cock, hard as steel behind the cotton of his sweats.

Hard for *me.*

"Does my defiance turn you on, baby?"

He cocks his head and glances between my eyes, his own narrowed and calculating as I continue to taunt him with my fingers.

After a moment, he steps back, shaking his head. "Nah, my hand around your throat does. Knowing all I have to do is snap your damn neck to shut you up for good." He adjusts himself quickly, turning his back on me to grab his bag on the table.

Meanwhile I'm frozen in place, unsure what my next move should be in this chess game we've begun.

He pulls open the door to the classroom and steps through the threshold, glancing over his shoulder at me. "If you were smart, you'd do well to remember that."

SEVEN
Rain

O f course, *of fucking course.*

As if losig tonight against Oregon in overtime wasn't bad enough, Coach had to throw this cherry on top of a goddamn shit sundae.

Since the game was late and away, we have to stay the night up in Portland before flying home in the morning. But Jesus Christ, the moment he called out my assigned roommate's name for the night, I was ready to start *walking* to Colorado.

Yep, you guessed it.

I'm spending the night alone in a hotel room with River motherfucking Lennox. Someone shoot me or lock me up in a jail cell, because there is no damn way both of us are lasting the night in a small space without murder being committed.

I don't know what it is about him, but it's like he gets off on making me uncomfortable or flustered with his witty comebacks and smartass comments. Sure, I know I brought it on myself a bit when I started acting like a douchenozzle once I found out he was bisexual.

But really? The shit he pulls…it drives me insane.

Snatching the key from Coach while we're still in the lobby, I turn to find River.

"Hey roomie." He grins like the asshole he is.

Yeah, he's enjoying this way too much.

"Don't call me that," I growl, hauling my duffle over my shoulder and heading to the elevator with him in tow before smacking the call button.

"Okay, *Rain*. Whatever you say."

I tense at the nickname only one other person has called me. Someone who meant the world to me, but like everything else, I screwed that up too. "Don't fucking call me that either."

The elevator dings before opening, allowing us to slip inside. I hit the button to our floor when he asks, "What *should* I call you then?"

Huffing out a breath, I turn a glare on him from across the miniscule elevator cab, begging for it to reach the tenth floor *any* faster. "Literally anything else."

River nods, glancing around the interior as he processes this. He still hasn't said anything when we stop at our floor. The doors to the hall begin to open, and that's when the asshole decides to finally speak again.

"Okay, grump ass."

This sonofamotherfuckingbitch.

I halt in the doorway with my back to him, perfectly aware the doors will try to close on me if I don't move. Hell, I might wait for them to be shutting to step out of the way, sending him back to the lobby. I could do with a few more minutes of reprieve from his obnoxious tendencies.

"Uh, you gonna get out there, grump ass? Or did you finally manage to find your manners standing in the doorway?"

My teeth close on my tongue so hard the familiar metallic taste of blood floods my mouth.

It's one night. Eight hours. Do not kill him.

Just. Fucking. Breathe.

He takes my non-answer in stride, slipping past and heading down to room ten-oh-four, leaving me standing in the doorway of the elevator until it closes on my shoulder, alerting me to get out of the way.

Coming up behind River, I watch him swipe the key card and step into the room, flipping on the lights as he goes. It's nothing fancy seeing as we're only here to sleep for the night, a regular double queen room with a television and attached bathroom.

My gaze follows him as he waltzes over to the bed closest to the window, tossing his bag on the bed before unzipping it, digging through its contents.

"You mind if I shower quick before we hit the sack?"

Didn't you just take a shower at the stadium after the game?

"Because you need my permission?" I grumble, throwing my bag onto my own bed, directly next to the bathroom, searching for a pair of sweatpants. One thing I can't stand about college football is having to wear a suit to and from the stadium for away games.

I understand the concept, showing up looking our best for the reputation of the school. Hell, it's what I'll be expected to do if I ever get to play professionally. But I've spent the better part of my life in the damn things when I'd rather be in literally *anything* else than this monkey suit.

Unfastening my tie and removing my suit jacket, I drape it over the chair near the bed before beginning to undress down to my boxer briefs. A quick peek in my peripheral shows me River is doing the same before he retreats to the bathroom, a pair of shorts in hand.

The door to the bathroom clicks behind him, the sound of a shower spray coming from under it not a moment later. Slipping into my sweats, I hang my suit on one of the provided hangers, and flop onto the bed to surf the channels for a movie to watch.

Under normal circumstances, I'd attempt to fall asleep. I played a tough game today and my body is already feeling the effects of the beating it took. But staying in a room with one of the few people on this Earth I despise and actually falling asleep?

Yeah, not happening. He'd probably shave my head or stick my hand in warm water, hoping I'd piss myself. When it comes to River Lennox, I'm a firm believer in the whole *sleep with one eye open* mentality.

Or in this case, not sleeping at all.

It's safer...for many reasons. The utmost being I don't need him to have anything to use against me, and he'd most definitely gain a shit ton of ammunition if he knew what plagued my mind while I'm asleep.

At least this hotel has Netflix, so I decide to settle in with *Silence of the Lambs* because who doesn't love a good mindfuck to keep them up at night?

Shit, maybe I'll do a Hannibal Lecter marathon. Keeping River up all night would be *hilarious*. You know, since the guy probably needs his *beauty sleep.*

Loving the idea a little too much, I start scrolling for the first film in the franchise, *Red Dragon,* instead. Just as I'm about to click play on the remote, I hear a strange, low humming noise.

Assuming it's the TV or some sort of static in the air, I hit play.

But then a couple minutes in, I hear a grunt I'm almost *positive* came from the bathroom. Where River has been in the shower for at least ten minutes now.

What the hell is he doing?

Rising to my knees, I press my ear into the wall separating the bathroom and rest of the suite, waiting to hear the sound again…

But nothing comes.

Weird. Must've come from the TV too.

Settling back into my bed, I resume the movie…only to hear it again. And this time, I swear to God, it's from the bathroom. No way on Earth it isn't.

Hopping off the bed, I make my way over to the door to the bathroom. The small gap from the bottom of the door the steam is pouring out of should allow me to catch the noise once more.

But I stand there for a good minute and nothing.

Just as I raise my hand to knock on the door, ready to tell him to finish off whatever self-love session he's got going on in there, I hear it again.

Except this time, the grunt is followed by a low, throaty moan, and holy shit, he's *actually* jacking off in there with me not five feet away from him on the opposite side of the wall.

Anger licks at me like a flame, but I make no move to distance myself from the door dividing me from a wet, naked River.

A wet, naked River, who is stroking his cock. Full of soap while his one hand is plastered to the shower wall to keep himself up. Water is pouring over his muscular back and shoulders, rivulets tracking down his body and — *Jesus Christ, what is wrong with me?*

I do my best to shake the mental image from my head, but it's ingrained there, seared into my mind on a loop. Like a never-ending, fucked-up fantasy featuring the bane of my existence. The soundtrack? Every groan and pant slipping through the panel of wood separating us.

My hand is plastered to the drywall of the wall between us, eyes clenched shut as my mind wars with itself to shut down the visuals rolling through my brain.

I'm not gay. I'm straight as an arrow.

But the way my mind is running wild with these thoughts? God, it's anything *but* straight.

The battle waged inside my head comes slamming to a ceasefire when the door is suddenly yanked open, revealing a dripping, flushed River...in only a pair of athletic shorts riding low on his hips.

Sans underwear.

And of course my stupid, *stupid* eyes travel further south to see the outline of his dick, clearly still half-cocked from fucking his fist. I swallow.

Fuck me.

River halts before practically slamming into me, seeing as my body is directly in his path out of the bathroom. "Whoa, if you needed to get into the bathroom, you could have pounded on the door, instead of standing outside it like a damn creep."

My eyes snap up from the eight-pack, the perfect definition on each individual muscle, to meet his questioning gaze. I pull back from the door, crossing my arms over my chest. "Would you actually have hurried up if I had? Or purposely taken twice as long?"

He shrugs, leaning against the door jamb. "Did you actually need to get in there or is this some hypothetical we're playing out?"

My brow raises. "Does it fucking matter?"

"Absolutely," he insists. "If this was a hypothetical, then of course I'd hurry up for you. But if it was real life…" He trails off, swiping this thumb over his bottom lip while wearing a wicked grin as his eyes trail over my body.

Cocksucker.

I'm damn near ready to tear him a new asshole — *figuratively* — when I notice his eyes firmly fasten themselves to my groin.

"Need some help with that?" The devilish smirk on his face while motioning to my crotch with his chin makes me want to knock him out. Until I look down to notice the tent in my gray sweats, and suddenly I'd much rather punch *myself* in the face.

All the air leaves my lungs in a rush.

Shiiiiiiit.

Internally scolding my dick for being a worse traitor than goddamn Benedict Arnold, I shoot River a glare. "Fuck off, I don't screw around with dudes."

He just laughs and shakes his head. I have to hand it to the guy, he doesn't seem to be phased by the assholery I aim at him, which in itself is a feat. Most people cower when I toss taunts and barbs their way, but somehow they only make River stand taller.

Unfortunately.

My desire to bend him until he snaps in two has become somewhat of a sick obsession ever since the party on Sorority Row, growing stronger and more vicious after each and every encounter ends with vile insults being hurled between us.

River slips past me and flops down on his bed, leaving me still standing at the door of the bathroom with a raging boner like an idiot.

"I'm being serious," he insists, throwing his hands behind his head as he cocks a brow at me.

Trying desperately not to stare more at his bare chest or the way his basketball shorts hang on his V, even lying down, rolling my eyes and letting out a huff, I reply, "So was I, jackass."

"Really, Rain. If you want someone to take care of it for you, I have no issue doing so." His shoulders hunch in a shrug, and his aqua eyes hold my gaze hostage. "A mouth is a mouth, doesn't matter if it belongs to a girl or a guy. Doesn't make you gay for letting someone of the same gender suck you off."

My shoulders tighten at his offer. Not because of him offering to suck my cock. No, it's the way he picked up on my fucking insecurity, reading me like a damn children's book.

Letting a dude blow me most definitely *is high on the gayometer. And I'm* not *gay.*

"Again," I grind, my jaw tight, "I'm not into screwing around with dudes. If I need to get off that bad, I'll hit up a bar around the corner or go take care of it myself in the shower like you just did."

Oh shit.

Wrong. Thing. To. Say.

River's eyebrows jump to his hairline before his dimples pop in his cheeks on a grin. "So that's what got you so worked up, huh, Grady? The sound of me fucking my fist gets you hot and bothered?"

"Hardly," I growl, my knuckles cracking from being squeezed so tight.

"From the looks of it, it's actually *very* hard," he retorts, letting his eyes fall back to my groin where my cock is still a steel pipe in my pants.

Fucking treacherous appendage.

Just as I'm about to snap at him with my own witty comeback, my phone vibrates in my pocket. And like the coward I am when it comes to confrontations with River, I thank my lucky stars for being saved by the bell.

Shooting a glare at River, I pull my phone from my pocket and check the screen.

And you remember what I said about luck and being saved?

Yeah, scratch that shit and erase it from your memory because it was a lie. Because I wouldn't call it luck when fate decided to be a royal cunt today by fucking me with a chainsaw. Sans lube.

My teeth are *this* close to cracking under the pressure of my jaw when I read the message on the screen from none other than my stepfather.

Him: We need to have a discussion when you get home from college for Thanksgiving break.

Yeah, the fuck we are, asshole. It'll be a cold day in hell before I sit across a table from you to share a meal.

My fingers fly over the screen quickly, attempting to deal with this shit before River decides to get nosy and peek over at the screen.

Me: We have nothing to discuss because I won't be there. Téigh trasna ort féin.

Okay, so telling him to go fuck himself wasn't *totally* needed, but…okay, who am I kidding? He deserves that and worse with the kind of bullshit *father figure* he's been since my mother married him when I was eight.

Telling him off in my father's native tongue just brings me *extra* pleasure since I know the dickhead doesn't have it in him to not break down and Google Translate the insult.

Which he does. Every goddamn time, I'm sure of it. Being the sociopath he is, he needs the knowledge, the control.

Him: Go fuck myself? Original, Ciaráin. Be an adult and show the fuck up, or I promise, you'll regret it.

This cocksucker. As if I would be able to come home to Philly from *Colorado* for less than forty-eight hours.

Then again, there are two problems with that scenario. One being he has no idea I'm in Colorado. Asshole still thinks I'm at Clemson. In South Carolina. Which he would know better if he gave a shit about anything other than himself and whatever will further his own agenda.

But isn't that exactly what I was banking on when I up and decided to make this switch?

And honestly, even if I was still at Clemson, I haven't been home for Thanksgiving, or *any* holiday since I left for college at eighteen.

So to go back there for a holiday only consisting of catering and schmoozing with a bunch of rich assholes and politicians when it is meant to be a *family* holiday? I mean, yeah, I haven't really had a family since I was a kid, but still.

I know enough to decide I'd rather shave my balls with rusty kitchen scissors. Blindfolded.

My eyes snap up to River, finding him staring at me with his brows raised in amusement, arms crossed over his chest as he leans back against the bathroom door.

"Fuck this shit," I mumble under my breath, tossing my phone onto my bed and yanking open my duffle in search for jeans and a shirt.

Doing my best to ignore River's eyes following my every movement, I slip out of my shorts and into the jeans as quick as I can. I'm still painfully hard despite the bucket of ice water those texts from my stepfather dumped on me. A fact that both River and I are well aware of, if the strained clearing of his throat while I adjust my erection in my jeans is any indication.

Throwing my shirt over my head, I slip into a pair of Nikes before I grab my phone, wallet, and key card to the hotel room.

"Where are you going?" he asks, pushing off from his position and following me to the door.

The slightest waiver in his voice has me looking up to meet his gaze. His thick brows are furrowed in harsh slashes above ocean eyes, a slight vulnerability to them.

Like he doesn't want me to walk out of here. Even though that makes absolutely no sense. And as much as I hate it, if I look at him any longer while that glimmer of innocence resides in them, I might stay.

He's probably just worried about me getting caught and he'll be implicated as well, fucking golden boy he is.

So I roll my eyes before gripping the knob angrily in my hand to jerk the door open with such force it hits the wall behind it with a *bang.*

"Fucking anywhere but here."

EIGHT
Rain

My Uber driver pulls up to a club downtown not more than twenty minutes later, and the second I step out of Dave's Subaru, I'm hit with the pulsing music coming from within the club.

I'm not huge into the club scene, but tonight, I need to dive headfirst into any vice I can find. Anything so I don't go back to the hotel hard-up and in need of an orgasm while River is there. Or worse, stuck thinking about the bullshit demands from my stepfather.

The line outside moves quickly enough and in less than five minutes later, a bouncer checks my ID before ushering me into a mass of hot, sweaty bodies. The club is dimly lit by black lights, and my eyes take a minute to adjust before observing everyone's clothing glowing while they grind and dry-fuck on the dance floor to some techno shit I don't recognize.

I scan the perimeter, searching for the bar. Spotting it on the back wall, I make my way through the throng of drunken idiots to get my hands on some booze. Because, boy, do I need it.

It takes a while to get the bartender's attention, people lining up to grab their drinks two deep, but eventually it clears out enough for me to grab a place near the end. Ordering a Jameson neat, my favorite homage to my father, I watch the people on the dance floor.

They lose themselves in the music, the atmosphere.

What I wouldn't give to live carefree, even if it was only for a night. One night of freedom from my demons seems like a small favor to ask of the universe. But still, it never seems to hear my pleas.

When the bartender, an inked up guy appearing to be in his late twenties, slides my two fingers of whiskey across the dark wood, I toss it back in a couple swift gulps, relishing in the warm fire burning down my esophagus and into my stomach. I signal to him for another before slamming down a fifty on the crowded counter.

He quirks a pierced brow at me, but doesn't say anything, simply refilling my glass with three fingers this time. Telling him to keep the change, I go to leave the bar, but a hand claps me on the shoulder, startling me.

I don't turn around right away, preparing myself to meet River's annoying stare of disappointment I'm sure is written all over his goddamn face.

Did he seriously fucking follow me?

But when I turn to see whose hand is on me, I'm surprised to find it attached to Jaxson Hopkins, one of the cornerbacks I played against tonight.

"I thought it was you, Grady!" he leans into my ear, hollering over the music. He gives me a drunken grin when he pulls back slightly. "You want to come party upstairs with us? Private room with the goodies up there."

At that, he rubs his nose, signaling what exactly he means by *goodies.*

Drugs.

And by my guess, it's one of my favorites.

The decision, while it should be an instantaneous *fuck no...*is the exact opposite. "Lead the way, man," I tell him with a smirk.

I follow closely behind him as we weave through the mass of bodies to reach the stairs to the upper level, housing a smaller bar and some private booths and even a few private rooms. Once he clears me to get into the VIP section with the bouncer at the top, I find myself in one of those rooms. The music is the same as it is out in the public part of the club, just set at a lower volume. As if whoever designed this place knew some people want to actually hear themselves think.

Lounging on red plush couches, I spot three other guys I played against tonight, a defensive end, the safety, and one of the offensive linemen... and a slew of girls.

Or maybe it's a harem?

I couldn't tell you, I just know the ratio of cocks to pussy is extremely low, and by the looks on their faces, was the entire point.

But what draws me in the most is the baggie of white powder sitting on the mirror-topped table.

Cocaine, my old friend.

I absently lick my lips, the blow calling to my blood like the long lost escape it is. I haven't touched the stuff in years. Part of my deal with my stepfather for making the night I can't seem to forget, nothing more than another skeleton tossed in the back of my closet.

But what was I saying earlier tonight? Wanting to forget my demons?

Jaxson must notice my eyes locked on the coke because he gives me a playful shove toward the table. "Didn't take you for anything more than a weed man, what with all the Heisman talk. But I'll play. Since your team lost tonight and you're our guest, I suppose you can take the first line if you want it."

Fucker, get real. I probably snorted more lines on my seventeenth birthday than you have in your entire life.

That alone should give me enough sense to not get high with a bunch of fuckwits I don't know from Adam.

Still, I'm not in the mindset to oppose.

Sinking to my knees, I take the rolled up bill a blonde girl with a huge rack is holding out to me before pouring a line onto the table.

A warning niggles in the back of my mind, telling me to stop. Years of sobriety are about to be tossed out the window, and for what? A night of fun, drowning my trauma with every vice in the book?

Alcohol, drugs...sex?

Shaking my head, I lean forward and inhale the powder in one swift move, the burn tingling my nostril and back of my throat is pure bliss.

God, I've missed this.

I take another line before handing off the bill to another girl, this one a redhead. My fingers wrap around my tumbler of whiskey I'd set on the table beside me, bringing it to my lips to take a long pull of the liquid. The burn of the alcohol mixes with the sting of the cocaine at the back of my throat, and I feel...good.

Really fucking good.

The best I've felt since...

My thoughts screech to a halt as fast as they can manage in this state because there's a dead body on the table where I took the lines of coke.

But it's not just anyone's body. *It's Deacon.*

His lips are blue and look as if they'd be cold to the touch, and his gray eyes I always thought looked like liquid silver are open, staring at nothing because...he's fucking dead.

No, no, no. Deacon has been dead for years.

Since that night in high school.

My brain tries to grasp at those straws of sanity, but it's not working because the body is still here, inches from me, dead as dead can be.

I blink a thousand times—a million times more—and he's still there.

No, my logic tries to reason with my inebriated brain. *He's not here. This isn't real. I'm just tripping out.*

But he's so lifelike, even for a dead person. So real and *right there.*

Looking down at my reflection in the small corner of the table that Deacon's body doesn't take up, I notice my eyes are bloodshot to hell. Pupils blown to hell.

Yep, definitely fucking high.

But this high is nothing like I've felt before. My skin itches all over and every time I go to scratch it, I think I do, but then…did I actually do it or only think I did?

I look up at Jaxson, who is sitting with the blonde girl who gave me the bill to take my line and *is it fucking hot in here?*

It is, isn't it?

I swallow down the rest of my whiskey in an effort to cool myself, but it only proceeds to make me warmer. It boils me from my stomach out, and *holy shit*, did I leave my stomach on the stove? Is that why it's boiling?

No, you idiot, the tiny piece of rational brain tells me, *you're out of your mind right now is all.*

"What the hell did I just bump?" I manage to ask. Or, at least I think I ask it. It's a question better asked *before* I took the hit, but better late than never, right?

But then, I must speak the words because Jaxson laughs at me. "It's a special mix. Got a splash of MDMA in there. Makes for some phenomenal fucking once you get past the initial paranoia."

Ecstasy?

My mind is racing at a million what-the-fucks per second.

I've done E before and I've done coke before. But never together.

And holy shit, I will never do them together ever again.

Ever, ever, *ever.*

Even in this bumped up state, I know I'm in for one helluva crash.

I watch transfixed as he pops the girl on the ass, motioning for her to get off his lap so he can rise to his feet. Extending his arm, he pulls me up, and he's *really* strong because I fly through the air but somehow still land upright.

"Why don't we go grab you another drink at the bar to get you through this first bit of the high," Jaxson says, his hand on my shoulder as he leads me back to the door. Glancing back, I see the little blonde following us. But more importantly, the table doesn't seem to have Deacon's lifeless body lying on it anymore.

So I've got that goin' for me at the very least.

"Kayleigh here can help you get what you're looking for once you've got your drink," Jax continues, oblivious to my internal ramblings that'd earn me a one-way ticket to a psych ward.

Help me get what I'm looking for? Shit, dude, all I'm looking for is a way to get home. I gotta go take my stomach out of the oven. Or was it off the stove..?

But then the girl…Kayla, was it? Or Kylie?

What's-her-fucking-name gives me a look. It says *hi, I'm down to fuck in the bathroom of this club and never see you again.*

Well, what do you know, Kandy, I'm down to be the one fucking you in said bathroom.

I smirk down at the blonde, finally starting to feel the ease of the high slide over me. The paranoia, the anxiety, it's long gone, and I'm exactly what I want to be.

Free.

At least for the whole ten seconds it takes to get to the bar on the second level. Because at the end of it, I see *him.*

A piece of my past, but this one isn't dead. No, he's very much alive. At least, according to his twin sister, he is. Neither of us have heard much from him for a while.

Well, maybe if you didn't ruin your friendship with the guy the night before he left for college…

Blinking rapidly, I try to focus. To see if it's really him. I know he moved out to this area for school, so the possibility is high. The coincidence would be nearly insane, but it's possible...

And when a set of dark hazel eyes meet mine, I know it's him.

"Let's get you that drink," blondie purrs, her fingers plucking at my shirt over my pecs. Her movement causes me to snap my attention back to her. It's only for a second, but when I look back up to meet *his* gaze again...he's gone.

Vanished into thin air.

Holy shit, I'm higher than the fucking Empire State Building right now.

Little blondie taps on my chest again, bringing my stare back to her. Looking down at her this close, I realize she *is* pretty. Pouty pink lips and huge icy blue eyes that scream *come fuck me.* And I'm certain they work well for her when it comes to that request.

Yet even in my coked up, drunken mind, I know fucking her is a bad idea. Try a *terrible* idea.

But it doesn't mean I'm going to walk out of here without getting laid. I can't go back to that damn hotel room still hard-up and sleep in a bed next to River Lennox all night.

Nope, I'm going to continue down the self-destructive path I'm paving for myself right now because *fuck* River Lennox, my stepfather, *everything.*

Fuck. It. All.

"Why don't we find somewhere more...private," the girl says in voice meant to be sultry, but it's loud in here so I can barely hear the words. Still, I nod in agreement and she takes my hand to lead me back down the hallway we came from, stopping outside the men's room.

I push open the door, and she's on me like a goddamn suction cup.

Yeah, I know that doesn't make sense but she has literally *suction-cupped* her mouth to my throat like one of those creepy sucker fish that attaches itself to the sides of fish tanks.

Shit, now I'm thinking about water and I'm thirsty again. I can't seem to remember…did I get another drink at the bar?

I guess it doesn't matter because Lady Dracula is currently leaving the world's biggest hickey on my neck and I'm getting seriously annoyed, even in this fucked-up state my brain is lingering in.

But that all changes the second she starts rubbing up against me, and my cock starts taking notice.

He never notices much if I'm being honest, but this little twitch is a good sign.

What can I say, he's a lot more picky than I am.

Not wasting any time, she cups me over my jeans, rubbing against my length with her palm and the heel of her hand. And it feels really good.

Atta boy, I praise my dick, being grateful he's going along with the game plan tonight. Namely, fucking a random chick so I get some relief and an escape from reality, if only for the short time I'm buried balls deep inside her.

My eyes slide closed while she works my jeans open, slipping her dainty hand into my briefs to pull out my cock. It's currently in half-chub form, but that's only because it was being ground up against by another body. In all honesty, a goddamn monkey could get my dick in half-chub territory, and I'm not into bestiality.

What the fuck are you even thinking right now…? Bestiality, Rain? Really?

Her warm fingers wrap around my girth, giving it a few quick tugs, but it doesn't do shit for me. I groan in frustration, wishing for once I was somewhat normal because the shit she is doing doesn't work for me. It *never* does.

That might be the most infuriating part of having sex as my preferred vice at this point in my life. I never am attracted to the girl the way I should be.

She could be the hottest woman on the planet, and she won't do anything for me down south. Not really.

Regardless of who she is or what she looks like, her hand is always too small, too smooth. Making me wish it was my own instead. And when her lips wrap around my length, the texture of her chapstick or lipstick or lipgloss or whatthefuckever is always too sticky on my length.

It doesn't belong there.

And don't get me started on pussy. It's always too soft, too warm, too…pink. I'd much rather screw a girl in the ass, but most one-night stands aren't down for back door play, so I've learned to take what I'm able to get.

All of this put together and adding in that I'm usually not sexually attracted to women and…yeah, I'm convinced.

I'm asexual.

It makes the most sense to me. It's what I *have* to be.

There's no other explanation for why I'd rather have my own fist wrapped around my cock, the hard, calloused skin stroking me to my own release, rather than be with a girl. Having to think of that kind of grip on me to even get it up for a girl.

But I'd be lying if I said it was always *my* hand I envisioned around my cock while I was being jacked.

No, I shamefully must admit, it belongs to another man.

Like right now, as this blonde chick strokes my cock in her hand, I'm not thinking about her. Or my own hand.

No, it belongs to *him*. The one I just saw — or *think* I saw — at the bar. His brown hair, now a disheveled mess from me running my fingers through it. In my mind, his dark hazel eyes bore into mine as he takes me higher and closer to the place I need to be.

And like every single time I think of him, I'm hard as a rock.

But only this time, those eyes I'm staring into inside my head shift and turn to the color of aquamarine. A deep teal, rather than a green-brown.

Only, I'm too fucked up to care that those eyes are all wrong, that they belong to my nemesis, because I'm turned-on and ready to get this show on the road.

Honestly, getting this high always seems to help when I need to fuck. It's like my brain needs the extra stimulants to get my body on the same page of what exactly it is I want when it comes to getting laid.

I don't know. Whatever it is, it works like a charm. Like it always did.

I slap the girl's hand away from my cock before I lift her in my arms. My hands palm each of her ass cheeks as she wraps her legs around my waist to open herself for me. Pressing her back against the wall, I thank Jesus himself for the creation of skirts as I move her underwear to the side and guide myself to her entrance, bottoming out in her after one deep thrust. Her eyes roll back as her head hits the wall behind her, letting out a breathy moan.

A moan too light and airy for my liking.

Shifting my hips, I begin moving inside her, grinding against her pelvis with each thrust.

And it feels...good.

I mean, sure, it almost always feels good. It's *sex*, for fuck's sake.

But every goddamn time, it's like there's something missing. And no matter how hard I try, I can never put my finger on it.

My mouth latches onto her neck, sucking the supple skin between my lips. I'm harsh enough to leave a serious hickey for her to remember me by in the morning and from the state of her incoherent mumblings and glassy eyes, she sure as hell isn't going to remember anything else.

Plus, it seems fitting, knowing I'll be sporting one to match.

I start pounding into her, not giving a shit about finesse or my stamina. This isn't about impressing some chick with my skills in the sack. I frankly couldn't give two shits what she thinks, seeing as I'll never see her again after tonight.

It doesn't take long before she's writhing in my arms as I drive into her with reckless abandon, moans of ecstasy coming from her mouth.

But God, those moans are too loud, too high-pitched, and they hurt my fucking head.

So I cover her mouth with the palm of my hand and fuck her harder, giving her the clue to shut up.

Spoiler alert, it doesn't work.

It doesn't matter though, because before I know it, my balls draw up and cum bursts from the head of my cock into the condom I don't remember managing to slip on before I put my dick inside her.

Did she give it to me, or did I have one?

Whatever, it doesn't matter.

I just thank God for small miracles. I don't need some cleat chaser trying to tie my ass down with a goddamn pregnancy.

I sway on my feet as I pull out of her, setting her back on the ground.

Her drunken smile tells me in no way, shape, or form if she got off, but at this point, I don't care. A fuck in the club bathroom is just that; a fuck. And from the looks of it, she's too far gone to give a shit either way, because she sashays out the door without bothering to right her skirt or fix her mess of hair.

Shaking my head, my hand works on peeling the condom from my softening cock before discarding it in the trash receptacle to the side of me. Tucking myself back in my jeans, my hands slightly blurred as I do, I sigh.

What the fuck am I doing? What the fuck did I just do?

Or more like who? Because I still don't remember what her name is, only I think it starts with a K.

Karlee?

Fuck me.

This was a relapse of the worst kind, I know it. All my vices rolled into one messy, screwed up package. And while part of me should give a crap about the possibility of drug testing, getting kicked off the team, the cleat chaser poking holes in the condom...I don't care.

Not one goddamn bit.

Shit, I'm still really fucked up.

Wiping the sweat from my brow with my wrist, I turn on the faucet and quickly wash my hands and face. I press my hands into the cool counter, holding my weight up with them as water drips from over my nose and lips, and close my eyes. Inhaling deeply through my nose before releasing the breath from my mouth, I war with my emotions, heightened to hell from the booze and blow.

It's all I can do not to vomit right now.

When the room stops spinning enough for me to open my eyes and not puke, I glance up into the mirror.

And I proceed to lose the contents of my stomach. Right there in the sink.

I'm hallucinating.

He wasn't here before, and he's not here now.

He didn't watch me fuck a random girl in the bathroom of a club.

I look up again, certain this is part of a bad trip. I know the coke was laced with something. E, right? Or it was the combination of the alcohol and drugs. Shit, maybe the fact that I've been clean for a few years now, save for one night, and this shit is just hitting me differently than it used to.

I don't know.

Whatever the case, it has to be the reason I'm met once more with the dark hazel eyes belonging to one of the many ghosts from my past.

NINE
Rain

My head is still pounding the following afternoon as I take a seat on Doctor Fulton's couch in her office, my face resting in my hands as I try to fight off the continuous urge to cut my head off to stop the headache.

Yeah, I'm back at therapy again.

And after last night, I think I need it.

If tripping out and imagining my dead friend on the table of the private room in the club wasn't bad enough, then hallucinating my ex-best friend *twice*, who I haven't seen or spoken to in years, definitely pushed me in this direction.

The second I cleared my thoughts enough to be able to move, I bolted from the bathroom and ordered an Uber to take me to Taco Bell. It was my only hope that some food might sober me the fuck up so I could walk straight back into the hotel room.

Because yeah, I was definitely still drunk as shit off the

whiskey I downed faster than a fish out of water. And the last thing I wanted in the entire damn world was to wake River up when the whole point of me going out to the club was to avoid him in the first place.

But alas, even though I was off my high and able to walk without running into anything in my direct path, I opened the door at half past three in the morning to find River sitting on his bed with the lights on, his head in his hands, looking like a wreck.

A feeling, something like guilt, tickled the back of my mind at the sight of him looking so helpless.

That all changed the second he saw *me*, though. Because he was on his feet and screaming before the door to our room was fully closed.

"It's after three in the fucking morning, Rain! We have to be on a plane at eight o'clock. Or did you forget that little tidbit of information when you decided to go out and get plastered out of your mind?" His *eyes darted to my neck, where I was correct in assuming my little blonde hook-up left quite the lover's bite, and he scoffed. "Of course. And to get fucked apparently."*

Yeah…

Needless to say, there wasn't a whole lot of talking the rest of the night between River and me. Or the plane ride home, which was thankfully short because I spent most of it fighting the urge to puke the entire time.

I even let him call me that goddamn nickname because I didn't have the energy in me to fight with him. All I wanted was to flop down on my bed, pass out, and hope to God the nightmares would stay away since I wouldn't be getting a ton of sleep.

I relived part of one in the flesh while I was high as it was, but that didn't mean the memories wouldn't torment me in the few hours of shut eye. Normally I'd fight the sleep off, and especially with River in the same room. But it wasn't worth it. I needed sleep because when the crash hit my body, it was like being backed over by a tank multiple times and then tossed over a cliff onto a ton of sharp, pointy rocks below.

You'd think it would be reason enough for people to keep off drugs, but apparently, I'm one of those idiots who never learn their lesson. Because I broke years of drug sobriety for the cheap thrill of a meaningless fuck in a semi-public place, and a quick way to chase away the demons for the night.

Again.

Only that didn't exactly work, did it? Because the damn things — persistent as ever — were still there the whole time.

But I digress.

"So Ciaráin, tell me what brings you back after your colorful departure the last time we saw each other," Doctor Fulton requests. I peek at her through my fingers to find her with a perky smile I want to wipe off her smug face.

And don't get me started on her cheery-ass voice. It's like nails on a chalkboard, making me want to rip my goddamn hair out with every syllable.

Jesus Christ, coming back here was a worse idea than getting lit up last night.

I remove my hand from my eyes entirely and glare at her, not giving a shit that I look like I want to kill her with my bare hands. Honestly, life imprisonment for homicide charges might be worth it if I never have to listen to her damn voice again.

You're here for a reason, I tell myself.

Namely, I fucked up by *getting* fucked up and the only way I'm going to deal with the resonating emotions from my actions last night is to *talk them out.* It sucks donkey dick, but there's no way around it. It's like I need someone else to absolve me of my sins in order for me to even attempt to move past them.

Though I'm rethinking this route, knowing it would be simpler and a lot less of a hassle to join a church and start going to confession.

Just tell her, Rain. Tell her what a fuck up you are.

"I..." I start, letting out a sigh. "Something happened last night. *A lot* happened, actually, but I honestly don't know where to start."

Doctor Fulton sets her pen on the notepad in her lap and leans forward in her chair, her forearms resting on her thighs. "Usually when you don't know where to start, the best place is the beginning."

The beginning of what? Last night? This bullshit with River? The bullshit that is my *life*?

Doctor Fulton must sense my apprehension, because she offers me a smile. Not one of condescension or annoyance, but a real, genuine smile.

"Ciaráin, it's okay to be hesitant to share after what happened with your previous therapist. I get that. But just know this is a safe space for you to get out whatever it is eating you."

And I don't know why, I really don't, but for some reason, I believe her. This is a place I can share what I need to in order to move on from my mistakes and transgressions and find closure from my past.

So, I do it.

I open my mouth and tell her everything that happened last night from the moment Coach announced River was my assigned roommate up until I was face down on the bed at three-thirty this morning.

The confrontation with River, the texts from my stepfather, the drugs, the girl in the bathroom.

The hallucinations.

All of it.

And when I'm done baring my soul to this *stranger*, we sit in silence while she digests the previous night's events. But there is no judgment in her eyes, no look of disgust on her face.

The only things I see are compassion and empathy, and *God* if it doesn't make my heart ache in my chest for being such a damn douche.

"Let me ask you this," she says after another minute, twirling her pen between her fingers. "What part of last night do you regret the most?"

Her question gives me pause, which it shouldn't. The answer should be obvious. I should be regretting taking the two lines of bumped up coke. If I hadn't done the lines, I wouldn't have hallucinated Deacon or Roman. I probably wouldn't have even fucked that girl. And for the life of me, I still can't even remember her name.

So that's exactly what I tell her.

"I know what I *should* regret the most." I sigh. "It *should* be drug use. Because if I had kept clean, I could have avoided so much of this other bullshit."

She nods and then prompts me to continue with, "But?"

But the thing I regret most isn't going to the club, getting drunk and high, or fucking that girl. No, what I regret the most… was coming back to the hotel to see River's face for the split second before he lit into me.

I've never seen another human look so…distraught.

Like somehow, me leaving him there and going out was the worst thing to ever happen to him.

Which makes *no* sense. But it doesn't stop me from feeling an immense amount of guilt for it.

"I regret my actions in general for keeping River up half the night wondering where I was," I mumble, putting my head in my hands. "And I hate that I don't know *why* I feel this way."

"He's really gotten under your skin, it seems."

Very observant, Doc.

"Yeah, he has." I sigh, rubbing my temples. "He's found every one of my buttons and makes it his life's purpose to push them until I snap. It drives me insane. And the worst part is, anything I say or do doesn't seem to faze him in the slightest."

"Say or do?" she asks, and I glance up to her, finding her brow raised.

I wince. *Fuck.*

How do I say this without sounding like a completely homophobic asshole?

"Look, I'm not saying I'm in the right because I'm not. I know that. But…" I swallow roughly and shake my head. "I've called him some pretty awful shit. Derogatory slurs or whatever. Pinned him up against the wall a couple times when he came at me with his silver tongue. But it was only ever when he pushed me over the edge."

Not exactly a lie...

Doctor Fulton scribbles something in her pad before looking up at me, still lacking judgment. "And do you regret *those* words and actions like you do the ones from last night?"

I shake my head, frustration building within me from her line of questioning. About the *topic* of questioning, more like it. "I don't know. I *didn't*. At the time I did and said those things, I felt, I don't know. Justified, almost? Like there was a *reason* behind them and he deserved them. Even last night when he was taunting me yet again about blowing me, I didn't feel bad about what I said or about leaving to go to the club. But when I got back to the hotel last night and saw him all…vulnerable or whatever, it's like it set off some alarm in my brain, and all I feel is remorse."

That's the kicker of this whole thing. I left so I wouldn't do and say more awful shit to him, but in the end, it probably was the worst thing I could have done. Because, for the very first time, I saw him *hurting* from my actions and seeing it only confused me more.

And now I don't know *what* I feel. Besides guilty, that is.

"Ciaráin, I know you said Roman is an off-limits topic, but part of me feels this unhealthy form of communication you have with River might be stemming from that."

I close my eyes and groan because she's right. I don't want to talk about Roman.

"I don't know. They're similar, yeah. But Roman, he would never push me past the limit I could handle. He'd get me to the edge, but he *never* sent me into free-fall."

"Except it might be exactly what you *need.*"

My brows furrow. "How so?"

"Ciaráin, it's easy to see you have this need for control. And there's nothing wrong with that, most people do. But with your past trauma, it's intensified the desire in you to have a hold on everyone and everything around you." She pauses and gives me a smile. "Again, not a bad thing. But I think you've reached the point where you need to relinquish some of it."

The good doctor has a point, unfortunately. "Okay. I mean you're not wrong. But what does my need for control have to do with Roman or River?"

She sets her pad and pen on the table beside her and leans forward. "It sounds like Roman let you have a lot of control during a time of your life when you needed it. Over your friendship as well as the end of it. So when he pushed you to the edge but never made it so you had to take the plunge, you still had a hold on your world. Which, at the time, was a good thing."

She pauses and gives me a little smirk. "But River? From the sounds of it, he refuses to let you tell him what to do, let you control him, like you're itching to do. But it's not just that, is it? He has this way of making *you* lose the control of *yourself* that you're so desperate to cling to. And I think it could be good for you. I think you *need* it."

Losing control is good for me? Yeah, I don't think so, Doc.

"I tend to disagree," I say through gritted teeth.

She scoffs. "Of course you would. Because it goes against your nature."

"Then why would you want me to purposely go against my nature?"

"This thing called self-growth, Ciaráin. River could be an opportunity to give it to you, just like Roman did at a previous point in your life."

I shake my head, adamant that this is not going to happen. "We're enemies. I don't want him to be in charge of *any* form of growth."

Especially one in particular...

"But you were willing to let Roman?" she counters.

"Roman was different. I'd known him for years, we were best friends. And it's not like I was aware he was leading me on some journey of self-discovery or whatever."

"And you had feelings for him."

Her words give me pause. *"What?"*

"Ciaráin, you had feelings for him. I've read all your files, every word about Roman in there. I see the way you tense when I bring him up or the look in your eye when we started talking about him. I know infatuation when I see it."

Fuck me.

My chest aches at her words, hating the validity to every single one of them.

"The day he kissed you, he didn't ruin your friendship because he was bisexual and came on to you. It was ruined because you trusted him, *loved him* even, and when he finally made the move to show you he felt something similar, it was too late. He was leaving for college. Leaving *you*."

I feel like I might pass out as the words slide over my body, constricting and squeezing around me like a snake coated in barbed wire.

She has to stop fucking talking.

"And I also think—" she says slowly, her eyes searching me as I war with myself, "you have some of these confusing feelings for River as well. This attraction you don't know what to do with *because* of how much he reminds you of Roman. And while you might not talk to Roman anymore, you still have a sense of loyalty to him. So, in turn, having these confusing feelings for River feels like a betrayal."

"You don't know *shit*," I growl.

"I don't?" she challenges, a brow raised. "How do you explain what you feel for River then?"

"I don't feel *anything* for him except disdain and contempt. Especially when he started being a cunt and egging me on just to get me to lose my shit."

"Lose *control*," she corrects. "But do you blame him for lashing out after what you said? Do you understand *why* he is acting the way he is?"

Of course I do. Does she think I'm dense?

I know he's only lashing out because of the shit I started. It all could have been avoided had I just been straight up with him from the beginning. The moment I found out about his sexuality from Elliott at the party.

But I'm the one who pushed *him* first. His retaliation is on me.

"Whatthefuckever," I snap, not wanting to think about any

of this shit anymore. I glance up at the clock, noting there is over a half an hour left in our session. But I can't be here for that long without *losing control* of my temper. "It doesn't matter. We're done talking about this."

Rising from my seat on the couch, I stalk over to the door and yank it open, pausing in the threshold as she speaks.

"You can't run from this, Ciaráin. Not forever. Sooner or later, you have to face it."

TEN

River

I swear to God, I need to see a shrink, because despite the shit Rain keeps pulling with me, I can't seem to let go of my fascination with him.

It's still early in practice, so Garrett and I are in only athletic shorts, T-shirts, and our red practice pinnies since we're in the middle of passing drills with some of our wide receivers. Including, of course, Ciaráin. I'm off to the side taking a break as Garrett throws about a forty-five yard bomb to Ciaráin down the field. Watching as the ball sails down the field, I'm in awe at the perfect spiral as it lands safely in Rain's hands at the opposite ten yard line.

I'm also in awe of the way Rain looks while catching the fucking ball.

Impressed as hell, I jog over to Garrett and slap him on the ass before gripping his neck and pulling his forehead to mine roughly. "That's what I'm *talking* about, man," I exclaim in pride, before shoving him away playfully.

The kid, while only two years my junior, has been struggling this season in adjusting to the tenacity and skill level required to play on a Division One team. Most of the time it's small shit, like his grip slipping or fumbling in practice due to nerves. I can't fault him, after all, he's only a freshman and green as hell, but today seems like a damn breakthrough. By the giant grin on his face, he realizes it too.

"You're looking good, G. A lot more confident than you did even a week ago," I tell him, which only stretches his smile even wider. "There's just *one* thing you need to work on with your stance. It's going to save your shoulder in the long run."

Tossing a football into his hands, I motion for him to get into a throwing stance. Once he's where I need him, I grip his elbow in my palm and adjust it slightly, moving it into the position it should be in.

"When you throw long, you need to make sure you're using the correct form." My hand slides down under his bicep to lift it up into the correct placement as I speak, channeling my inner physical therapist. "It isn't natural for the body to throw overhand. It's harsh enough on all the joints and ligaments, making it much more prone to injury. You don't need to throw out your arm, tear a rotator cuff, or fuck up your elbow when it can be prevented by something as simple as proper form."

Slipping my hand up further to his shoulder, I begin to make the necessary adjustments there as well. Once I'm satisfied he's in the stance that'll save his arm, I step back and motion for Drew to head out for a deep one. Once he starts jogging out, I nod for G to let it fly. Sliding around as if in the pocket during the game,

I watch his arm move flawlessly this time, letting the ball sail through the air and into Drew's hands about fifty-yards away.

"Shit, dude. Keep throwing like that and I'll be out of a starting position." I step up to Garrett with a laugh, clapping him on the shoulder before giving him another quick pat on the ass. "Continue to work on your form and—"

My words are cut off by a sharp, shooting pain through my left wrist and all the way up my arm. It takes me a moment to realize the reason behind it is none other than Rain. His hand is wrapped firmly around my wrist, almost in a crushing grip. He tugs it back at an awkward angle, causing the ache in my shoulder as well.

My eyes fly up and over my shoulder to meet his, finding them on fire and filled with unchecked fury. His lips are pulled back in a sneer as he twists my wrist even further, pulling it behind my back between our bodies. I feel the bones grind together under the pressure of his hand and wince. Panic floods my senses and my brain works for ways to get myself free from his grasp before he breaks my wrist in half or dislocates my shoulder entirely.

Rain tightens his grip even more, and a small whimper escapes me. "You might be the captain, but you need to watch where you put your goddamn hands while you're on this field before I fucking break them." His hot breath hits my neck and shoulders, telling me his mouth must be close to my skin.

Confusion hits me like a Mack truck.

Put my hands? What?

I squirm in his hold, spinning around to face him, so at least my shoulder isn't being extended backward.

"Uh, Grady, is everything good here?" Garrett slowly asks, stepping into my peripheral view.

Rain's head snaps to the side, startled to realize someone has walked up on him practically assaulting me on the football field.

Using his distraction to my advantage, I snatch my arm out of his grasp and bring it to my chest. "What the hell, man?" I hiss. Grimacing when I rotate my wrist, I pray to God he didn't injure me. Rolling my shoulder in its socket, at least I find it's not nearly as painful.

Small fucking miracles.

I glance up at Rain, letting out a long, calming breath to put myself in check before I bite his damn head off, or worse, start throwing punches. But the second I go to open my mouth again, Coach is already on us, so I don't have the chance to demand an explanation.

"Grady! Get your ass out of here. You're done for the day." My eyes fall on Coach to see steam practically shooting out his ears as he storms over to where we're standing.

God, he's pissed.

I suppose he has every right to be when his two golden geese are at each other's throats during practice. "I'll see you in my office. Tomorrow morning before you suit up." His tone is sharp, leaving no room for debate.

Rain just scoffs, shoving past me with a rough bump to my shoulder before jogging off the field and out the tunnel, my gaze trailing him the entire way before the blackness overtakes his form.

"What in the hell is going on between you and Grady?" Coach

Scott barks in my face, causing me to flinch as my attention is brought back to him. "I can't have my star wide receiver breaking the arm of our starting quarterback when it's the ticket to a goddamn bowl win."

He says it as if he hasn't known me my entire life, which rubs me the wrong way. My cheeks heat as I do my best not to get mouthy with him, knowing full well it won't do me any good.

"Fuck if I know, Coach. Maybe you should ask him."

Well... that plan didn't work, since the look on his face tells me I'm about to get my ass reamed.

Nope, definitely not the right answer, River.

Whipping his hat off his head, I prepare for his verbal lashing, but he only lets out a sigh. "River, can you take one for the team here? Literally? Go apologize for whatever smartass comment came out of your mouth to piss him off?"

I open my mouth to object to his assumption that my mouth is the problem between Rain and I, but the way he raises his brow at me in challenge lets me know he isn't putting up with my shit today. Guess that's what happens when I practically lived in his house during my time in school with Taylor.

By now, he's clearly picked up on my infamous toxic trait of biting off more than I can chew.

"Yes, Coach," I grumble, rubbing my hand over my face. "But for the record, in this *particular* instance, I haven't done jack shit to merit him attempting to snap my arm in half."

Pinching the bridge of his nose between his thumb and forefinger, Coach shakes his head in exasperation. "Damnit, just go. You're done for the day."

With a nod, I grab my water before heading off the field.

"Ice your arm tonight!" Coach shouts right before I reach the tunnel to the locker room, to which I wave him off.

While I appreciate the hell out of Coach Scott for the mentorship and all he's done for me as a second father figure, I can't help but feel irritation for his comment. For thinking I'm always the root of the problem because I *sometimes* like to be a smartass a *little* too often.

Or at inappropriate moments.

Shit, okay, I guess he has a point. Doesn't mean I have to like it.

The door slams open against the wall behind it as I enter the locker room, still salty about the entire incident. Steam is rising in the air and I faintly hear the sound of water spraying onto tile, signaling Rain is in one of the showers. At least, I think it's Rain, seeing as everyone else still has easily another two hours of practice before they'll be done for the day.

My mind latches on to him in the other room, naked and dripping wet, and my cock springs to life behind my athletic shorts.

Fuck me.

I can't stand this attraction I feel toward him.

Whipping my shirt and pinny overhead, I toss them in my locker before slipping out of my shorts and underwear. I grab a clean towel from the bin and head over to one of the shower stalls, careful to pick one as far as humanly possible from Rain.

Last thing I need is for him to attempt to drown me in the inch of water puddled on the floor of the shower room.

I make quick work of rinsing off my body, seeing as I haven't sweat much in the short amount of time I was actually practicing today, and hop out of the shower. Sounds of water splashing still come from the stall Rain occupies as I wrap my towel around my waist and head back out to my cubby. Redressing in a clean shirt and jeans is slightly difficult with the ache in my wrist and shoulder, and my fingers tingle slightly when I tie my shoes, but I don't think he managed to do any major damage with his vice grip.

I'm running my towel through my hair when Rain comes into view in only a towel sitting low on his hips, leaving his abs, Adonis belt, and the perfect line of hair trailing below his belly button on display for my wandering eyes.

And *fuck*, do my eyes wander.

I've always been *very* considerate with my teammates and their privacy, seeing as I'm openly bisexual and it might make them feel awkward to be changing in front of me. Never have I ever openly ogled them half or fully naked while in the locker room. Or even at all.

I need their respect as their captain, and the last thing I want to do is mess with the chemistry we have going by getting an eyeful of man candy.

Not that it's been difficult, seeing as I've never been attracted to any of my teammates while playing for CU.

Until Rain, that is.

My perusal works its way down to his crotch, where a slight bulge is present behind the rough, white fabric. He's not hard, *at least, I don't think he is*, but from the size of said bulge, it's apparent he is *very* well-endowed.

More so than I realized in that classroom those few weeks ago.

Subconsciously, I find myself rolling my teeth over my bottom lip, my thoughts straying to the night in Portland when I offered to suck him off.

Before I realized he was hard *because of me.*

After that, I wanted a fuckton more than just his dick in and around my mouth.

And great, now *I'm* hard thinking about him while *he's* hard. While he's standing in front of me with nothing but a towel on.

Fucking perfect.

Like he can read my goddamn mind, Rain turns his attention my way and catches me blatantly checking him out for probably the...what, thirtieth time since we've met? Honestly, I couldn't tell you how many times it's happened.

But...at least every other time he wasn't practically naked.

A scowl instantly mars his rugged face, his dark brows creasing in the center, furrowing over a pair of whiskey eyes. Combined with the slight scruff dusting his jaw, and he looks like a darker, pissed off, fuckhot version of that singer Jack Gilinsky.

"Are you serious right now? Do you want me to *actually* rip your fucking arm from your body?"

"Uh, no?" It comes out more like a question than I mean it to, as if I'm really contemplating on letting him dismember me.

That sounds like a hard pass.

"Then stop looking at me like you've seen me naked." The snarl evident in his tone should be warning enough. I'm treading down a dangerous path and if I want to leave this locker room on my feet rather than in a body bag, I'd better shut up real quick.

Then again, I've always liked to live life on the edge.

"I mean…you kind of are…right now."

And just like that, I find myself being lifted by the neck only to be slammed down, my back against the wood bench that is positioned in front of the row of cubbies.

"You're asking for a good ass kicking, Lenny," he murmurs, low and wicked. "In any other circumstance, I'd be more than happy to give it to you. But hell, I think you'd enjoy it a little too much."

"You're not wrong," I taunt, refusing to back down despite the dizziness hitting me from his brutal manhandling of my body.

So what if he knows I'm attracted to him? Knows this little dance we do with each other only serves as the best kind of foreplay?

I'm many things; a liar isn't one of them. There's no way I'm going to start now just to appease him.

His smirk is filled with venom, and I instantly know I'm not going to like what he has to say next. "Too bad the only way I'll even consider touching your ass is if it were to bury you six feet under after snapping your fucking neck like a twig."

With that final barb, he releases his hold on me, heading back over to his own locker to get dressed. Leaving me disoriented with the beginnings of a killer headache.

Pulling myself into a sitting position, I stare at his back as he starts pulling clothes from a duffle inside his cubby, wondering how in the ever-loving fuck he has this much hatred brewing inside him for me alone.

"Stop *staring* at me."

I don't stop staring.

His eyes flick up to mine and he throws his duffle back into his locker, stalking back to me once again. "You need to get this through your goddamn skull. Hate isn't a strong enough word to describe what I feel for you. The only reason I bother interacting with your queer ass is because football means the world to me. Stop messing with it." His face is so close, I can feel the dampness of his skin, sending a chill through me. "Stop staring at me like you want to fuck me. Stop with the witty bullshit that never fails to fall from your arrogant mouth. Jesus Christ, if you stopped *breathing* around me, that'd be preferable."

My blood boils at his words, the infuriating way they make me want to do the exact opposite of what I know I *should*. I'm not normally a hothead, but something about this guy has me bursting with animosity.

"What the hell is your problem?" I roar, getting in his face and pushing him in the chest. My fingers slide against the smooth muscles of his pecs, small droplets of water clinging to them, and I have the urge to lick every single one of them.

Fuck. Why do I have to want the one guy on the team, hell, in the school, *that hates me?*

His lips curl back in a sneer, just about knocking me off my feet; it's filled with that much disdain. "How many times do I have to answer that? You're my problem! Jesus Christ, can I make it more obvious to you?"

Blinking rapidly, I shake my head in an attempt to make sense of what is happening, but to no avail. "No, please. Tell me. What *exactly* is it that I do that gets you this *fucking* pissed off to the point you would be willing to risk injuring your *fucking* quarterback in the middle of the *fucking* season?"

He tosses his hands in the air. "It's everything you do! Don't you get it? You walk around on this field more arrogant than God, and smacking the asses of your teammates when you're *bisexual.*" He spits the last word as if it's something disgusting, a word that has no business coming from his mouth. "It's uncomfortable to watch, so I can only imagine how the guys you do it to feel."

My eyebrows shoot up to my hairline. "No one on this team has *ever* mentioned ass smacking has made them uncomfortable. In all the years I've played ball, in the amount of time I've been openly *out*, not a damn person has mentioned it to me."

At least, I don't think.

Running through my time as an "outed" man, I can't find a time where any of my friends or teammates have had jack shit to say about my sexuality. In all honesty, they shouldn't have an issue anyway. Who I fuck is of no concern to them.

Or in this particular circumstance, to Rain.

A scoff leaves his lips as he crosses his arms over his sculpted chest. "Because they'd be *so* willing to tell you, right?"

Okay, true.

"Come on, Grady. It's not a big deal unless you make it out to be one. Plenty of guys slap ass in football. Stop being a damn homophobe about something that literally *does not concern you.*"

"Doesn't *concern* me?" he bursts in outrage. "It's practically sexual harassment, River! You could be kicked off the damn team for shit like that if someone decided to report it." His words come out with a sharp bite, snapping at me with ferocity. "So it *does* concern me. I didn't move across the goddamn country to play for a team with a subpar backup QB. I'm looking to get a damn bowl ring this year, so do us a favor and keep your hands to yourself."

"You didn't seem to give two shits about bowl rings when you were crushing my throwing wrist not more than half an hour ago *on the damn field.*" Being the sarcastic asshole I am, I smirk and release another taunt. "In fact, I don't think it has anything to do with bowl rings and *everything* to do with the fact that it's not *your* ass my hands are on. Am I right? Are you *jealous?*"

It's comical the way his eyes practically bug out of his skull at my comment, giving me a stupid amount of pleasure at his discomfort. "What? No. *No,*" he sputters, his eyes flying around the locker room. They land on the floor, the lockers behind me, the bench to his left. Basically anywhere but my face.

What the hell? There's no fucking way...

But the flush coating his face, the set of his jaw...it all speaks truth to my statement. Which is...shocking to say the least.

I can't keep the incredulity from my voice. "Wait, *are you* jealous?"

His amber eyes are on mine in a flash. He's composed himself quickly enough, but I know what I saw. I *know* I'm right.

"No, I'm not fucking *jealous.* I just told you it makes me feel awkward as shit."

Awkward... *okay.*

I smirk, having caught him between his lies spewing from his mouth like a waterfall. "It's just the two of us here, Rain. You can take off the mask." Stepping into his personal space, I press my palms into the cubby on either side of his head, caging him in. "That's why you haven't put your money where your mouth is?

Why you haven't hit me or done anything more than wrap your hand around my throat? You want me all for yourself, yeah, baby?"

His eyes search mine and the amount of panic in them makes me smile. I take a deep breath, loving that I can practically *smell* his fear and anxiety in this moment.

Oh, how the tables have turned.

"It's okay to admit it, you know. Because I don't mind giving you a piece of the action too." Rolling my teeth over my bottom lip, I slide a hand down from the locker, gripping his chin in my hand. His breaths come out in short, staggered pants as my gaze moves over his face, resting on his cheekbones, his jaw.

His lips.

The top slightly thinner than the bottom, but still pink and perfect and *right there* for the taking.

He must notice what has caught my attention because he grabs my jaw and yanks my head up, forcing my eyes to meet his. "If you kiss me, I swear on my life, I'll fucking kill you and everyone you've ever met." His growl is missing its usual bite though, and when my fingers graze down his obliques, I swear he trembles under my touch.

"You're full of death threats today, huh, baby?"

"River, I fucking swear—"

"Relax," I soothe, cutting off his protest. "Who said anything about kissing?" I knock his hand off my face and move in again, rubbing my nose down the length of his jaw. Tightening my hold on his chin, I pull his head to the side to give me access to his neck. My lips brush against the pulse there, a whisper of a touch, and this time he really does shudder.

I grin before nipping at his collarbone as my free hand fingers the edge of the towel wrapped around his waist, slowly creeping toward the knot holding it together. "I'd much rather bite. Lick. Suck and fuck. Leave marks on you that a kiss just doesn't accomplish."

And then I drop my knees.

Bringing down the only barrier of decency he had with me.

ELEVEN
Rain

Panic floods my veins as my towel drops from my hips to the floor, landing at my feet between us.

No, not between us. Under him. Under his damn knees.

Because the cocksucker is on his goddamn knees in front of me, naked as the day I was born, staring at my dick like it's a lollipop, and all he wants to do is take a lick.

And that isn't even the worst part.

I'm also—to my horror—*hard*. Harder than stone. Granite. A fucking diamond.

No. No. Fuck me. No!

The way he grins up at me before snaking his hands around the backs of my thighs, right below my ass cheeks, has me clutching the sides of my cubby behind me so I don't lose my balance entirely.

Because the look he's giving me—*my cock*—is like a kid on

Christmas morning. Effectively tilting my entire world on its axis.

"Looks to me like you're ready to take me up on my offer of a nice blowie after all, huh, baby?" he taunts before his wicked tongue lashes out, swiping against the tip of my cock at an agonizingly torturous pace.

A groan slips from my lips without permission, and I curse myself—and him—for the precarious situation I find myself in. My knuckles blanch as he runs the flat of his tongue from my base to crown in a long, languid stroke, flicking the tip at the sensitive underside of the head.

It's torment and bliss wrapped into a single six-foot-two package.

"Fuck," I breathe, my eyes begging to close and allow my brain to enjoy the pleasure being wreaked on my body. But I can't look away.

Before I can make a move to push him away, *because that's what I should do*, his tongue travels down one side of my V. It slides across my lower torso, just above the base of my dick, then back up the other side. He pays special attention to the inked line of text on my hip, nibbling at the tattoo with his perfect fucking teeth before lapping at the imprints he left behind.

"*Some rise by sin, and some by virtue fall*," he murmurs, his hot breath whispering across my hip as he reads the Shakespeare quote, written in a gothic font. The one I got the day I turned eighteen, if only to remind me the dirty, ugly truth of this world is the vile and corrupt will always claw their way to the top, and the good never get what they deserve.

I should know. I've seen it. Lived it.

And to my shame, embody it.

His teeth latch onto the word *sin,* and my fucking God, what it does to my cock is just that.

Sinful.

Every inch of my skin tingles where he touches me. And even where he isn't. Fire and ice lick through my veins with every swipe of his tongue and harsh bite of his teeth, making my brain short circuit in pleasure.

A pleasure only serving to cause me self-loathing and agony.

Jesus Christ, I've died and gone straight to hell.

Moving his assault to below my belly button, he traces his mouth down the thin happy trail leading back to my aching cock. It bobs with need as his mouth comes near again, pleading for his attention.

"And here I thought you didn't like me." He laughs against my skin, the sound husky and threaded with desire.

"I don't," I hiss through gritted teeth, begging my body to get on board with my mind. But my cock has a mind of its own, and he is firmly in what camp gets him deep down River's throat. And my body continues to betray me, throbbing and desperate to cum on the spot when one of his hands brush across my taint on its way to wrap around my dick.

"Your cock begs to differ."

And then his mouth surrounds me, enveloping my length in the most glorious way I've ever felt. I don't think anything—mouth, pussy, or otherwise—has ever set each and every nerve ending in my body on fire from a single touch.

His mouth...it will be my undoing.

My eyes snap closed on impulse as he takes me deep in his

mouth, working me back down his throat. He's not gentle or shy about the way he touches and sucks and fucks me with his mouth, moving faster and more assured than any other person ever has while bobbing on my cock.

All except one.

And when I open my eyes again, it's not the teal oceans of River's eyes staring back up at me, but two chocolate orbs I despise.

My lip curls back in a snarl as I watch my length disappear down his throat with every pump of my hips, but his eyes never leave mine. They always watch me, never look away for even a moment. As if he doesn't want to miss a second of what he does to me.

Without a second thought, my fingers fly to the dark blond hair at the top of his head, tangling through the strands as I struggle to get a better grip. Clutching his hair for dear life, I start slamming my hips forward, hitting the back of his throat with each measured thrust. Water wells in the corner of his eyes, but he still holds my gaze.

Look away. Look away, goddamnit.

But he won't give in, no matter how hard and fast I fuck his face, using my hands to pull his mouth on me at a rapid pace while at the same time pounding forward into him. His hands cup my balls and he kneads them gently in his palm, pulling and tugging at just the right moments, when my cock is in the deepest part of his throat, to have me seeing stars.

But then something strange happens.

His eyes, they shift from brown to aqua for a split second just before…they close. They fucking close as he releases my cock, moving down below it before sucking one of my balls into his mouth.

He's never done this before.

His fingers gently brush my inner thigh, his touch a light, teasing caress, as his tongue swirls around my sac, licking and milking it as if it's the last thing he'll ever do. A moan slips past my lips at the thought of him never being able to do this to me again.

Because he won't. This will be the last fucking time.

When his mouth disengages from my balls, I groan.

Damn him for making this feel so good.

I feel his tongue trace a lazy path down my taint before descending down the inside of my thigh in hot, open-mouthed sucks.

Another new piece added to this never-ending nightmare.

"I had a feeling you'd like having your balls sucked, baby," he *mumbles against my skin, but the voice is all wrong, just like the words. It's not deep enough, not filled with the memories of verbal lashings and torment.*

And he never speaks, not until after.

"I bet you'd love it even more with a finger in your ass. Or maybe you'd prefer my tongue."

My eyes snap open, dazed and confused as I see a head full of brown hair making its way back up toward my cock. River's ocean eyes latch onto mine for a brief moment before sliding closed as his mouth surrounds my length once again.

River.

I shudder, not only from the pleasure his mouth is giving me, but out of relief.

Thank fuck. It's just River.

Fuck. Wait. No.

It's fucking *River.*

It's been him…this whole time.

Mortification slams into me at a neck-breaking speed because, *for fuck's sake*, I just…he's…and I'm…

I need to end this, before it goes too far, or even further than I've already taken it, but my brain can't formulate a thought past the ecstasy his mouth is giving my body.

My fingers slide into his hair in an attempt to pull him off me. But it doesn't work. He doesn't *let* me. Just keeps working me over with his tongue that lashes right back at my most brutal insults. Those lips that smirk each time he realizes he's weighted and measured me, only to back me into a corner.

Exactly where he wants me.

Like he has right now.

As if sensing my thoughts, his eyes snap back open to mine.

Blue as an ocean. Not brown.

Not. Brown.

I watch, transfixed, as he moves up and down my length, eyes locked on mine. And the sight of my cock between his pink lips, his gaze staring deep into my soul, it has me fighting so damn hard not to shoot my load into his mouth.

"You on your goddamn knees for me…it's a good look on you." Shifting my hips, I roll them into him, letting him take me impossibly deep down his throat. My fingers, still wrapped in his hair, clutch at the strands, and I hold him steady while I fuck his face again.

But this time, it's him I see.

Only him.

He gives me control over him, the one thing I've craved from him since the beginning of this fucked-up mess between us, and it does something to me.

He lights a fire inside me I've never felt before, burning brighter than the sun, consuming me in flames and embers. Its dangerous intensity threatens to char each and every inch of my perfectly crafted facade of indifference toward him.

Because as much as I can't *stand* it, I'm not indifferent to him. I feel the chemistry buzzing between us. It's liquid hot. I'd have to be deaf, dumb, and stupid to not feel it.

Doesn't mean I *want it.*

A low moan comes from River while my cock is lodged deep down his throat, so deep I swear I can see it moving behind his Adam's apple. His eyes ensnare mine as he practically swallows my cock whole, the sensation causing me to go off like a rocket, spilling into the back of his throat before I can stop it.

He continues to suck my dick, swirling his tongue around it as I grunt, continuing to spray the longest orgasm of my life into his stomach. And he keeps licking, like it's a goddamn sucker. Not letting up on his assault on me until my hand releases its hold on his hair.

Once he's satisfied to have sucked and lapped every last drop of cum from me, River leans back on his heels and glances up at me. His chest is heaving as he attempts to regulate his breathing. Unspoken words flash between us, the most prevalent being this…never fucking happened. I'm screaming it in my mind, but my lips can't form the words. All I can do is gape at him.

Stare at the tiny glistening spot of cum at the corner of his mouth.

His tongue flicks out to lick his lips and he must taste or feel it, because his thumb reaches up and wipes it away before bringing it out in front of his face to look at the transferred fluid.

And then the strangest thing happens.

He smirks at my cum on his finger. Breaks out into a huge grin, actually, like the sight of it is the funniest damn thing in the world.

To be clear, it's not funny. At all.

It's actually *really* bad.

He's had my cock in his mouth. Tasted my skin. My cum. My fucking *desire* for him.

And it's so fucking wrong.

The glimmer of liquid sitting on the pad of his thumb shows… he finally *got to me.*

He licks his lips as he rises from his knees and laughs, a sound so rich and decadent, like warm honey. I hate that I like it.

And when he's directly in front of me again, our eyes at the same level, I swear to God he's about to lick that drop of cum off his finger in the vulgar way men do after eating pussy.

It's honestly a move I can see River pulling, the dickwad fuckboy he is.

I open my mouth to tell him off, to tell him to leave, to say *something,* but the second I do, his thumb is inside it. Brushing against my tongue, leaving behind the salty tang of my cum.

Mother. Fucker.

His thumb presses against my tongue with enough pressure to keep me from speaking, and he leans forward, his lips brushing against my ear. "I love the way you fight me, baby. It makes the taste of your cum that much fucking sweeter."

And then he pushes off the locker, grabbing his bag on the way to the door.

Not bothering to look back.

TWELVE
Rain

I hear my name being called as I open the entry door from the quad to the weight room, just wanting to get in a quick workout before the next couple days off. When I spin around, I spot River halfway across the open

I'd never admit it, but I've been avoiding him ever since the… incident…in the locker room.

The incident being the best blowjob I've ever received.

By none other than River motherfucking Lennox.

But it's not like he's seeking me out either.

It's been weeks since then, but shit is still so awkward. We don't fight each other, don't make snide or taunting remarks. We don't even make eye contact when we're in practice, like we've come to an unspoken agreement. The night in the locker room never happened if we pretend the other doesn't exist.

It's been working pretty damn well so far, in my opinion.

So why is he breaking the stalemate now?

My teeth grind together as he jogs my way, stopping at the bottom of the steps. He quirks a brow and nods to my gym bag slung across my chest. "What are you doing? We aren't scheduled to lift today. Or practice. Next two days, we're home free."

"I know," I bite, "but I don't have anything better to do, since Pennsylvania and I aren't exactly on speaking terms right now, so I'll be around here for the next few days with nothing to do."

His brows furrow. "You aren't going home?" he asks, completely ignoring my sharp tone.

I scoff. "For two days? No, I won't be."

"Then what are you doing for Thanksgiving?"

I sigh, rolling my eyes because *Jesus fuck* he's nosy. "Do you actually care? Now if you don't mind, I'd like to get the hell inside to lift before my grandkids are born."

River is up the steps and in my face faster than Rocky fucking Balboa. "Would it kill you to be civil, you inconsiderate douchenozzle? I was about to invite you to *my* Thanksgiving since you won't be able to spend the day with your family."

I take a step back, confused.

"What? Why the hell would you do that?" I narrow my eyes at him. "As if I would even accept your goddamn pity invite."

River sighs, clasping his fingers together on the back of his head atop his backward hat and starts backing down the stairs with a stupid amount of ease, not the least bit concerned he might trip and fall. "Sorry for trying to be a decent human being. Forget it, Rain."

He used that *damn* nickname again.

"I thought I told you not to call me that?" I hiss, my grip

tightening on the handle of the door.

He cocks his head to the side, as if to think about it. "Did you? Huh, I must've forgotten after you willingly fucked my mouth in the locker room."

There it is. Motherfucker.

I'm down the stairs with my hand around his throat in an instant, backing him into the waist height stone wall lining the staircase up the building. His eyes, more blue than green today, shine with delightful recognition of the fury he just brought forth in me.

For some messed up reason, he loves riling me up.

And for some goddamn reason…I let him.

Every single time.

"We don't speak of that. *Ever*," I growl, my nose brushing his as I speak. "It *never*. Fucking. Happened."

River leans into me, forcing his windpipe against my palm even more. "Or what?" he whispers, probably because he can't speak at any louder volume. His mouth is hovering over mine, soft and taunting, and I feel my dick twitch behind my zipper at the feel of his body against mine.

Goddamnit, what the hell?

"What are you going to do, Rain? Fuck me in an attempt to bend me to your will?" He smirks, and I *feel* it against my mouth, and *fuck yes*, that's exactly what I want in this moment. "Sorry to disappoint, baby, but you should know by now I'm anything but docile."

His hand somehow has snaked its way up and is latching on my throat before I can protest, catching me off guard. Taking full advantage of my shock, River spins us around, pressing *me* back into the wall with his entire body.

I still have a grip on his neck, but his hand feels much tighter around my throat. Then I feel the thick ridge of his erection rub against my leg and my traitorous cock decides he loves it, stiffening painfully in my pants, despite my mental revulsion.

Shit.

"In fact, some would even say I love having the upper hand, holding all the cards." His eyes flash to mine and his smile is wicked. "Being the dominant." His mouth moves to my ear and he gives the lobe a soft bite, right there in the *fucking* quad for the entire *fucking* campus to *fucking* see. I'm horrified someone might catch us.

But also…turned-on.

So turned-on, I don't even notice my hold on his throat has vanished.

"With all that said, it should come as no surprise that I usually get what I want," he taunts, removing his mouth from my ear and pulls back to look at me. "And what I *want* is to not feel like a fucking prick on Thanksgiving while I eat with my family, fully knowing you're spending it by yourself."

He shoves off me, stepping back, and starts heading down the stairs.

"I'll pick you up tomorrow at four. Don't make me wait."

"I thought I told you I didn't want your pity invite?" The snarl in my throat is evident as River pushes me aside to let himself in my apartment. "And how the fuck did you find my apartment?"

It's exactly three minutes after four, and true to his word,

River's here to pick me up and take me to *family Thanksgiving.*

Like a date or some shit.

River slams the door to my apartment behind him, stepping into the entry. "Coach," he says simply. "And I thought I told you I don't take no for an answer," he snaps, taking in the apartment for a brief moment before his glare lands on me. "And that I didn't want to wait."

"I'm not going," I growl, but that was the wrong move.

River is on me in an instant, gripping me by the collar of my shirt, and practically drags my ass to the door like he pulled me out of class that day.

"Put your goddamn shoes on and get in my car, Grady."

I don't even attempt to erase the scowl from my face as he throws my shoes at me.

Well, at least I'm Grady again and not Rain.

Once we're in his Range Rover, he pulls out onto the streets of Boulder, heading back in the direction of campus. We pass by familiar sights of the city in silence, my gaze locked out the window on the infamous Flatirons in the distance.

It must only be ten minutes before we pull into the driveway of a two-story craftsman style home in an upper middle-class neighborhood. It's nice, white and slate gray with a large, covered front porch, complete with those signature white columns. Truly, it's nothing ostentatious, but the area of town tells me it must have cost a pretty penny.

I know River comes from *some* form of money, seeing as he went to Summit Academy with the Benson twins and Coach Scott's son. But from the looks of it, he was probably one of the least wealthy kids who went to his prep school.

Which is saying something, because he drives a fucking Range Rover.

Grinding my teeth, I yank the door handle and push the car door open with unnecessary force. I round the car and start heading to the door, River hot on my heels.

He doesn't knock on the door after we climb the steps, just walks in. The aroma I distinctly recall from the past as the scent of Thanksgiving hits me hard, causing my chest to ache. Before I can stop it, thoughts of the few Thanksgivings with my father prior to when he died come rushing back to me.

Mom was never a good cook. Honestly, she sucked at it, much like she sucks at life in general these days. But when she and Dad were married, it didn't matter. He could cook well enough for the both of them, so naturally, he made everything for our Thanksgiving dinner every year.

I remember one year, he woke up at three in the morning to start prepping the turkey for cooking. He had decided to buy the biggest damn turkey I'd ever seen that year. That was the last year he was alive; I was almost eight.

We played football in the backyard after dinner every year, just the two of us, while Mom sipped a glass of wine on the deck and watched. He's the reason I grew to love football, though *his* love for it made no sense because he was from Ireland. But I played for him, even though I was more drawn to art from an extremely young age. I gave it a shot. He was even coaching my peewee team when I caught my very first pass in a game, and from that day on, I loved it too. The way it bonded us.

When he died in Afghanistan during his deployment, I kept playing.

It was the only way I continued to feel close to him.

Grief catches in my throat and I do my best to shake the thoughts away as we enter the kitchen after passing through the foyer and then the living area.

I find a tall, thin blonde woman, maybe about fifty, in the kitchen, looking like the typical Stepford housewife, complete with frilly dress, hair dolled up, and...heels.

In her own house.

"Mom," River says behind me, sliding past to catch her in a hug as she floats around the kitchen with ease. She pauses with a pan of rolls in her hand, startled, before spinning around with a huge grin on her face.

"Hi, sweetie," she exclaims, setting the pan on the island before wrapping her slender arms around River's neck. She plants a kiss on his cheek and something like...jealousy floods through my veins.

I know I shouldn't feel it. Of course his mother adores him. Any *sane* mother loves and dotes on their child. Even when they mess up.

But my mother was never like this, warm and affectionate, not after my father died. The day two men in military uniforms came to our front door to tell us my father had been killed in action, it was almost as if both my parents died.

Little did I know the death of my father would be the turning point in my life entirely.

"And who is this?" River's mom says, snapping me from my

thoughts. She gives me a warm smile as she releases River.

"Yeah, uh." River rubs the back of his neck, clearly anxious. "Mom, this is Rain. Rain, this is my mom, Kathleen."

"Hi, Rain. It's so nice to meet you. River didn't tell me he was bringing someone home for Thanksgiving." She glances over her shoulder at River and I try not to wince at the phrase *home for Thanksgiving* like it holds some sort of romantic connotation. She gives me another smile before stepping into my space and wrapping her arms around me in a similar fashion she did with her son.

And my heart clenches, knowing it's anything but normal to hug a complete stranger and somehow finding yourself feeling at home in their arms.

But I'm also livid. Because he didn't even *tell them* I was coming today.

"It's actually Ciaráin, ma'am. But it wasn't exactly planned for me to be here until last night, so I'm sorry to have caught you by surprise."

"Oh, nonsense, Ciaráin. You're more than welcome. We have plenty of food to go around." She releases me and turns back to place the rolls in the oven. "Dinner will be ready in less than ten, so you're welcome to head into the dining room and grab a seat." Glancing up at River, she nods over to the counter. "Can you set another place for your friend, sweetie? And call up to Willow and let her know it's almost time to eat? Your father should be arriving shortly so it's best we're all ready to go when he gets here."

"Sure, Mom." River smiles, seemingly forced, and kisses her on the cheek before grabbing a plate and utensils from the cabinets and heads across the hall into a formal dining room. I follow behind closely, taking my place at the seat he just set out and glance up at him.

"What the fuck, River? You didn't tell her I was coming for *Thanksgiving dinner*? Are you nuts?" I grind through my teeth, my blood boiling.

He glares down at me, fire in his eyes, and I'm honestly a little surprised. "Don't screw with me right now. I didn't have the chance to tell her, and to be frank, it is better this way." The sound of the door opening from the front of the house signals that his father must be home. I watch as a vein in River's forehead makes an appearance before he grips the back of my chair and the one next to it, leaning down into my personal space. "Just do us both a favor by sitting here and looking pretty, okay? I'm sure that should be easy enough for you."

"I'm not going to pretend to be your *boyfriend* at your fucking *family Thanksgiving*," I practically spit the words at him, I'm so pissed.

Who the fuck does he think he is right now?

"Believe me, Rain. The last thing I want is my family thinking you're my boyfriend." His growled words sting a helluva lot more than they should as he stands back up and heads out of the dining room, probably to greet his father or call for his sister per his mother's request.

Fuck him.

I didn't want to come here, he forced me into it. And now he's going to act like that? Make me sit here and act like some piece of eye candy during his family dinner. All to look like a goddamn saint for bringing in a stray? So I can sit here and let their perfect little family life eat me alive on the inside because I haven't had or seen one in years?

Yeah, fuck that.

Fuck. Him.

I'm halfway out of my seat when River walks in, a dark blonde girl behind him, probably a couple years younger than us, followed by a man who is clearly River's father. Both River and his sister, Willow I think, look like carbon copies of their parents mashed together.

His father's eyes, a dark shade of green, latch onto me the moment he enters the room, and I instantly still. He's locked me in place, in an awkward half squat, as his gaze takes me in, a stranger, at his dining room table.

God, this was a terrible idea.

Clearing my throat, I continue to get up and extend my hand to the man, hoping the fervor behind his stare lessens once I introduce myself. "Hi, sir. My name is—"

"Ciaráin Grady. Yes, I know."

What the fuck? Is River *talking about me* to his family?

It's official. I'm going to kill him.

River's father finally gives me a wry grin and grasps my hand. "Roland Lennox. And don't look too shocked, son. You were the talk of the town when you transferred out here from Clemson. Plus, you've backed it up with one hell of a season, if I might add. If I understand correctly, you've got to be close to, what, eighteen hundred receiving yards this season?" He releases me and motions to the table, so I return to my seat, River sitting to my left and his father at the head of the table on my right.

"Uh, yeah, actually." I swallow, feeling slightly less distressed with the football talk. "Riv has been throwing me some bombs. I'm really impressed with how well we've, uh, synced in such a short time," I admit, and it's not false. Eighteen hundred receiving yards puts me in the top ten of all time for a single college season, and we still have a couple games left. I've never had a season like this in my life, even with the QB at Clemson who I went to bowl games with the last two years.

River and I just...connect. On the field, that is. No other way to describe it, honestly. There are times I feel like there's a line linking our hands. One the ball has no choice but to follow.

It's magnetic.

His father, rather than smile and relax with my praise of his son, stiffens and flashes a glance between us. Giving us a tight smile, he nods. "Yes, well, that's all we can hope for to get us a National Championship this year."

Just then, Kathleen enters the dining room carrying the biggest turkey I've ever seen as River's sister sits across from me.

They're both pretty, I suppose. If you're into the typical perfect woman who goes to church on Sundays and gives you two point five perfect kids in your perfect house in the suburbs.

But that shit doesn't interest me, and neither do they.

Unfortunately for me, I *usually* tend to attract those girls regularly. I blame the tattoos and the *I don't give a fuck* attitude radiating off me in spades.

"Hi there," the sister pipes up from across the table with a small wave. "Daddy said your name is Ciaráin? I'm Willow, River's younger sister. So glad for you to join us." She says the greeting with an overly sugary sweet voice, but the way she looks me up and down, pausing on my chest and arms, tells me this "good girl" definitely has a bad side.

Not fucking interested, sweetheart.

River's mom finishes bringing in the rest of the meal, and once Roland cuts the turkey, we begin digging in. The food and the conversation, while still a little awkward, isn't terrible. Kathleen and Willow chatter on about her cheerleading bullshit while Roland and I continue to talk a bit of football, River sprinkling in a few words but, strangely enough, otherwise keeping quiet.

The guy never seems to shut the fuck up any other time I'm around him, but it's as if he's a completely different person around his family.

Briefly, I find myself wondering if they know he's *out*. I highly doubt it, since I'm not so sure it fits into this perfect little family persona they have going on. But then again, people often surprise you.

They also never fail to disappoint.

And the way I notice Roland throwing subtle jabs at River and the way he keeps glancing between us and taking large sips of his drink, like he's expecting us to jump each other at the dinner table, makes me think the latter.

I catch an undercurrent of animosity toward his son, the golden boy, and it's most definitely the latter.

As dinner winds into dessert, Roland is on his third drink, and by the looks of it, definitely starting to catch a buzz. I'm in the midst of a bite of the best pumpkin pie I've ever eaten in my life, sans whip cream because that shit is nasty, when Roland lets out a gruff laugh and walks to the liquor cabinet at the other side of the room and pours more amber liquid into his tumbler from the decanter.

"Are we going to pussyfoot around the elephant in the room?" Roland asks the table once he is seated again. I glance over at River to my left, seeing his shoulders go rigid and his knuckles blanch around the fork in his hand.

But my attention moves back to this cocksucker who clearly has an issue with my presence at his precious Thanksgiving dinner. The entire dinner, the football talk, the kind words, was a goddamn front. Not unlike my stepfather used whenever we had guests to hide the true emotion he held for me.

Fuck. I knew I should have refused to come today.

"I'm sorry, sir—" I manage through gritted teeth.

Roland cuts me off, aiming a glare at River. "You couldn't go one day in your miserable life without parading around your *boyfriend* in front of us, could you?" The word *boyfriend* leaves his mouth like an insult and my blood begins to boil. "You had to take a holiday meant for family and turn it into...*this.*"

My stomach clenches, fists curling so my nails dig into the palms of my hands as I seethe.

This douchebag.

"You're a fucking disgrace to this family and its values. It's disgusting, this *lifestyle* you're choosing to lead. *You're* disgusting," his father spits, venom and ice dripping from his voice. Roland swirls his tumbler, filled with maybe two fingers of what looks like whiskey before swallowing it down in two gulps, hissing through his teeth at the burn.

I'm on my feet before I even know what's happening, my

chair scraping loudly against the hardwood of the dining room floor. My eyes flash to River, who is gaping at me in what seems like pure terror. The blues of his eyes are looking at me like they want to drown me and use me as a life preserver all at once, and for some reason, the only thing I want is to drag him from the toxic storm about to hit his home.

My attention snaps away from him, zeroing in on the piece of garbage spewing some ridiculously vile shit to someone who is his *family*.

"Where do you get off?" I say, getting into Roland's face as he rises to his feet again, albeit a little unsteadily. "That is your fucking *son* you are speaking to. *Your son,* who is one helluva human being, I might add. He invited me to dinner tonight— no, he *forced me* to come—when he found out I was spending the holiday alone." I glance over my shoulder at River, but he's staring at the table. My heart seizes in my chest for him.

Whipping my head back to his father, I start in again, "Not that it is any of your concern, but you're completely off base. I'm not interested in cock, and honestly, River and I aren't even friends, let alone anything more than that. Yet he still took me in like the stray I am because he is a good person. Which is a fuckton more than I can say for you."

Fury ignites behind his eyes as they darken and squint into slits, narrowing in and analyzing my defense of his son. Roland goes to open his mouth and I smell the liquor on his breath, I'm that close to him.

I don't let him get a word out before my fist connects with his jaw and Roland flies to the ground, not expecting the punch.

"River deserves so much more than the likes of you for a father," I growl down at him before turning and heading for the front door.

The cool Colorado air slides over me, instantly making me regret not bringing anything more than the hoodie I'm wearing. It's already after dusk, being late November, and I look around the lamp-lit street before heading in the direction of campus.

Once I'm a block away and out of sight of the Lennox house, I pull out my phone and begin to order an Uber. I'm not a far walk from my apartment, but I'm not about to do it in the dark while it's freezing.

Just as I'm about to order the Uber, River pulls up in his Range Rover and rolls down the window.

"Get in," is all he says.

I let out a frustrated sigh before pocketing my phone and conceding to his request by climbing into the car. He looks at me for a moment in the dim lighting of the dash before pulling back onto the road, every so often tossing glances down at my hand. It's fine, not broken, just going to be sore in the morning.

If anything, I'm more concerned about having to explain the swelling to Coach Scott tomorrow.

"It's fine, River." I sigh when I catch him looking at it for the millionth time when we stop at a red light.

He nods slowly, glancing back at the traffic light. I will the damn thing to change, so I can be home and forget this entire day.

After the longest and quietest car ride of my entire life, even more awkward than the one *to* dinner, we arrive outside my apartment building. Despite wanting to be inside, I feel bad for the guy and the chaos that ensued at his expense with his family.

"I'm sorry for decking your father," I mumble, still staring out the windshield. "I mean, I'm not sorry I did it. The guy is a fucking douche. But I'm sorry if it causes any problems for you. That wasn't my intention."

I hate the words as they leave my mouth. I can't stand apologizing, admitting I was wrong. And while I might not be *wrong* in this circumstance, I'm most definitely *not* in the right.

I also hate the kinship I'm feeling for him right now.

Seems we aren't all that different when it comes to the relationships with the men who raised us. They are both complete trash.

River reaches up, turning the volume dial of the radio down, letting Deadset Society's "Like A Nightmare" fade softly into the background.

"My father..." River starts, taking a deep breath as he turns in his seat to better face me, "he had a hard time accepting it when I came out as bisexual back in high school. And since, most often, I leaned more toward men, it was even worse." His eyes shoot up from his lap, looking at me with pleading in his eyes.

What he wants from me? I have no idea.

To listen? To understand? To *get it*?

"I don't want to hear your queer pride story, Lennox," I growl under my breath. The way he winces, I immediately regret being such a dick.

But...what the fuck?

Why would he think he should be sharing this with *me* of all people?

One disaster of a Thanksgiving with his family and a shared

hatred of his piece of shit father does not make us friends.

Swallowing hard, I break eye contact and fiddle with the door handle. I'm stewing with how uncomfortable I am sitting in this car now.

River lets out an anxious laugh and my eyes dart back to him as he pulls his snapback off and runs his fingers through his hair before putting the hat back in place. It's a nervous tick if I've ever seen one, but it's out of place. Sure, I've seen him flustered, but never to this extent. Even on the football field or in the locker room before a game, he's cooler than a penguin on ice skates.

I think back to the first game this season, the way he sat there tapping his hand on his knee to his favorite song of the week, and I catch his hand twitch, as if to tap along to the beat of an imaginary song. I briefly wonder which song.

Probably Beartooth again.

"What song?" I whisper, before I can stop myself, moving my gaze from down the street to his face.

River looks down at his hand on his knee, subconsciously tapping in slight movements. "'Hated' by Beartooth," he says softly after a moment.

Called it.

And I hate that I know that about him.

That I would think to care.

Fuck me, but that's all he wants right now. I can see it written all over his face.

"I'm sorry," I whisper, guilt rising. "If you need to get it off your chest, you can. I can't promise to be nice or whatever, but…" I trail off, glancing up at him.

He gives me a nod and a soft smile filled with gratitude before continuing.

"That night, he and my mom fought about it while I was up in my room. They shouted at each other and my mother told him she was just as *displeased* by my announcement, but they were still my parents. And she told him if he can't get behind that, he needed to get out. Apparently he was so against it, so furious about it, he did just that." I watch tears well in his eyes as he shakes his head, looking down at his hands in his lap again. "Afterward, he came up to my room and when he looked at me, I could tell it was only going to get worse. He yelled at me, screamed even. He was so disgusted with me, he even had the audacity to ask me to *just be straight* until I went away for college. When I told him I couldn't pretend to be someone I'm not, someone he could *live with*, he packed a bag and he just. Fucking. *Left*." He clears his throat, focusing his gaze out the windshield. "He moved out and filed for a divorce not even a week later. It broke me, and I don't think I've ever fully healed."

My pulse quickens as his revelation sinks in, burning me alive from the inside out. I know more of what he is saying than I'm willing to admit.

A family, the worst kind of scum to walk the Earth.

Being told you have to keep a piece of who you are hidden from the world.

It's for different circumstances, sure.

But I know what it feels like all too well.

"He comes by for weekly dinners and we spend all our holidays together, which is probably the worst part. He likes to feel like he still has control over the three of us. Me, most of all." He lets out a sigh and licks his lips before shaking his head. "I've never told anyone that before. Besides Taylor," he whispers, finishing his thoughts before meeting my eyes. I can see the truth in them. They're coated with a glossy sheen, and my cold, dead heart actually manages to ache for him.

It's stupid of him to say this to me, his sworn enemy. The amount of ammunition I gained from his disclosure is astronomical if I ever decided to use it.

Only, I know I won't.

I let out a breath, the heaviness sitting on my chest making me feel like I'm drowning in his pain. My jaw ticks, my teeth grinding while I debate what to say in response.

Because I have to say *something*.

I nod once, twice, before sighing and rubbing my jaw. Opening the door, I prepare to bolt.

But then I speak the truth.

"You aren't disgusting, River. He is."

THIRTEEN
River

"C'mon guys, get your heads in this. We're only down by ten. This game is far from fucking over," I hiss to my offensive line in our huddle on our opponents forty yard line.

We're starting the fourth quarter in the last game to clinch a spot in the playoffs.

And we're losing.

Not by a lot, it's completely conceivable that we could come back and win this game.

Well, maybe if a certain wide receiver got his head out of his ass and started playing the way I know he can play, because the number eighty-three on this field is not the Ciaráin Grady who was nominated for a Heisman two years in a row.

No, the guy playing right now would be picked dead last to play badminton in gym class, that's the level of trash he's playing at right now.

Truth be told, he's been off his game ever since that day in the locker room. We'd barely spoken three words to each other up until that day outside the gym when I forced him to come to Thanksgiving.

Fucking Thanksgiving.

Shit, after that disaster this past week—the most awkward Thanksgiving in the history of the holiday, by the way—it's like he turned into a fumbling idiot.

Literally.

The idiot has fumbled the ball *twice* in the first half of this game. If he could have kept his shit together on either of those passes and *not* ended up turning the ball over to the other team, it would have resulted in some kind of score.

And for the life of me, I can't understand *why*.

Yeah, it was awful by any *meeting the parents standard*, but this wasn't even that. He was there as my guest because contrary to what he might think, I do my best to be a genuine, nice person. That's how I was raised, and even if my father can't accept who I am at my very core, I still hold onto those values he and Mom instilled in me as a kid.

And *he* decked *my* father, not the other way around.

Rain's threatened to punch and even maim and kill me without batting an eye, yet he gives my father what he has coming and now he's, what? Embarrassed?

Nah, that shit doesn't fly.

"Grady," I growl at him, attempting to get his attention, but he won't look up at me. He hasn't looked at me once since the night he got out of my car and practically ran into his apartment. *After he told me I wasn't disgusting.*

I don't even have it in me to unpack the meaning behind that one because I'm so sick of having hope we'll be anything but the bane of the other's existence. Even when all I *really* wanted was friendship.

"Grady," I snap again, grabbing the front of his facemask, yanking his head until it's directly in front of mine. And for the first time in almost a week, I'm met with the golden hazel eyes that haunt me.

And they look...exhausted. *He* looks exhausted.

"Are you good? Can you get your shit together enough to help win this game so we can get in the playoffs?"

He doesn't answer, just narrows his eyes at me.

Whatever.

I release him and cast a glance at Drew, who is watching with amusement. *Just like the other eight guys in this huddle.* "Can I count on you if I need to go long?" I ask him, cocking my head.

"Always." He nods, but not before his eyes flash between Grady and me.

I haven't said much to E or Drew about the shit going on between Ciaráin and I. Shit, I haven't talked to *anyone* about it. Not even Taylor.

But how exactly do you call up your best friend and ask for advice in this situation? How the hell do you slide that into a conversation?

Hey, T. I know you're busy with your own shit and getting ready for baseball season, but I blew my arch nemesis in the locker room during practice after your dad kicked us out for an altercation on the field. And then to top it off, I invited him to Thanksgiving where he proceeded to

punch my *father for insinuating he and I were screwing. But anyway,*
how have you been?

Yeah, not gonna happen.

Breaking the huddle, I shake my head as I watch Rain jog over into position. Even the way he's moving, it's off. Slow and sluggish.

Has he not been sleeping or something?

God, why do I even care?

I can sit here until I'm blue in the face, screaming to myself that it's only because we have a damn game to win, but deep down I know I care just because *I fucking care.*

I wear my heart on my sleeve, caring about people who couldn't give a damn about me, and unfortunately, it's a fatal flaw. One I can't seem to break free from.

Positioning myself behind my center, Aiden, I call out the play and the ball is in my hands not a moment later. Looking downfield, my eyes immediately catch on Drew, who is being double covered.

Of course.

The defense knows Rain has been off his game, otherwise he would be the one they'd have under double coverage.

My eyes find number eighty-three down the field as I dance around the pocket, looking for an opening. He's got a bit of space between him and his defender, so trusting my gut, I launch the ball in his direction.

I watch as it sails through the air, a perfect spiral, and lands safely in his arms at the twenty yard line. But the moment he turns and starts making forward progress, he's slammed into from behind by his defender.

And the goddamn ball is loose on the field.

For the *third* time today.

And all I can see is red the second the opposing team scoops up the ball and starts running it back toward me. I continue to watch in horror as he evades three of our players before finally being tackled on their own thirty yard line.

Jogging over toward the sidelines, I spot Ciaráin with his helmet off, rubbing the back of his neck as he runs toward me to get to our bench. But like he can sense me, he looks up and fury instantly crosses his features.

"What the actual fuck, River!" he screams at me when he's only ten yards away from me.

I go to grab him and pull him off the field when he rips my hand from its hold on his jersey.

"Don't fucking touch me!" he screams as our defense starts running onto the field around us. "What the hell was that crap? You said you were throwing to Benson!"

I yank my helmet from my head and scowl. "That might have been the plan, but you have to be ready for anything. When you're on this field, you are ready to have the ball thrown at you. He was in double coverage and you were open, so I made the choice to throw to you."

"You could have run the damn ball!" He shouts the words, getting in my face.

I roll my eyes, feeling my temper rising to dangerous levels. "We needed yards I can't run, Grady. Use your head and think about what you're saying."

"Well, your *decision* just caused us to turn the ball over again!"

I scoff, getting up in his face, our noses brushing against each other as my hand grips his collar. "I made the decision to throw you the ball, yeah. But don't sit here and try to pin your fuck-ups on me because you're the one who fumbled the ball *again,* and that's on *you and you alone.*"

"Yeah, well, maybe if we didn't have a faggot for a QB whose only focus is staring at ass instead of making proper play calls, we would actually win this goddamn game."

Actually?

I laugh in disbelief at his audacity. Gripping his collar tighter in my fist, I move my lips to his ear, whispering directly into it, "Or maybe if your homophobic ass could stop thinking about how good it felt to have your dick down my throat, then you could actually manage to hold onto the fucking ball."

With that said, I give him a hard shove and turn away, heading to the sidelines until I'm needed on the field again.

Only I don't make it more than two steps before he grips my arm, yanking it so I spin back around. I don't even have to look to know it's Ciaráin. The way my skin is scorching under his hand is confirmation enough. It's searing, actually. The way our sweat mixes on my arm, adding to the burn already present any time he touches me.

It's so distracting, I don't even feel it at first when his fist meets my cheekbone.

My head snaps to the side as a throbbing pain radiates from the spot where he landed the punch. I stumble back a couple steps, wincing at the pain as a hiss escapes my lips. My hand makes its way to my cheek, cupping it in my palm as I glance up at this asshole.

My first thought is *this fucker actually just hit me.*

And, fortunately or not, my second is an immediate *I'm the quarterback. I can't hit him back.*

No matter how much I want to.

But what I *can* do...?

My hands are on his chest pads, shoving him as hard as I can away from me. "What the hell is wrong with you?" I shout at the top of my lungs, the words ripping from my throat in a snarl.

He pulls back for another punch, but I'm prepared this time, ready to block or dodge him.

Only, I don't have to because Aiden is behind him, restraining him in a headlock while he fights and struggles to get at me. Drew steps in between us, a palm on either of our chests when I feel someone's hand on my throwing wrist, holding me in place.

Glancing up, I find Elliott at my side, his eyes on his twin, Aiden, and Rain.

"Think about who you're throwing punches at, Grady," Elliott says in a low voice, eyes narrowed on him. "Because it isn't a fair fight when you know he won't hit back."

Ciaráin doesn't have the chance to respond though, because everyone is crowding around us now, including Coach Scott and the officiating crew.

"Eighty-three, eighteen, those are flagrant personal fouls," the white hat says. He turns to Coach, nodding his head at us. "I have to toss these two, Coach. They need to hit the showers."

"I understand, Al," Coach Scott says to the referee, his glare aimed at us. "You two. Locker room. Now. And you'll wait there for me until after the game."

Anger bubbles inside me.

Ejected.

I was just ejected.

Yanking my arm from Elliott's grip, I stalk toward the tunnel, not bothering to look back at the team. I can feel their stares of disappointment searing into my back, every single eye burning holes into my skin. Hell, the entire *stadium* is in pandemonium, shouts and boos rushing over me in waves.

Fuck.

Never in my life have I been ejected from a game.

Never in my life have I gotten into an altercation with another player for any reason.

And never in my fucking life would I have thought both would happen in the most important game of the season, maybe even my career.

Pushing through the locker room door, I rip my pads over my head and toss them into my locker, the plastic banging against the wood with a *crack.* I quickly slip out of the rest of my uniform and toss that in too. Grabbing the towel from the top shelf, I head to the shower.

As I stand under the spray, I attempt to let it wash this bullshit off me, along with my shitty attitude. But the water does nothing to curb my anger. Instead it feeds it, soaking into my pores like toxic venom until I'm ready to burst.

I hear a stall slam closed and another shower start, signaling Ciaráin must be in here finally. What took him so long to get in here, I don't know.

Nor do I care at this moment.

Fuck him.

The rage inside me is a new feeling, one I'm not used to coping with. I'm a laid back, go with the flow kind of guy. Some would even say happy-go-lucky. Rage does not mix with *any* of that.

But unfortunately, that is the emotion Ciaráin Grady seems to bring forth in me more than any other.

Turning off the shower, I exit with the towel wrapped around my waist and head back to my cubby to get dressed in a pair of sweats and a long-sleeve tee. I wince as the fabric brushes against my face, already having forgotten I'm going to sport quite the shiner for the next week or two.

I head over to the mirror in the bathroom, glancing at my cheek.

It's not terribly swollen, but it's red and angry and most definitely will be black and blue in the morning.

"Aw, damn. Checking out how bad I messed up your pretty face?" Ciaráin's voice says from behind me, causing me to meet his gaze in the mirror.

I give him a glare, noting the asshole is once again only wrapped in a towel. It brings me back to the day only a few weeks ago, when I said fuck it and tugged it off him to give him the best blowjob of his life, even if he would never admit it.

Cocking my head, I turn to face him, leaning against the sink with my arms crossed over my chest. "The joke's on you, because you're the one who has to look at it every day, not me."

He taps his chin as he looks over my face and lets out an exaggerated sigh. "Well, shit, in that case, I'm regretting not giving you a matching set."

I bite my tongue so hard it starts to bleed because if I don't do *something*, I most definitely am gonna hit the dickhead.

And that would be very, very bad. Because this damn hand is my ticket to tuition free college. Which is extremely *helpful* if I'm going to be in school long enough to get a doctorate in physical therapy.

Buuuuuuuuut that doesn't mean I have to keep my mouth shut.

"Well, why don't you?" I taunt, raising my arms out to my side to offer myself up to him. "I fucking dare you."

Ciaráin takes a step toward me, his eyes narrowed into slits like a snake ready to strike. And I try really, *really* hard not to notice how the knot in the towel around his waist slips slightly with the movement, revealing more of that tattoo inscribed on his hip.

A tattoo that I've licked and sucked like it was my own personal piece of candy.

You've licked and sucked a lot more than just his tattoo, you idiot. That's why you're in this mess in the first place.

"You don't think I will?" he asks, stalking closer and closer until he's right in front of me, his face less than a foot from mine. I can feel the heat radiating off his bare chest, seeping into me through my shirt.

And I hate it.

That his proximity does this weird thing to my body, and I can't seem to get a hold on long enough to fight it.

My eyes meet his, hard and determined, and I smirk. "No, I think you *will*. I want you to, in fact. Do it again. Please. So Coach has no choice but to suspend you from the team. Or better yet, kick you off entirely because I sure as *fuck* have no interest in playing ball with you ever again. Especially for the shit show you put on out there." I look him up and down, purposely pausing on his cock for a moment too long before meeting his glare once more. "Heisman worthy, my ass."

His hand is around my throat a second later, his face only inches from mine as he sneers at me with malice. "Maybe I'll just kill you instead. Snap the golden boy's pretty little neck like I promised in that classroom. Because my world will sure as hell be a much better place without you in it."

Fighting fire with fire, I lean forward, bringing my lips a millimeter from his. The grip he has around my throat becomes more constricting as I bite out my response.

"Do it."

The words, less than a whisper, float off my lips and onto his, making him shudder at the contact.

A snarl works its way out of his throat, and it's the most animalistic sound I've ever heard come from a human. But it's quickly cut off when we're interrupted by a door being slammed open followed by both of our names being shouted.

Coach.

"In my office, right now!" he shouts, snapping us out of the stand-off we were in the midst of.

Rain releases his hold on me, stepping away and heading back to the locker room to get dressed while I stare after him. The rage still bubbling under the surface is begging me to go after him and giving him a taste of his own medicine, but I tamp it down. Just barely.

Instead, I head down the hallway to Coach Scott's office, stepping inside only a minute before Ciaráin does, now dressed similarly to me.

"Shut the door and have a seat," Coach bites out, barely

sparing us as glance after we enter. And I know immediately, this is going to be bad.

I've seen Graham Scott mad *once* in all the years I've known him. Which is since I was born.

And this…I can tell it's about to be time number two.

Ciaráin and I both take a seat, not looking at each other while we wait for Coach to ream us a new asshole.

But he doesn't. He simply takes a seat behind his desk, resting his elbows on the wood with his chin on his joined knuckles.

And he stares at us for an uncomfortable amount of time. So long I'm ready to start squirming in my seat under his penetrating gaze.

"In the game of football," he starts with a sigh, rubbing his temple with an index finger, "we win as a team and we lose as a team. That is something I've ground into the minds of every player I've ever coached because it's what was instilled in *me* since I learned how to play the game. *Everyone* is held accountable, regardless if you set foot on the field during the game or not. We are in it *together*."

I know this. I've seen it and experienced it. Even as a kid, it was something he always taught the twins, Taylor and me. And it's a motto I've played this game with from the time I was able to throw my first completed pass.

"But tonight? The loss we just suffered?" he continues, his gaze drifting between us before he shakes his head. "I can't let those guys out there be held accountable for that. How can I when it's *the two of you* who gave the other team the win the moment you decided whatever bullshit is happening between you is more important than the *team*."

Coach rolls his teeth over his lip, clearly trying to keep a more cool and collected tone with us because how can he lecture the two of us about keeping our heads when he can't practice what he preaches?

His gaze lands on Ciaráin for a moment, pinning him in place. "I know Coach Donaldson from Clemson well. He spoke highly of you, which is why the second your transfer came over my desk, I jumped at the opportunity to get you on the team." Tapping his finger on his chin, he exhales. "Your talent knows no bounds and you could go places if you chose, Ciaráin. But your attitude? The chip on your shoulder? Combined with that temper of yours, it will get you into some seriously deep shit."

His eyes leave Ciaráin and land on me, causing my heart to stop in my chest.

Because in those eyes, I see it. The one word I fear most coming from the man I've idolized for most of my life.

Disappointment.

"And you." He sighs, pinning me with a frustrated stare. "I've known you since you were a child. Helped raise you with my own son. You *are* a son to me, for all intents and purposes. So I know *for a fact* you were taught better than this. *This* is not the quarterback, nor the person, I know you to be." He pauses again, rubbing his hand over his face. "Disappointed doesn't even *begin* to cover how I'm feeling right now."

And there it is. Goddamnit.

My heart seizes in my chest and if I'm being honest, I'd rather him be screaming at us and telling me I'm doing suicides for an hour every day for the rest of the time I play for him at CU.

I'd rather have him do *anything* other than say that one word. Kick me off the team, even.

"First that stunt in practice, and now this?" he grumbles, tossing his hat on the desk. "I have *no idea* what to do when it comes to the two of you. Not a damn clue. It's not like I can leave you trapped on an island or ship you off to couple's therapy to work out your crap."

Oh, Coach, don't make me laugh at the irony behind that last statement.

Coach is silent again, his eyes slipping back and forth between the two of us as he works out our punishment in his mind. From what I've gathered, we lost the game which means our season is officially over in a game playing capacity. He could carry a suspension over into the next season, maybe.

I honestly don't know.

He taps his hand on the desk after what must be an eternity, finally coming to a decision he's comfortable with.

"You know, maybe you two *do* need to…*get away.* Figure out a way to work your shit out in a more…*therapeutic* environment." His hard glare dances between us as he speaks the words that damn near stop my heart. "Lucky for the both of you, I know just the place."

FOURTEEN
Rain

DAY ONE

"**Y**ou've got to be fucking kidding me."

I've never been this irate in my life. Even when I was told I'd have to spend the next five weeks of winter break at a "getaway" with River. Because for some insane reason, I thought Coach might be sending us to the damn beach or something.

Instead, I find myself sitting in Coach's truck, glaring out the front window at a motherfucking cabin.

In the woods.

In the mountains.

In the middle of *nowhere*.

I might as well be in a horror movie. At this point, that might be *preferable*.

"Not at all, son. Now come on, let's get you boys situated so I can show you how things run around here."

After climbing out of Coach's truck, I follow him and River up the deck steps, taking in the cabin. Sure, it's nice. An A-frame style with a hammock stand on one side of the deck, sans hammock, and one of those moveable fire pits and patio furniture on the other, sans cushions.

There's also a good eighteen inches of snow on the deck and ground, which is just *awesome*.

Walking through the side door, I take in the massive open floor plan of the cabin. I'm surprised at how large it is, the gourmet kitchen with a large island and bar stools on the left, a small dining room table set up just beyond that. Directly to my right is a sunken living room with a huge fireplace on the side wall with the entire front one full from floor-to-ceiling with glass windows looking out of the cabin at the stream flowing beyond it.

The place is stunning, I'll give it to Coach.

Glancing to my left, I notice a hallway running down the back of the house, probably where the bedrooms are. I start heading down the hall to grab a room before River can because, yeah, I'm that level of petty and pissed off right now, when I hear Coach continuing to chatter with River.

"River, you know where everything is. Nothing has changed much since you've been here last. There's plenty of wood stocked up in here, but the shed key, along with the ATV key, is hanging by the door. Just remember…"

His voice fades off in the distance as I make my way down the hall. The cabin is much larger than it seems from the outside, seeing as there are a ton of doors to choose from down the hallway. Five in total, two on each side and one at the very end.

Assuming the very end is the master suite, I head straight back and to the right, opening it to find a bedroom with a queen mattress, a dresser, and desk. Nothing too fancy, but there is a lot of open floor space which is perfect for what I have planned.

Which is to avoid the fact that I'm stuck here with my nemesis who, for some reason, can't take the hint I'm not interested in getting into his pants. *Because I'm not fucking gay.*

And the one way I can think of doing that?

Art.

That will be the only thing keeping me sane while I'm here. It's why I have five cases filled with my supplies under the cover on Coach's truck bed. It's the only form of escape away from this nightmare that's become my reality.

Because yeah, if I thought spending a single night on an away game in the same hotel room with River was bad, five weeks under the same roof *alone* is bound to be detrimental to my mental health.

And more than likely his physical well-being if he keeps being an idiot.

"Grady, get out here!" Coach yells from down the hall.

Sliding my duffle from my shoulder, I toss it on the bed and head back out to face the music.

"Yes, sir?" I ask when I'm met with his authoritative gaze.

A piece of me really wishes I didn't respect him as much as I do. It would make it so much easier to just cut my losses and leave the team or even the school to prevent this prison sentence from actually being carried out.

"River has been here plenty of times, so if you have any questions, please ask him for help."

I roll my eyes and scoff. Of course the dickface has been here before.

I shouldn't be surprised. I've heard both Drew and Elliott tell stories about their group of five, all the shit they'd get into with Taylor and a kid named Asher.

And of course, River. The kiss ass.

I'd be lying if I said I wasn't jealous as hell.

That kind of mischief was something I never got to do growing up. Without Siena and Roman, I probably would have lost my mind or cut off my ear like goddamn Van Gogh before the age of twelve.

But we never got to explore the mountains, spend time in the woods, do the things kids should do. We didn't get into trouble, cause chaos or disorder. They were always expected to be prim and proper, as was I, being who we were.

High class. Children of powerful men.

Perfect little dolls, only meant to be seen and not heard.

Fuckin' bullshit.

Coach gives me a stern look before continuing, "Everything you need is here, save for maybe a grocery run or two for things like milk and whatever perishable foods you boys might need. But I made sure the fridge and pantry is fully stocked for at least the first two weeks of your stay. You'll be able to take the ATV into town if or when you need anything else."

I just nod, attempting to accept that I am indeed being exiled to this mountain home for five. Fucking. Weeks.

He gives me a sympathetic smile before patting me on the shoulder. "It won't be that bad. Trust me, there are worse things than getting away to get your head back on your shoulders. The two of you make an excellent team when you aren't at each other's throats. You need this, if not for the team's benefit next season, then for your own personal growth." He sighs, rubbing the back of his neck. "I mean, you boys can't go punching someone when you have a disagreement. On or off the field."

I know this, I promise I do. It's common sense, really. But I swear, River makes me do some stupid shit when he opens that mouth of his.

There are times I think I would do anything—literally *anything*—to shut his goddamn mouth. Punching him out in the middle of a game seemed like the right route to go at the time.

Still, I can't say I regret it.

"C'mon, let's get those boxes you brought loaded in here before I take off," he says, motioning to the side door.

Once the truck is completely unloaded of all the shit we brought to last us the next five weeks, Coach heads back out to his truck to leave with the two of us in tow to see him off.

And I'm this close to begging him to take me back with him and telling him to kick me off the team instead. But then I think of my dad, his love for the sport, and I can't do it.

I have to see this through, if only for him

I'm just grateful River has seemingly been on his best behavior since we've arrived, barely speaking a word unless it was in conversation with Coach Scott.

"I think you're about set for me to take off. The landline works if your cell service is shit, but I'd suggest you use this time to reflect on why you're here. Don't spend your time on your phones or in front of the television. Get to know each other. Find shit in common with the other."

"How the hell would we do that?" I mumble under my breath.

But clearly Coach has the ears of a hawk because he nods out toward the cabin before speaking. "You could start by taking to the outdoors. There's plenty of good hiking around here, but the one up to the lake overlook is by far the best. I marked a path up to the trail just behind the cabin."

"I know, Coach. Don't forget I've been here a time or two." River grins.

Yeah, we get it, River. You're in tight with Coach Scott, NFL superstar, and his kid. No need to rub it in more.

"And so then you know the way back? It's been a few years since you guys have been out here." Coach raises his brow, questioning Len.

River smirks and shakes his head, which only makes Coach chuckle in return, both of them clearly in on the inside joke I'm not privy to.

"Someone want to enlighten me, so I don't get fucking lost in the middle of the mountains if I decide to take a nice stroll...and don't end up throwing myself over a cliff?"

Sounds pretty fucking good right now. Actually scratch that and point me to the nearest death drop, thanks.

Coach shakes his head and glances at River. "When these guys used to come out here with us when they were younger, since maybe about ten, they've been exploring these woods. They know them like the back of their hands *now*. But the first time we let them wander a little too far out of our eyesight, they were lost for almost two hours."

River laughs at that. "I still am convinced I knew where we were the entire time, but *your son* was convinced we were going the right way until I managed to convince *him* otherwise."

My brow quirks. "And this has fuckall to do with finding my way back to the cabin…how?"

River rolls his eyes. "Because dumbass, you just have to use common sense."

Coach's eyes snap between us. "You two going to be okay up here for this long of a time? I don't really feel like walking in on a bloody crime scene in January when I'm back to pick you idiots up."

"You wouldn't have that problem if you didn't force us to come here in the first place," I growl, unamused. "Just tell me how to get out of the damn woods if I have trouble."

Coach sighs, pinching the bridge of his nose between his thumb and forefinger. "Look, Grady, it's simple. If you think you're lost, just follow the river."

Follow River. Is he fucking serious?

My eyes shoot between them, annoyed as hell. "This some kind of joke you two think is funny? Because I'd rather let a blind woman lead me across the interstate than follow River anywhere."

River rolls his eyes before pushing off the railing of the deck. "He said *the river.* Not *me,* River." His gaze shoots passed me to look at Coach. "Although I stand by the fact that if Taylor would have followed me that day, I'm sure we would have been back a lot sooner."

Coach shakes his head and lets out a deep laugh. "We can definitely go with your story, but don't tell my son that. It would bruise his ego since he never picked up a sense of direction for being a born and raised mountain kid."

Yanking open the door to his truck, he hops in and starts it. "Don't kill each other, please. I don't want to have to explain it to your parents."

Don't have to worry about that one, Coach. Doubt they'd give two shits either way.

We watch from the deck as his truck disappears over the bridge of the stream and into the forest on the other side, back to civilization.

Since I don't particularly want to sit outside freezing my ass off and I'm definitely not looking to sit around the fire and knit sweaters with River, I head back into the cabin, finding refuge in my room.

Thankfully, River took the one diagonal from mine, so he's as far away from me as possible without sleeping outside.

I start opening the different bins I brought with me, setting the first on my desk, and begin pulling out the supplies I need to start painting. I want to start setting up my makeshift art studio as quickly as I can, needing the small slice of freedom from my thoughts and tormentor already.

"What are the crates for? Decided to move in?" River asks from the doorway not even a minute later.

Why didn't I think to shut and lock the fucking door?

Rolling my eyes, I slam the lid back on the one I was digging through and spin around to give him a mocking smile. "No, they're to hide all the pieces of your dismembered body when I end up killing you before these next five weeks are over."

His brows furrow, glancing at the five or so crates, stacked in the corner, not knowing they are filled with paint, canvas, and pads of paper, then at the one on the desk in front of me. "Okay, but we're in the middle of the mountains with literally no one around. Why wouldn't you just toss me out back for a mountain lion or something?"

Jesus Christ, leave it to River to think of a better way to dispose of his own dead body.

I shake my head. "I can't with you right now."

"You never *can* with me, Rain, so—"

I round on him in an instant, pressing him into the doorframe with my forearm on his throat. "For what might be the thousandth time, don't call me that," I snap. "In fact, don't call me anything."

"Kinda hard when we're stuck out here for over a month," he gasps.

I crush my forearm against his trachea more. "No, see Lenny, this is how shit is going to go while we're here. I'm going to stay in this room and when I'm not, you're going to be in whatever place *I'm not*." I lean in, my face inches from his and growl out the rest of my demands. "We are not going to talk. We are not going to interact. We aren't even going to breathe the same air. This will be the last time you set foot in this room, the last time you see me, the last time you bother me with the annoyance of your presence for the next five fucking weeks. Are we understood?"

River licks his lip, drawing my eyes down to them. And of course, he notices and smirks.

"Whatever you want. Just know these little rules aren't going to last long or you'll go fucking mad." His hand wraps around my forearm, ripping it from his neck. "And honestly, baby? I think it's cute how you think your cock won't end up in my mouth again before this little *vacation* is over."

My jaw ticks, and *goddamn it,* it's been ten minutes since Coach left and I'm already itching to make good on my threat to murder and dismember the asshole.

But I don't let his taunts gain the hold he wants.

No, instead, I get in his face and shove him hard out the threshold of my room, slamming the door shut and locking it for what might be the next five weeks.

FIFTEEN
River

DAY TWO

I awake with a jolt to the sound of shouting.

Confused and disorientated, I snap up to a sitting position and try to rub the sleep out of my eyes. It takes me a moment to realize I'm not in my apartment, but in the cabin Coach brought me and Grady up to yesterday afternoon.

Grady.

He's probably watching some horror or action movie in the living room at full volume just to piss me off.

Glancing over at the alarm clock on the nightstand, it tells me it's barely past two in the morning. Jesus, we haven't even been here twenty-four full hours, and he is already trying to do his best to make me fucking miserable.

With a groan, I roll off the bed and pad my way across the room, my feet hitting the freezing wood floors.

Shit, he's awake and can't even throw logs on the fire or in the wood stove?

Asshole.

Throwing on gray sweats, my *Colorado Football* hoodie, and a pair of socks, I slip out my door and head down the hall to the living room, ready to rip him a new asshole. Except, when I pass through the opening into the living area, I'm surprised to find it dark and empty.

Huh. Weird.

I know there aren't any televisions in the bedrooms, since Taylor and I have come up here in high school for long weekends when we wanted to go snowboarding.

So what the hell was that sound?

I brush it off, heading over to the fireplace to grab some logs and throw into the wood stove in the corner of the room. Maybe it was my subconscious shouting about how freezing it is in here, even by the standards of a Colorado native.

Once the stove is burning nice and hot, I grab a blanket off the back of the couch and settle in to watch a movie. The cabin isn't freezing per se, but between that and whatever startled me awake, I'm not tired anymore.

Flipping through Netflix, I settle on the new movie about Ted Bundy, because why the hell not? I love horror, suspense, and thrillers, but my guilty pleasure is anything true crime. It's not like I decided to watch *The Wrong Turn* or *The Cabin in the Woods* when I'm stranded at a cabin in the mountains with no way to leave.

I'm not a masochist.

And if I'm going to be stuck here, at least it is with a sexy as sin asshole who hates my guts in an attempt to "work out our shit."

Yeah, that was sarcasm.

Except, Rain *is* fucking sexy. Dark hair, amber eyes, and some truly phenomenal ink covering the tanned skin of his arms. I still remember the taste and feel when I ran my tongue across the tattoo running down the right side of his V.

Okay, maybe I am a masochist.

I sigh in frustration.

I don't know how the hell Coach thinks this will work.

Sure, I know he had success with this tactic in the past, before I came to CU. Hell, he's even threatened to send the twins out here because they are constantly at each other's throats for no reason. For sharing the exact same DNA, they are completely different, and I think that is most of the issue in itself. But at the end of the day, they're *brothers. Twins*, for fuck's sake. They have an undeniable bond with each other, and I tend to agree that them spending time out here to work their shit out would be helpful.

Ciaráin Grady and I are a completely different story.

We don't have a bond so strong it can withstand anything. We barely know each other, and what we do know, we don't fucking like.

I hate his arrogance, like he is above me because I'm bisexual. I hate how he has to antagonize and torment me about anything and everything. I hate how he refuses to grow up and just accept that, yes, not everyone in the entire world is straight.

But I also hate how stupidly turned-on he makes me when we face off against each other. How his muscles flex when he lifts weights in the gym. How we somehow have this unspeakable connection on the football field, like his hands are a beacon for my arm to throw to.

Most of all, I hate how, if things were different, I wouldn't hate him at all.

Even now, I don't know if I actually do.

I shake the thoughts I don't want to hear from my mind, focusing back onto the movie in front of me, or maybe on being able to fall back asleep now that I'm not as frozen as a popsicle.

I'm around an hour into the movie, at the part where Zac Efron, who plays Bundy, starts his trial in the state of Florida when an ear-splitting scream comes from down the hall, causing me to jump.

Scrambling to my feet, I rush down the hall to Rain's room, where I hear him shouting on the other side of the door.

"No, stop!" he yells, despair evident in his voice.

Is someone in there with him?

I grip the doorknob and twist, but it's locked.

"Rain!" I call, pounding on the door as loud as I can, as if he could come unlock it if someone is in there with him.

Panic rises as I continue to listen helplessly to his shouts, which quickly turns to pleading.

"Please. Please don't do this," Rain sobs, and the sound fucking rips my heart to shreds. "I'll be good."

Wait. *What?*

That doesn't make sense to say to someone who is coming in to, what, kidnap him? Kill him?

Is he… dreaming?

My brows furrow, but I continue smashing my fists into the door, willing it to open. Of course, it doesn't.

"Rain, it's River. Are you okay? Fucking talk to me!" I keep slamming my fists and yell his name, desperate for a coherent response from him.

Suddenly, the shouting stops, and I hear the telltale sign of feet moving across the floor just as the door flies open to reveal Rain.

He's drenched in sweat, covering his exposed chest and abs, even coating his dark hair to his forehead. My gaze slides down to find him wearing only boxer briefs, and my eyebrows shoot to my forehead when I notice his impressive erection tenting them.

What the…?

"What, River?" he snaps in irritation, forcing my eyes up to meet his. They're dark and angry, but I also see something new and unfamiliar behind them.

Fear, maybe?

"Did you really wake me up just to gawk at me half naked? Because I swear to God, if you keep looking at my cock like that, I'm going to make good use of it and shove it down your throat. Again."

I clench my jaw, doing my best to keep my temper under control.

But for fuck's sake, he was shouting and screaming and *sobbing* in his sleep moments ago. Sue me for giving a shit.

"I heard yelling," I state calmly. "I was checking to see if you were okay. When you didn't respond…" I trail off when I see his dark brow quirk up in amusement.

Fuck him, he doesn't deserve my worry.

"What, you were concerned for my well-being?" He scoffs. "Tell me something I'll actually believe. Because the idea of either one of us actually giving a flying shit about the other is more far fetched than flying pigs on Mars."

I do my best not to wince at his words. We might be enemies, but I'm not so demented that I wouldn't care if something bad happened to him. Still, he must catch my flinch, because he lets out a low, unamused laugh, and shakes his head.

"I'm fine, River. Go back to fucking sleep," he says with a growl before slamming the door in my face for the second time today.

SIXTEEN

River

DAY FOUR

I'm lounging on the couch in the living room, a paperback in hand when Rain comes barreling down the hall in a blur.

He made himself scarce after the first day we got here, not leaving his room unless it was to take a piss or grab something to eat from what I can tell. Who knows what he is doing in his room alone for twenty-hours a day other than doing his best to avoid me?

I can't say I blame him. I want to be stuck here with him for a month as much as he wants to be here with me.

Not at all.

"Where's the fire?" I laugh in an attempt to defuse any tension when he almost trips on his own damn feet.

We haven't spoken a word to each other since the first night, when he woke me with his shouts and screams from what I'm assuming is a nightmare.

He's had them every night since we got here.

I know, because for the past couple days, I'm startled awake in the dead of night to the sound of him battling whatever haunts his dreams. And every night I grab a blanket and pad over to his room, sliding down the wall to sit and wait. Listening to make sure he's okay. Waiting until he manages to evade his demons and slip back into what, I hope, is a more peaceful slumber.

The lack of sleep on my end is a bitch, but at least I know nothing is hurting him.

Physically, that is.

"There isn't one, that's the problem," he grumbles in a huff as he storms over to the fireplace. He begins building a fire, the muscles of his back and arms taunting me as they flex under the fitted long sleeve shirt he's wearing.

Why couldn't the bastard be less attractive?

The saying might go all good guys are either gay or married, but they forget to mention the sexiest ones are always homophobic assholes.

Case in point? Ciaráin fucking Grady.

"Need a hand?" I offer, dog-earring my worn copy of Orwell's *1984*.

"I've got it," he grunts as he strikes a couple matches, tossing them into the pile of logs and newspapers. Soon, the fire is roaring to life, giving the living room a little more heat.

He unfortunately discovered the first night that this cabin, while stunning and on a gorgeous, secluded plot of land, doesn't have electric heating like all the resorts and homes down in the town of Vail.

Rain grabs a blanket from the basket beside the recliner adjacent to the couch I'm lying on and wraps it around himself before sitting on the floor directly in front of the fire.

"Jesus Christ, how do you people survive these kinds of winter? My hands are fucking freezing."

"Feel free to put them down my pants."

The words tumble out of my mouth before I have the chance to think twice. It's a crude comment, one I'd make with any friend and it would almost always be laughed off.

Except, this is Rain.

And by the way his spine just snapped to attention, I'm about to regret my lack of filter.

"The fuck did you say to me, Lennox?"

In all honesty, there are two ways I can play this. One would be to apologize, say I didn't mean anything by it.

On the other hand...

"I mean you'd get your hands warm and I'd get some action in the process. Sounds like a win-win to me, Grady."

Goddamn it, River. Why do you have to antagonize him at every available opportunity?

But I know why. As strange as it is, fighting with him is my favorite kind of foreplay. I'd be lying if I said it didn't get me a little hot and hard.

Rain shoots up from the floor and is instantly hovering over me, both hands plastered to the back of the sofa on either side of my head. His face is so close I can smell the mint of his toothpaste on his breath. I have the urge to close the space between us and taste his mouth.

Attraction is a strange thing, and the kind I have for him is dangerous.

Makes-me-stupid-and-reckless kind of dangerous.

Ruin-my-life kind of dangerous.

"Why, River? Why do you have to egg me on when you know it will blow up in your face every time?"

I grin. "You make it so easy. Like right now? There are so many things I could do with that 'blow' comment you just made. But I'll keep it to myself if you promise I'll get rewarded for being a good boy."

I feel Rain clench the fabric of the couch cushion in his fists and watch in fascination as he winces slightly before his stubbled jaw ticks in anger. My breath hitches when I think about what it would feel like to run my tongue along it, then down his neck, nipping at his pulse before trailing wet kisses down his pecs...

Fuck, now I'm hard...*er.*

"Stop fucking with me. Especially with *anything* related to blowing. Or shit is gonna get ugly."

"Not my fault you can't handle me giving you the best blowjob of your life, man."

"You didn't, not even close," he spews, his voice laced with venom.

I cock a brow. "Really? So you're telling me you didn't grab onto my hair and fuck my face until you came so damn hard down my throat, my voice was hoarse the next day?" I nod my head in mock acceptance before continuing, sarcasm dripping from the words. "Okay, yeah. I believe you."

"That's not—"

"What happened? Oh, I know. Not at all." An indignant laugh escapes me. "Why can't you just accept it? It's not a big deal a dude blew you and you liked it."

Rain pushes off the couch with a huff. "I don't even like *you*, let alone what you did to me in that locker room."

What. A. Liar.

Rolling my eyes, I stand and get in his face. "I think you like me a lot more than you're willing to let yourself admit."

"And I think you're delusional, and Coach locked me up here with someone who is certifiably insane."

"And *I think* I'd rather be batshit crazy than be so uncomfortable in my sexuality to the point where I have to constantly lie about being attracted to someone of the same sex."

The pulse in his neck is beating rapidly and I can practically see the steam coming from his ears.

Good, I'm getting under his skin.

"In fact," I continue, "I think the real issue you have is you're also bi. Just unwilling to acknowledge it. You know, methinks the lad doth protesteth too much and all that."

Jesus, I'm asking to get decked today.

Again.

"Fuck this," Rain mumbles, brushing past me to head down the hall, and I'm sure, to the safety of his room.

But do I let it go and relish in my victory?

Nope.

I chase after the douche canoe, reaching his door as it slams closed. Trying the knob, I find he's already locked himself inside.

"Let me in, Rain," I growl, pounding my fist against the wood.

"I thought I told you not to call me that?"

Yeah. You did. But all it accomplished was giving me something to use against you.

I ignore his question. "You need to face this head-on, man. You can't run away and hide from me for an entire month. And especially not from the truth about who you really are."

His roar is muffled by the closed door between us. "Just watch me, Lenny!"

I scoff before yelling back, "I mean, yeah, you can *try*. I guess I never took you for a fucking coward!"

From the other side of the door, I hear a slam and a fist connecting with the wall.

Looks like I hit a nerve with that one.

Satisfied with his little meltdown, I spin around and head into the bathroom we've been sharing. I desperately need to relieve my aching cock from his excitement our little tango caused. Stripping out of my clothes, I turn on the water to the walk-in shower.

Coach might've skipped on some first world necessities, such as central heating, but he most definitely made up for it with the bomb-ass design of this bathroom. Well, mostly this shower, with the glass divider and door separating the rest of the room from the river rock mosaic floor and rough stone wall of the shower. They contrast with the smooth, cut tiles on the adjacent walls situated with the shower heads. There's two of them, allowing water to pour down from both sides.

Pulling out my phone, I connect it to the bluetooth speaker. The sounds of Palisades' "Hard Feelings" fill the bathroom.

Ironic.

After testing the water's temperature, I step through the opening and under the spray, the glass door closing behind me.

I allow the water to cascade over my body, wetting my hair and skin before grabbing some body wash from the small alcove in the stone wall. Just as I'm lathering some suds in my hands, I hear the sound of the glass door banging closed.

Before I know what is happening, Rain's hands are forcing my chest and stomach against the stone wall, using his whole body weight to keep me there. My vision blurs and I realize it's because his initial push caused me to hit my head on a rock jutting out from the wall. The rough material scrapes against my skin where it makes contact, and I can already feel blood trickling down from my busted brow.

I don't have long to formulate a thought, let alone a plan on how to escape him, when his hands grip my ass cheeks and spread them wide, his chest pressing me harder against the wall.

And even though I know it's coming, nothing could prepare me for the moment he slams his cock into me, hard and fast.

I suck in a ragged breath through clenched teeth, exhaling on a hiss.

The first thing I feel is discomfort, followed by a thousand knives cutting me open as he buries himself inside my tight hole. It's a sensation I'm not used to when it comes to getting fucked. Since it's generally a common *fucking* courtesy to prep your *fucking* partner before you slam your cock into their ass.

You know, instead of going in as dry as the Sahara *fucking* Desert.

Contrary to popular belief, water does not substitute as lubricant. My intuition tells me Rain knows that.

He wraps an arm around my body and grips the front of my throat, his forearm resting flush against my chest between the valley of my pecs. His grasp is just strong enough that he constricts my airway, but it's not to the point where I can't breathe.

Not that it matters, I'm still completely breathless from the shock and pain of his cock filling me.

My lungs are desperate for air when he starts moving inside me, sliding in impossibly deeper until he is fully seated with his hips flush against my cheeks. The friction is causing my ass to throb with each of his movements, the ache only getting worse. He might as well be ripping me in two.

"Lube," I choke, my voice strained from his grip on my throat and the pain coursing through me.

"Fuck you," he growls in my ear, thrusting into me once, twice more.

If it weren't for the agony I'm currently in, my first retort would have been *you already are.* But instead, a cry escapes my lips and I breathe out an anguished *please.*

He pulls his cock from inside me, his fingers still wrapped around my throat as he reaches for the bottle of body wash in my peripheral. At this point, his hand on me is the only thing keeping me upright. My knees shake as torment and rage wracks my body with a vengeance.

A few moments later, when he's nice and soaped up, I feel his crown back at my crease. He nudges the head past my rim and I wince, the intrusion agonizing from him entering without lubricant the first time. Adding the soap only causes more of a burn, and I bite my lip hard as he slides in smoothly this time, stilling once he's completely inside me.

God, he's fucking huge.

Obviously I know he is. I had him in my mouth and down my throat only a few weeks ago.

But I've never been fucked like *this* with a cock built to split me in half.

"Hands on the wall. Brace yourself." His words come out as a barked command, and immediately I obey, thankful it gives me a moment to adjust to the sting and his presence this time before he starts moving again.

My ass feels like it's on fire as his length works the soap into the fissures and cracks I'm sure are now present inside me. Even my first time bottoming didn't hurt nearly this bad.

I grit my teeth and adjust my stance, spreading my legs a little wider in hopes of easing some of the discomfort. Rain takes full advantage of this and with his other hand, grabs onto my hip, using it and the leverage from his grip on my neck to impale me on his cock. His thrusts are long, hard, and deliciously slow, reaching deeper than I've ever experienced before.

After a minute or two, the pain gives way to pleasure and I start moving with him, pressing back into him with each thrust. Soon our bodies are slick with the mixture of water and sweat. Lust ignites in my veins and my cock feels impossibly hard between my legs.

He feels so damn good.

I fucking hate it.

I should be fighting him off, pushing back, trying to gain some goddamn control in this encounter. But *fuck*, submitting to him in this moment, letting him have his way with me, is only making me hotter.

Rain groans and starts fucking me harder and faster, squeezing my throat so tight I start to see stars, only to loosen his grip right when I think I might pass out.

His hot mouth licks at the muscles of my neck and shoulder before he bites down on my trapezius. Hard. He pierces the skin, and I gasp when I feel him lick up the mixture of water and blood pooling on my shoulder.

Another moan blended with pleasure and pain escapes me.

"I knew you'd like it rough," Rain grunts as he pistons his hips in quick, fluid motions, railing into me without abandon.

Fucking Christ, he feels good.

The burning pain of his initial thrust is long gone, replaced by toe-curling bliss with each and every pass his cock takes over my prostate.

My own dick aches between my legs, so stiff it might explode. I whimper, needing more contact. It's begging for his attention, for relief.

Knowing he won't give me what I need, I remove one of my hands from the wall to stroke myself, but Rain slams into me harder when he notices, forcing my palm back to the wall to keep my balance. It's either that or end up with my face pressed against the rough stones once again.

Rain leans forward, his hot breath wafting over my neck and ear as he grips my throat tighter. "Is it everything you thought it would be, Riv? Me fucking your ass from behind, hard and fast?" His taunts only serve to turn me on more.

God, I need him to touch me, jack me, *something.*

"Yes," I pant, pushing my hips back to meet him thrust for thrust, desperate for more.

"Good to hear. Because make no mistake about it. The fact that I don't have to look at your face as I pound you into the wall is the best fucking part of playing out your little fantasy."

His words are like a bucket of ice water being thrown on me. My desire and building orgasm quickly dissipate from a raging fire into nothing more than a dull twinge.

This asshole. Using my own words against me.

He must know I'm about to come back with a snappy retort, because he practically crushes my windpipe in his palm, effectively shutting me up before I even have the chance to speak.

His hips moving in sporadic, uneven movements, I can tell he's close to climax. I'm prepared to let him ride it out, using me as the human fucktoy he clearly views me as, when he pulls out suddenly, taking advantage of his already tight grip on my throat to turn me around and force me to my knees.

My bones crack against the uneven stone floor and I wince. Before I have time to think, to breathe, or to protest, Rain yanks open my mouth with one hand, the other gripping my drenched hair, and shoves his cock in my mouth with brutal force. My gag reflex kicks in when the tip hits the back of my throat. I know he loves the sensation of my throat working his cock, but screw him. I'm not about to give him the satisfaction.

His hands cup the base of my skull and he starts fucking my face, his cock sliding in and out my throat. I feel him throb against my tongue right before hot spurts of cum slide effortlessly down my esophagus.

I swallow every drop, even though I don't have any choice in the matter, hating myself for letting this happen.

For letting it get this far.

How did we end up here?

Never in my fucking life would I have imagined the guy I met that first day of practice would be this sadistic and pure fucking evil. I never asked for an enemy just like I never wanted to start this game, this battle of wills, with him.

And all this because I'm bisexual?

Rain pulls from my mouth and immediately turns away from me, not sparing me a backward glance as he begins washing his softening cock with soap on the other side of the shower.

I look away from him, glancing down to the floor in disgust, noticing the pink tinge to the water on the floor.

Shit, I'm still bleeding.

From where, I have no clue.

I run a hand across my forehead and shoulder, my fingers coming away bright red.

Fuming, I shift my position from my knees to my ass. The pain ravaging my entire body at the movement causes me to grimace.

God. I don't think a single piece of me went untouched by him.

I still feel him everywhere and instantly know it was his goal.

"I hate you," I murmur dejectedly, and I don't know if it's the harsh truth or the greatest lie I've ever spoken.

"Maybe. But that doesn't mean you wouldn't let me fuck your tight ass every day of the week and twice on Sundays if I wanted it." He doesn't look at me when he says it, just rinses his cock and abs before shutting off the water.

Shit.

It's like he sees straight into my mind and is able to pick out the most fucked up thoughts, dying to bring them to light in hopes that airing them out will force me to bask in my shame.

Except I have no reason to feel shameful.

I'm openly bisexual. I love fucking both men and women. And yes, I do love receiving a nice dicking too. For fuck's sake, men have a prostate for a reason, so anyone unwilling to use it is wasting a gift from God himself.

But this?

This went beyond a sexual experience about mutual pleasure.

This was vile, sadistic, and just... degrading.

Never in my life have I been treated less than human.

Until today.

And so knowing I would still let him inside me again if he asked? *That* is downright heinous.

But I can't help the way my body wants him, even when my mind and soul fracture every time we interact, whether it be from his vicious words or the wicked way he uses his body against me.

What just occurred in this shower with him was the best sexual experience of my life. Until it wasn't.

I've never felt so euphoric. Until I didn't.

I hear Rain open the shower door to climb out, letting it close with a bang behind him. He won't fucking look at me, and out of this entire torturous encounter, that's what pisses me off the most.

The fact that I don't have to look at your face as I pound you into the wall is the best fucking part of playing out your little fantasy.

My body quakes with fury, resentment, and fire. The need for vengeance is crawling up my spine and I have no desire to stop it.

I study him closely as he wraps a towel around his waist with an expression of indifference on his face before pulling open the bathroom door. I let the words slide off my tongue in a low, menacing threat, only loud enough so I know he won't miss a word.

"Make no mistake about it, Rain. I will make you regret this until your dying day. I don't know when and I don't know how. Mark my words, it will happen. And this pain is going to be worth it when I finally bring you to your fucking knees."

He doesn't turn around. Doesn't respond.

I knew he wouldn't. Not when he won this battle.

But he's been warned.

This war has only just begun.

I wait until I hear the click of the door latching shut before I curl into myself and sob.

Cold, mangled, and defeated.

SEVENTEEN
Rain

DAY FOUR

With my back to the door of my bedroom, I sink to the ground and place my head in my hands.

What the fuck have I done?

EIGHTEEN
River

DAY SEVEN

Three days.

Three goddamn days and I can still feel the aftermaths of Rain's brutal onslaught on both my body and mind.

I don't know if I'm more damaged physically or emotionally at this point.

And the worst part?

I can't stop thinking about him.

Even sitting here on the couch, *Fahrenheit 451* in my hand, I find my mind drifting to thoughts of him.

What is he thinking? Is he regretting what he did to me?

After he left me in the shower, he went to his bedroom and didn't leave it for over a day. At least that I could tell. It's as if he waited until he knew I was out hiking or sleeping or something before getting food or using the bathroom.

I haven't actually *seen* him in those three days, only glimpses of his shadowed figure moving in the hallway.

At this point, I can only be grateful for that. Ignoring each other, while it never lasts long, is preferred to constantly being in each other's faces, ready to throw down at any second.

I was already sick of constantly living on my toes, always having my guard up any time we are in the same room. I have a feeling it will only be worse now, after what happened in the shower.

The. Fucking. Shower.

His cruelty has known no bounds since he found out my sexuality all those months ago. I've become used to it, almost numb in a way. He isn't the first person to hate or dislike or shun me because I'm into both sexes. At a certain point, you grow thick skin and it all just slides off your back, making you stronger.

That's what it's been like with him. Hurled insults and punches, nothing but sticks and stones and words that try to hurt me. And in all that time, they never succeeded.

But what happened in the shower? It went beyond torment.

The word *rape* plays around in the back of my mind, but deep down, I know I could have stopped it if I wanted.

But I didn't want to stop. I wanted it. *Him.*

Ciaráin Grady is many things I've come to learn in these months of knowing him.

Cruel. Antagonizing. Intoxicating. Yes, absolutely.

But a rapist? No, I refuse to believe that.

Still, that doesn't stop me from hating myself for the conflicted emotions running through me every time I see, hear, think, touch, smell him.

Because there is one thing he will always be.

My enemy.

Rain is the first one to break our stalemate. If I can pride myself about anything when it comes to him, it's that I'm never the one to give into the silence surrounding us due to his malice.

I'm maybe thirty pages from the end of my book when he comes down the hall, looking, dare I say... chipper?

Okay, that's not true. Just less broody than usual.

His hair is slightly damp from a shower and he's wearing a black hoodie and jeans, holding his backpack in his hand. I watch as he slides his shoes on and shrugs into a jacket, all the while avoiding making eye contact with me.

Turning my attention back to my book, I hear the familiar sound of the fridge opening and water being poured into a glass.

It's not for a couple more minutes until he speaks.

"I'm heading down into town on the ATV, I need to grab some stuff from the store. Do you need anything?"

Glancing up at him over the back of the couch, I make eye contact with him for the first time in three damn days. His golden eyes don't give much away, they usually don't when his armor is on, but I think they seem to be slightly softer when he looks at me today.

I can only hope that's a symptom of guilt.

"I don't think so, but thanks," I reply.

At least he's being civil...

But then something crosses my mind.

The door opens behind me and I call out, rolling over the back of the couch before Rain steps outside. "Hey, actually, can I go with you?"

He pauses in the threshold and faces me. "I guess, but you're riding bitch."

Rolling my eyes, I grab my shoes, sliding them on and toss on a jacket before following him out to the shed which houses our only means of transportation.

He starts the engine up with ease, pulling it free from the shed, which I close behind him. My eyes move to the small seat behind where he's sitting. Where I'm supposed to sit.

"Well, are you coming or not?" he snaps.

Biting my lip, I step onto the footholds and swing my leg over the seat. I do my best to keep distance between us, my fingers gripping the rack on the back, but as we begin moving down the mountain, I can't help my body sliding into his due to gravity.

Still, I try to give him his space, clutching the bars behind me for dear life, my arm muscles straining with the effort. After slipping down and pulling myself back about fifty times, Rain reaches back and grips my knee with one hand, glancing at me over his shoulder.

"For fuck's sake, just hold onto me, I'm sick of you sliding into my backside," he shouts over the roar of the engine.

Oh, there's so much I could do with that.

Still, I keep my mouth shut.

Taking a deep breath, I uncurl my fingers from the storage rack and wrap my arms around him. I try desperately not to think about how good his back feels pressed against my torso, even with the empty backpack between us, or how my fingers are itching to slip under his jacket and sweatshirt in search of the smooth, warm skin of his abs.

I promise, I try really fucking hard.

The last thing I need is to pop a semi, or worse, a full blown boner from our bodies, fully clothed, smashed together.

We arrive down in town about thirty minutes later, and my face and hands are frozen from the wind since my dumb ass didn't think to grab a pair of gloves before following him outside up at the cabin.

Slipping off the back as Rain kills the engine, I notice we're outside a Walgreens.

"Can you grab the stuff on this list while I go to the store across the street?"

"Sure," I tell him, taking the paper from him and looking it over. It's simple, nothing crazy, milk and a few other groceries. When I glance back up, I see him heading across the street to a couple small shops.

Okay, then.

I spin and enter the store, heading past the checkout counter and over to the grocery aisle, quickly collecting everything from the list Rain gave me. Once that's taken care of, I grab the items I wanted for myself before heading to the cashier.

After paying, I head out with my bag and the gallon of milk, seeing Rain reaching this side of the street, empty handed, which I find strange.

He extends his hand to me, taking the milk first, slipping it into his backpack he set on the seat of the ATV.

"You're going to have to wear this on the way back up, unless you're keen on snuggling a carton of milk and whatever else is in the bag," he tells me, taking the plastic bag from me, quickly glancing inside.

And he freezes, his shoulders going rigid.

Shit.

When his eyes snap up to mine, they are brimming with rage, and I notice his whole face is flushed. He's practically foaming at the mouth, he's seething that intensely.

Double shit.

"Condoms and fucking *lube*? Are you shitting me right now?" His voice is low, full of disdain and venom, and he steps toward me in a predatory stride. "What the actual *fuck*, River?"

"We're both consenting adults," I grind, my temper beginning to get the better of me, but I back up, hitting the wall behind me at his advance. "But next time you want to fuck? I'd rather have some goddamn lube and condoms on hand instead of going bare and fucking *raw*, so I took some precautions."

He slams his hips into my body, pinning me against the side of the building as he gets in my face. "What do you think this is gonna turn into? Some *Brokeback Mountain* type shit? Well, newsflash, Lenny. I'm not into dick. So do us both a favor and get those sick thoughts out of your skull before I bash it in with a fire poker." His words come out in a snarl, but I don't back down.

No way, not this time, for one damn reason.

He's such a fucking liar. And we both know it.

I honestly have no clue what his issue is, but I have a feeling it isn't really with me. I'm just the one taking the brunt force of whatever shit he's trying to work through in his own mind.

Still, he's taking it a little far at this point. Being bisexual isn't the end of the world. Not in this day and age.

But for some reason, it scares the ever-loving shit out of him.

"Let's call a spade a motherfucking spade, Grady. I'm bisexual, so are you. Maybe it's time you get the *fuck* over yourself and just *fucking* accept it. Because a straight man doesn't decide to shove his cock in another man's ass or fuck his face like it's the last thing he'll ever do."

My eyes dart over his face, taking in his fury. "And on top of that? I'll let you in on another little secret. While I might be the one pinned to the damn wall right now, I also hold all the power."

My cock is rock-hard in my pants from his assertion, and from the heat and shock flaring in his eyes, he feels it too. Taking advantage of his momentarily stunned state, I grip his jacket to flip us around and pin *him* against the wall.

His breaths come out in short spurts as his eyes lock on mine, a battle of emotion raging behind them. I grind my dick against his leg and I'm *thrilled* when I feel his start to thicken behind his jeans as well.

"Because it's simple, really. You're not immune to me, no matter how much you wish you were. You might hate yourself for it, you might not be able to handle it and what it means about who you are as a person. But make no mistake about it, baby. You won't be able to fight it for long, I'll make sure of that."

Rain squirms under my stare, and I smirk, fully aware it pops my dimples. When his eyes flash to them, then move to my lips, I know I've got him right where I want him. Putting one hand on the wall next to his head, I slide the other between us and cup his length over his pants.

Thick and long and damn near fucking perfect.

Like it was made for me.

Using the palm and heel of my hand, I stroke his dick through the rough material, loving the way it feels in my grip, even with layers separating our skin. I'd be lying if I said I'm not dying to unzip him and take him in my mouth right here and now. If we had the coverage of nightfall, I most definitely would.

Guess you could say I'm somewhat of an exhibitionist.

I'm so turned-on it's painful, but I grind against his hip to alleviate some of the building arousal. My mouth meets his jaw, and I lick and kiss and nip a path back to his ear and down his throat.

Then something happens.

But what surprises me isn't the hiss that comes through his clenched teeth or the groan rumbling from deep within his chest. It's the way his hips rock with the movement of my hand, proving my theory has been right all along.

He's just as desperate for this as I am.

Grinning against his neck, I let out a soft chuckle before moving my lips to his ear, my palm moving fast against him.

"I'm determined to get my mouth on you again. On your chest. Your hips. Your cock. It's driving me fucking insane how much I want you," I declare, nibbling on his lobe. "But more than that? I can't wait to have you at my mercy." My tongue flicks the shell of his ear. "I meant it when I told you I would bring you to your fucking knees. And when it happens, it'll be *my* cock down *your* throat. Because you know that's what will happen. Sooner or later."

I squeeze his dick the best I can, my fingers digging into the denim of his jeans, and he moans.

Fuck. That sound goes straight to my cock, and I'm embarrassingly close to coming in my damn pants like a preteen.

"And when I fuck you? When I get to sink into that tight ass of yours and fill you with my cum? *Goddamn*, you're going to be fucking ruined. You'll never want anyone else. That is my promise to you."

Pulling back, I find Rain's head bowed back against the wall, his eyes closed as our bodies grind together. The look on his face, pure agonizing bliss, tells me he's close to bursting.

Just where I want him.

"Just know this. I won't give my cock to you until you're begging for it." Leaning forward, my mouth centimeters from his, I remove my attention from his cock and take his face in my palms. He groans in protest, his eyes snapping open to meet my gaze. I press my body in further against his, our cocks aligning and causing the most exquisite pressure.

"Because, baby, unlike you, I don't take *that* unless it's willingly given."

With his lips so close, I'm tempted to have a taste once and for all. But I know if I do, there is a very real and highly likely chance he will leave my ass here and go back to the cabin on his own. That's not exactly a hike, or a risk, I want to take.

Pulling away when I know he's right there—because I am, too—is like tearing a limb from my body, but I can't give him anything more.

Not until he realizes this playing field isn't as uneven as he thinks it is. He isn't superior to me, he doesn't get to belittle me and then get off.

Not again.

And it's time to remind him of that.

Pushing away from him, I lock him with a glare as his eyes harden into pools of frozen amber.

He doesn't even offer me a backward glance as he storms past me, hopping onto the four wheeler and starting it. I half expect him to drive away, so I'm shell-shocked when the next sentence comes from his mouth.

"Get on the fucking ATV so we can go home

NINETEEN
Rain

DAY NINE

I'm holed up in my room again.

Yeah, I know. Real mature.

But I *can't* handle being around River right now. Not without wanting to rip his damn clothes off and shoving my cock into his ass.

Or his mouth.

Again.

At this point, I just want him however I can get him, which is so fucked up.

I don't *like* guys, let alone want to shove my cock in any of their fucking orifices.

But River seems to be the goddamn exception.

So I shut myself in my room, painting, drawing, and reading to pass the time. But it only helps take the edge off. I'm starting to understand why Rapunzel despised being locked up in that tower.

At least she had her lizard thing to keep her company instead of a sexy quarterback to hide from. Although, I have a feeling she might agree to a trade with me any day of the week.

There's an idea...

Now all I have to do is figure out a way to get River *into* the tower and snatch the little lizard without getting caught...

Jesus Christ.

I'm going insane if I'm plotting ways to kidnap a fictional *cartoon* chameleon.

I need to get out of this cabin. Now.

My phone's weather app tells me the temperature is around forty degrees, positively *balmy*.

Whatthefuckever. I'll gladly let my balls turn into ice cubes than stay locked in this room for one more minute.

Shoving my watercolor pens and pad into my backpack, I get ready to make an escape. If only for a little while.

I pad out of my room on quiet feet, silently shutting the door behind me, and pray River is in his room and not the living room. As I pass his room, my ears catch the distinct sounds of From Ashes To New's "Crazy" flowing from under the door.

I smirk, knowing it's most likely his song of the week, seeing as I've heard it plenty of times in the last couple days.

At least I'm not the only one feeling insane.

Slipping into my winter gear and boots, I throw a set of snow spikes in my backpack, as well as a blanket and a bottle of water, before slinging it over my shoulders. I set out for the lake Coach had mentioned was a short hike from here.

I put my headphones in my ears and quickly flip on the same

song River was listening to when I snuck past his room. He has good taste, as much as I loathe to admit it.

Letting the music pour into me, I move at a steady pace, following the well-marked trail starting right behind the cabin next to the creek. My body is flooded with endorphins from the fresh air and the music pulsing through my veins. I hike for just under half an hour before reaching the lake overlook that we were promised was worth the steep incline.

He wasn't wrong.

A turquoise blue lake sits completely frozen in the bowl of the surrounding mountains. Their jagged, rocky peaks are imposing when paired with the snow covered pines and silence of the afternoon.

I'm utterly alone.

And I feel it.

As much as I hate to even think it, I wish River was here, so I had someone to share this with.

Shaking the thought from my head, I lay the blanket out on a log and pull out all the necessary supplies in order for me to paint the scene before me.

I know I won't do it justice.

Not because I doubt myself or my skill when it comes to art. It's just *that* beautiful.

For a while, I manage to lose myself in the music and the task in front of me, allowing my hand to relieve my mind of worry, if only for a short while.

When I begin to focus my attention on painting the lake the most vivid shade of aqua, I'm reminded of a set of eyes, matching them almost perfectly.

Those eyes, not only as blue as an alpine lake, also hold the same depth. But they are twice as captivating.

River's eyes.

Shit.

Inhaling a harsh, cold breath into my lungs, I let out a sigh.

Even when he isn't here, he manages to worm his way into my thoughts. It's like I will never evade him. No matter the amount of space I put between us.

Before I even know it, my mind wanders to the other day, him pressing me into the side of the convenience store, and the look in his eyes.

His resilience amazes me. Even after all the shit I've spewed his way, he still manages to come at me with determination and purpose.

Even when I have him in a position that screams of his vulnerability and begs for his submission, he has a knack for flipping things on me, showing his strength.

He's done it time and time again. At this point, I've come to expect nothing less than a fight from him. If it were anyone else, I'd destroy them with the snap of a finger for daring to challenge me.

But not River.

For some reason, his defiance…turns me on.

Which, unfortunately, he knows all too well. He's so much as called me out on it before.

And the way those aqua eyes bored into mine while he stroked my cock back in town told me everything I need to know.

He's getting to me. We both know it.

I pride myself on being in control. In knowing when I'm outmatched and it's time to tap out. In having all the cards in my hand, just waiting for the right time to let them play out.

But when I opened my eyes and saw his gaze fixated on my lips, I almost lost it entirely.

Control slipped, and I sat there, daring him to do it. To try to take the upper hand from me.

And hell, the worst part of it all?

At that moment, I wanted him to do it.

To defy me. To challenge me.

I fucking wanted him to kiss me.

The sun dipped below the mountainous horizon ten minutes ago, but I can't bring myself to head back to that God forsaken cabin.

Back to him.

Still, I find myself gathering my shit, throwing it into my backpack, and trekking back down the way I came. The only indication of the path I have are the lonely set of footprints serving as proof of my journey to the top.

As the cabin comes into view, I see the lights in the living room are on, signaling River must be in there. Probably waiting to ambush my ass the moment I step in the door.

Shocker.

I glance up and notice the black smoke billowing from the chimney, rising and fading out into the dusky sky. That sparks an idea.

Firewood.

We've been here nine days and neither of us, from what I can tell, has restocked the pile in the living room for the fireplace or the wood stove. And since I'm damn near desperate not to go back inside, I'll take the extra few minutes of reprieve from River and the toxic cesspool of the cabin.

Swinging the door to the shed open, I begin grabbing pieces of wood stacked against the wall. At this point, I'm glad Coach had enough foresight to put the wood *inside* the shed and not stacked against the *outside* like most people would. There is easily a foot of snow on the ground, if not more, and trying to get to the wood under a pile of this shit would be a nightmare.

As if being stuck here with River Lennox for a month isn't a nightmare in itself.

"Need some help?" I hear River's voice call from behind me. My spine instantly goes rigid.

Goddammit.

I only wanted five more minutes without him trying to... shit. Do anything to me? Talk to me? Bully me?

Fuck with me?

Fuck me?

"I'm good," I say, spinning around and heading back to the door.

But of course, in true River fashion, he doesn't listen.

He's already stepping up to the stack of wood, gathering some in his own arms.

Fine. Let him help. No way he will carry in more than this load. I can just throw my shit inside and take a few more trips to get a little more time outside.

Away from him.

When I head back out into the night after stacking the pile of logs next to the fireplace, I feel River following close behind again.

My molars might crack by the time we leave this damn cabin with how often I grind my teeth to keep from biting his head off.

The thing I might dislike about him the most has to be the fact that he's genuinely a nice guy. Too nice. Even though he calls me out on my shit, bickers with me, and threatens me with revenge after what happened in the shower. When he has every reason to leave me out here to freeze my nuts off, he doesn't. Because he's a good person.

And I can't fucking stand it.

"I've got it, Lennox," I call to him over my shoulder as I quickly stomp back to the shed and pile more wood into my arms. I'm already in the doorway of the shed when he reaches it, effectively blocking my way.

"It's getting colder and it's pitch black outside already. Let me help you. I don't mind."

"I mind," I spit at him, my temper rapidly increasing to dangerous levels.

Knock-down-drag-out levels.

He doesn't budge from the doorway, though. I'm forced to look at him, really fucking look at him, for the first time since we got back to the cabin from town three days ago. He's dressed in a dark sweatshirt and jeans, a beanie on his head and snow boots on his feet. His jaw is riddled with scruff, as if he hasn't shaved in a few days.

I hate that it makes him even better looking than he already is, with those eyes as vivid as polished turquoise and ever-tousled brown locks.

At least he's wearing the beanie, so I'm not tempted to run my fingers through his hair. Maybe grip onto it while I drive into him from behind.

My dick stirs behind my zipper, liking that idea entirely too much for my comfort.

Fuck.

His brow quirks up in surprise at me snapping at him. "What the hell, man? Are you seriously incapable of accepting help? Or is it just because *I'm* the one asking?"

"Doesn't matter. Move. Get out of the way. Before I freeze my damn nuts off standing in the doorway."

He doesn't budge. Instead he crowds in further, so close that if I didn't have this stack of logs in my arms, our chests would be touching.

"That's okay. I'd rather stay right here. If your nuts get cold, I'll gladly warm them up for you with my tongue." His mouth is centimeters away, his lips brushing mine lightly as he speaks. "After all, I know how much you like it when I suck them into my mouth. How quickly it gets you going."

And then the asshole flicks his tongue out in a wicked caress against my lips.

Oh, fuck this shit.

My arms drop the woodpile, not giving a flying fuck if they land on either of our feet. Because I'm about to lose my damn mind and completely forget the task at hand.

No, not collecting firewood.

Ignoring him. Avoiding yet another confrontation.

I shove him in the chest. Hard. I must've caught him off guard, because he stumbles back, tripping over a log that landed behind him. My hands connect with his pecs again, pushing him to the ground while he is still off-balance, sending him to his ass in a mound of snow.

I stare down at him, both lust and fury raging through my veins. The fact that fighting with him like this gets me hard as a rock only serves to piss me off more.

It's an endless cycle and from the grin on his face, he seems to thoroughly enjoy it.

"I'm fucking done with your shit, River. I'm *over* it." My hand slices through the air in outrage as I shout the words at the top of my lungs. Screw being quiet or civil, I'm not afraid of anyone hearing our dispute. My heart is pounding inside my chest, as if it might explode right along with my mental fortitude. I drop my voice, letting it drip with ice. "Stop taunting me. Stop trying to mess with my mind like it's your favorite game. We've been here nine days and we have at least twenty-five more to go. You're driving me insane, *on purpose.* Do us both a favor and don't test my fucking patience. Or I swear to God, I'll bend you over right here and fuck you into submission."

I don't bother waiting for a response, just spin and start for the house. Except I don't make it more than three steps before a force slams into my back. I stumble into the side of the shed and grip it for balance, but River is there, yanking on my shoulder until my back is pressed into the rough wood siding. Before I have the chance to make a move, River's hand is gripping the front of my throat, the other resting against the shed above me, and his hips pining me in place.

I can feel his cock, thick and stiff against my thigh.

From the sinful smirk on his lips, I'm painfully aware he can feel how hard I am too.

"I'm not the one submitting tonight," he growls fiercely.

"Riv —" I start, but my protest is cut short when he crashes his lips into mine.

His mouth is hot and insistent against mine as he pours his pent up rage into this kiss. It's harsh and volatile.

It's fucking transcendent.

He tastes of peppermint and rivalry and forbidden desire and something addictively masculine. A flick of his tongue against my lips causes me to gasp, which he takes full advantage of by slipping his tongue inside where it tangles against mine in a brutal battle for dominance.

My hands fly to his chest and I grip the fabric of his sweatshirt between my clenched fists as panic floods my body.

Fuck, this is the first kiss I've had in four years and it's with the most infuriating motherfucker I've ever met.

Whether or not the bigger issue of my thought is that I can't stand him or that he is a *he*, I can't say at this moment. All I can do is attempt to push him away, off of me.

Because I don't want this.

But for some inexcusable reason, my hands do the exact opposite and hold onto him for dear life. Even when he is the very thing causing me to feel like I'm drowning in the first place.

The dual sensation of his lips on mine and his body pressed tightly against me causes my dick to get impossibly harder, and when he moans into my mouth, deep and husky, I almost lose it completely.

River's hands move to grasp each side of my face and tilt my head for better access. For more control.

It shouldn't surprise me that the way he kisses matches the way he teases and taunts and fucks with me every chance he gets. Making me desperate. To make it stop or for him, I couldn't say. And hell, the confidence in it. The insistence and demand, taking what he wants from me like he *knows* I'm going to just stop everything to give it to him.

And. I. Fucking. Do.

But the second his hips shift, causing his erection, and subsequently my own, to grind behind our clothing, I manage to detach my lips from his for a brief moment.

That only seems to spur him on more, though. He moves his mouth to my throat and his hands fly between us. The fumbling of his belt and zipper greet my ears as wet, open-mouthed kisses are plastered against my neck, from my jaw to my collarbone and back up again.

"River. No," I pant, the lust in my voice causing the words to come out no louder than a hoarse whisper.

Either he didn't hear me or he doesn't give a fuck, because he doesn't stop.

"Why do you fight it, baby?" he whispers, his breath hot on my neck. "Why do you deny yourself when you know I can make you feel so good?" It's not a taunt, but a legitimate question. One, for the life of me, I don't have the answer to.

His fingers swiftly unfasten the button of my own jeans right before his hand slips down inside both them and my briefs to make contact with my aching cock. A hiss escapes my lips as his fingers curl around my length, but it is promptly hushed by another scorching kiss. With a firm grip on me, he starts jacking me slowly, using his free hand to tug my jeans down past my ass.

"River, stop." The words, like my protest, are weak.

Powerless.

We both know it.

Still, River releases my cock, and I groan in protest. Or thanks? After all, he did what I asked.

Except he *didn't*, because then he drops to his knees right there in the fucking snow and takes me into his warm, velvety mouth, sucking me deep just like he did in the locker room. His head bobs on my cock, the tip hitting the back of his throat a few times.

I've got to hand it to the guy. Even though I'd never admit it aloud on my deathbed, he gives the best head I've ever received.

And deepthroats like a fucking champ.

"Please," I plead.

He has to stop. We can't keep traveling down this path of destruction.

This. Has. To. Stop.

Because I'm not gay.

His words from the hotel after the away game in Portland come rushing back to me.

"A mouth is a mouth, doesn't matter if it belongs to a girl or a guy."

Fuck. Me.

River releases my cock with a pop, causing me to shudder at the now cold, icy feeling wrapping around my length from the frigid temperature in the air. It doesn't last long, though, because the fire between us continues to ensue.

He pulls his own cock from his jeans and I take a moment to marvel at it. I hadn't seen it in the shower the other day, so this is my first glimpse of it.

And sweet Jesus, it's fucking...more than perfect, whatever that might be.

Thick and long, rivaling my own nine inches, with the slightest curve upward and a silky mushroom crown. Pre-cum glistens against the tip and I'm horrified by the instinctual urge I have to lick it clean.

River rises from his knees, catching where my gaze is focused, and smiles. I feel the tips of my ears burning red as he licks his lips and leans in, his mouth a whisper from my own.

"It's okay, Rain. You can look all you want. I already know you want me too."

It's on the tip of my tongue to deny it, but I don't have the chance before he spits in his palm before pressing into me again, taking both our cocks into his large hand. His mouth descends on mine once more and he nips at my bottom lip as he begins jacking our cocks together.

Shit. This is going too far.

I'm able to rationalize his blowjob and even fucking him in the shower. Those are things that could and did happen with any number of the girls I've been with.

But two dicks rubbing together?

No one with eyes could stand there without coming to the conclusion that this is about as gay as it can get.

And for fuck's sake, *I'm. Not. Gay.*

I. Don't. Want. This.

Except...I do.

"River," I cry against his lips. My resolve is beginning to crack as the contradiction of my mind and my desire rip me in two. Never in my twenty-one years of life have I ever felt such extreme pleasure and anguish at the same time.

It's catastrophic.

Because Jesus Christ, I've never done anything like this. And if that isn't terrifying in itself, let's add in the fact that nothing has ever felt *this* good.

"Rain," he groans, repeating the nickname that...fuck, I don't hate it from his lips anymore. Not right now, in this moment.

Our cocks slide together in his palm, coated with his saliva. He twists his hand around the heads, gathering the pre-cum from both our crowns and spreads them down our lengths. My hips can't help but jerk with his strokes, the added lubrication from our mixed juices helping our dicks glide against each other without friction.

I feel my balls begin to draw up in the telltale sign I'm about to come.

Shit.

"River, *please,*" I sob out the plea, but I don't know what I'm begging for anymore. My mortification of this encounter will only increase exponentially if he finishes me off. Because I can't write off this untamed desire for a third time. Because he will know, without doubt, my body wants him, even when my mind doesn't.

And he will have gained the upper hand.

But even still.

I don't want him to stop.

River takes my bottom lip in his mouth and tugs it between his teeth, biting hard enough to draw blood at the same time he squeezes our cocks in his firm grasp on an upward stroke.

"Fuck, Rain. I need you there with me," he pants, licking the blood from my lips.

And as the coppery taste of my own blood fills my mouth and our dicks are clutched together so tightly they might as well be one, I come like I've never come before.

Pleasure shoots up my spine and straight to my brain as my hot, sticky cum spills out over River's hand. He continues to stroke me through my orgasm and bring himself to his own climax, all while still lapping at my wounded mouth and pride like it's the best thing he's ever tasted.

To him, it might be.

That might be the most agonizing part of all of this.

Even with every fight I put up and every victory I claimed against him, they all just became completely meaningless.

Because while I may have won countless battles, he's won the fucking war.

I look down at the mess of cum and spit and fucking dignity between us, a couple silent tears of defeat sliding down my cheeks. They mix with the blood dripping over my lip before he manages to lick those from my face as well.

Fuck me, I haven't cried or found myself vulnerable with another human in years.

It had to be *him* who changed that feat.

Releasing me, River bends to wipe his hand off in the snow, and like the animal he is, picks up a handful to clean off his cock as well before tucking himself back into his clothes and standing in front of me.

I expect the look on his face to be smug or even triumphant.

Instead, I only see conflict.

Gentler than he has ever touched me before, he cups my tear-stained face in his hands and places a soft, sweet kiss on my swollen lips. His tenderness is giving me whiplash. It's like he is a completely different person now.

His lips move over mine, and goddamn me, I kiss him back.

Once. Twice.

A third time.

He pulls back and brings his forehead to rest against mine, our mouths a whisper apart. I keep my eyes closed as I feel his breath caress my lips.

"Accept this is who you are, so you can start to enjoy being stranded in a fucking cabin in the woods with me for another four weeks."

TWENTY

Rain

DAY TEN

Sitting at the desk in my bedroom, paint brush in hand, I do my best to forget.

About my parents and how they are pieces of trash. About this mess I'm in. About my demons that haunt me.

About *him.*

But I can't forget. Everything in my life has come to a tipping point and all I can do is helplessly wait to get flung overboard. To be tossed off the cliff I'm desperately clinging to, just like Doctor Fulton said I *need.*

And it's a lonely, bleak existence, constantly waiting for the other shoe to drop.

The forbidden moments with River, first in the locker room, the shower, then against the shed were the only times I didn't feel like I was drowning. Like I could finally breathe.

An escape from my life. My problems.

Myself.

But as soon as I was alone again, no longer in the warmth of his presence, my demons began to devour me. Just as they are right now. They always know which emotions to pick at in order to eat me alive. Ever since that morning in the shower, it's been one emotion.

Guilt.

You raped him, my conscience screams at me.

What the fuck does that say about me? That I got off on his torment?

I always knew I was fucked up but, Jesus Christ, this is downright depraved.

Sadistic.

But the way his ass felt wrapped around my cock was pure magic.

I want to feel it again. Fuck him again.

I've never craved someone like this in my life.

But. I'm. Not. Gay.

That's been my mantra since the first run-in at school in the locker room. It's been my mantra since I was four-fucking-teen. It's my mantra still. But River broke down the barricade around my mind outside the shed, and I'm struggling to rebuild it.

And goddamnit, no matter how hard I try, I can't stop replaying his words.

Accept this is who you are, so you can start to enjoy being stranded in a fucking cabin in the woods with me for another four weeks.

Shit.

I don't want him to be right. But he is.

I don't want to want him. But I do.

Four weeks is a long damn time to sit around this cabin,

avoiding him and his tempting as hell ass. It hasn't even been two weeks and I already feel like my sanity is slipping away.

And I'm grasping at straws, coming up empty when I try to think of how to hold on. Nothing is working.

Except River.

Whenever we fight, I stop thinking and worrying because all I want is to rip his clothes off and fuck him into submission. It's explosive.

It's chemical.

So maybe…

Goddamnit, I'm going insane to even consider this.

"Screw it," I grumble, slamming the brush down and shooting up from the chair.

Ripping open the door, I head down the hall to his bedroom. I knock softly on his door before calling out to him, hating the butterflies flying in my stomach.

"Riv?"

I wait a moment, head canted toward the door to listen for footfalls. Nothing.

I open the door, letting it swing into the room and look around to find it empty.

Nothing.

My brows furrow as I pull the door back shut and continue down the hall to the living room.

"River?" I call, when I notice that room empty too. Same with the kitchen.

Dread floods my system and before I can stop myself, I shout his name at the top of my lungs, my voice thundering against the walls of the cabin.

Relax. There's no way he left you here. You would have heard the four-wheeler start. A car door slamming. The crunch of tires under the snow.

Just relax.

I can't fucking relax. Where is he?

Yanking the front door open with enough force to rip the door from its hinges, I swing my head around the porch in search of River.

"River?" I yell into the silence of the forest.

Fucking. Nothing.

I check the shed for the ATV to find it still sitting where we parked it last week, as I figured. Glancing at the ground, I scan the area for fresh tracks, but there hasn't been snow in a few days, and since I'm no motherfucking boy scout, I can't differentiate the fresh from the old.

"River!" The scream comes from deep in my soul, I don't even care that the panic is present in my voice. His name echoes off the trees and the mountains and the snow. But when the echoes fade, I'm left with nothing.

Just silence.

It's been five hours of pacing and panicking, and still no sign of River. I've called his phone, but no answer. Not like I get the best reception out here, anyway.

I glance at the clock above the stove.

Shit, it's going to be getting dark soon.

Okay.

If he isn't back in thirty minutes, I'll take the ATV into town and…

And what?

Jesus Christ. I'm a rich fuck from suburban Pennsylvania. I'm not equipped to deal with this kind of MacGyver bullshit.

As I'm about to head down the hall to change into sweats, the front door swings open.

My heart stops when I see it's River.

Relief instantly flows through my body at the sight of him, clearly in one piece. His cheeks are red, probably from the wind, and he looks a little out of breath.

He doesn't notice me standing at the edge of the hallway, so he lifts his feet, one at a time, resting them on the bench next to the door to take off his boots. His ass flexes beneath his jeans, causing my dick to thicken behind my zipper.

Fuck, I want him.

It's the most confusing and infuriating thing I've ever experienced.

Whipping off his jacket and beanie, he tosses them on the hook behind the door, then spins around to face me. He pauses, finally catching me staring at him. I track his hand running through his brown locks, attempting to fix his unruly hat hair.

I want to be the one to run my hands through them.

What. The. Shit. Where is this coming from?

Pulling his AirPods from his ears, he tucks them into their case and tosses them on the kitchen island before meeting my eyes again.

"Hey," he says softly.

And I just…snap.

I'm pinning him back against the island, my hips pressing firmly into his, my hand around his throat before I can even blink. My teeth grind together in aggravation.

Hey?

He's been gone for *hours*, I didn't know if he left me here or if he was fucking dead in the forest being eaten by a mountain lion like he said were out here that first day.

And he says *hey*.

I'm fucking seething. "Where the fuck were you? You've been gone for hours. You didn't answer my calls, you didn't leave a note. I was freaking out thinking you left me here. I thought…" I cut myself off, swallowing harshly.

Shit.

"I thought something terrible happened to you."

Shock crosses his face. "I went for a hike. Kind of like you do without telling me? I didn't think you'd care."

I sigh and release my hold on his throat, bringing my forehead to rest against his. My heart is pounding a mile a minute. "Of course I care, River," I whisper.

"*Why?*"

His question gives me pause. I pull back to look into his eyes, more green than blue today, my brows furrowing. "Why?"

"Yeah, why? Why do you care when you clearly hate me?"

I clench my jaw. "I can hate someone and still want them to be alive and well. They aren't any fun to torture if they're dead."

River presses his hands into my chest, pushing me off his body. "Of course, Rain. You threaten to kill me *multiple times,* but you want me to be *alive and well.* You want your victims to feel it when you hurt them. I get it now. Really. I think I understand that more than anyone."

"Fuck you."

"Do it yourself," he taunts with a smirk. "But I'd appreciate an orgasm out of it this time. Didn't anyone ever tell you it's rude to leave your partner hanging?"

I narrow my eyes at him. It didn't take long to catch onto the game he plays, but for the life of me, I can't keep myself from playing it. "First, you aren't my damn *partner*. And second, I know all about getting my *actual* partner off." I pause, getting closer again, speaking against his lips. "You asked if you'd get rewarded for being a *good boy*. And you were anything but, Riv. So why would you ever think I'd let you come when you never know when to shut your fucking mouth?"

Shit, just talking about his mouth makes me stupidly hard. Maybe just stupid in general.

Because I'm not gay.

But I want to capture those lips with mine, seeing as I can't stop staring at them half the time, and put our tongues to other uses than fighting and taunting.

Goddamnit.

River licks the seam of my lips with the tip of his tongue, a wicked grin spreading across his face. "Well, baby, you know what to do to get me to shut up. Put your gorgeous cock in my mouth."

Baby. My brain catches on the word.

I know he uses it as a barb, just like he always does.

But *this* time? I swear I hear something else in his tone.

Tenderness?

"You'd like it too much," I tell him, currently reeling on the idea of River wrapping those perfect pink lips around my cock again. Inhaling deeply, I attempt to calm my erratic thoughts.

But he smells so damn good. I swear to God, his cologne or soap or natural fucking scent sends a signal of raging desire straight to my dick anytime I catch a whiff.

I can't believe I'm even contemplating this…

"But maybe if you show me how *good* you can behave, then I can be…" I glance up into his eyes before continuing, "…generous enough to make these next few weeks a lot less… confrontational, and a lot more… pleasurable."

"What are you saying, Rain?" he mumbles, the sound of my name, *that name,* on his lips getting me ridiculously hard.

"I want to fuck you again," I whisper into his mouth, giving into temptation and grabbing his bottom lip between my teeth and tugging. "And I *hate* it. I can't stand that I want to fuck your tight ass more than I want to escape from this goddamn cabin," I say in a frustrated exhale. "I hate that I'm driven by this uncontrollable…lust for you, even when I hate you."

"That's because you don't hate me at all."

I sigh against his mouth, letting the lie slip off my tongue. "I couldn't hate anyone more if I tried."

"Better be careful, Rain. Love and hate are two sides of the same coin. You'll be falling in love with me before you know it."

"Unlikely."

He pushes me back again and rolls his eyes. "Is it so hard for you to admit you like me?"

"Yes, because I don't. So, I'm not going to say it because I'm not a liar."

Liar.

"You like me enough to want to fuck me. That's what you're attempting to ask for, right? A good fuck? Something to pass the time while we're stuck in this hellhole?"

River's lips quirk up in the corner and his eyebrow inches toward his hairline as well.

Damn him for being so receptive.

"That's not what I'm saying at all," I deny. But we both know my argument is weak and the furthest thing from the truth. Because the unthinkable is happening.

The asshole is starting to grow on me.

So naturally, I keep digging the hole deeper, knowing he will have a witty retort on the tip of his tongue for anything I have to say.

"This changes nothing. I don't like you. I never will. And I won't like fucking you, either. It's a means to an end, that's it. *If* we were to do this, then when this little social experiment Coach is putting us through comes to an end, so does the... arrangement between us."

"Fine by me."

I raise a brow. I was expecting him to put up more of a fight.

"And no one can know about it when we get back to school."

"I'm not agreeing to that."

Ah, there it is.

"But—"

"Shut up and let me finish. I'm not agreeing to that." He pauses, checking to make sure I'll keep my trap shut this time. "I refuse to go back into the closet for anyone or anything. But that being said, you shouldn't have to worry about people back at school finding out if we end this the day Coach comes to pick us up." He quirks a brow in amusement. "Or are you already planning on breaking that rule, trying to hunt me down when you think you need a good dicking?"

"You won't go anywhere near my ass," I snap. "And before you even think about it, I'm not blowing you, either."

He laughs. "Fucking bet."

"I'm serious. In this agreement, I'm the top only. I'm in charge."

River shakes his head. "No deal, man. I'm not a human blow-up doll. I deserve to get off just like you do. Every time. Not only when you think I *deserve it*."

I grind my teeth, conceding that he does have a point. Begrudgingly.

"Fine. I'll make sure you get off. But I stand firm on the anal."

River just smiles and steps into my personal space. His hands, so much larger than any other that has touched me like this, slide under my shirt and over my abs. My dick jolts, loving his hands on me in any capacity.

Fucking hell.

I'm not gay.

Riv moves his hands from my abs around my waist to my lower back, fingers trailing softly against my flesh. Goosebumps break out over my skin as he slips two fingers under the waistband of my jeans and briefs, teasing the top edge of my crack. "I'll take this ass one day. And don't worry, baby. You'll love every second of it."

I tense. It's on the tip of my tongue to call this bullshit off and ignore him for the rest of the month, even if I go insane in the solitary confinement of my bedroom. But his hand shoots up and he places a finger over my lips, silencing me.

"These lips don't need to do anything right now except seal this deal with a kiss. So do us both a favor and shut the fuck up."

Before I have the chance to object, his mouth smashes into mine, his tongue probing my mouth instantly. In search of a sparring partner. It only takes a minute of our tongues tangling before I completely forget the protests I had to his terms.

What were they again?

Hell if I know, because kissing him makes me damn near mindless.

I press River back into the counter with my body, locking him in with my arms and pinning him in place with my hips. My erection is thick and heavy in my jeans already, begging for release from its confines.

"Get naked," I murmur against his lips before whipping my shirt over my head in one fell swoop. My hands fly to my belt and I unbuckle it hastily before unbuttoning my jeans.

"Someone's eager," he laughs huskily in my ear before his mouth trails down my neck and across my collarbone in slow, leisurely kisses. He nips and sucks at the skin on the other side of my neck, I'm sure leaving hickeys in his wake. "I'm fine going slow. I'd love to mark every inch of you first."

"Later," I growl, beginning to undress him from the waist down. The minute I have his jeans opened, my hand dives into the front to grip him.

Shit.

This is the first time I've touched him.

A shudder of pleasure racks my body when I pull his cock free, getting close enough so I can grasp my own dick in my palm too, like he did out by the shed. I give us two slow vertical strokes, loving the way it feels to have his cock pressed to mine.

Why does something so wrong have to feel so good?

"I need to fuck you," I tell him while he drives me insane, still biting and sucking at my neck.

"Then fuck me," he murmurs against my skin before pulling back to aim a self-satisfied grin at me. "Preferably with lube this time."

I can't help but smirk. "Go get it, jackass. Since you were so sure of yourself to buy it in the first place."

He just laughs and I can't stop staring at him. His chiseled jaw, those dimples that could win wars, and his lips. God, my eyes are glued to them. He quickly grabs his wallet from off the counter, fishing out a condom and packet of lube, tossing them both at me. Being the star wide receiver I am, I catch them with ease and glance up at him.

"Jesus Christ, were you a boy scout or something?"

"It pays to be prepared." He grins, pulling my mouth back to his with a grip on the front of my throat.

He sure can fucking kiss.

River breaks away and finishes undressing quickly, shucking all his clothes in any which direction while I slide out of my own jeans.

And then I take a minute to really admire his body.

Sure, I've seen him in only a towel plenty of times in the locker room and his back half-naked the one time in the shower a little over a week ago.

But I'm allowed to look this time.

His chest and arms are perfectly sculpted, hard and smooth in all the right places. A couple tattoos run down his left arm in sporadic placement, and though I've seen them easily a hundred times at this point, I can't help but stare. There's a small cross on his inner wrist. A mountain range and treeline wrapping all the way around his forearm, just below the elbow.

On his ribs, I see a quote in script.

Into the forest I go, to lose my mind and find my soul.

I move my gaze down his torso and over his abs. They ripple and flex under my perusal, forcing my eyes down further, to his cock. It stands at attention, long and thick and just as perfect as the last time I saw it. It jumps suddenly, as if sensing my thoughts, and my eyes fly up to meet River's.

He wears nothing but an arrogant smirk on his face.

I frown. "If you say *anything* stupid, I promise, you're going to regret it."

He lets out a throaty laugh before ripping the condom from my hands, tearing open the foil and rolling the latex over my cock. "I was going to offer that you could take a picture, since it'll last longer."

I roll my eyes as I open the packet of lube, applying a generous amount to my length.

This time, despite my threat, I don't have any desire to hurt him.

I want to be the only one making him feel *good*.

"How do you want me?"

I bite my lip and glance around the open floor plan of the cabin, but my attention keeps snapping back to the kitchen island.

"Up here," I command, patting the stone countertop.

River doesn't waste a moment, hopping up, only to let out a hiss as his bare ass hits the cool surface. But then he laughs and pulls me between his legs. His mouth is on mine again in an instant, molding against the shape of my lips, his tongue dancing with mine.

I could drown in him, in the euphoria of being like this with him.

But that doesn't mean it's not confusing as shit.

Slipping my fingers into his hair, I tug his head back and trail soft, wet kisses down his throat, my tongue flicking out against his Adam's apple.

"Lean back," I mumble against him, pressing my palm against the warm skin of his pecs, forcing his back against the counter. My fingers dance over his chest and abs, relishing in the way his muscles tense under my touch.

A low groan slides past his lips when I trail the pad of my index finger down his length from tip to base. "Stop teasing me."

Chuckling softly, I grip his hips and shift his body to where I want it, his ass at the edge of the counter, the backs of his knees draped over my forearms. "You think *that* was teasing? Oh Riv, you're in for a rude awakening." After slicking two fingers with the lube on my sheathed cock, I slip my hand under him and tease his crack, coating his hole before easing the tip of my index finger inside him.

He's hot and tight, making my dick ache to be inside him again and actually be able to *enjoy it* this time.

Not that the shower wasn't intoxicating in its own right. Hate fucks are pleasurable, the undeniable charge in the air is something that only comes from pure, unfiltered lust.

But right now, taking our time and learning each other's

bodies? It's just...*more*. Seeing someone in their most vulnerable state and knowing you are the one who holds the power to make them quake in fucking ecstasy. That is when true chemistry is formed between two people. That is *real* pleasure.

River starts to squirm as I begin pumping the single digit in and out of him, slow and tantalizing. Curling my finger to brush along his prostate on every downward stroke.

I drop to my knees in front of him, letting his legs dangle over my shoulders and trace my lips up his inner thighs. Adding a second finger just as I give him a slight nip right where his hip and torso meet causes him to buck off the counter.

"Jesus Christ, my toes are tingling," he gasps when both fingers rub against the hidden button of pleasure inside him. Continuing to nibble at his skin, licking each and every little bite mark I leave behind, River shoots into a sitting position. His hands twist into my hair and he uses his hold to anchor my head in place. "You're fucking killing me."

Smirking, I lick his hip. "Don't die on me now, Riv. I haven't even gotten to the good part." My taunts spread warm breath across the sensitive skin near his groin.

He shivers, his foggy gaze meeting mine. With quick lashes of my tongue over his V, his hips, I work my fingers faster. Eyes locked on him, watching every intake of breath and heave of his chest, I press him back into the counter again, forcing him to release my head.

"More," he pants, bearing down on my hand, fucking himself harder with every twist and thrust of his hips. "I need more."

I bite his skin, harder this time, in an attempt to keep from smiling.

Patience, Riv. They call it a virtue for a reason.

Rising back up to a standing position, I slide my arm under his knee again and spread him wider before me. For a brief moment, I watch him while his eyes are closed. His body moves in rhythm with my hand in the way we always seem to be in sync.

And I've never been *this* turned-on in my entire life.

River's body is a masterpiece, sculpted and molded after Adonis himself. Something I've been desperate not to notice up until this point, yet always did.

But it's not just his body. It's fucking *all of him.*

His intelligence and quick wit. The sharpness of his tongue when he lays into me, letting me have a taste of my own medicine. When he smiles and laughs and is fucking *secure and honest* with who he is. And while I'm insanely jealous of that freedom, it might also be the biggest turn-on of all.

I'm beginning to realize resisting him was a futile effort from the start, and I thank my lucky stars I don't have to anymore. Because right now?

He's all fucking mine.

With a grunt of satisfaction in knowing I'm about to be balls deep inside him, I remove my fingers from him. A shudder wracks his body and his head snaps up.

His chest is heaving, and his eyes narrow into slits before he bites out, "That is the exact fucking *opposite* of more."

I can't help it, I burst out laughing at his little meltdown, a huge grin taking over my face. Which, of course, only causes him to frown harder. But his eyes soften, so at least he isn't actually pissed at me for stopping when he must've been close to coming.

Instead, a small smirk plays at his lips as his eyes dart between mine. "You should do that more often."

I quirk a brow, gripping the base of my dick and swiping it up and down his crack tauntingly. "Stop when you ask for more?"

"Fucking laugh, you jackass," he rasps as his body squirms, pressing toward me as best he can. I keep myself from sliding home into his tight ass, despite the urge flooding me. Even though it just about kills me.

"Maybe you should make me then, yeah, Riv?" I continue teasing my length against the puckered hole before aligning myself with it, ready to drive into pure bliss.

"The only thing I want to make you do right now is *fuck me*."

And with that, he wraps his legs around my hips and impales himself on my cock. We groan in unison, delirious with how damn *good* it feels to be joined like this.

I could spend the rest of my life inside his ass and it wouldn't be enough time.

"Move," he commands as he attempts to sit up, but my hand flies out to his chest to keep him down on his back.

"You're not the one in charge here," I tell him, sliding my forearms back under each knee, my hands finding hold on his hips as I give a powerful thrust forward. His hands claw at the edge of the counter above his head, gripping for dear life as I start pounding into him.

My balls seize for a moment and I internally curse. I need to focus on not coming prematurely like a goddamn preteen at each pump of my hips and every clench of his ass around my cock.

River's head hits the counter as his back arches with each swipe I make over the tiny button inside him, unleashing the rawest, impassioned sounds from his lips. Those moans only spur me on, fucking him with quick, confident strokes. Tightening the grip I have on his hips to a bruising level, we build and climb toward ecstasy.

"Fuck, you feel too damn good," I pant, using my shoulder to wipe the sweat from my brow as I slow, rolling my hips and bottoming out inside him.

River's eyes roll back in his skull as one hand moves from his grip on the counter to grasp his own cock. My eyes latch on to the sight of him stroking himself in time with my movements, fucking his fist like I'm fucking him. A small bead of pre-cum gathers at his tip after a few minutes, glistening in the light and taunting the hell out of me.

It makes my mouth water and for the first time…the thought doesn't have me in a fit of rage.

So I don't know if it is the high I'm riding from being balls deep inside River or if I've gone completely insane, but before I can think twice, I lean forward and lap at the tip of his cock. The salty tang of cum hits my tongue instantly, shooting a bolt of desire down my spine as his hips jerk off the counter.

The first thought that processes through my brain is…*I want more.*

And I don't care how wrong it is.

My eyes shoot up to his face to find him watching me, his heated gaze scorching me from the inside out. The haze clouding his eyes overwhelms me with the most powerful feeling I've ever known. Holding his eyes in place with my own, I continue to fuck him. I'm still bent over his body, each pant and sigh leaving my mouth caresses his cock, causing it to twitch.

At that small movement, lust overtakes me, allowing me to

flick my tongue over his tip again. Keeping my eyes trained on his, I watch as he finally submits to the control I have over him. I've never felt this level of dominance over someone.

"Suck it, baby," he moans, his smoky voice raw with lust.

My tongue swirls around the head of his dick before taking him deeper into my mouth. Not much deeper, seeing as I'm not *that* flexible, but it seems to be working for him based on the rumbles coming from his chest as his head hits the counter once again.

A gravelly *fuck* leaves him, and I smile around his cock.

Yeah, no fucking kidding.

My hips keep pistoning, now in more sporadic strokes, while my lips and tongue work the first couple inches of his length. Hollowing my cheeks, I suck hard, letting my tongue play with the underside of the head. It's driving him wild based on the way he's clawing at the counter. Which only spurs me on more, leading me to close my eyes and give into the task of sending him to heaven via my cock and mouth while he continues to stroke himself.

And fuck me. The way he takes control of his own pleasure, owning it with confidence and ease…I'm in awe.

I feel the tip of his erection twitch in my mouth, a surefire signal he's close to finishing, when one of his hands grips my trapezius and squeezes.

Realizing what he's trying to tell me, I give him one final suck before releasing, leaving him to pump his entire shaft as he pleases.

"*Fuck me,*" he demands, his eyes wild with passion as he starts jacking himself faster, the muscles of his abs straining with effort. The hand that was on my neck finds its way to my waist and he tugs me to him, emphasizing his request.

Tightening my grip on his hips, I fuck him mercilessly. Grinding. Climbing. Chasing my climax as his tight channel starts spasming around my cock. I lose all sense of time, of surrounding, of my-fucking-self in him when his release spurts from his cock, coating his stomach and chest.

"Shit," he groans, licking his lips as his eyes flash to mine, holding steady as he continues to work himself. The sight sends me over the edge right behind him, spilling my cum into the condom while I'm lodged deep in his ass.

"Fuck, Riv," I breathe, slowing my thrusts dramatically, every ounce of semen milked from my body by his tremors.

And when I stop altogether, I'm left a sweating, panting mess.

My hands leave his hips, gripping the edge of the counter as I gasp for breath. I pull from his body slowly, my head bowed over him as I attempt to calm my erratic heartbeat.

What the hell just happened?

River's palms grab each side of my face, causing me to start. He yanks my head up, making room for him to move into a sitting position. My heart clenches at the sight of the dopiest, sated smile on his face before he leans in and places a rough, chaste kiss on my lips.

No tongue, no teeth.

Just his lips on mine and for some reason...it feels more intimate than the fuckhot sex that happened not more than a few minutes ago.

He rests his forehead against mine after he withdraws, our breath and sweat mixing together as we continue to come down from the high of our orgasms. Reaching down, he rolls the condom off my softening cock, tying it off and placing it on the counter beside him.

"I meant it, you know," he tells me after a couple minutes, pulling back to look at my face. The expression on his... I can't place it. But whatever it is, I'm sure it has everything to do with this bridge between enemies and lovers, just having been dismantled entirely.

I feel my forehead crease. "About what?"

River rolls his teeth over his bottom lip, before smirking. "You laughing more. It's sexy as hell. And I'm selfish enough to want to hear it all the time."

My eyes roll of their own accord as I grimace. "Okay, River."

His smile is contagious as he shoves my shoulder. "I'm fucking serious. I'm about to make it my mission to hear it every single day we're here." He pauses to tap his chin. "And twice on Sundays, seeing as it's the *holy* day and you love to be inside of *my* holes."

I blink at him, a small smirk on my own lips, and he shrugs before continuing.

"What? It's only fair to think I should get *something* out of it."

I just stare at him some more, attempting to process his cocksure attitude and misplaced entitlement...only to realize we're having this conversation bare-ass naked in the kitchen of our Coach's cabin...covered in cum and sweat after the hottest sex of my entire fucking life.

And for the second time today, I just can't help it.

I laugh.

TWENTY-ONE
River

DAY SIXTEEN - CHRISTMAS EVE

"You ready for this shit?" I ask Rain over my shoulder. I'm digging through a clear bin I found in the hall closet that housed a few Christmas decorations, smiling like an idiot. Nothing fancy is inside, just white string lights and some standard buffalo plaid ornaments. I'd found it there the other day when I was searching for a second pair of snowshoes before remembering they were out in the shed with all the other sporting equipment.

But the minute I found them, along with a tree stand, I sent Coach a text asking if it would be okay for us to set up a tree. He agreed, so long as we tore it all down before he was here to pick us up at the end of our stay.

Hence, where we are now. Me and my die-hard Christmas-loving ass asking for Rain to help me decorate for the holiday.

"Do we have to?" he grumbles, leaning over the back of the

couch, staring at me.

My brows raise in disbelief. "You're kidding, right?" I scoff when he nods in affirmation. "It's Christmas Eve and we chopped down a damn *tree* for this and hauled it back here. Of course we're going to decorate the damn thing, you nutsack."

Yep, that's right.

Two days ago, I dragged Rain into the forest in search of the perfect tree for us. It only took an hour to find one I thought was manageable enough to both cut down and haul back to the cabin, but Rain bitched and moaned about it pretty much the whole time.

Such a Grinch, this one.

And even after our fuckhot rendezvous in the middle of the forest that I *swear* could have melted the snow on the ground around us.

"All part of *your* brilliant plan, I might add."

"I don't appreciate your tone," I snip as I drag the box over to where the tree is held up in its stand, just next to the fireplace. Pulling free a strand of lights, I motion for him to join me. "Let's go, Scrooge."

Rain lets out a huff of indignation before rising to his feet and crossing the room to me.

"You're such a pain in my ass," he gripes as his hands snake around and palm *my* ass.

I simply smirk, not saying a damn word until he realizes the opening he left me. Because there is *always* an opening when it comes to the shit he says. I mean, *come on.* I'm a bisexual man and you're talking about *pain* in the *ass*. It doesn't take a rocket scientist to decode my thoughts on that one.

Still, it takes a moment, but his eyes widen, then he frowns at me. "You're such a child."

"Oh, really?" I laugh, grabbing the back of his neck with my free hand and bringing his mouth to mine in what is meant to be a quick kiss…that quickly turns into a full-blown make out session.

It's honestly a little surreal, being with Rain like this.

Open. Free. Affectionate.

And still, it's not always perfect. I can tell there are times when he starts to feel uncomfortable with how we touch each other. Moments when he hesitates. Whether it's when our lips first touch, or the first seconds my hands or mouth are on his cock.

He still fights the attraction flowing between us, and in turn, has what I've dubbed *mini meltdowns.* Where I watch the wheels turning in his head and the tick of his jaw set, like he's preparing for battle.

There have been a couple times where he's snapped at me over the past four days, but in all honesty, I expected it. I'm not looking to change who he is as a person. He wouldn't be Rain if he wasn't a little bit of an asshole, and I like him exactly how he is.

Especially when he's deep inside me, which in itself is mind-boggling.

When we fuck, pure and animalistic and…hot as hell, it's like we channel all the rage and disdain we held for each other into making the other feel good instead. We're more attuned to one another now, as if it were even possible because I already swear he can read my damn mind.

In short, it's the polar opposite of the vibe we've had flowing between us up until a few days ago when he flipped out on me, thinking I left him here on his own.

Because, apparently, I'm the kind of person to do that to someone.

I'll never admit it to him, but that hurt me more than anything he's ever done or said to me. Never in my life have I claimed to be perfect or upstanding at every moment, but there are a few things I would *never* do. Abandoning someone, that's high on the list.

Especially when I know what it feels like.

A nip on my bottom lip pulls me out of my thoughts, and I'm left panting when I pull away from him, but there's a huge smile on my face. When he sees it, his mouth lifts into a small grin too.

That fucking smile.

It might be the best part of this whole arrangement we have going on, getting to make him smile. And shit, I almost got another laugh out of him the other day. He played it off, attempting to cover it with a cough, but I heard it. The decadent sound will be ingrained in my mind forever, making me wish to hear it as often as I can.

I meant it when I said I would try everyday to make it happen.

"Come on, you just got laid this morning," I chide, removing myself from his tempting grasp.

We've hardly kept our hands to ourselves in the past few days, even with Rain's issues adjusting to our new status quo. But God knows we need to learn how to handle being in the same room without getting naked and fucking on whatever surface might be available before we become addicted.

"We should do this while we still have a few hours of daylight, so we can enjoy it."

Starting at the bottom, I begin stringing the lights around the tree, only to find Rain staring at me and...

Holy shit, he's actually standing there pouting. I mean, sort of. In a more masculine, *I-could-rip-you-limb-from-limb* way.

"Who are you, a male version of Cindy fucking Lou Who?"

I smirk at his movie reference, knowing he's full of the most random ones. He even quoted *Mean Girls* the other day. His asinine use of the phrase *boo, you whore* in a valley girl accent damn near brought me to my knees, I was laughing so hard. He says he learned them from using an obscene amount of GIFs in texting chains with his friends in high school, but I don't believe him for a second.

Besides, when it comes to the usage of *Mean Girls* references, the limit does not exist.

"I think that would be Tiny Tim?" I laugh as he finally joins me in running the lights around the tree. We work in tandem, me handing him a length of lights and him working them through the branches of the tree.

"Nothing tiny about you, babe."

My heart stutters at the endearment, and I freeze. Rain doesn't notice right away, just holds his right hand out for more lights as his left fiddles with the section he laced through the branches of the tree moments ago.

His attention snaps my way then, probably wanting to know what the hell my issue is, but my stunned expression brings him to a pause.

"What? Why are you staring at me?"

I don't answer, just continue staring.

I can tell the moment he realizes what he said, because red tints his cheeks and the tips of his ears.

"Sorry, it kind of slipped out."

I bite my lip in an effort to keep from smiling, but it's no use. Before long, I'm grinning at him like a full-blown idiot. I'm always fucking smiling at him. Because, as strange as it might seem, especially with everything we've gone through to get to this point...I'm happy.

Really happy.

More than I should be, literally sleeping with the enemy.

If that's where I'd even slot him these days.

Clearing my throat, I start handing him more lights. "Don't be sorry, I don't mind," I tell him, and it's true. It's not like I don't call him baby, though it's usually in a taunt or in some sort of heat-of-the-moment kinda thing. "I guess I wasn't expecting it is all."

He keeps stringing the lights, not meeting my gaze, but he lets out a strange noise somewhere between a laugh, cough, and groan as a blanket of uncomfortable silence settles over us.

Shit.

We keep working, and after all the lights are on the tree, Rain finally speaks as he digs out some ornaments, starting to place them sporadically around the tree.

"At least you aren't making us listen to fucking Christmas music while we do this."

I laugh, but on the inside, I'm actually surprised. *How the hell did I forget that piece of tradition?* "Thanks for the reminder, *baby*." I smirk, gripping the back of his neck and kissing him again. The emphasis on the word *baby* makes him shake his head once we pull apart, but at least the ice has broken once again.

Still holding his neck, I call out to the Google Home on the kitchen counter, asking to play a Christmas playlist. A few seconds later, she's blasting some good ole "Frosty the Snowman."

Biting my lip, I chance a glance at Rain, who is glaring daggers at me.

Damn, he really isn't into the Christmas spirit.

His palms grip each side of my face and I'm actually a little scared he might go all *Game of Thrones* on me and squeeze my brain into mush through my eyeballs, The Mountain style.

Moving his mouth forward to hover over mine, he whispers, "This is one of those moments when I really wish I still hated you," before latching his lips onto mine in a possessive kiss that curls my toes, not letting my mind linger on the fact he inadvertently admitted to not hating me anymore.

His kiss is fierce and bubbling with desire and unspoken promises. His tongue thrust into my mouth, and I groan when it makes contact with mine. We're desperate, fucking each other's mouths with greedy stokes, begging to dive deeper.

I don't think I'll ever get used to kissing him, tasting him. Just *him.*

But *goddamn,* I want to. Part of me hopes I never lose whatever this is with him. That same part of me is dreading each and every passing day.

I realize this line of thinking is dangerous, damn near insane. We've been messing around for only a handful of days, and I'm already finding myself far too attached for comfort.

And honestly, how could I not be concerned?

Ciaráin Grady was tailor-made for heartbreak.

And *apparently,* I'm the idiot who volunteered as tribute, putting my heart and body on the line, allowing Rain to test drive where he falls on the "gay spectrum".

As if there is such a thing.

Sure, there is a difference between being gay and bi and straight. But it ends there. You can't be *kind of* gay or *sort of* bi. You can't *sometimes* like fucking a guy's ass or a dude's lips wrapped around your cock like you would *sometimes* like mustard on a hotdog.

Yes, sexuality might be extremely fluid as a whole, but there are no gray areas when it comes to this.

You either like cock or you don't. You're into guys or you fucking aren't.

The way he responds to me when I touch him, kiss him, fuck him with my hand and mouth and tongue? Jesus, it tells me everything I need to know.

He likes it. And he is.

I feel the ridge of his erection pressed into my leg as our lips continue devouring each other. His hand slides down to cup me through my pants, but it only serves to remind me of the shit we need to get done. Namely, Christmas tree decorating.

Sex can wait another hour, after all.

Wrenching my mouth from his, we're both left breathless, panting like we just completed a marathon in record time. If it were possible, I'd say I could hear his damn heart beating at a rapid pace matching my own.

"We need to finish this up," I point out, stepping from his hold quickly before he manages to suck me back into his orbit.

I'm not quick enough though, because he drags my mouth to his for a final, chaste kiss before allowing me to step away. "Fine, but only if you turn this shit music off until *after* I get to fuck you."

I'm pleased to announce, after decorating the tree and then the *hottest* sixty-nining session of my life, followed by being bent over and officially learning what the term *pillow biter* means, I have managed to de-grinchify Rain.

Okay, well not completely, but I'm going to take credit where it is due here and just be grateful he's no longer bitching about the Christmas music or the decorations or generally anything pertaining to my favorite holiday.

Glancing up from the pan of this cheeseburger casserole Rain wanted to try, I spot him coming down the hall with an oversize envelope in hand, slightly larger than a four by six photograph.

Setting down the glass dish on a potholder and slipping off the oven mitt, I nod toward the envelope, "What's that?"

Rain shifts on his feet before setting it on the stone island counter, biting his lip. He stares at it for a good minute like it's a damn bomb about to detonate, completely ignoring my question.

"I, uh…" he starts, clearing his throat. Twice. His whiskey eyes raise to meet mine and he sighs. "Look, Riv. I…fuck." The curse comes out in a harsh bite before his hands fly to his hair, tugging at the strands before he takes a seat at one of the bar stools. Hands slipping from his hair to cover his face, he shakes his head.

What the hell…?

I start to move over to him, but I barely take a single step before Rain holds up one of his hands.

"Please don't touch me right now. I'm fine. Just give me a minute."

But he looks anything but fine. His skin is more pale than a ginger who has never seen sunlight and he looks like he might legitimately toss his lunch right here on the kitchen floor.

Even still, I don't move a muscle. Hell, I don't dare to breathe.

Because if I've learned anything about Ciaráin Grady in the past few months, it's in moments like this, if you push his buttons, you're in for the fight of a lifetime.

And his wrath is not the kind you want to be at the receiving end of.

That doesn't mean I'm not practically *dying* to ask him what's wrong. I need to pull his head from his hands and look into those eyes that entrap my every waking thought to figure out what's wrong.

How I can make it better.

Instead, I wait. Biting the inside of my cheek so hard blood coats my tongue. I watch as one of his hands reaches out to play with the envelope in front of him, fingering the corner and spinning it in slow circles.

I realize then it's not a piece of mail. There's no address written on the outside and the seal looks to be unbroken.

Meaning...what, exactly?

"It's for you," he mutters softly, as if reading my thoughts. Hell, at this point, I wouldn't put it past the guy. It would explain why, even when we were at each other's throats, we always managed to stay in sync.

I open my mouth to ask...what, I'm not sure. But it doesn't matter because he cuts me off before I even have the chance to make a sound.

"Just let me say something before I give this to you, yeah? Because...fuck I have to say this before the guilt eats me alive."

He pauses to swipe a hand over his face, letting it linger over his eyes before dropping it down to the counter. Then those amber orbs latch onto mine and the amount of regret painted in them causes me to catch my breath.

"What I did to you…it can never be undone. No matter how much I want to take back that day, I don't have that kind of power over the universe. And it just about fucking kills me." He takes a deep breath, anxiety crossing his features. His fingers twitch against the counter for a second before they find themselves running through his hair roughly again.

"An experience like that can shape who you are as a person. I mean, you hear horror stories about rape and non-consensual sexual encounters and most of the time the people come out the other side fucked up beyond belief. It's sickening and for the life of me, I don't want that to happen to you."

Hold the motherfucking phone.

Rape?

Is that what he thinks happened in the shower?

But yet again when I go to open my mouth to speak, I'm cut off. This time by a glare cast from Rain.

"River, let me…fuck, please just let me talk." The hoarseness of his voice sounds as if he swallowed gravel. "I crossed the line. You've taunted me and antagonized the ever-loving hell out of me for months. I held out on anything more than a punch and a few harsh words for the most part. But something inside me snapped and it was like all these pieces fell into place, and the only way I could formulate a plan to get you off my back was to pull a stunt so fucking heinous you wouldn't have a choice but to ignore me the rest of the time we were here. Or risk having it happen again."

Shame takes over his handsome face, and I hate it. I hate all of this.

That we found ourselves rooted against each other for no damn reason when we could have been *friends* from the beginning. That he feels this shame and guilt for what happened when...shit, I *never* said no.

Mostly I hate that he felt the need to go to such extreme measures to ward me off. I was driving him so crazy he felt the need to...

"You wanted me to be afraid of you," I whisper in revelation, holding his gaze.

He nods, his throat working to swallow. "I did. It wasn't right and I understand that. There were a million other things I could have done. Hell, I could've hiked my ass to town and gotten a hotel for the night. Called an Uber to take me back to Boulder or fucking *anything* else other than the course I chose to follow."

I can tell by the set of his face he believes the bullshit coming from his mouth like they were words spoken by Jesus himself.

And it most definitely *is* bullshit because here's the thing. Rain had a goddamn *meltdown* when he thought I left him stranded in this cabin only a couple days ago. Full out screamed at me about it, reamed me a new asshole for not letting him know I went for a damn *hike* when that's something he's done regularly since we've arrived.

So, do I think he would leave me here on my own for another three plus weeks and just *leave?* Nah, it'd never happen.

Finding a sasquatch riding a unicorn would be more likely.

"You don't mean that," I mutter, my nostrils flaring because *fuck* letting him sit here let guilt eat him alive. "You would never."

He doesn't respond, just clenches his jaw rapidly. I watch, transfixed on the pulse point coming from the action. Neither of us speak for a moment, letting the agitation in the air grow to uncomfortable levels. I'm not about to speak more, not when the ball is in his court to keep this conversation moving forward. So I keep my eyes trained on him while he bites his lip, trailing his fingers over the envelope.

What the fuck is in there that has him so worked up?

"I'm so fucking sorry, River. I can't even begin..." He trails off and shakes his head before glancing up at the ceiling. "Just know I would give anything to take back that morning in the shower. To erase it from history, so it never happened."

My heart aches at the anguish present in his voice.

Regret and remorse are normal emotions to feel when you fuck up. Every person in the world, except maybe the population who are full-blown sociopaths, feel them. I get that.

But to be at the point where he wants to alter the course of our history? It means he's holding onto this too hard. Up until now, I hadn't realized that morning had a lasting impact on him as well. I guess it's ingrained in both our memories, never to be forgotten.

And yeah, does it suck the first time he was inside my body, the first time we had sex, my consent was dubious at best?

Yeah, it sucks a whole damn lot. But neither of us can change it at this point. What's done is done.

"But it *did* happen," I reply softly. "It happened and it's useless to live in the past, drowning in our regrets." Biting my lip, I tap the edge of the counter anxiously to the beat of the song in my brain.

It's started changing a lot more frequently now, which I've found odd but I'm rolling with the punches. Something *Rain* clearly needs some practice in.

"How can I not live in regret when I think of what I did every time I look at you?"

I try not to wince at his words, but they gut me. Not for the reason someone might think, though. I know I'm not some scared and frightened animal attempting to lick my wounds the big bad wolf inflicted on me.

I'm strong. Resilient. I've more than proven I can stand on my own against him and even come out on top.

I've done so multiple times.

No, what hurts about his words is the broken way he says them. That he can't see past his mistake and look at the past few days through different eyes.

Because hell, these past few days not fighting with him have been, dare I say…*fun*. He's a lot of fun to be around when he's not being a brooding douchewaffle who has his mind set on making me miserable.

"Let me ask you something, Rain," I say, looking at him down the island, loathing the space separating us still. "Did you ever once hear me tell you *no*?"

That gets his attention. His hand freezes on the envelope at the same time his head slowly rises. I watch a war battle in his eyes while he thinks back on that morning. Most likely in vivid detail, judging from the way his eyes sink closed once again.

I remember it well too.

The burn of the soap, the vindictive words he spoke in my ear.

Yeah, I remember it all, and honestly? I don't have it in me to hold it against him. Even before he apologized.

Clearly, since I've let him fuck me *multiple* times since then.

"No," he responds with a voice being cut open by glass. "You never said no."

I nod, knowing he's correct. "And did I ever ask you to stop?"

He licks his lips and shakes his head, eyes still closed. "No."

I nod again, but I can see I'm still not getting through to him. He won't open his eyes, he won't look at me still. And I can't fucking stand it.

"Look at me, Rain." It's a request, a plea.

For him to see we're *equals.* The other morning was just another bump in the already treacherous road for us to get to the point we're at right now. Which, if I'm being honest, I don't know what it is.

Fuck buddies, I suppose. Sounds much better than sleeping with the enemy.

But even as I wait a moment, he refuses to meet my eye. To listen to me. Not that I'm at all surprised. Rain doesn't do anything he doesn't want to and he kneels to just about no one.

"I said, *look at me*," I demand sharply, not bothering to keep the bite from my tone. And it works, because he obliges, giving me his full attention. "I want you to stop this pity party you're having. Because that is what it is."

The way his eyes widen, nostrils flaring, tell me he's about to go off on me, but that's not going to happen.

"Shut up and let me talk," I growl, rounding the counter to stand in front of him. "You're sitting there stewing in your guilt and it's doing nothing, fucking *nothing,* to heal the wounds we've caused each other. And we both know I can stand here and forgive you a million times and you will *still* feel guilty." I quirk a brow, daring him to disagree, but the smart man he is, he keeps his trap shut.

"Do I wish things would have progressed between us differently? Absolutely. But Rain...that was some of the hottest sex of my life, even if it wasn't exactly..." I trail off. How do I tell him I *liked* what he did to me? He might be a little fucked in the head for doing it, but *I* am the idiot sandwich who actually enjoyed it?

"Look, I'm not mad. I don't hold it against you. I forgive you, absolve you of your sins. Whatever you fucking need to get past this." My hands itch to reach out and touch him, but I keep my fist balled at my sides. "I wouldn't have hopped into bed with you *willingly* if I thought for one second you're a rapist. Which is exactly what you're painting yourself as right now."

"But—"

"No. No *but.* Not unless it is one of *ours* getting *fucked,*" I bite, ticking my jaw. "Do we have an understanding? You are not a rapist. I am not a victim. We are two people who are making the best of a shitty-ass situation by enjoying each other's bodies. *Consensually.*"

I wait for a sign of his agreement. A nod, a word, *something.* And while it takes a minute, his sigh of concession is more than enough for me to soften again. And I'm glad.

Being harsh with him, having to *put him in his place* so to speak, I hate it. It makes me itch and feels so...uncomfortable.

Unnatural. Which is odd in itself because I love having the upper hand with most people. The control, the dominance.

But with him, my preference is to submit.

Still, there are times like this where I just know he needs someone to make him back down. Bend him enough to show his hand.

Force him to kneel, if only for his own good.

And honestly, isn't that what I've been doing from the beginning with this battle of wills we waged? Giving him someone who was strong enough to fight back. Who was strong enough to *win*.

Isn't that what he needs?

An *equal*.

Licking my lips, I shake my head. Because even though *I* know I am, I'm not sure he will ever see me as that. "Christ, Rain. Can I touch you yet?"

He smirks and nods, giving me the go ahead. I slip between him and the counter, so I'm positioned directly in front of him before hopping up, his torso and shoulders between each of my dangling legs.

Rain wraps his arms around my waist and presses his forehead into my sternum and lets out a sigh. "How the hell can you go from sweet to dominant as fuck, then back to sweet again within a minute?"

I shrug, wrapping my hands around the back of his neck, teasing the short hair I find there with my fingers. "God given talent? Human sour patch kid? Unclear."

He lets out a soft chuckle. "Tastiest sour patch kid I've ever had in my mouth."

My brows shoot up. "Oh, so you're a jokester now?"

"No," he shakes his head with a wicked grin on his face. "Just making sure you remembered how well I milked every drop of cum from your cock earlier with my mouth."

I grip the back of his neck, bend down, and bring his mouth to mine giving his lips a quick nip. "That will be damn near impossible to forget," I say against him before kissing him. It's meant to be a quick peck, but as always, our tongues end up in a tangled mess until we're panting and breathless.

"As much as I love your mouth on mine, I'm *dying* to know what is inside the envelope you brought in here." I lick his lips with the tip of my tongue before pulling away, glancing to my side where it sits on the counter.

Picking it up, he hands it to me with an uneasy look back on his face. I pluck it from his grasp with a smile before giving him a soft kiss again. It's heavier than I thought it would be, and thick like cardstock.

His forehead finds the space right below my pecs and his arms tighten around my waist. Snaking my arms around his neck, I slip my finger into the seal of the envelope and tear it open carefully and pull out…a piece of what looks like…painting paper.

But it's blank.

I feel my brows crease as I flip it over and my heart…it stutters in my chest.

Rain must know, because he squeezes me for a brief second, burrowing his head against me like he'd like to get inside my ribcage to make sure my heart is still beating.

It's a painting. A watercolor.

And it's stunning.

It's a place I recognize well having been there with Taylor, Drew, and Elliott plenty of times in our youth whenever we'd come up to the cabin during the summer months. Or even in the winter when it was snowboarding season down at the resort in Vail.

The jagged, snow covered peaks and lines and clusters of pine trees surrounding a vivid aqua lake. It's absolutely perfect, captures the beauty of the place better than any photograph ever could.

"I was up there one day," Rain mutters, his voice muffled slightly by my shirt, "and I was so fucking sick of fighting with you. But I was even more tired of hiding from you, so I slipped out and hiked up there to see what all the fuss was about."

I remember the day he's talking about. I heard him slipping out of the cabin, seemingly undetected, looking ready to set out on a winter hike. He was gone for a long time, almost to the point I started to worry when I saw him out the window going into the shed off to the side of the cabin.

It was the night I first kissed him.

"And when I got there, I figured it out, you know? I didn't realize it immediately because I was busy painting, trying to lose myself in the task. But when I started on the lake, it hit me. How can you stare into something so blue and not just drown in its depth?" He pauses and slips away from me, my hands with the painting falling from around his neck and onto my lap. His gaze searches mine for a second before he continues in the softest whisper, searing my heart entirely. "The color...it reminded me of your eyes."

He says it in a way like it's a simple fact and he didn't just flatten my world like a pancake with less than ten words. Like the fact that this...is more special to me than any apology he could ever give me.

My eyes drifting back down to my lap, I let my fingers trace the edges of the painting, the soft perfect lines and the mixture of colors, in awe of his talent.

He thought of me when he painted this?

Rain lets out a nervous cough, grabbing my attention in time to see he's rubbing the back of his neck with his palm. "It's like even when I was trying to escape from you, it only made me think about you more. And I'm done letting my thoughts of you drive me mad. To send me to the brink of becoming the kind of person who..."

He doesn't finish his thought, but he doesn't need to in order for me to know.

Fights people. Hurts people... Rapes people.

"Anyway, um," he starts, licking his lips before sighing. "Just...Merry Christmas, River."

Christmas.

I can't believe even with the decorating today, it slipped my mind the moment he stepped into the kitchen. Guess that's what happens when you're given a gift transcending beyond the meaning of the holiday.

And no, I'm not talking about the painting in my hand.

Setting the watercolor on the counter beside me, I glance up for his eyes to capture mine. And the second they do, I see more vulnerability in them than I ever thought possible from him.

I feel my hand reach out and curl around the collar of his shirt. Something like confusion crosses his face when I start tugging him to his feet. But when I simply wrap my arms around him and squeeze, he relaxes into me and returns my embrace.

"Thank you," I almost choke on the words, my fingers twisting into the back of his shirt as I inhale his scent with a deep breath. "Thank you."

TWENTY-TWO
River

DAY SEVENTEEN - CHRISTMAS DAY

L ast night, something strange happened. There's been a shift in our dynamic.

I don't know if Rain can feel it, but I definitely do… and it's absurd to even be thinking it. Feeling it.

Part of me knows if I even *mentioned* it to Rain, to see if he noticed as well, it would send this progress we've made a million steps backward. Which is the last thing I want.

But it's there, festering under a thin layer of avoidance.

I don't feel like his enemy anymore. Not at all.

I don't have the urge to fight with him tooth and nail.

What I *want* is to be his friend. His *actual* friend. Not just a friend you happen to fuck because we're stuck in the middle of the mountains with nothing better to do than get each other off.

I'm talking, real ass, going to the movies, hanging out after practice, studying together, enjoying each other's company…*friends*.

Whether or not the sex would still continue after we returned to school? If we decided to pursue this in other facets? I... shit.

I don't know.

I just. Don't. Know.

Because the sex is fantastic. Mind-altering. Dare I say, the best I've ever had, with either a guy or girl. And coming from a guy who is used to topping more often than not?

Like I said, mind-altering.

Because I love the way he controls me when he's inside me, yet he lets me have my way with him even when I'm bottoming. Yes, I'd be lying if I haven't thought about sinking inside him more often than is probably mentally sane, but I would be happy to live the rest of my life never sinking my cock into anything other than a mouth if it meant getting fucked by Rain Grady.

Which in itself is...problematic.

I'm twenty-one years old, and the last thing I should be thinking about in my junior year of college is *settling down* because of a good lay.

My gut clenches, rejecting my line of thinking. I know this is more than a good fuck. I see myself getting in way too deep with him, especially after last night.

And yet...I'm not about to stop this.

No chance in hell.

Groaning, I roll to my side and slide out of bed, sore from spending half the night on the floor yet again. I don't have it in me to care though, as long as I'm close enough to him if he ever decides he needs me.

I just wish he would let me in there with him. Or spend the

night with me in my bed. But I'm not about to rock the boat with a suggestion and risk fucking up this…arrangement we have going on.

Goddamn, I'm so fucking screwed.

I slip into some clean clothes and decide not to dwell on whatever I'm feeling or not feeling for Rain. I have time to figure it out later.

I'm shocked to find Rain sitting at the kitchen table, cup of coffee in hand, when I make my way down the hall. It's only a little after seven, and usually he isn't up much before ten, what with his nightmares waking him frequently.

Last night wasn't nearly as bad, though. For some reason, he only moaned and sobbed for twenty minutes before falling back into a more peaceful slumber.

That doesn't mean I didn't spend a good two hours on the floor outside his room to be sure.

I haven't attempted to talk to him about them at all since the first night. It's not like we sleep in the same bed. Hell, we barely even *fuck* in a bed. Maybe once, in the week we've been…sleeping together? Having sex? Fucking?

Shit. Things are already getting too complicated.

"Morning," he says, standing from his seat and heading back to the coffee pot. He pours himself another cup, then grabs a second mug to pour some for me as well. Handing it to me, a nervous glimmer flashes across his eyes. "You sleep okay?"

"Yeah," I say, and it's not entirely a lie. When I'm asleep, I sleep fine. The ground is just a hard place to try to make that happen. I take a sip of my coffee, loving the bitter taste on my tongue, and smile at him. "So I might have something pretty fun planned for us today."

His thick brow quirks up. "Is that so?"

"Sure is. It's actually a good thing you're awake already. Means we can get started early before it gets too busy."

"Too busy?" he asks, confusion on his face, to which I bite my lip, attempting to keep my grin from growing larger.

Ever since Rain told me he had never been to the mountains, let alone skiing or snowboarding, I've wanted to take him. Yet, knowing Rain, he'd never want to be seen with me in public more than possible.

Though I'm not so sure that's true anymore.

And after last night? Giving me such a thoughtful gift and expecting nothing in return?

Yeah, no. Not fucking happening.

"We're heading into Vail," I tell him nonchalantly before taking another sip of my coffee. "I got us lift tickets for the day."

Rain's eyes practically bug out of their sockets at my words, then they narrow skeptically. "Is this a Christmas gift?"

"Does it matter? They are already paid for, non-refundable, and no, you can't give me money for yours." I shrug. "I've been wanting to hit the slopes since we got up here. It's more for me than you, since you don't even know how."

Again, not a *total* lie.

The look he's giving me tells me he is still doubting my motive, but he doesn't disagree. "You'll teach me?" The question comes out so defenseless, I'm almost shocked speechless.

Rain fucking Grady, nervous.

It's a sight to behold.

I smile behind my mug. "'Course, baby. I'll hold your hand the entire time down the bunny hill."

Not more than an hour later, we're dressed in the winter gear we brought with us to the cabin — thankfully, I brought a second pair of snow pants for Rain to borrow — and we're on the ATV into town. At least on this time riding bitch, I get to fuck around with him, teasing him by running my palms across the skin of his abs, chest, and back under all the layers of his clothing.

He might have pulled over and threatened me to knock it off before he drove us off the road, but he didn't seem *too* mad.

After renting a couple boards and helmets and showing Rain the basics of moving with one foot locked in a snowboard, we're setting off one of the chair lifts to the top of the mountain.

I glance out over the surrounding landscape as we rise up over the mountain on the lift, finding myself grateful as hell I was fortunate enough to grow up in such a beautiful place. So many people never get to experience what a beautiful world we live in, how small we are in the grand scheme of life, and being in the mountains always seems to put that in perspective for me.

Not just me, either. There's a reason Colorado is growing so fast, and it's definitely because of the good ole Rocky Mountain high.

A small twinge of guilt hits me, knowing this has been my backyard for most of my life, yet before today, Rain has never set foot on a ski resort. It makes me thankful I'm giving this experience to him. Though he hasn't opened up to me, shown me his scars and demons, I know he battles them each day. I hope a nice dose of nature might give him a break from it.

If only for today.

"What song?" Rain asks out of the blue, snapping me from my thoughts.

"Huh?"

"What song are you playing in your head right now?"

"I'm not—" I begin to deny, until I realize I've been tapping my glove-covered hand absently against my snow pants, lost in my thoughts. Rain takes said hand in his own, lacing our padded fingers the best he can.

That's new.

My brows furrow, looking at our intertwined hands and glance up at him as he gives me a smirk.

"You were saying?"

I feel my cheeks heat, even with the cold wind whipping around us, and glance away, suddenly anxious being so close to him with no escape.

"I don't think…I wasn't thinking of a song," I lie, still looking out over the slopes, which are relatively empty since most people are with their families on Christmas Day.

"Why are you lying to me?"

My eyes snap to him, not used to being called out by him. At least not for this. Because I never tell him lies. Stretch the truth? Sure. But even when we were at each other's throats, I didn't ever fucking lie.

My jaw ticks. *Goddamnit.*

"River," he growls, gripping my chin. "I've asked you what fucking song every single day in the week since we decided to do this…thing between us. What's the issue? Where the hell is your mind right now?"

"Everywhere," I mumble, staring into the depths of his amber eyes. "My mind, it's running rampant and I just..." Jesus Christ. How do I explain what I'm thinking, what I'm *feeling* for him?

I shouldn't be wanting to kiss him for the world to see or hold his hand as if to claim him as mine. It's not what we agreed to and is certainly more than a fuck buddy would feel. Which is all we are while we're stuck up here.

Right?

Letting out a frustrated breath, I give in to my desire, gripping the back of his neck under his helmet and slam my mouth to his, not giving a flying fuck who sees.

At first, he freezes, and I think he's going to push me away. Hell, I think he might push me *off* the damn ski lift, sending me plummeting to my imminent death.

Surprising me, he nips my bottom lip between his teeth before molding his mouth to mine in the perfect fit.

"Are you trying to distract me from finding out what song it is?" he pants against my lips between kisses. "Because as much as I enjoy making out with you, it's not working. In fact, it makes me want to know more."

"I just wanted to kiss you," I gasp, and this time, it's not a lie. "So, kiss me."

And kiss me, he fucking does. So well and for so long, I'm insanely hard once we're almost to the top of the lift, ready to dismount for our first run of the day.

We quickly move over and out of the way of the lift to the top of our first run. One of the easier green circles at the resort. Rain, the stubborn ass he is, was adamant he would not be spending time on the bunny hill. So this will be...*interesting.*

Latching my left foot into my board, I glance over at him just in time to see him topple over as he attempts to do the same with his right. I cough to cover my laugh, but he most definitely catches it if the glare he casts my way before he locks himself in from a seated position this time is any indication.

And then there is his less than graceful efforts trying to stand back up, which, I'll be honest, is hilarious and cute as shit. Seeing Rain off balance, figuratively and literally, makes something inside me grow a little bit warmer.

Taking pity on him, I hop over and extend my arm to him to help him up.

"You're fucking laughing at me already?" he growls, gripping my forearm.

"Damn straight, baby. It's my prerogative as your teacher. I get to laugh as much as I want at you today when you fall on your ass."

Rain smirks and tightens his grip on me, pulling me to the ground with him instead of using my outstretched hand to rise to his feet. I land with an *umph* on top of him, our legs and subsequently, our boards getting tangled together.

"Now look what you did. Is this what you wanted?"

"No," he groans, shifting beneath my weight as I try to disengage my legs from his. "I just wanted to make you shut up by making you fall."

I'm starting to think you have...in more ways than one.

"Well, jackass, mission accomplished." I laugh, righting myself before giving him a hand to get back up, which he thankfully takes and actually *uses* this time.

Once we're both stable, I glance up at him to find the biggest smile on his face. Bigger than I think I've ever seen.

It makes my heart stop completely.

"What?" I ask, sure that the sound of the word, no more than a whisper, is lost in the cool winter wind.

"Nothing. I'm just happy."

And the truth behind his words show. The glint in his eyes, the smile still on his face. I've never seen him this way.

Free.

I'm desperate to take this moment and bottle it, download it, find some way to save it so I can remember it for the rest of my life. To remember the way it feels to have him look at me like this.

To remember, if even for a moment, I was the source of his happiness.

And it's the most powerful feeling in the world.

I squeeze his hand in mine, leaning forward to brush my lips against his. "Me too."

His arm snakes around my waist as he drags me closer to him the best he can with the snowboard strapped to my feet. His lips are soft against my own, but still rough, insistent, and demanding.

All things fitting when it comes to Rain.

In all honesty, I still can't believe this is actually happening. That I'm kissing him like this, careless of our surroundings; that everything about him is mine to touch, taste, smell, if only for the time being.

My hand snakes under the back side of his helmet and I tilt his head to deepen this kiss. His tongue begins wrapping around mine and things start getting a little too heated for a public place. Not that I care, really. But knowing Rain, he might be uncomfortable if he knew people could see us, are watching us.

Because they most definitely are when the loud curse of *"fucking faggots"* is heard clearly from somewhere in our vicinity.

Rain's mouth freezes instantly on mine, his entire body going stiff as a board. He pulls back to look in my eyes and tries to yank free from my hold, but I don't let him.

Shit.

My other hand slips up to cup around his neck and I hold his eyes with my own while rage starts to build within them. "Hey. *Hey.* Rain, it's okay," I soothe the best I can. Because this must be the first time he's been subjected to any sort of homophobic slur in his life.

And yeah, no matter how thick your skin is, the first time hearing it...fucking sucks.

"Don't listen to them, baby," I murmur, my gloved thumb rubbing against the pulse point on his neck. It's visibly racing, manifesting from his anger. "There is *nothing* for you to be ashamed of. Not one goddamn thing. So, fuck them. Fuck them *all,* and the ignorant, hateful horses they rode in on."

I watch as his teeth work over his bottom lip and I see the gears turning in his head as he attempts to calm himself down.

"Breathe, okay. They have no say in what we do. It's the twenty-first century, they can get the fuck over two guys kissing each other. Love is love."

His eyes widen at my last words, and *shit,* I didn't mean to bring love into this situation.

"You know what I mean," I add quickly, praying to God my little slip didn't freak him out even more.

Because…I don't love him.

No, this is just sex. Sure, we are slowly becoming more like friends than straight up fuck buddies at a *very* rapid pace.

But I don't *love* him…

Right?

"Don't let them ruin our day, okay?" I plead, needing that look from only a few minutes ago back in his eye. "I know the first time someone says that…it's like a shot to the stomach. But don't let it get to you."

Rain shakes his head, coming out of whatever pissed off trance he was in. When his eyes connect with mine, they have a sadness in them, making me want to find the fucker who yelled our way and rip his nuts off.

Because *fuck him* for making this harder than it should be; for being so closed-minded he causes other human beings to question whether or not they are allowed to be the person they truly are.

Fuck their fear and their hatred of the things they don't understand.

For thinking that deviating from social norms coincides with being *inferior.*

Screw that bullshit thinking from *generations* ago, so we can move into a time of acceptance. Let people shine in their most authentic form.

Rain's helmet taps against mine as he leans into me. "Fucking asshole," he mutters, his grip on my waist tight, even through the layers of gear.

"I know." I sigh. "I'm sorry. I didn't mean—"

"Don't," he cuts me off, pulling back to look at me again.

"Don't apologize to me for the bullshit someone else said. That's not on you."

"True, but—"

"Shut up," he growls, kissing me roughly before I have the chance to speak further. His words come out in a harsh breath against my lips. "If anyone should be apologizing, it's me. Not for them, I don't give a shit what they have to say. I only care that I've used the same word as a weapon against you."

My chest constricts at his declaration, knowing now it wasn't those dicks that had him freezing up. It's that he's still holding on to so much guilt for the crap we did and said *before*. "Rain, it's sticks and stones. Words have no power to hurt you unless you let them."

"And let me guess," he says, licking his lips and pulling back from me, his eyes liquid fire. "You're about to lie to me for the second time today and tell me the crap I said never hurt you."

He doesn't give me a second to answer though, because he's already pushing off me, aiming his board down the mountain. I can tell that he's already hardening, shutting himself off from me once again.

"Let's go, babe. No use dwelling on the shit we can't change."

With that, he starts down the mountain, leaving me wondering if I somehow managed to fuck up this entire day with one fucking sentence.

TWENTY-TWO
River

DAY SEVENTEEN - CHRISTMAS DAY

I t seems my dumbass mouth and I didn't ruin the day after all, thank God.

After the first run, where I found Rain was surprisingly agile on a snowboard for his first time down a mountain, we got in line and it was almost like the whole damn thing on the mountain never happened.

He smiled more, kept giving me glances when he thought I wasn't looking.

Flirted with me, held my hand. Kissed me when he pleased without shame or hesitation.

For the last few hours, it's been nothing short of the perfect day.

And it felt like…a date, or something.

Which begs the question, *can you* date *your fuck buddy*?

I'm pulled from my thoughts as I'm slipping back into the lounge area of the lodge from a quick bathroom break. This place never gets old, with the vaulted two-story ceiling, all the exposed wood beams giving off that mountain lodge feel people pay insane amounts of money to experience. Especially with the massive wall of windows to the left facing the mountains with a wooden deck attached; the place screams *Colorado* in all the best ways.

Glancing around the spacious room, I look for Rain. He's not by the stacked stone fireplace getting warm, nor sitting on one of the brown leather sectionals filling the space. Checking the upper balcony, I don't see him at one of the tables in the dining area either.

But when I glance over to the wall I just walked through from the bathroom, I find him. His back is to me, attention trained on the TV mounted on the wall broadcasting the news.

I take a second to watch him without his knowledge, observe him in his natural state.

But something seems…off.

His hand is clutching his jacket he removed when we got inside so tight, his knuckles are whiter than the snow outside. The veins on the back of his hand are popping out of his skin from the strain. And his shoulders…they're rigid. Tense beneath the cotton of his long sleeve shirt.

Moving my gaze from Rain to the television, I read the subtitles on the screen to see they're talking about that senator, the one who apparently was raping a kid.

Sick, depraved people these days, using their power to abuse people. *Children*, for God's sake.

No wonder Rain is agitated. I am too, seeing this kind of thing on the news, probably about to be swept under the rug like it never happened. Because that's what money and power can buy you in this country.

It's sickening.

And taking into account how he feels about what happened in the shower… Fuck.

Moving up behind him as quietly as I can manage, I lean forward and bite down on the base of his neck, right above the collar of his shirt. He startles slightly, but he must know it's me because the hand not holding his jacket reaches out behind him and grips my shirt.

"You look like you could use a massage," I murmur in his ear, slipping my hands up to knead his shoulders. They instantly relax under my touch and I smile against the skin of his neck. "That's better, yeah, baby?"

He groans when I continue working out the knots from his shoulders, wondering when was the last time he had someone do something like this for him. Touch him, give him affection just for the sake of making him feel appreciated and loved.

God, there's that damn word again, running rampant through my thoughts.

Nuzzling my nose behind his ear, I do my best to relax his mind as well as his body. "I see what you're doing. The way your head is spinning," I whisper, continuing to massage his shoulders, needing to take his mind away from the places it's clearly going. "But we went over this last night. You didn't rape me, I never said no. There's no need to compare yourself to that man."

Rain sighs, leaning his head back against my shoulder, his back pressed against my front. "I know, Riv. I know," he tells me, letting his head loll to look at me before brushing his lips lightly over mine. "And as good as this feels, I need you to stop before I have to go searching for a private place to bend you over and give you *your favorite* kind of massage."

My ass clenches and cock twitches at his words, knowing full well what he means. "You know I would be perfectly fine finding a broom closet to have a little rendezvous in."

"Let's put a pin in that plan, yeah, babe?" He smiles and his soft laugh against my lips just does something to me.

Good things. Wonderful things.

Fucking dangerous things.

He turns around in front of me, my hands sliding off his shoulders and back down to my sides. "I'm going to grab something to drink," he says softly. "You want anything?"

I bite my lip to think of drink options, which is really fucking hard when all I really want is to revisit the broom closet idea. "Maybe hot chocolate? Hot cider? Something warm?"

"How about some eggnog? That'll warm you up real quick." He grins deviously.

Shaking my head, I chuckle. "Don't you dare, one of us has to be sober enough to drive back up the damn mountain."

But the shithead he is, he just starts backing up toward the stairs to get our drinks, calling out for me to find us a place to sit.

Okay, I'd much rather go find a damn broom closet though.

Damn him for putting those kinds of ideas in my head.

"Lennox! That you?" a deep voice shouts from behind me, causing me to start. It's one I recognize well, but it doesn't belong to Rain.

Spinning around quickly, I spot my best friend in the world sitting on a couch in the lounge area, a petite girl about our age with brownish red hair at his side.

Which normally wouldn't be a shock, but I haven't seen him since August when he left to go back to Michigan. "*Taylor Scott? Do my eyes deceive me?*"

He leans forward, pulling his arm from around the girl's shoulders and motions for me to join him. "Don't be a dick and get the fuck over here." He laughs, standing from his place on the sofa before offering his hand to his… friend? Although from the way his eyes are glued to her as he helps her up or the way his fingers linger on her skin…I'd wager they are much *more* than just *companions.*

He hasn't mentioned anything to me about a girl, other than the two he lets run his life back in Michigan like two tiny dictators, as he calls them. Part of me wonders if this is one of them.

His eyes, a similar shade to mine, dance with a hint of mischief as he pulls me in for a quick hug. "Hey, man, how are you? Dad said you were out this way at the cabin."

My brows enter my hairline. "He told you I was out here?"

He nods, bobbing his head of light brown hair. "Yeah. When I asked to use the cabin for break, he mentioned he sentenced you and a teammate to exile for fighting?" Taylor shakes his head, laughing. "What the hell, man? You've never been one to have a hot head."

He's not wrong. But…he's also never met Ciaráin Grady.

"Shit changes when you aren't here to keep me in line, T." I grin, referring to him by his nickname from our childhood. "What brings you out? Skiing? Where are you staying?"

"Oh, we rented an AirBNB near the edge of town." He gives a half-smile, white teeth peeking out. "Not as good of a view as the cabin, but it works."

"And um, who is *we?*" I ask, glancing down at the girl beside him. Her hair, while a beautiful dark auburn color, is nothing in comparison to her ridiculously vivid green eyes. So damn green, I swear I could count individual blades of grass in them.

Taylor smiles that smile he always got when he would talk about baseball or gaming or whatever else held the source of his passion. And he looks down at her before wrapping his arm around her shoulder and squeezing it, fire lighting up his eyes.

And it's in that moment I know my best friend is in love with whoever this woman is standing next to him.

"River, this is—"

"Siena?" Rain's voice asks from behind me. I glance over my shoulder to see him standing with two mugs of something steamy, probably spiked knowing him, and a look of complete confusion on his face.

"*Rain?*" the girl, apparently Siena, shrieks as she slips from Taylor's grasp to head over to my man.

Wait... Fuck. Not my man.

Although I'm not above pissing on him. Staking my claim. Letting whoever the fuck this girl is know he's *mine*.

Rain sets the two mugs on a side table quickly before Siena basically jumps into his arms, wrapping her entire body around him like a damn spider monkey.

Now, I wouldn't necessarily care about that. While I'm possessive of the things I deem as mine, I don't get jealous.

And believe me, there's a fucking difference.

Jealousy is wanting what someone else has. She doesn't have Rain. Okay, maybe she has him in her literal hold but not in the way that counts. But possessiveness comes with making sure everyone around you doesn't let their jealousy try to take what's yours.

Marking your territory, so to speak. Letting the world know not to fuck with it.

But he isn't yours, my asshole brain likes to remind me.

I watch them as he spins her around in a circle, her legs locked around his waist, a giant smile on his face while he hugs her to him with an insane amount of comfort and familiarity.

And I see fuckin' red.

"Is that Ciaráin Grady, the wide receiver who almost won the Heisman twice?" Taylor asks, his brows furrowed as he watches Rain set Siena on the ground, her hands moving animatedly as she talks a mile a minute. Rain's still got that damn smile on his face, and fuck me, that smile is *mine.*

And then...she says something that makes him laugh, and I just about lose my shit entirely.

"That'd be him," I grind, keeping my temper in check. "He was my new wide receiver this season. Damn good player, so he deserves the Heisman hype."

Taylor turns to me, removing his stare from Siena for the first time for more than five seconds since he called my name. "Is he the one Dad sent you up here with?"

Meeting his questioning gaze, I nod in response before returning my attention back to the two of them across the room. I feel Taylor's eyes on me while I watch them, my jaw ticked so hard it starts to ache.

"I really hope you're not staring at them because of my girl." Taylor laughs, but it lacks humor.

His girl.

Okay, well, that makes it better I guess. Taylor has a great sense about people, so I can't see him getting in with someone who would be willing to drop him for a more semi-famous college athlete.

"No, I'm too busy trying not to become a jealous fucking prick because *your girl* has somehow managed to get a smile and a goddamn laugh, both of which I have to work really fucking hard to get, from *my man*."

Taylor grabs my chin and turns my face toward his again. "Grady is into dudes? And wait, I thought Dad sent you up here because you and him were fighting? Brawling on the field during a game and shit?"

I sigh. "We fought, yeah. It was pretty bad. That's why we're here."

He raises a brow as his eyes search mine, trying to get a better read on the situation. That's what Taylor does, I learned early on. He has this uncanny ability to read between the lines of what you're actually saying. Like right now, I know he dissects every single vibe I'm giving off and sifting through to come to a conclusion "But now you're, what? Dating?"

Biting my lip briefly, I let out a sharp exhale. "No, we're not dating."

"Then what, just fucking? Because Riv, the way he's looking at me right now..." He laughs, shaking his head before releasing his grip from my chin. "Hell, he looks ready to commit murder for my hands being on you."

I allow my gaze to travel over to Rain and Siena to find them engrossed in conversation, but even as Rain's mouth is moving and smiling at Siena, his eyes are latched on me and Taylor.

And indeed, there is a fire in his eyes most people who aren't as receptive as Taylor wouldn't catch. I'm not even sure Siena can see it and she is standing right in front of him.

His attention darts between the two of us, and I catch the subtle lift of his brow before his eyes harden on Taylor and then back to me.

The question in his eyes is clear.

Have you fucked him?

And shit, it might be toxic as hell to feel as happy as I do by that. Because…I fucking get it. I felt it when I just watched him with Siena. Or when I saw the hickey on his neck that night in Portland.

Seems jealousy and possessiveness aren't one-sided with us like I thought it might be, regardless of how unhealthy it is.

My eyes stay locked on Rain while I respond to Taylor. "It's the best sex of my life, T. Mind altering. And all it's supposed to be is sex." I flash my eyes to Taylor. "But something changed in such a short amount of time and now it's become…complicated."

Understatement of my fucking life.

Taylor nods. "Sex always has a way of fucking shit up. I get it, man. I do."

I let out a sigh, thankful as hell that my best friend never ceases to put me at ease, even if it's just by confirming something I already know to be true.

"Taylor!" Siena shouts, a huge smile on her face as she waves us over to where she and Rain are standing.

When Taylor immediately starts walking over, I cough,

"whipped" under my breath, which earns me a shit-eating grin and two middle fingers from my best friend. Following him to where they stand, I smile at Siena.

"Siena, right? I think our introduction was cut a little short. I'm River," I tell her, sticking out my hand. My eyes flash up to Rain's when she slides her palm into mine for a brief shake.

"So nice to meet you, River. Taylor's mentioned you plenty." She smiles prettily up at me, and I can immediately see why T is so taken with her. She looks over at Rain then, quirking a brow. "How do you guys know each other?"

Rain shrugs. "Football. Riv is my new QB."

And for some reason, his simple explanation sends ice through my veins. *Yeah, Rain. Not like we're fucking multiple times a day or anything. Let's go with football.*

She nods, accepting his non-answer just as Taylor raises a brow in disbelief at me. Rain, however, catches Taylor's movement and glares.

"River and I are also kind of..." Rain trails off, biting the inside of his cheek in search of the correct word. "...together?"

"Remove the question mark off the end of that sentence, and yeah, that's accurate," I say, smiling at Rain, making him roll his eyes.

What, baby, you think you're the only one who wants to stake a claim? Try again.

Siena's eyes widen but her smile grows immensely. "Oh my gosh, that's great to hear! In that case, I'm even happier to meet you, River." She flashes a glance to T. "Rain and I were talking about the four of us maybe grabbing dinner later? What do you think?"

T looks at me, and I shrug. "Fine by me," he answers, giving

Rain a once over before continuing. "Gotta take a minute to get to know the guy who's caught my boy's interest. Meet you guys here at, say, six?"

Agreeing to the plans, Taylor and Siena give us a quick goodbye and head off and out the doors back to the cool winter day.

Before I even have the chance to look at Rain, he's gripping my shoulder to spin me around. "Who is he to you?"

My brows furrow. "That's Taylor. As in Coach's *son*. My best friend?"

Rain's forehead creases. "Did you fuck him? Or vice versa?"

That makes me laugh. "What? No, of course not. I never even looked at T that way. Or Drew or E." I smirk. "Why? Did you fuck her?"

And the way Rain's face visibly pales, I know his answer. My stomach drops along with the smile on my face. "Of course, you did." I scoff. "I shouldn't even have to ask."

He shakes his head, grabbing my face with one hand. "It's not what you think, Riv. She was actually my first, yeah, but it was never anything like..."

"Like *what*?"

"*This!*" he says, gesturing to me with his free hand.

I roll my eyes, as if that comment is supposed to make me feel better. "Well, considering she doesn't have a cock for you to suck on, I'd assume it would be very different indeed."

Yeah, I know I'm being petty right now. But holy goddamn, I wasn't expecting this bomb to be dropped on me today. Not when we were in this...bubble of happiness.

"You know what I mean," he growls. "Don't act like you

don't have exes you've fucked before me."

"I do, but at least I don't sit you down at dinner with them when they're currently dating *your best friend*."

"She wasn't just some *fuck*, River. She and her brother were my two best friends in high school. I was trying to get my shit together and find out what I liked, and she offered." He sighs, rubbing his temple with his free thumb. "It was only the one time. She isn't anything more than a friend."

I exhale sharply and give him a brief nod.

God, I hate my insecurity right now. The feeling is usually so few and far between, but right now, with him, it's like it's been magnified for some reason. Like the fact that we had such a volatile start to this thing between us had a way of enhancing all the shit I suppress.

"I believe you. I'm sorry, I just…"

"Got jealous." He smiles, his thumb brushing my cheek. "It's okay, babe. I don't mind it. I'm not gonna lie, it feels good. But you don't have a reason to be."

"I don't?" I furrow my brows at him.

He laughs, still the greatest sound to ever grace my ears as he drags me down onto the couch, handing me my mug of now lukewarm cocoa. "Nah, you're plenty for me to deal with. No way in hell I could handle adding in a side piece."

Despite my initial fears and protests, dinner wasn't nearly as uncomfortable or dreadful as I thought it would be. It helped that Taylor, the chill guy he is, already knew all about Rain and Siena.

Their childhood, their friendship, the sex — all of it.

But, much to my delight, Siena is actually really fucking cool too.

Down to Earth, sarcastic, and funny as fuck. Honestly, I completely understand what drew Taylor to her.

After dinner, we decided to stay for a couple drinks. Well, *I* decided to drink. Rain is staying sober, at least enough so we can drive back up the mountain on the four-wheeler safely.

I'm standing at the bar waiting for my new drink, watching Rain and Siena talk out the corner of my eye at the high top table we moved to after dinner when Taylor comes up beside me. He catches where my gaze is directed and lets out a low hum from the back of his throat, a mannerism he has always done when he wants to say something but is attempting to bite his tongue.

I've heard it hundreds of times, but he's never done it directed at *me*.

"Say what you want to say, T. We don't have secrets." I sigh, fingers tapping absently on the bar.

"You have feelings for him?"

I scoff and laugh.

Yep, there he is. Taylor has never been one to beat around the bush, and honestly, I'm thankful for that, even in this circumstance.

Turning away from Rain entirely to face Taylor, I roll my teeth over my lip. "I don't think it matters if I do or don't. It's over the minute we're back to Boulder."

Taylor shakes his head and smirks. "We're two of a fucking kind. Always wanting more than what someone is willing to give."

I lift my shoulder absently, hating that he's right. We've always been cut from the same cloth. Far more attuned with our emotions than the rest of our friends. It's probably why we've always had this unbreakable bond where we can tell each other whatever is on our minds.

"We're too young to be wanting that kind of shit, anyway."

T glares at me. "Riv, don't be dense. You and I both know that when you know, you just fucking know. It doesn't matter if you're sixteen, twenty-one, or thirty-something. When the person you're meant to be with is tossed in your path, you grab them and hold on for dear life. In whatever capacity they'll have you."

Perceptive as ever, this asshole.

Because yeah, at this point I'll take Rain however I can have him.

"This is different, T. It's not as simple for us."

He shrugs. "It never is. I'm not saying it's simple for me and Siena. She didn't even want to start sleeping together. Made a goddamn list of rules for us to follow if we were going to. And I've already broken every fucking one of them. It could wind up screwing me over, leaving me absolutely heartbroken in the end. But having her is better than not, for no matter how long."

"Are you trying to tell me you think she's the one?"

Licking his lips, he lets out a soft chuckle. "I've loved her from the moment I met her freshman year, Riv. I'd propose right now if I thought I had any chance of getting her to say yes. I want it all with her. Marriage, kids. Growing old and senile as fuck together."

"But we always want more from them than they are willing to give," I murmur, repeating his sentiment.

Taylor nods again, and the bartender chooses this moment to place my drink on the bar. I grab my gin and tonic, taking a swift drink before setting it back on the bar.

"Look, Riv. You're my best friend in the entire world. I only want what's best for you, for you to find the person you can't stand the thought of walking out of your life for good."

"I know, man." I laugh, not sure where he's trying to go with this. "Of course, I want the same for you."

He grins. "I know, dipshit. This isn't about me, though. It's about you and that guy you can't take your damn eyes off of for more than a few seconds. Shit, I even saw a flare of jealousy earlier and I'm going to be honest, I never pictured you as the type to feel that emotion. You're too carefree for it."

"Yeah, T? It seems that I'm full of surprises."

He rubs the back of his neck and smirks. "It tends to happen when you fall in love, bud."

There's that word again. *Love.*

But hearing it come out of Taylor's mouth, who knows me better than probably anyone on this entire planet? It makes me itchy.

"I'm not in love with him. I like him, sure. But damn, man. Just a few weeks ago we were ready to kill each other. We hated each other."

Taylor smirks, and for the first time, I want to deck my best friend in the damn face for thinking he knows something I don't. That he knows more about Rain and me than *I do* from observing us for, what? A couple hours?

"It has nothing to do with you two specifically. I've seen something just like this with a couple of my friends back in Michigan," he tells me. "Passion is passion. All-consuming, raw, and even toxic at times. It's all in how you decide to harness it that establishes the line between love and hate." He pauses, tapping his fingers twice against the bar before grabbing my own hand to force it into silence.

He's always tried his best to let me cope that way, but I know it annoys the ever loving shit out of him.

"Sorry," I tell him, putting my hands in my pants pockets.

"Don't let it make you anxious. Stop fighting it. There's no use being afraid of it."

I scoff. "I'm not afraid of love or passion."

T bites his lip and nods, but it's one of those that he gives me when he's thinking *you're so full of shit and we both know it.*

"I'm *not.*"

"Sure you are, Riv. I don't blame you for it either. Did you forget I watched you go through your parents divorce once you came out? What you thought was a marriage built to withstand the most brutal storms was blown to smithereens the second a tiny little gust of wind hit.

"And worst of all, your dad decided you weren't worth being his son anymore, as if being bisexual was a *lifestyle choice* when we should know by now it's who you are in your damn DNA. So the day your dad walked out on you? He proved his love was conditional."

I clear my throat, attempting to work the knot that lodges itself there out. "And what does this have to do with me and Rain?"

He rolls his eyes and shakes his head. "You're afraid of love, knowing what it feels like to have what you *thought* was unconditional love ripped away. Turning your life upside down in the process. River, you're afraid of loving someone, only for them to not love you enough to stay."

Shit. If he didn't just read me like a damn book.

"When did you become such a fucking expert?"

He laughs at that. "You forget, my friend. You and I are two sides of the same coin, just etched a little differently."

I nod, knowing the truth behind his statement. Though we didn't grow up exactly the same, Taylor always had it a little rougher than I did. Even with a superstar NFL player for a father.

Or maybe *because* of that.

"Look, man. The point I'm trying to make is to not be afraid. If you are, you'll never be able to end up on the same side of the line as Rain. The *right* side this time."

"I don't know if that's possible with us," I shake my head. "It's been *a week* since we stopped clawing each other's eyes out. This can't be anything more than sex."

"Love, passion, desire. None of it has a timeline, man. Again, you know this."

I sigh, hating the logic in his argument. "There's so much more in play here. So much he's keeping close to the chest. I don't...I don't even know if *he* knows where he falls, you know? He's definitely not *out*."

"In this case, I don't think it matters, Riv."

My brows furrow. "What makes you say that?"

He grins and looks up and over to where Siena and Rain sit. I follow his gaze, finding the two of them are watching us intently.

And the grin on Rain's face...*fuck.*

"Because he looks at you the exact same way you look at him," he says simply, keeping his eyes on them. "With the same kind of passion."

TWENTY-FOUR
Rain

DAY NINETEEN

"**G**et on your knees, boy," he hisses, pushing roughly on my shoulder.

Like the good boy I am, I fall to the floor.

My knees hit the rug with a crack. Still, I wince in pain, because I know.

I know what's coming next.

What always comes next.

I watch him unbuckle his pants. The same pants he wore to dinner with my mom and me. Pulling his dick out, I see it's half-hard already. He always gets hard when I'm on my knees in front of him. At his mercy.

That's what gets him off the most, I've noticed.

The way I listen, always listen and do whatever he says.

I do whatever he tells me, because I'm his good boy.

He steps closer to me. His pants slip down further past his butt to reveal his entire length to me. He brings it to my lips.

"You know what to do," he growls.

There's no use in fighting it. Fighting him. I'm so much smaller than he is. I know it would be pointless.

It's never worked in the past, so why would it now?

If I let it happen, it will be over sooner. And that's all I want every time. For it to be over as soon as possible.

So I open my mouth immediately and allow him to slide inside with ease over my tongue. The taste is familiar, one I've come to know well.

He starts thrusting instantly. Working his dick deeper into my throat.

I try not to gag, but I can't help it. I'm not any good at this, even though I've done it more times than I can count.

Because I'm not supposed to be good at this.

Because...I'm a boy and boys don't do this to other boys. Or to grown men.

Heck, I'm only twelve years old. Today, in fact. I should be playing video games with Roman after dinner or doing my math homework Mr. Chutney assigned in class.

I should be celebrating my birthday.

I shouldn't have a dick in my mouth.

Especially one belonging to my mother's husband.

It's wrong, so, so wrong. But I can't do anything to stop it.

Suddenly, he pulls from between my lips. I suck in a breath and cough as he yanks me to my feet. He is quickly shedding the rest of his clothes before unbuttoning my own pants. He's on his knees before me, yanking my pants and underwear down and off me. Before I can blink, his lips wrap around my own dick.

It's hard already and he's barely touched me. Which means I must like what he's doing to me.

What I do to him.

That's what he tells me, at least. That's what my health teacher confirmed for us this past semester.

If it's hard, that means I like it.

But I don't like this...

He stands after he's made sure I'm harder than a rock. But he licks the tip of my dick one last time before moving over to the bedside table. I hear him rummage around in the drawer. Looking for what, I don't know.

When he turns around, I spot the two items in his hand.

A bottle, small and white. What it contains, I can't tell from here.

And handcuffs.

My stomach rolls at the sight of the restraints. He hasn't ever used those before and...I'm scared. Terrified, actually.

I don't fight him. Ever. I'm good, I always listen, so why does he want to handcuff me?

Or does he want me to use them on him?

My question is quickly answered when he snaps one around my wrist before tossing the bottle on the foot of the bed.

"What are you doing?" I ask, but he doesn't respond. Instead, he pulls my shirt from over my head before turning me to face the bed.

"Put your hands on the footboard," *he tells me, and like his lap dog, my fingers curl around the wrought iron of the footboard.*

Listening to his command.

I always listen, because that's what good boys do.

And he said, as long as I'm a good boy, he won't hurt me.

That's why I never fight. I never kick or scream or make any noise at all.

If I do, he might hurt me and I don't want that.

He slips the second half of the handcuff around the metal before latching that side around my other wrist.

Locking me in place.

Sweat breaks out across my forehead. Panic bubbles up within me. It's so much, too much, so I can't help but break the rules and talk. Ask questions. "Please, just tell me what is happening. Why do you need these? I'm always a good boy, I do what you say."

He picks up the little white bottle, one reading lube *on it. My heart rate kicks up.*

My senses are on high alert and my body trembles in fear, in panic. Instinct tells me to fight and run. But how can I, now that my arms have been restrained by the cuffs?

Still, I try. My arms attempting to tug my wrists free from their confines. The metal of the cuffs bite into my skin, causing me to wince. But I still do my best to squeeze my wrist through the hole.

It's no use, though. I'm stuck.

Helpless.

I hear the cap of the bottle being flicked open. The squirting sound of the gel being squeezed out and smeared around on his fingers.

His hand grips my waist, tugging me backward. It forces my arms into an extended position. I feel the wet and cold sensation of the lube be rubbed against my buttcrack, his finger teasing my butthole.

He's done this before, when he's had my dick in his mouth.

It's okay, Ciaráin. You're okay. *I chant those words to myself. Like if I say them enough I might actually start to believe them.*

His first finger enters my hole, the second quickly following. I groan softly, biting my lip from crying out.

It hurts, it always does at first. But it also feels good, especially when he hits the spot inside me that makes my toes tingle.

I don't know which is worse.

A moan slips past my lips as his fingertips touch that place over and over. He strokes and kneads me there until I'm pressing back against him, desperate for more pressure.

My dick, it aches between my legs. Like every time, I'm mortified by how good his fingers feel inside me. When it's so very wrong.

Why do I like this?

I shouldn't even know what this feels like, let alone have some sick addiction to it.

But as quickly as his fingers entered me, they're gone. I let out a whimper at the absence. My entire body is lit on fire by the way he's turned me on.

The sound of more lube being squeezed out sets my body back on edge. Every muscle in me tenses.

And then I feel it, the head of his dick, so much larger than his fingers, against my hole.

I tense more, my butt squeezing together on reflex because…I don't want it back there. It won't fit, there's no way. Not without splitting me in half.

"You are a good boy, Ciaráin. Always such a good boy. And you know I won't ever hurt you." His words wash over me in a soothing tone, and for a minute, I relax again.

He won't hurt me, not really. He's only ever made me feel so, so good.

But then he presses his hips forward, just slightly. It's enough to start to enter me, and I let out a soft cry, no matter how hard I try to keep it in.

"No, no. Ciaráin. You have to keep quiet. That's what good boys do," he tells me, "I need you to bite the comforter if you think you're going to be loud. It's very important."

"Why?" I ask, breaking the rules again. But I do as he says, anyway. I bend myself over the railing that my hands are cuffed to, taking the silk fabric between my teeth like he said.

Because I'm a good boy, he won't hurt me.

I feel his hand on my back, gently touching my spine as he shifts my legs further apart. "That's it, Ciaráin. You're such a good boy. So good, in fact, I'm about to give you a special birthday gift."

And with that, he slams his hips forward. Entering me in one, brutal thrust.

I scream out in pain, but the sound is muffled by the fabric in my mouth. It feels like I'm being ripped in half from the inside out. And the pain. It only gets worse and worse as he starts moving inside me.

"No," I howl, keeping my face pressed into the mattress, but I know I'm loud enough for him to hear me. "No, no!"

Tears stream down my face, staining the comforter below me as I cry and cry and cry some more. My body is quaking in agony, trembling as I do my best to keep myself standing like the good boy he wants.

It doesn't matter though, I don't care that I'm not listening. That I'm not being a good boy anymore because I'm shouting at the top of my lungs for him to stop, to please, please stop.

I tell him he's hurting me, but he doesn't listen.

He just continues to hurt me, all for his sick, sick pleasure.

"Please stop! I don't like this. It hurts too much!" I wail into the silk. Its smoothness is the only thing giving me any sort of comfort. "You told me I was a good boy, that you wouldn't hurt me!"

But his assault only continues, his pants and groans mixing with my cries and the noise of skin slapping together.

"Stop fighting it and it won't hurt, my good boy," is all he tells me.

Then a few minutes later, something happens. The pain stops. The physical pain. It's replaced with something that feels...good.

Good like it does when he fingers are in there. Good like...like I like it.

But that's wrong. It's so wrong and I need him to stop.

"I'll do anything," I sob, snot and tears coating every inch of my face. *"Please, just stop this."*

But nothing works. He doesn't stop.

And once I realize my efforts are futile, I cry silent tears. I choke on the bile that keeps rising in my throat. It threatens to spray all over the bed if I open my mouth again.

I fight the pain coursing through my head as his body makes me feel so good, like he promised. It's confusing, how I can like something I don't want. It makes me sick. So sick I want to puke all over his fancy bed.

I want to be anywhere but here.

And I can't help but wonder what I ever did to deserve this.

When all I ever did was obey his every demand like a good boy should.

But suddenly, something shifts, my reality morphing into a new scene entirely.

I don't feel his thrusts, the pain is gone, and I'm not a twelve-year-old cuffed to the bed anymore.

No, I'm an adult.

I'm me, the twenty-one-year-old college student. I look down to see my arms, covered in tattoos.

And a sense of relief washes over me.

That is, until I focus to see...

Now I'm the one...doing the things he did to me.

"Please, please stop," the voice pleads as I drive my hips forward, *fucking him hard and fast. The request is soft coming from his lips, like*

music to my ears as I ignore him. He says it again, and the tone of voice is familiar somehow.

But I can't place my finger on why.

"Ciaráin, no. Please," he says again as I swivel my hips and hit him deeper than I was before. His ass is so tight, it feels phenomenal clenching around my cock.

I could cum at any second if he would just stop his bitching.

My fingers slide into his hair, gripping the brown strands tightly in my fist before pressing his face down in the mattress to shut him the fuck up.

He screams into the mattress as I fuck him, taking what I damn well please from him, from his body. My free hand glides across the smooth muscles of his shoulders and back in a soft caress. I love the way it feels against my skin.

It's electric.

My fingers slide down to his side and over his ribs, and it's there I notice a tattoo.

Two lines in a script font.

A quote I know to be from John Muir.

Into the forest I go, to lose my mind and find my soul.

It's a quote I've seen before, also as a tattoo, in fact.

In this exact same place...

He cries into the mattress again, but it's muffled, so I can't make out his words. Pulling his head back, I lean over him and whisper tauntingly in his ear, "What was that? I couldn't hear you."

"Rain!" *he cries out, a plea ripping from his throat in a guttural sob.* "Rain, stop. Please stop. You're hurting me! I don't want this!"

My nickname off his lips startles me, causing a hitch in my movement, just for a second, before I continue with my onslaught on his body.

But a word, one single word, snags in my brain.

Rain.

He called me Rain.

There are only two people in the world who call me by that name.

Both of them have brown hair. A deep, smoky voice that slides over my skin like perfectly aged whiskey.

But only one of them has that tattoo.

"Rain." *His voice comes out choked, thick with emotion. Barely more than a whisper this time. "Please."*

Horror washes over me, recognition of his voice finally settling in.

I loosen my grip on his hair and cup the side of his face, slowly turning it to confirm my worst suspicion.

And the second those eyes, the color of an alpine lake, meet mine, my whole world shatters.

River.

My eyes snap open as my body jackknifes in the bed. Cold sweat chills me to the bone and my throat aches, in need of water to ease my vocal chords.

Fuck.

Years, fucking *years* of living with these nightmares and it never gets any easier. I can never seem to fight them off. But they don't usually wake me from a dead sleep like this.

For some reason, it felt more real tonight. Like I was actually living it.

Again.

But…River being there, that was unexpected. And far more torturous than reliving the horrible things that happened to me.

I allow my erratic heart to calm, taking deep, soothing breaths as I stare at the ceiling, letting the darkness of night bring me to peace. Usually it only takes me twenty minutes or so to get to the point where I can go back to bed until morning, but there is no way in hell I'll be able to lull myself back into sleep tonight.

With a grunt, I roll off the bed and pad quietly to my door. I might as well take a shower, cool off, and maybe watch a movie before River wakes up at the crack of dawn like usual.

I don't know how the guy can be awake and chipper so early in the day. I'm still grouchy as hell when I wake up after ten.

I'd say he has some sort of sunshine or rainbows shoved up his ass, but I know for a fact—

My thoughts come screeching to a halt when I turn the lock, drag open the door to my room, and trip over something lying directly next to the door.

What the hell?

"Shit," I curse, catching my weight against the wall right as River scrambles up into a sitting position, startled and clearly groggy as hell if the way his head is snapping in a million directions is any indication.

Wait...*River?*

"Rain? What's wrong? Are you okay?" he asks in quick succession, alarm and gravel present in his voice, as he scrubs a hand over his face.

"Why are you on the floor?" I demand rather than answer his question.

He's most definitely still half-asleep, since he sways getting to his feet, picking up his blanket and pillow and starts dragging it to his room like a little kid.

"To be close by. If you need me. 'Cause of the nightmares."

My. Heart. Fucking. Stops.

Has he...?

No.

He's halfway through his doorway when I grab his wrist to stop him. The knot lodged in my throat is massive as I attempt to swallow, to breathe, to fucking do *something* other than stare into his sleepy eyes.

"That isn't the first night you've slept there, is it?" The words are barely audible. Hell, I wouldn't even know if I actually spoke them aloud or just thought them in my head if it weren't for the flash of guilt I see across his face.

The look in his eyes, the apprehension, tells me he's planning to lie to me.

Again.

Using my grip on his wrist, I pull him into my chest, blanket, pillow, and all, and cup his face. "Don't fucking lie to me, Abhainn. We're past the bullshit. How long have you been sleeping outside my room?"

The way he searches my eyes in the dim glow of moonlight, with clarity and focus, lets me know he's fully awake now. And by the looks of it, in full anxiety mode. I can even feel his hands twitching to whatever song is running through that beautiful brain of his.

"Every night," he whispers, biting his bottom lip. My thumb brushes against it, tugging it free from his teeth. I'm about to speak again when he quickly adds, "Only for a couple hours. During the bad parts."

I swear to God, if holding onto his face wasn't anchoring me in place, I might float away. Or disintegrate into finely ground dust, right here on the spot.

I've never been this mortified in my life, yet so eternally...moved.

Every. Fucking. Night.

He's been sleeping on the ground, outside my room *every night*.

"I'm sorry," he mumbles, his voice cracking. "It's just that, after the first night...I didn't want... fuck, Rain. I won't do it again."

The vulnerability written on his features is shredding me from the inside out and I can't stand the way he's looking at me right now, like at any moment, I'm going to flip the switch back to the asshole I was to him not even two weeks ago, and then I realize...

He thinks I'm *angry* with him when all I want to do is...hold him.

Fucking forever.

And I make the decision to do just that, for as long as I can.

"You're right, you're never going to do it again," I tell him softly, smoothing the worry lines marring his face. Grabbing the blanket and pillow from him, I carry them to the bed, which he clearly slept in for a few hours before ending up in the hall. "You're not going to spend another night on the damn ground attempting to get to me, to comfort me. Because I know that's what you were trying to do." Sliding in between the sheets, I keep my eyes on his.

"I know. I'm—"

"Stop apologizing and get in the bed," I growl, my temper rising. Lifting the sheet, I indicate to the vacant spot beside me.

"But—"

"I swear to God, River, I need you to listen right now." My tone is sharp, but I hear the plea in my voice, hoping he does too. "If I need to spend every single night in this bed with you to make sure you don't end up on the floor, I fucking will. The thought of you — *goddamn*, it *guts* me," I say, my voice breaking. "If the nightmares come — and make no mistake, they will — I'll be right next to you. Not keeping you at arm's length, letting you freeze on the floor."

River crosses the room to the bed before slipping in beside me, laying on his side to face me. "You don't have to — "

"I know that. Just like *you* didn't have to. But you *did*, even after *everything*." A sigh escapes me, and I wrap my arm around his waist, pulling him so our bodies are flush. "That shit? The fighting and the bickering and the fucking games? It's all over. If there's one thing you can believe, it's that." I rub my nose against his once, twice, before resting my forehead against his and close my eyes.

My stomach is in knots and my heart still aches for how many times he's shown me that, for some ungodly reason, he cares about me. No matter the messed up shit I've done or said. When I don't let him in, when I push him away, he still fights for a way to gain even a glimpse past the mask.

It's about time I let him have it.

"Every night, for the rest of the time we're here, this is how it's going to be. Maybe because it makes sense or because I feel guilty, I don't know. Whatever it is, the most important reason is I'm a selfish bastard, and when I want something, I take it." My throat works at the knot residing in it before I let out a shaky exhale. "And what I *want*? More than anything? Is to finally have something to hold onto to make it through the night."

River stays silent, rolling to his back and I take the opportunity to tangle our legs together and burrow into the warmth of his skin, his presence.

Him.

It's easy to be together like this in the dark. As if we're in another world, another time. Where this thing happening between us is real. Tangible. Even if we both know, when dawn breaks, it will end. We both would rather relish in the dream, even if it can only take place in the dead of night.

After what seems like years, he finally asks the question I'm sure has been burning on his tongue.

"Are you going to tell me what they're about?"

No.

"Not tonight, Riv. Tonight, just distract me. Tell me about the songs. They've been changing more frequently since we've been here." I nuzzle into River's neck before wrapping my arm around his stomach.

"You've noticed that?"

I've noticed so much more than that, Abhainn.

"Yeah. I guess being stuck here doing nothing would make you want to change it up a little more often."

"You're not wrong." River chuckles softly, his minty breath wafting over my head. "Ever since…that morning in the shower, it's been changing more frequently."

I swear my heart stops at his mention of the shower.

"What did it change to then?"

A real, honest-to-God laugh leaves his throat this time. "You really want to know?"

My jaw ticks, and I nod, my face rubbing against the smooth

skin of his pecs.

"'The Enemy' by I Prevail."

I can't help but laugh at that, no matter the guilt eating at me for what I did to him in that shower. Because I know the song and *of course* it makes all the sense for him to pick it.

"And outside by the shed?"

"'Tapping Out' by Issues."

"The night when we agreed to…this?"

I feel the grin on his mouth against my hair before he presses a kiss to my temple. "You Me At Six's 'Loverboy.'" He laughs. "I thought I was funny as fuck and so damn clever."

My skin heats at the sound of his laughter, true and genuine. It's the most deliciously addictive sound I think I've ever heard. It might be better than the way he says my name when he's taking my cock deep in his ass.

"What about the day on the ski lift?"

This time, he hesitates. "Why? Why do you care?"

Acknowledging in order to get this piece of him I need to give up something in return, I give him the unabashed truth. "Because they're a window into your mind. To know what you're thinking but not saying. And as much as I don't *want* to, I *need* to know. Your thoughts. Your feelings. Not of just the world, but of *me*. Of this side of who I am."

He lets out a sigh and wraps his arm around me tighter. "If you want to know those things, all you have to do is ask," he argues, still avoiding.

Tou-fucking-ché.

Not wanting to push any further and risk pissing either of us off, I let it slide, choosing to focus on his fingers playing with my hair and the steady rise and fall of his chest. The warmth of his body and the beat of his heart have almost completely lulled me back into sleep when he speaks.

"It was the same one that's in my head right now," he whispers. "It's called 'Right Here' by Ashes Remain."

I don't know it, and even if I did, the haze of unconsciousness is too heavy to attempt an analysis. But still, the corner of my mouth lifts.

That wasn't so hard now, was it?

Kissing his chest, I murmur, "Thank you, Abhainn."

"Is that Gaelic?"

I nod.

"What does it mean? You called me it earlier too." He lets out a soft chuckle. "It probably means asshole or something, right?"

Shaking my head, I release a long breath, allowing sleep to continue dragging me under. "It's your name, Riv. Just your name."

Then a dreamless, blissful slumber takes me once again.

TWENTY-FIVE
River

DAY TWENTY-FOUR - NEW YEAR'S EVE

Rain has gone back to his mopey, shut off self once again, and for the life of me, I can't figure out why. It's like ever since that night he tripped over me in the hall and decided we would be sharing a bed for the remainder of our time at the cabin flipped a switch in him again. And every time I try to go flip it back off, he's standing there, holding it in place and refusing to budge an inch.

I'll admit, Rain's brooding nature is a massive part of his allure, seeing as the strong silent type always seem to carry the most sex appeal. But Jesus Christ, I'm at my wit's end here. If he keeps withdrawing from me, I'm gonna fucking snap.

This morning at breakfast, I asked him if he wanted to do anything special tonight for New Year's Eve, even stream the ball dropping in Times Square from one of our phones since this is his first time experiencing the holiday not on the East Coast and making stir fry, but he only shrugged, telling me *whatever is fine.*

Sigh.

I get that he's guarded, that he isn't happy all the time. But he's given me glimpses of who he is, what he's like when he's being himself, and I'd be lying if I said I wasn't craving more. Ciaráin Grady opening up and letting go is a beautiful sight to behold.

But the problem is it makes it difficult to keep emotions out of this arrangement of *just sex.*

Who am I kidding? Difficult is the understatement of the millennia. Try fucking impossible for a more accurate description.

Because the trouble is, I *know* I'm already falling.

Right here, right now. No safety net in sight.

Sitting on the couch with yet another paperback to read, *The Catcher in the Rye* this time, my mind spins in circles, trying to come up with something, *anything* to get him out of this funk he's found himself in. Because I want him to enjoy tonight with me.

It's New Year's after all.

I know drawing and painting makes him happy, or at least less of an asshole. *Sometimes.* But I can't do either of those.

I could always cook stir fry like I said, seeing as we have all the ingredients, and find a movie for us to watch. Low-key and simple, which is something I know he'd like. The only issue is that option leaves him stewing in his room all day still, like he has been again a lot more recently.

We could go for a hike to the lake, even though we've easily done that a dozen times between the two of us. Or maybe take the ATV into town and grab a few beers at one of the local microbreweries?

Tapping the spine of my book to my knee, I continue to weed

through the ideas as they come to me, but nothing seems quite right.

Think, River. Think.

My eyes float around the cabin, grasping at straws for some sort of idea.

And when my eyes land on a huge basket of blankets in the corner, I have a brilliant one. One that I can't believe I didn't think of sooner.

Scrambling from my spot on the couch, I walk over and grab the basket, hauling it to the center of the living room in front of the fireplace to set to work.

I used to come out to the cabin at least twice a year with Taylor and his family, if not more. In fact, I can only think of one year, the year his dad won his last Superbowl, when we didn't get to come out to the cabin more than twice.

Most of the time, T would only bring me with, but sometimes Drew, Elliott, and our friend, Asher, would tag along. But the times the other guys would come, even as kids, we would get into so much shit.

Like the one time we were eleven, Coach and Taylor's stepmom went down into Vail on a "date night", leaving the five of us boys at the cabin for a maximum of four hours.

But in a four-hour period, we managed to build the most *bomb-ass* blanket fort. It was multilevel—not sure how we managed that one, but I think we stacked some *very* unstable furniture—and took up the entire living room. And this cabin isn't small, so that tells you something right there.

When T's parents came back those few hours later, needless to say they were less than pleased at the state of their cabin. Well,

Taylor's dad thought it was hilarious, but his stepmom threw the biggest bitch fit I've ever seen, especially seeing her *precious Taylor*, as she'd call him, hanging out in the upper level of the fort.

I mean, yeah, it wasn't exactly safe, but it was hardly worth the screaming match it caused with Coach and her after we cleaned it up and went back to the two bedrooms that we all slept in.

But that fort, man. It was such a fun night. I can still see the damn thing in my head and fuck if I'm not tempted to build a replica of it now.

Rain doesn't talk much about his life growing up, but his silent and brooding nature had to stem from something. And while he might keep those stories close to his chest, I can deduce the biggest reason might be his childhood wasn't all that great. Not filled with love and laughter like it should've been.

Not like mine was, at least until my father decided to practically disown me and divorce my mother because of my sexual orientation in early high school.

Decision made, I start moving the furniture in the living room around, creating the most space I can right in front of the fireplace before I set to work at the hardest part, the draping of about ten sheets and blankets.

By the time I'm finished with that portion of the task, I have to say I'm really fucking pleased with the results. It doesn't look exactly like the one we made as kids, but I honestly think this one is way better.

And a fuckton safer and more structurally sound too.

It's gotta be, if two twenty-one-year-old college football players, both well over six foot in height, are planning on spending the night inside there. More than likely fucking at some point as well.

After adding some finishing touches, including all the spare pillows I could find and stringing Christmas lights around the interior, I slip into my room to grab a comforter and a few pillows. I set up the inside of the fort as well in preparation for spending the rest of the night inside it.

It's not exactly the way I envisioned myself spending New Year's Eve, but honestly? This might be even better than hitting up the bars and getting plastered out of my mind with the boys.

A night of fun and sex with Rain? I think that'll *always* beat going out to get lit.

Giving my handiwork a final once-over, I decide the fort is completed to my liking and I can't help but grin like an idiot in pride. I know there is an *extremely* high possibility Rain will think it's stupid, but I don't care. It's the thought that counts, and since I can't paint worth a damn or do anything creative along those lines to cheer his ass up, this is the best I've got.

Lying back in the recliner I pushed out of the way to make room for the fort, I pull out my phone and scroll through my contacts in search of Rain's name.

Me: Come out here, I have a surprise.

I flip the TV on and surf through Netflix, selecting *The Witcher* because fucking *duh,* while waiting for his response. It comes about twenty minutes later.

Rain: Can't. Busy.

Rolling my eyes, I pause the show. I should have expected this response from the beginning. Biting my lip, I try to think of a way to get him to drop everything.

Me: But I'm naked and horny...

That ought to get his ass out here in a hurry.

When my phone dings with an incoming text not more than a minute later, I'm prepared for something witty or dirty. Not what I actually find.

Rain: Again, busy. Later.

Okay, what the actual fuck?

I have half the mind to send him a damn dick pic just to get him out here. I'm bound to have one on my phone somewhere...

Wait.

A shit-eating grin spreads across my face as my idea takes hold. There's no way he'll be able to resist this.

Unfastening my jeans and slipping them and my underwear down past my ass, I pull myself free. I'm already half-cocked from my idea alone, and it only takes a few languid strokes before my dick is standing at attention, ready to make his first FaceTime debut.

Settling myself into the recliner more, I continue stroking my cock with my left hand, holding out my phone with my right. Propping it up on my knee I tap the video camera icon with my thumb and wait, making sure I'm positioned right for him to get the full effect.

He answers on the fourth ring. He must've propped the phone on the nightstand after he accepted the call since the camera is showing him sitting on his bed with his sketchbook in hand from a side angle. He's still focused on what he's drawing when he says "River, I told you *twice*, I'm busy."

I let out a low chuckle, working my length in view of the camera. "Baby, why don't you bring that thing out here and draw me instead of whatever nature scene you've got going on in there?"

Rain tenses visibly through the camera, his hand pausing its movements. "I'm not…" He sighs, bringing the hand holding his pencil up to his head to scratch at his hairline. "Abhainn, can we just do this — " he cuts off abruptly before the word *later* can leave his lips because that's the moment his eyes finally lock on the screen of his phone.

Wetting my lips before dragging my teeth over my bottom one, I smirk. "What was that, baby? You wanted to wait 'til later?" I shake my head slightly as my fist rolls over the tip of my cock, collecting the pre-cum seeping from the blunt tip. His gaze latches onto the movement and I continue, "'Cause I hate to break it to you, but if I wait much longer, I'm going to have to take care of this solo."

Rain tosses his sketchpad and pencil on the bed before reaching over to grab his phone. He settles himself in against the headboard, one arm behind his head, amber eyes darkening with lust as they connect with mine.

"You're that impatient for my dick, huh, babe?" he drawls slowly, his eyes moving back down to my cock. "You couldn't let yourself wait just a little bit longer? And now you're threatening to finish yourself off without me?"

My chest rises and falls rapidly as I watch him watch me. God, it's such a turn-on, I feel my cock pulse in my hand.

"Cat got your tongue now?" he taunts, a devilish half grin painting his face. "Well, go for it, then. Fuck your fist while I watch you."

My hand freezes.

Holy shit.

When this idea went through my brain, all I wanted was to

get Rain into a better mood by acting like kids again in a blanket fort. I never imagined it would end in FaceTime sex with him just down the hall in his room.

"Lick your hand, River. Get it nice and wet," he orders, cocking his head slightly, waiting for me to obey.

And, as if I'm in a damn trance, I do. My cock slaps against my abs when I release it. Bringing my hand to my mouth, licking a path up my palm twice, coating it with saliva, all the while keeping eye contact with him through the screen. I hear a slight groan from him and catch him shift on the bed, making me smile.

You ready too, baby?

"Wrap your hand around your cock. Imagine it's *my* fist. Or better yet, my mouth," Rain demands, fixated on my hand as I bring it back to my dick, working my length. "I'm teasing you, taunting you. Turning you on so much it's painful."

Fuck me. I might have been used to being the more dominant one in bed, even when I bottom, but giving up control to Rain is the most sensual experience of my life.

Every. Fucking. Time.

"I don't want your mouth or fist," I pant, feeling a slight tingle in my balls already. "I want to imagine your ass milking my cock as I fuck you."

A wicked grin appears on his face, showcasing bright white teeth. Pulling his arm from behind his head, he reaches down at the same time he moves his phone out to the side, showing me his hand palming his ridiculous bulge behind his sweatpants.

"That's going to be tough. Because *my* cock is going to be milked by *your* ass later," he goads seductively, rubbing at his hard-on. "That is, as long as you listen and don't come until I tell you that you can."

A moan slips past my throat and my cock throbs in my grip, desperate for release. It's ready to blow as it is, I don't know how much longer I can hold on at this pace with his lust-filled voice controlling me and his heated eyes burning holes into me.

"I'm close," I tell him. "I'm going to come soon, baby."

"Don't you fucking dare," he growls, jackknifing up in the bed. "You wait for me."

My breathing increases rapidly as my hand begins moving in more sporadic and uneven motions. "I can't stop."

"River," Rain hisses, leaning forward as he watches me continuing to fuck my fist. Closing my eyes and leaning my head back against the smooth leather of the chair, my hips start thrusting slightly with each downward stroke I take on my dick.

"*River*. Open your eyes and look at me, Abhainn."

Fuck, I love when he speaks in Gaelic to me.

I don't listen, though. My eyes stay glued shut as I jack myself faster, climbing and chasing a release that seems so close, but too far away.

A hand wraps around the one on my cock and my eyes instantly snap open in time to see Rain's head descend on my length. His warm, silky mouth envelopes me, and I groan in pleasure, dropping my phone, both my hands flying to his hair and gripping for dear life. His eyes are closed as he focuses all his attention on bringing me pleasure.

His tongue swirls around the tip of my cock, paying special attention to the sensitive spot under the head, and slipping me back past his lips.

I watch in awe as he licks and sucks my shaft, taking me deeper to the point I touch the back of his throat. He's never deep-throated me before, and goddamn, it might be the best thing I've ever felt in my life.

My balls tighten as a bolt of pleasure shoots up my spine, straight into my brain. I'm about to cum, and right when I go to tell him, his eyes open and meet mine, and I fucking lose it at the intensity of his gaze.

My release rockets out of me as Rain drinks down the hot liquid, his throat working to swallow, wringing me completely dry.

Rain pops off my length, giving me one final lick, before rising up and kissing me harshly. The taste of myself on his tongue is intoxicating and somehow I feel ready to go again even though all the semen in my body was just shot out of my dick in the most epic orgasm of my life.

"I thought I told you to wait for me," he mumbles against my lips, stealing another kiss before rising to stand. I shift my hips, bringing my underwear and pants back into place before standing as well.

"And I thought I told you I couldn't," I retort with a smirk. "Clearly, you listen better than I do."

"Clearly." He laughs, the decadent sound washing over my body. I would give my left arm to hear it more often. Which is saying something, since I kind of need it to throw a damn football.

"Abhainn, I'll make you a deal," he begins, heat from his eyes scorching me. It's then that I look down and realize his impressive erection tenting his gray sweats. "If you give me five more minutes to finish what I was working on, I will milk your prostate like it's the last thing I'll ever do. First with my fingers, then my cock." His head tilts to the side, watching me through a hooded gaze. "Can you give me five more minutes?"

He takes a step away from me, taking my silence as a confirmation, and that's when my surprise catches his attention.

"What the fuck?" he asks, his brows furrowed. "Is this what you wanted to show me?"

My tongue runs across my bottom lip as I nod, taking a step toward him, gripping his shirt in my fist. "Yeah, it was. Now, baby, since you're *clearly* the one who can listen better..." I trail off the taunt, a half smirk teasing my lips. Leaning forward, I lick his jaw, simultaneously grabbing his bulge in my palm, before whispering against his lips, "Get in the fucking blanket fort."

TWENTY-SIX
Rain

DAY TWENTY-FIVE - NEW YEAR'S DAY

The fragments of my nightmare pull me from my slumber, and I find myself disoriented when I crack open my eyes. My vision is blurry, but even still, I can tell I'm not in River's bed.

Oh, right.

The blanket fort.

I tense. I haven't had a nightmare since the night I found myself crawling into River's bed last week, my mind begging for an ounce of peace. We've spent every night together in his room after that. And for some unknown reason, it seems to keep the nightmares at bay.

It's as if my demons can't catch hold of me when he's around.

Guilt rises in my throat when I think about all the nights I probably kept him awake with my screaming and shouting when we first arrived.

He's been so fucking good to me, even though I don't deserve it.

I roll to my side, praying to any God who might answer that I didn't wake River with my flailing while I rode out the memories that plague me, even in my sleep. It's still mostly dark, so I know it must've been only a couple hours since we fell asleep. Maybe three in the morning. But even in the dark of night, I can usually see him, hear him. Like a patch of brightness in my black reality. A calming melody in my silent world.

He just exists on a different frequency.

Reaching an arm over, I find the blankets beside me empty, but warm.

"Riv?" I call out, my voice hoarse with what I hope is just sleep, and not the remnants of my screams from the horror story in my mind while I'm unconscious.

"I'm here," he whispers from the entrance of our make-shift fort near my feet. I lift my head to see his shadowy form squatting down in just his underwear. After crawling in beside me, I quickly curl into his side, relishing in the warmth and security his body provides me when his arm is wrapped around me. The hard planes of his muscles mold against mine and I run my fingers over his abs, the pads tracing each individual indentation.

The level of comfort and contentment flowing between us begins to relax my racing heart. It's all because he's here, holding me, keeping me safe, even from myself. This is a feeling I can't imagine living without ever again.

It scares the fuck out of me.

At some point, he became a necessity, even when he was never meant to be anything more than an enemy.

"Where'd you go?"

"To brush my teeth, since I was a little occupied before we went to bed and forgot," he murmurs, his lips brushing my forehead.

"This late?"

He's quiet for a moment. "Yeah. You kind of woke me up," he says slowly. "But it's okay. I don't mind."

Just as I feared.

"I'm sorry," I mumble into his chest, pressing my cheek into his pec.

Silence settles between us, nothing but the sounds of our breathing and the soft sounds of River's "Mellow" playlist coming from the Google Home in the kitchen, still playing on a loop from earlier. Just when I think he's passed back out on me, his soothing voice speaks out again.

"Are you ever gonna tell me what the nightmares are about?"

I freeze.

Fuck.

My nightmares have been my affliction since the time I was twelve. It is recurring, coming to haunt me on a regular basis. I think I can count with my fingers the number of times I've slept in peace without them.

Seven of them were this past week, with him.

And then when I was eighteen, after a night I wish I could forget, a new nightmare began to torment my dreams. The night I watched my friend Deacon die, overdosing on the very drug that ran my life for *years*.

So they take turns now, and I never know which will rear its ugly head on any given night.

I take a deep breath, inhaling his scent, to put me back at ease.

I've told this story, my story, twice.

Once to a person I trusted with my life, but no longer have a relationship with.

Once to a person who betrayed me in the worst way possible.

And somehow, I find myself opening my mouth, and my soul, to spill one of my darkest secrets to the man beside me.

"I was nine and a half the first time my stepfather molested me," I say softly. So quiet, if Riv wasn't right next to me, he would have missed my admission. It would have drowned beneath the sounds of The Fray's "You Found Me" playing faintly from the speaker.

He tenses as he processes the words, but quickly relaxes and begins to run his fingers through my hair. The desire to nuzzle into his contact shoots through me, but if I don't get this out now, I never fucking will. I take a deep breath and continue, "At first, it was just hand jobs. He would jack me off, then make me do the same to him. That wasn't so bad. It's not like I was old enough to understand what was happening. Though, soon enough, I did know better. Yet he wanted more, no matter how wrong it was. He wanted me to put my mouth on him, and vice versa."

I bite my lip, trying to fight back the tears burning my eyes. "I was ten the first time I tasted cum."

"Rain—" River starts, but I shake my head, dislodging his fingers from my hair. It distracts him enough to let me continue.

"He was satisfied enough with that for about another year or so. But as time went on, his fingers began wandering while he blew me. Together, we learned I loved having my prostate milked well before I hit puberty. Something I shouldn't have discovered for another four or five years at the very least."

I pause to inhale River's masculine scent of citrus and salt as he begins drawing patterns with the pads of his index and middle fingers across my forehead, smoothing out the frown lines I'm sure are present. I can't help but relish how it sets me at ease, even in this moment.

If only for a moment.

My throat seizes, knowing the words that'll come next. Words I can never take back once they are spoken.

"For my twelfth birthday, my gift was a cock in my ass for the first time. I tried to get him to stop, of course. It was in vain, though, since I was still really small at that age and couldn't do much about it. Only beg and plead. I never really stood a chance. He bent me over, handcuffed me to the footboard of his and my mother's bed, and fucked me raw."

My jaw ticks and I keep pushing the words out, focusing on the sound of River's deep breaths beside me. "God, did it fucking hurt. Sure, he worked up to it with his fingers. But I was twelve, for fuck's sake. And it wasn't long after, maybe a week or two, when he made me fuck him too." I let out a humorless laugh. "I liked that a lot more than taking it. At least I could fuck him hard and fast, attempt to make him feel a fraction of the pain he caused me. And what do you know? As if I couldn't possibly loathe myself anymore, I actually got off on it." My voice cracks without permission on the last couple words.

There it is, all my shame and resentment, bared for him to see.

At least, all the pieces I'm willing to share.

He doesn't need to know about the string of girls I fucked once I turned fourteen to numb the pain. He doesn't need to know

I drowned the demons caused by that fucking bastard in pills and blow and booze, almost losing my scholarship to Clemson. He doesn't need to know the real reason why I switched schools in the middle of my college career was to escape once again. He doesn't need to know a few weeks before I was offered this transfer, I was ready to end it and finally escape once and for all.

He doesn't need to know I looked down the barrel of a gun... and fucking flinched.

He doesn't need to know he was right. I'm a fucking coward.

He doesn't need to hear those things.

Not tonight.

Not ever.

"When did it stop?' River asks quietly after what seems like an eternity of silence.

"When I was fourteen. I got big enough the summer before high school, thanks to football training camp. One night he came at me, and when I fought back, I actually won. Sent him to the hospital with a couple broken ribs and everything."

"And he never came for you again."

I nod. "But it was too little, too late. He already took all my firsts. Every damn one of them."

A tug on my hair brings my forehead to rest against River's. My eyes close and I take the moment to simply be here.

With him.

Just us.

"But he didn't get all of them. He didn't get your first kiss. He didn't get to be the first person to make your heart leap in your chest when you saw him. He didn't get to be your first love. And he most definitely won't get a single one of your lasts," Riv whispers, his hot breath, smelling of toothpaste, wafts across my mouth.

"That might be true. But he took everything from me. Not just my firsts. He took my fucking sanity. He made me question everything about myself. Who I am as a man. What I like when it comes to sex. Who I let myself—" I cut myself off before I utter the word *love*.

River runs his fingers again and again through my hair as he presses a gentle kiss to my throat. "I'm sorry those things happened to you, Rain. I'd say it helped make you stronger, but I have a feeling that's exactly the kind of thing you would hate to hear."

"You'd be right," I mumble as I play with his fingers resting on his chest. "I didn't need to be made strong. I was a fucking child. I just..."

"Needed to be kept safe."

I pull back and my eyes lock onto his teal ones. In them, I see a level of kinship and understanding I've never experienced in my goddamn life. How he knows what I was thinking, what I wanted to say, I don't think I'll ever understand.

It has nothing to do with the fact that we've been fucking like rabbits. Nothing to do with the fact that we are both attempting to navigate the world as a minority frequently shunned, though only one of us is honest about it.

Those things might have bonded us. But this goes deeper than that.

He just fucking *gets me*.

He's pulled back the layers no one before him has dared to go near.

He's put up with my moody, irrational ass for almost four weeks in a cabin in the woods in the middle of the fucking Rocky Mountains.

He's seen the good, the bad, and the ugly. *And stayed.*

Not like he has much of a choice. But he didn't have to keep trying to make an effort with me.

All despite the massive douchewaffle I've been to him since I found out he was bisexual.

The realization makes my heart squeeze in my chest.

Fuck. Me.

"Exactly," I whisper, my gaze holding his.

I'm still naked from our romp in the sheets earlier, and Riv is quick to discard his own underwear after sliding out from under my hold. He rolls on top of me, his arms braced on either side of my head. His soft lips press against my own once, twice, in sweet kisses before his tongue slides against the seams, begging for entrance.

Not being able to deny him a thing at this moment, I open and greedily take everything he has to give. My cock hardens again from the feeling of his tongue tangling with mine and the presence of his body hovering over me.

Goddamn, I'm so fucking fucked.

River nips my bottom lip and tugs hard before moving his assault from my mouth to my jaw and then to my throat. His hand slips between us, grasping both our cocks in his grip and jacking them in long, slow tugs. Not that he needs to get me worked up and ready, I'm already harder than granite.

"Fuck, Riv," I pant, gritting my teeth. The sensation of our dicks rubbing together feels so good.

Too good.

And nothing that feels this good is ever meant to last.

"It fucking kills me, knowing you went through that, baby. With no one to fight for you, to stand up for you," he tells me between kisses across my pecs. "And while I might be too late to keep the nine-year-old Rain safe, I'm here now. I've found you."

Even in the shadows, his turquoise eyes say more than his mouth as he repeats his declaration once more. "I've found you and I'm here, and I promise I will always be your safe place for as long as you need one."

His words send waves of desire coursing through my veins, springing me into action.

I cup his jaw, stubbled and sharp and carved by God himself, with both hands and bring his mouth back to mine in a searing kiss of lips and teeth and tongues.

Desperate. Demanding.

Mind altering perfection.

My soul begs for this. For more. For him.

Jesus, I just want him. And I don't care if that makes me gay or bi or whatever.

It doesn't fucking matter right now.

While I'm still lost in our kiss, River begins moving above me, sliding the hand that was stroking our cocks down to cup my balls and knead them with expertise. As my hands begin to roam his body, I feel his finger sliding over my taint and to my ass. I clench my cheeks on instinct.

No.

River leans back and grabs my chin with his other hand, his

fucking finger still playing against my hole. He forces me to meet his gaze, sensing my panic. His eyes, filled with lust and desire, soften as he sees the fear written all over my face. I'm sure he can feel my nerves buzz through my body and into his own where our skin touches.

"Don't worry, baby. I've got you," he pleads with his eyes for me to trust him. "I promise, you're safe."

Jaw clenched, I give him a curt nod.

I trust him. With all of my black heart and damaged soul.

And fuck, if that isn't the hardest thing in the world for me to do anymore, I don't know what is.

River removes his hand from my ass and reaches over to the edge of the blankets for the bottle of lube we brought in here last night. Uncapping it, he squirts a good amount on his index and middle fingers, rubbing them together to coat them completely.

"We'll go slow," he whispers, moving back over me to trail warm, wet kisses down my chest and abs. "If you want me to stop, tell me, and I will."

When his lips brush the tip of my cock, I groan.

Fuck, I want him so bad. I'll let him do whatever he wants to me. I don't fucking care. I just want him to erase the painful memories, the touch of the wicked human who did those vile things to me.

"Touch me, Abhainn," I plead. "You're already driving me crazy."

I feel him grin against my pubic bone before he gives it a light nip. "In good time."

"*Now*," I demand.

"Baby," he murmurs, licking the underside of my cock with

a long, slow stroke while he meets my gaze. "I told you I would stop if you wanted me to, and I will. But make no mistake about it, it's about damn time I'm the one *officially* in charge."

My cock jumps at the command in his voice.

God, and when I didn't think he could get any sexier.

Moving his coated fingers back toward my puckered hole, he takes the crown of my cock in his mouth and gives it a firm suck, still holding my eyes. The pad of his thumb brushes over my taint as he takes me deeper into his mouth. Eyes closing, he gives into his task, moaning around my cock as he swirls his two fingers around the rim of my ass, never breeching it.

My hips buck on reflex when the tip hits the back of his throat. He takes advantage of the movement, beginning to ease one finger through the tight muscles of my ass.

It burns at the first intrusion in years, but it doesn't hurt. Slowly, I allow myself to sink down on it completely, both of us moaning at the sensation.

Fuck, even with the burning, I forgot how good this can feel.

River slides in his second finger, working me open for him while taking my cock deep into his throat. His head bobs up and down a few more times, allowing nearly all my length into his mouth before he presses the pads of his fingers on that little button inside me at the same time he lightly scrapes his teeth against the underside of my cock on the upstroke.

My toes start to tingle, and I see fucking stars.

"Abhainn. I'm gonna come, baby," I groan as he continues to work me over. He slides a third finger into me and at this point, I'm practically riding his hand. I'm lost in the sensation of his fingers, his mouth.

Just lost in him.

River rubs against my prostate and takes me deep, sucking hard, and I can't hold on any longer. I bear down on his fingers as hot cum spurts from my cock, harder and faster than a bottle rocket, sliding down his throat. He keeps sucking me and fucking me with his hand, milking every last ounce of cum from my orgasm, and I swear to God, I lose all feeling in both my legs.

"Oh, shit," I pant as he pops off my cock and brushes kisses against my hips.

My mind is blank, and my entire body is in bliss while River leans over and sheathes himself with a condom, smearing the latex with copious amounts of lube. He leans down and presses a kiss to my lips before settling himself back between my legs, the tip of his cock pressing against my hole.

And just like that, I'm on full alert once again. Except this time, it's not panic or fear.

It's anticipation. Desire. Need.

My cock is already beginning to harden against my abs, because I'm fucking insatiable when it comes to River Lennox.

Having him is like taking your first hit of weed or line of blow. You didn't know what to expect from it, but fuck, the high sure does make you feel on top of the world.

"Are you sure?" he asks softly.

"Please, I need to feel you. I'm fucking begging you."

Even in the darkness, I can see him smile and his eyes light up as he slowly presses his hips forward, crowning me.

The burning begins again, seeing as his cock is much larger than his fingers, and I wince, breathing deep through clenched teeth.

Slowly, painfully fucking slowly, River continues to sink into me until he bottoms out, hips flush against my ass.

"Fuck," I groan, feeling so full of him.

His cock, yes. But also just... *him*. I'm beginning to realize there's no part of me he hasn't taken for himself.

Including what's left of my heart.

"You gotta move," I plead, desperate for more friction.

He leans down, our hot breaths mixing as our lips brush against each other. "What did I say about who's in charge?" he asks, still unmoving.

"River," I start, but he cuts me off.

"*Who* is in charge tonight, Rain? Who has their cock in your ass? Who is about to fuck you?"

"You. You are," I tell him, not giving one flying fuck about relinquishing control to him. Tonight, I'll submit. I already know I'll love every minute of it.

He can have whatever he wants, I'll gladly give it to him.

My obedience is rewarded with his mouth crashing into mine. He nips at my lip as he begins moving inside me in long, slow stokes. I pant into his mouth, loving the way his cock feels deep in my ass while our tongues tangle.

Nothing in the world could ruin this moment.

The sky could come crashing to the ground and it wouldn't make a dent in the blissful bubble we're in right now.

River moves his hips more quickly, building up speed, and I find myself lifting my hips, desperate to meet him thrust for thrust. Every brush of his cock against my prostate shoots lightning up my spine and straight to my brain.

It's never been like this.

Full of passion and emotion and... hell.

Love.

His movements become jerkier and more sporadic, so I know he must be getting close. I grasp my dick between us and begin tugging it in tandem with each stroke of his cock, but as soon as River takes notice, he bats my hand away, gripping my length in his palm.

"Your orgasms are mine," he tells me, leaning back and fucking me with reckless abandon, his hips slamming against my ass cheeks. "I'm the one who gets you off."

"Yes," I huff, pleasure sailing through me. "You. Only you."

River grabs my hip, his other hand still stroking me, and fucks me harder and faster and deeper.

Needy. Damn near frenzied.

His thumb spreads the cum leaking from the head of my dick around the tip before rubbing against that spot right under the head as his cock makes pass after pass on my prostate. I can't stop myself. I go off again, my entire being sent into a state of pure ecstasy as cum bursts from me, coating my torso.

River lets out a throaty groan as he finds his own climax, his thrusts slowing dramatically. Soon, he stops moving completely, just leans down to kiss me softly before pressing his forehead to mine.

Our sweat and breaths mix, our pounding hearts trying desperately to come back to Earth.

After kissing me again, soft and sweet, River eases out of me and climbs off my body. "I'll be right back. Don't move."

I hear the sound of a toilet flushing down the hall and the sink running briefly before River returns, a damp washcloth in hand. He gently wipes my stomach clean of my release, not meeting my eyes as he does so.

Which is not River-like at all.

"Hey," I say, grasping his chin in my hand. "What's wrong?"

He bites his lip, glancing away. "I didn't hurt you, did I?"

I huff out a laugh. "No, babe. I loved every second of it."

He visibly relaxes and finishes cleaning me off before discarding the cloth on the ground beside us. Slipping under the blankets again, he lays on his side to face me, so I mirror his pose. I reach out and take his hand in mine, keeping my eyes locked on our hands while I play with his fingers.

"Thank you for trusting me," I hear River whisper after a few minutes. "I know that was probably the hardest thing you've ever done after what he did to you."

Thoughts of my stepfather cause me to stiffen.

River is nothing like that man.

River's kind and caring and loving and everything that *he* isn't.

Everything *I'm* not.

"I don't want to be like him," I whisper, allowing my worst thoughts to be brought to light as I look up to meet his aqua gaze.

"You aren't *anything* like him."

"Yes, I am. I was. That first time in the shower." My next words catch in my throat. "I *raped* you."

"No," he says immediately, his voice firm. "We've talked about this, Rain. At Christmas. I never said no. I never asked you to stop."

He's right, of course. Doesn't mean I don't carry that burden with me every single day, though.

"That might be true, but it was close enough."

River looks like he wants to disagree at first, but then he nods slowly. I see it written all over his face, how much torment I put him through that morning, not even four weeks ago.

"I'm still so fucking sorry, Abhainn."

Just when I think his silence might kill me, he sighs and looks deep into my eyes.

"Are you ever going to do it again?"

I shake my head. "I'll never take what you aren't giving me willingly."

A small smile graces his gorgeous lips. "Then you aren't him."

Leaning into him, I place a soft kiss on his mouth.

Wishing I could believe him.

TWENTY-SEVEN
River

DAY TWENTY-FIVE - NEW YEAR'S DAY

I wake up a few hours later, my eyes burning from lack of sleep as I open them to find Rain still passed out beside me in the blanket fort. His hair is disheveled, strewn over his forehead haphazardly as his chest rises and falls with his deep, steady breaths. His fully tattooed arm, the one covered in a Celtic sleeve, is tucked under his head as a makeshift pillow because somehow, through the night, they both ended up on my side of our makeshift bed.

I watch him for a while, taking in his sleeping form, admiring this brave human who decided to open up to me in ways I never imagined last night.

He let me into his mind, his heart, his *body*.

And while the last one might not seem like such a feat, I know the amount of trust he gave me in that moment.

My own heart on the other hand, it's in some deep shit. As each day passes and we get closer to our departure from this little slice of Eden we've found ourselves in, I know I'm in for a rude awakening.

Because this thing between us, it's become so much more than *just sex, fuck buddies, frenemies with benefits,* whatever you want to call it.

It's none of those things, not anymore. To be completely honest, I don't think it ever was, apart from that first time.

Maybe even then.

I watch him sleep, how peaceful he looks, and I hate that this is the only time he seems to find some semblance of freedom from the ghosts of his past that haunt him.

I hate that man for what he did to him. To a kid he was supposed to *protect.*

I know that's what the nightmares are about, not that he has told me explicitly. But how can they not be? That kind of trauma... there's no way it doesn't stay with a person throughout their life.

Kissing him softly on the forehead, I slip out of the fort and make my way to my bedroom down the hall. I rummage through my duffle, in search of the small baggie of weed I brought with me.

I'm not much of a smoker, I hate it, in fact. The smell is God-fucking-awful and inhaling anything *other* than oxygen into my lungs isn't exactly something I like doing. But sometimes, when my anxiety is at an all-time high and I can't seem to stop stressing, I take a hit or two from a blunt, if only to help myself relax.

And it works.

So maybe, just maybe, it could help Rain too.

Finding what I'm looking for in one of the pockets, I grab it and turn to head back out to Rain, only to find him standing in the doorway. The sight of him causes me to jump, dropping the baggie I was holding that contains the couple blunts.

"What are you doing?" he asks, rubbing his eyes before blinking at me. "It's like seven in the morning, why are you awake already?"

I shrug, grabbing the blunts from the ground. "I'm an early riser."

"Yeah, I know, but we barely slept last night." His voice is still gravelly and husky, sending shivers down my spine. Sleepy Rain is the sexiest version of him, in my opinion.

I smirk at him. "And whose fault is that?"

He smiles back and takes a step closer to me. "Yours, mostly." As he reaches out to take my hand, his eyes land on what is in my hand and he blinks rapidly before looking back up at me. "Is that weed?"

"Yeah, I might have a little something for us," I tell him with a grin.

He steps back, shaking his head with confusion written on his face. "I didn't think you smoked pot. Golden boy and all."

I do my best not to roll my eyes at the *golden boy* comment. "Only when I'm stressed or whatever. Usually never enough to need more than one of these in an entire year." I close the space between us and peck him on the cheek. "I thought it might get your mind in a better place. And if not that, help you sleep, maybe."

Rain lets out a sigh and rubs a palm over his face before walking over to the bed to take a seat. His fingers mess with his hair as he bites the inside of his cheek, watching me.

I see the gears turning in his mind, trying to work out what to say without...what, upsetting me?

It's just weed. Perfectly legal in the state of Colorado.

"I can't have that," he tells me after a minute, nodding to

the weed.

My brows furrow as I take a seat beside him, bringing one knee up to rest on the bed. "Okay, that's fine. I wasn't trying to pressure you —"

"No, Riv." He sighs, taking the bag from my hand containing the blunts. He turns them over in his palms, staring at them like they're a live grenade in his hands. His eyes snap up to mine and he gives me a sad smile, holding out the bag for me. "I appreciate you trying to do this for me. But I've already gone down this road before in an effort to numb the pain."

Taking the blunts, I give him a confused look. "I don't understand. Baby, it's only weed. It's not a big deal, it's legal."

He bites his lip and shakes his head again. "Look, when...shit got bad, I turned to weed and booze to help me cope."

"That's not what —"

"I know it's not what you're telling me to do, Abhainn. Just let me talk, okay?" His eyes beg me to shut up for once in my life, so I nod for him to continue.

"My senior year of high school, I dove headfirst into weed and alcohol. It helped numb some of my pain, kept the demons away for a little while. At least while I was awake, that is. But of course they never helped at night. Soon enough, they weren't even enough when I was conscious." He licks his lips and laughs uncomfortably. "That's when I turned to coke. E. Whatever I could get my hands on that would make me forget."

His eyes grab mine, ensnaring me like they always do, and I get lost in the sadness I find in them.

Baby, let me take your pain away.

But I stay quiet, urging him silently to continue. To tell me more.

I need his truths, all of them. Every single thing he is willing to share, I'll eat it up and still beg for more. No matter how dark and fucked up it might be.

The darkest parts of his soul, his past, are what make him, him.

"It got really bad, to the point where I'd show up wasted to school and take bumps in the middle of practice. Pop a tab of molly before a game. Whatever it might have been. I was an addict, basically. I couldn't stop myself, even if I wanted to try."

His cheeks heat, a flush of crimson taking over the skin from his neck up, even the tips of his ears.

"Don't be embarrassed," I tell him, tossing the weed to the side to snatch his hand and hold in both of mine. "I don't judge you for the way you handle your pain. Hell, I had a Xanax prescription and therapy twice a week for years after my dad left us. Yeah, that might not be nearly the same thing, but it helped." Shaking my head, I let out an exhale. "The point is, no one has the right to tell you how to fix yourself."

He nods and I squeeze my hands around his, wishing I could do something, anything to help him.

"Can I ask what made you stop?"

I watch as his teeth roll over his bottom lip, gnawing at it. "A friend of mine...he died. Overdose. And it gave me the wakeup call I needed, I guess."

Shit.

"Fuck, Rain. I'm sorry."

He shrugs. "Don't be, it's not on you. I got clean, started going to therapy and figured out some other forms of coping that weren't going to kill me. But with that said, I won't even touch weed. I still drink, rarely, but I don't think it was ever the problem."

I smile, rubbing my thumb over the back of his hand. "Well, I'm glad. Was that the last time you used?"

Rain winces, and my heart stops.

"When?"

"The night in Portland," he says, his voice hoarse. "At the club I went to, I took two lines of coke. They said it was laced with E for a cloud high, but I don't even know. I was hallucinating, I ended up throwing up…" He shakes his head and the look on his face, it's agonizing. The guilt he feels, it's written all over his handsome face. "I fucking wish I didn't. I threw away my sobriety that night."

I feel my forehead crease. "Then why did you do it?"

His eyes dance between mine, reading what he sees there before licking his lips and casting his gaze away from me.

And I know.

"It was because of me, wasn't it?" I whisper, my throat catching on the words. "It was me. I was pushing you in the hotel room, egging you on. And then you left and…"

Oh, God.

My mind is spinning, and I think I might be sick. I slip my hands from his and turn away from him, my head in my hands.

I did this.

He threw it away…because *I* was being an asshole that night.

"*No,*" he says adamantly, grabbing my chin in his hands to force me to look at him. "You remember what you told me that night on the field when I decked you? That I can't put my fuck-ups on you?"

I nod, barely, but he feels it because he continues.

"Good. Because I won't let you beat yourself up for them either. They are *on me*, like you said." His eyes search mine and I see unshed tears in them. "I was the one who made the decision to get high, not you. *I* am to blame."

I wince at his words, swallowing harshly. "I feel so guilty. If I could —"

He shakes his head vehemently, cutting me off. "It doesn't do to dwell in the past, Abhainn. You'll forget to live."

I let out a choked laugh. "Did you just inaccurately quote *Harry Potter* to me?"

He grins, his thumb running across my cheek. "I'm not sure. It's something like that, I think." His smile sobers, but his thumb keeps sweeping over my cheek. "There is so much shit I've done wrong in my life. So many things I wish I could take back. But I can't, so all I can do is learn from it and try not to make the same mistake twice."

He's right. We all screw up in some way, but we just have to use it to better ourselves.

And that's what he's trying to do. I see that now more than ever.

"I'm still so sorry," I tell him, my hand coming up to grab his wrist. "I'm sorry for everything I did and said before…" I trail off, clenching my jaw. "I'm sorry."

His soft smile warms my heart, stopping it entirely when he places a gentle kiss on my lips. "I'm sorry too. I would say for everything but…" He trails off, bursting out laughing. "I don't know if I'm sorry for hitting you. It was nice to see the golden boy can be tarnished."

I laugh, my mood lifting immediately as I push him away before rolling on top of him.

"Only by you, baby. Only by you."

TWENTY-EIGHT
Rain

DAY TWENTY-EIGHT

Y ou know how everyone always has that classic bullshit "New Year, new me" mentality the first few weeks of January? They stick to their resolutions for a month, maybe two. But all of a sudden, its mid-March and they haven't lost any weight, they've stopped working out, they started drinking soda or coffee or what-the-fuck-ever all over again.

And so they say, *maybe I'll try again next year.*

This isn't one of those times.

I didn't have any intention of opening up to River the way I did a few days ago in that blanket fort. And then again the next morning in his room. But I fucking did, and when those moments were over, I made a vow to myself to keep letting him in.

It might only be the fourth day of the month—the year—but this is a promise I intend to keep in whatever way I can.

Giving him small pieces of me, no matter how insignificant

they might seem.

Eventually, when it's time, I can give him the darkest scraps of my soul, the fragments that never are able to see the light of day. The parts no one would love or understand, but I know he will find a way to see the good in them.

That's just who he is.

Which is why I find myself holding River's hand as I drag him to my bedroom door, where my makeshift art studio has taken over the space. I haven't slept in here since the night I slipped into his bed that first time after finding him in the hallway, but I have found myself in here a few hours a day when we aren't busy wrapped in each other.

He gives me a warm smile, but there's confusion in his eyes. He hasn't set foot in this room once since the day we arrived at the cabin, so the furrow of his brow and way the fingers on his free hand tap absently against his leg screams not only of his discomfort, but also *what the fuck is happening right now?*

I swallow the lump in my throat and turn the knob, still gripping his hand tightly with my other hand. "I want to show you something."

And I really do want to give him this piece of myself. More so than I already did by giving him that painting for Christmas. It's the least I can do for him at this point.

I still might not be confident admitting to the world, or even myself, who I am to my very core. I don't have the courage to show the world the "real" Ciaráin Grady instead of the person they think I am.

But I do know, when I'm with River, I'm who I'm supposed to be.

I open the door all the way and let him step into what was my little slice of sanctuary from before, when we couldn't stand the sight of each other. He slides past me, taking in the bright bedroom, artwork strewn about the entire space.

He's quiet for a minute, taking in the disaster of my workspace, complete with a canvas laid out on the floor I still need to cut down before I can start working on it. There are several finished acrylic pieces stacked together in one corner, piles of completed watercolors on the desk, bedside table, and even the floor. The crates I brought to put them in have long since overflowed in the past four weeks.

And don't even get me started on the paint. It's literally *everywhere*. Watercolor brush pens, along with actual watercolors, are scattered across the desk and there are boxes of acrylic paints amassing on the floor. Anywhere and everywhere I could find the space to put them.

To River, whose room is neat and tidy, it probably looks like a tornado and a hurricane and then a bull ran through the place. But to me, it's organized chaos.

River looks at me, a huge grin on his face, and fuck me, I love being the reason it's there. I'll never tire of seeing him smile, those dimples popping in his cheeks.

"Can I look at them?"

"Sure," I whisper, walking over to the bed to clear off some space so we have a place to sit. "They should all be dry. Just be careful of the canvas on the ground. That's the last of what I have until we leave."

I stack the watercolors that were set out to dry in a pile, careful to keep my eyes and hands busy while I feel him looking around some more.

God, this is harder than I thought it would be.

Art is subjective, certain kinds don't always appeal to everyone. Some of it is dark and tortured, while some are bright and fresh and new. Yet each piece and style has its own beauty and place in the world.

But that doesn't take away the fear of rejection, of not fitting in where you want to belong.

I've come to learn, because of River, people are like that too.

River lifts a crate full of watercolors to look through and places it on the bed next to me before climbing over me like I'm some sort of jungle gym or something. As he settles in beside me, his grin only grows larger. He catches me looking at him and literally beams.

"What?"

"Are you actually this excited about looking at artwork?" I laugh nervously. "I mean, art isn't really your thing."

Leaning over, he presses a light kiss to my lips, licking the steam with the tip of his tongue. "I know it's fucking cheesy as hell to say this, but *you're* my thing. It's part of who you are. Of course, I want to look at them."

He slides his tongue into my mouth, and I groan as it makes contact with my own. My dick is already thickening in my pants and the last thing I want to do in this bed right now is look at watercolors. But all too soon, he breaks away and rests his forehead against mine, panting slightly.

"Thank you for sharing this with me."

"Thank you for caring," I whisper over his lips.

He pulls away after another quick peck on my lips and grabs his phone to put on his favorite "Mellow" playlist I'm really starting to love before he begins digging through the crate, pulling out each and every painting that's inside. Over the next thirty minutes, he goes through damn near a hundred paintings of the surrounding landscapes, the cabin, the city of Vail. Some dark and moody, the style I prefer to paint, with an abundance of neutral tones, and others more vibrant and lively like the one I painted for him. It doesn't escape my notice the more vivid works are also the more recent ones too.

After taking in each one, he passes it to me to put back where it belongs, always meeting my eyes with a smile, and hell, I can't help the thrum I feel in my chest. Because I can't believe doing something like this would truly make him smile at me the way he is right now.

Once the last painting is in place, I hop off the bed to take the crate back to where it belongs. I start straightening up the desk, grabbing the remaining pile of paintings to set on top of the others when I hear a loud smack against the hardwood.

Glancing up, I catch River picking up a black book off the ground. My sketchbook from the looks of it. I go back to my task of picking up my desk when I tense.

Wait.

Shit.

My. Fucking. Sketch. Book.

I spin around as he flips the cover open to the first page and immediately stiffens.

So do I. Because I know what is on the first page.

A sketch of his hands and wrists, the small cross tattoo over his pulse point sketched there as well.

I know what is in the rest of the sketchbook too. I fucking drew them.

Him.

All the parts of his body I've memorized over the past weeks. Every line, curve, and muscle. Every piece of ink that adorns his skin.

It's all in there.

Ohfuckohfuckohfuck, this is bad. Worse than Thanos getting all six Infinity Stones bad.

Alarm slides its way into my very soul when he lifts those blue-green eyes to meet mine.

I can't read them.

"Riv," I say as gently as possible, almost as if I'm talking to a skittish animal rather than the man who has become the most important person to me in the world, even in this short amount of time.

He doesn't say anything, just takes a slow step toward the door, his eyes still locked on mine.

And because I know him as well I know myself, I know he's about to make a break for it.

As I predicted, River jumps over the canvas on the ground and makes a dash for the door, flying through it at a neck breaking speed. "Riv, wait!" I shout. I'm right behind him, out the door in a flash, but the fucker is faster than I am. He makes a beeline for the bathroom and slams the door shut just as I reach it. I try for the handle, but to no avail; he's already locked himself inside with the artwork I treasure the most.

Himself.

TWENTY-NINE
River

DAY TWENTY-EIGHT

I let out a breath of relief that I made it to the bathroom without Rain getting his hands on his sketchpad. Don't get me wrong, I feel guilty as hell for locking myself in here with something he clearly doesn't want me to see.

But shit.

He drew me?

"Abhainn, it isn't what it looks like," Rain denies from the other side of the door, pounding it with his fists.

Normally, I'd love the sound of his begging, but the sound from him right now makes my heart squeeze in my chest, utterly ripping me apart. Under any other circumstance, I would give in to his requests or demands. I'd submit, like he fucking loves.

But submission isn't in my nature.

Only sometimes, and only *ever* for him.

I don't answer him, instead moving to the vanity and slide

to the floor, my back against the base cabinets. Taking a deep breath, I do my best to drown out the sound of Rain begging and beating at the door.

But it's fucking difficult.

I hope he doesn't rip the damn thing off its hinges, trying to get to me before I have the chance to look through this.

"River, open this fucking door right now!" he yells, anger rising in his voice as the doorknob continues to rattle.

I don't respond, letting him stew in his rage.

He *drew* me.

He drew me.

He. Fucking. Drew. *Me.*

No matter how I think it or how many times it crosses through my mind, it doesn't make sense.

"Babe, *please.* Just do this one thing. Open the door and I promise we can look at it together."

Ah, he's already trying to make a deal with me.

A lot of people don't know this, but the stages of grief apply to more than loss and death. Rain, whether he realizes it or not, is already on the third step: bargaining.

I open the pad to the next page, then the next, and the next after that.

It's page after page of sketches.

All of me.

My tattoos.

My chest.

Arms.

Abs.

Lips.

Eyes.

My entire fucking face.

It's all here in graphite and paper, staring back at me like a mirror.

I don't know how long I sit flipping through page after page of his sketchbook. I must go through it half a dozen times, still unbelieving that he almost filled an entire pad with nothing but *me*.

When did he do these?

I've never seen him with this pad before. He's never sketched in front of me, save for that one time on the FaceTime call. He hasn't taken any photos of me, that I know of, to sketch from.

Which means this is all straight from his mind.

Which also means…each time he touched and kissed and licked every single inch of my body…he wasn't just worshipping it.

He was memorizing it.

My heart pounds in my chest and my palms start to sweat as I stand on shaky legs. I feel like fucking Bambi just learning to walk as I cross the bathroom and open the door.

I expect to find Rain still right in front of me, but in my reverie, I must have missed that he was no longer banging against the panel of the door. Instead, I see him sitting on the ground across the hall from the doorway, his head in his hands.

Stage four, depression.

He heard the door open from the way his shoulders stiffen as I step into the hallway, but he makes no effort to look up at me or say anything.

Squatting down in front of him, I place the closed sketchbook on the floor to the side of him, but he still doesn't look up.

"You drew me?" I whisper, my voice shaking and full of emotion. It wasn't meant to be a question. Or maybe it was.

I have no clue what this means, and I'm sure he doesn't, either.

That's probably why he didn't want me to see them.

Look at me, baby, I plead silently, my stomach clenching with anticipation.

As if he can read my mind, he lifts his head from his hands, his amber eyes meeting mine. They're red around the rims, as if he's been holding back tears, and I hate the idea that this caused him pain. It was never meant to, but I can't help being selfish sometimes and only thought of my own desire in the moment.

I watch as a stoic mask slides into place over his face, one he hasn't worn around me in weeks, and I have the urge to grip his shoulders and shake him out of it.

We aren't like that. Not anymore.

And then I realize.

Stage five, acceptance.

But acceptance of what? My anger or outrage when there isn't any?

Grabbing his wrists with both hands, I haul us both up to our feet before taking his face in my hands. My heart feels like it's trying to claw its way out of my chest to get to his. If only to let his know mine has never felt so completely whole.

I love you.

The words are there, have been for a long time, waiting to make their presence known. But I don't say them.

All they would do is scare him away.

But I beg silently, searching his eyes for any recognition that he understands the way I feel about him. That this is the most beautiful thing anyone has ever done for me, inadvertently or not. That he just gave my heart wings and let it soar.

That I fucking *love* him.

And I do. Goddamnit, I do.

I'd give anything to be able to tell him at this moment.

But I can do the next best thing.

Show him.

I crush my mouth to his in a blistering kiss, backing him against the wall. Biting at his lower lip, I flick my belt open, unbutton my jeans, and slide down my zipper in one quick move before beginning on his own.

"Your talent is so fucking sexy," I murmur against his lips, sliding my tongue along the seams before gripping my shirt and tugging it over my head. I toss it to the floor of the hall and walk back to his room, yanking off my jeans before crossing the threshold. As I do, I hear SayWeCanFly's "Pavement" coming from my still open Spotify app on my phone, giving me an idea.

"You aren't mad?" I hear Rain ask behind me, uncertainty evident in his rough whisper.

In only my underwear, I step around the canvas on the floor and start digging through the containers holding most of his acrylics. "No, not at all," I tell him as I grab a couple large bottles of paint. Foregoing the small hole of the squeeze top and just ripping the entire lid off before crushing the bottle in my hand and dumping royal blue paint all over the canvas laid out on the ground before me.

"What are you doing?" Rain asks, a tremor in his voice.

I glance up at him as I unscrew the other cap on the second bottle of paint, this one forest green. He's standing barely out of reach on the other side of the canvas, naked down to his boxer briefs and hard as a fucking rock. My mouth practically waters at the sight.

Showing you that I love you.

I squeeze out every drop of the paint from this bottle, too, spreading it all over the canvas and not giving a damn if any gets on my hands, arms, or any other part of my body.

Once the bottle is empty, I toss it to the ground with the other and turn to face him, sliding my underwear down my legs and throwing them across the room. I reach over and grab his hand, giving it a swift tug, and force him to step onto the paint-covered canvas.

Slipping my fingers into his waistband, I smear the mixture of paint against his hips as I tug down his boxers, kneeling before him as I go.

"Making art."

Cool paint slides and squishes under my knees as I run my tongue up his length, from taint to tip, sucking the head into my mouth while my fingers lightly feather up the back of his calves and knees, causing him to shudder. I suck him slowly for a few seconds before popping off and dipping my hands into the paint below me.

The urge to brand him as mine in any way I can is raging through me like a tidal wave, and I allow it to take over my senses.

Bringing my paint covered hands back up, I grip the backs of his thighs just below his ass in my palms. I lean up further on my knees, licking down the V of his hips with the flat of my tongue and then up the other side the way I know he loves, paying special attention to the ink on his left hip. Biting at the skin there, I pull it with my teeth, causing his cock to jump beside my face. When I release and pull away, I see the tiny white crescents from my teeth indenting his golden skin.

Imprinting him.

I want to mark every part of him as mine. Every damn inch.

With my teeth.

My tongue.

My hands.

Mine.

And he is fucking mine. I don't give two shits if he's "out" or if we make it official or if I have to wait until he is ready to give this a real shot.

He. Is. Mine.

Licking his cock again with a long, slow brush of my tongue, I keep my eyes on his face. His attention is fixated on me, kneeling before him, vulnerable and submissive.

"Put your cock in my mouth, baby," I say with a husky demand, causing his brows to quirk. I smirk at him, knowing full well he'll listen, even when he is seemingly the one with the power.

You have no idea how wrong you are, baby. I might be on my knees for you, but you're about to see what it's like to completely lose control.

He wars with himself for a whole three seconds.

And then the underside of his dick is sliding along my tongue into my mouth.

My hands knead the backs of his thighs before using my grip to take his cock deeper into my throat. Rain groans above me, sliding his hands into my hair to help me take him even further, his cock twitching when I moan around it.

Fuck, I love having my mouth on him.

I continue to work him over, my head bobbing on his length in fast, shallow passes before slipping into the back of my throat, licking and sucking every damn inch. My teeth run gently back up his length and it makes him go wild.

His grip on my hair gets harder as he begins thrusting into my mouth, panting and groaning while I cup his balls, kneading them with my paint covered hands, careful to avoid his ass.

"I'm close, Riv," Rain grunts as he continues to fuck my face. "Where do you want me?"

I remove my hands from him to pat my sternum with my fingertips and he's quick to follow, pulling out of my mouth and stroking himself through his climax, coating my chest and pecs with his release.

"Shit, what are you doing to me?" Rain growls and drops to his knees in front of me, taking my face in his palms and kisses me, rough and passionate. One hand moves down between us, grasping my dick firmly before giving it a couple fast tugs. He nibbles on my jaw before licking his way down to my collarbone as my fingers graze down his back.

"Put your cum on my cock," I tell him with closed eyes, lost in the sensation of his mouth and his hands on me. His mouth pauses for a brief second as he processes my request.

His fingers are running across my chest a second later, collecting his cum before gripping my cock and slicking the length with his release. A groan rumbles through me at the feel of his hand stroking me, coating me with his essence.

"Stand back up and turn around," I murmur, needing his hand off me so I don't blow a load before I even get inside him.

This time, he obeys without hesitation.

I grip his taut ass in my palms, spreading his cheeks to expose his puckered hole to me. I've never done this before, but fuck it, I dive in, my tongue caressing the tight bud. And surprisingly, I find eating ass isn't unpleasant at all. Flicking the tip of my tongue against him, I feel him shiver.

"Fuck. Babe," he pants.

He fucking likes it.

That only spurs me on more.

I spread his cheeks wider, continue lapping at his ass, slipping my tongue inside him, coating him with saliva the best I can. There's no way I'm not about to break away, covered in paint, to try to find a bottle of lube in my own bedroom.

Rain's body continues to shake and I can't fucking take it anymore.

I need to be inside him.

Pulling away, I move to sit back on the canvas covering the ground, slippery with a mixture of blue and green and teal.

Rain gazes down at me, a concoction of fear and excitement present in his eyes.

"Come here, baby," I demand softly, a smile spread across my face as I lean back with my hands sliding through the paint below me. "Come slip my cock in your ass and ride me."

This time, I do see uncertainty cross his handsome face, but I do my best to give him all the reassurance I can with my eyes.

I love you.

Whatever he sees, he trusts, because he steps over me before kneeling down, straddling my torso.

Along with eating ass, I've never topped another guy from the bottom before either. Tonight is a night of firsts, it seems.

Then again, it's not every day you realize you're *in fucking love* with the most beautifully infuriating man you've ever met.

I lean back further on my forearms, the chill of the paint on my skin sending goosebumps across my skin. Rain grips my dick, still slick with his cum, and before I have time to think or breathe, he lets out a shaky breath and sinks down on my cock. He lets out a low hiss as he takes my entire length in him for only the second time. Using my abs to sit up, I run my hands across his chest, his arms, his stomach, leaving behind smears of color.

Fucking beautiful.

And so goddamn perfect.

After adjusting, Rain begins to move above me, fucking himself on my cock. Riding me like he was made to do just that.

Probably because he was.

My dick slides in and out of Rain's ass with ease, and I grip his hips in my hands and help him move up and down on me, enjoying every moment of being inside him.

"Just like that," Rain gasps, shifting his hips so my dick will scrape against that spot of pure bliss inside him.

He's so incredibly brave.

So strong.

I want him to love this, to take back his pleasure from that fucking cocksucker who stole his innocence.

But more importantly, I want him to *want* to love this.

Humans were built to find pleasure in sex, but for victims of assault, they question the ecstasy that comes with it. They can feel guilt over their enjoyment.

I don't want that for him anymore.

Because I love *fucking* him.

Almost as much as I fucking love *him.*

"More," he moans roughly as he continues to move on my shaft.

"Take what you need, Rain," I say breathlessly.

My hands continue to frantically drift over his body as I watch in awe as he uses me for his own pleasure. I trace the planes of his muscles, leaving streaks of blue, green, and teal in their wake across his skin. He seems to pick up on my goal to paint every available inch of him, so he joins in, sliding his hands through the paint below us before gripping my shoulders and sliding his palms down my arms.

Rain's knees start slipping, making it harder for him to keep a steady pace as he continues to work himself over my shaft, so I wrap my arm around his back, the other hand on his ass and quickly flip our positions.

Hovering over him, I trail my lips across his jaw as I thrust my hips into him with quick, smooth movements. He pants against my neck and sweat starts trickling down my back when his slick fingers work their way into my hair. Tugging at the strands, he pulls my mouth to his.

"Baby," I murmur in protest, thinking about where my mouth and tongue were not long ago.

"I don't fucking care," he growls before grabbing my face, coating teal paint all over my face, and crushing his lips to mine. His tongue is immediately probing my mouth to find mine, and I fucking love it. I kiss him fiercely, fucking him harder and faster as we slip and slide over the paint-covered canvas.

Soon, too soon, I can feel myself getting close.

I need him there with me.

Reaching between us, I grip his length and slide my fist in rapid strokes, using the paint as lubricant.

"Get there, Rain," I growl into his mouth before moving my mouth to his Adam's apple, licking it despite it being covered in paint.

Fuck it, it's non-toxic. I checked.

"I am," he groans, his hips bucking to meet my thrusts. "When you go, I'll go."

"Where do you want me to cum?" I pant, bringing my mouth back to his.

"Wherever you want, babe. One of the best things about art is the mess you get to make while creating it."

Goddamnit, I love him.

I smile against his lips, nipping the bottom one and giving it a soft tug with my teeth before pulling from his body. Gripping both our cocks in my hand, I jack our dicks together, coating them with paint and sweat. I finish first, spilling all over his paint-splattered stomach, his own release right behind mine.

Struggling to catch my breath, I reach down and rub my hand through the milky liquid, mixing our cum together with the paint across his abs.

Claiming him.

Mine.

Creating a fucking masterpiece.

Ours.

I might not always understand art, but I sure as hell feel it. It's messy and never perfect, but it's always beautiful in its own way. It's a visual representation of not only time and effort, but of passion. It's a way of putting a piece of your soul on display for others to see, and trusting them to find similarities in their interpretation. It's open to vulnerability, knowing not everyone will see it in the same light.

Just like the love I have for him.

And from the drawings in his sketchpad, I'm willing to bet the love he feels for me too.

A love like ours will never be perfect. Putting in the work won't always be easy. Sometimes we won't work quite right and others we will have to take a step back and try to see what the other sees. And there will be times when people think it's wrong. But I have no doubt it will always be intense and passionate.

A chaotic flurry of adoration and desire.

Yet as messy as this love is, it will always be beautiful.

Because it will always be *ours*.

THIRTY

River

DAY TWENTY-NINE

Paint sex is a lot of fucking fun.

And the aftermath, washing each other clean in the shower? Equally as enjoyable.

But what isn't a good time? Trying to clean off dried acrylic paint from hardwood floors.

What can I say? I don't always think my brilliant ideas through completely.

This was most definitely one of those times.

Even still, I don't think I've ever smiled as much as I have this morning, watching Rain scrub the floor, bitching and moaning under his breath about my asinine ideas, only to look up and catch me staring.

And then…he'd smile back.

Not a smirk, but a genuine fucking smile, and I think part of me died right there.

I want nothing more than to be the reason behind it, for as long as I can be.

Oh, and the canvas? It turned out really fucking cool, so I'd say it was well worth the cleanup hassle.

It's like I said before.

Art, like love, is messy.

THIRTY-ONE
Rain

DAY THIRTY-FOUR

We leave tomorrow.

And it's honestly the most sobering realization in the entire fucking world.

I think neither of us wants to leave. I *know* I don't want to.

Living here at this escape from the real world has been like our own little paradise. Once we got past the bullshit, that is. But we *do* have to leave, so we decide to make our final day here as just the two of us as memorable as possible.

The day started with eating breakfast on the porch, even if it was cold as shit. We didn't care, simply lit a fire in the pit on the deck and curled up in blankets together while devouring the best fucking breakfast burritos I've ever tasted. I swear, the thing I might miss most about waking up in a house with River is his breakfast skills.

Okay, that's not true. I'm also going to miss waking up with my cock in his mouth and the copious amounts of sex we've been having.

But after that, I'm going to miss the food the most. The guy's cooking rivals what I remember of my father's.

Then we spent a couple hours back in bed, to no one's surprise.

By that time, it was nearly lunch, so we packed some sandwiches, thermoses of hot chocolate, and blankets for a hike up to the lake overlook. The same one I painted and gave to River.

And it was perfect. Everything I could have asked for on our last day out here.

Now it's after dark and we're lying in the hammock River was desperate to set up for us, though it's not very comfortable with two six-foot-plus football players in it.

But I don't care. The second he said he wanted to look up at the stars, saying it was how he always liked to spend his last night in the mountains, I caved.

I always seem to be caving when it comes to him.

And then he said something, I swear to God, I'll remember until the day I die.

Staring up at the night sky, it's the best way to remember we are so much smaller than we make ourselves out to be.

And the second he shut off the exterior lights and I looked up, I understood. I felt it, deep in my core.

So here we are, curled up under a pile of blankets and a sleeping bag rated for thirty below because it's fucking *freezing*, in a hammock that might break any second from all the weight.

And I'm exactly where I'm supposed to be.

Which tells me I'm not ready to leave this place. Not now, when we've found some peace, both within ourselves and in each other. I couldn't tell you when it happened or why, but over the course of the past five weeks, River went from being my enemy to…my everything.

My friend, my lover.

The keeper of my secrets.

My saving grace.

And for the life of me, I don't want this to be over between us.

"You might be silent, but your thoughts are loud," he tells me after a while, his fingers playing with the strings of my sweatshirt, tapping them absently against my chest. "Wanna talk about whatever's eating you?"

Not particularly.

"I'm just thinking about tomorrow. Leaving," I say, which isn't exactly a lie.

"Don't think about it. Not when we still have tonight."

I know he's right. And I don't want to ruin what little time we have left here by being a pessimist about it.

We both knew our time was limited. Five weeks isn't a lifetime. It's finite.

So why am I wishing five weeks is the equivalent to forever?

"Tell me something true," he says, pulling me from my thoughts. "Something I don't know."

"I like you," I whisper immediately, and it doesn't feel wrong to admit that.

Quite the opposite, in fact. It feels *right*.

"I already know that." He laughs, glancing up at me. "I mean, what's not to like?"

Cocky as ever, this one.

"Nevermind, I take it back," I deadpan, which only makes him grin more.

"I like you too," he whispers, brushing a kiss against my lips before snagging my hand resting on my chest. "But that wasn't what I meant, and you know it."

I think on his request for a moment, rolling over the options in my mind. Because there are plenty. So much about myself that he doesn't know.

So much he will never find out.

Deciding on a safe route leading to the least amount of questions, I start to speak, "Back home, I went to this super uppity prep school called Foxcroft Hall. Right outside of Philly. It was filled with rich assholes I couldn't stand. I mean, some of the wealthiest families in the state sent their kids there. Kids of politicians, media moguls, all that."

River gives me a half smirk. "Is this an inadvertent way of telling me you're loaded and are going to be a sugar daddy one day?"

A laugh escapes me, and fuck, it feels good. I never realized before staying here with him that I didn't laugh nearly enough. "Is this an inadvertent way of asking to be my sugar baby?" The urge to smack myself immediately overwhelms me as words tumble out before I have the chance to think about what they imply.

River and I being together. *Really* together.

A future we both know we don't have, because this all ends tomorrow.

"I wouldn't say no. I'd make one helluva sugar baby." Thankfully, River doesn't press that any further, just snuggles closer to me and plays with our joined hands resting on my stomach.

When I remain silent, he switches back to the original topic. "It couldn't have been too bad. I'm sure you had friends. Your teammates, maybe?"

I smile and press a kiss to his hair. "I wasn't one to hang out with the popular crowd, though I most definitely was considered a popular kid as a jock. But I had a couple friends," I murmur, memories of my days in high school flooding to the front of my brain. My smile grows when I think of the two people who kept me sane while at that hellhole. One of which I recently saw for the first time in *years*. "I actually grew up with this set of twins. Fraternal, a boy and a girl."

"Siena and Roman?" he asks softly.

"Yeah," I whisper, clearing my throat. "They're a senator's kids, grew up in heavy politics. Extremely wealthy family that holds a lot of power and clout. They were a year ahead of me in school, but they were my lifeline during the years we were at Foxcroft together. Si, she's great, as you've seen. A real firecracker, always busting the balls of any guy who gave her shit. Including her brother and myself." I let out a chuckle and grin at him. "I honestly don't know how Taylor puts up with her."

River lets out a sigh and shrugs against me. "He loves her. And people will do really crazy shit for the person they love."

I nod. "That they do," I say, my voice suddenly hoarse with emotion. "That they do, Abhainn."

And I'm starting to understand that now. Little by little, I'm learning what it means to let someone in and trust them with the pieces of myself I don't particularly like.

I wouldn't do *that* for just anyone.

Tell him about Roman, a small part of my brain whispers. *Better yet. Tell him everything. And then maybe, just maybe, you can keep him.*

But deep down, I know I can't. I can't tell him.

I can't keep him.

Because why the fuck would anyone, especially someone as put together as River, want to be with someone who can't even slay their own demons?

Can't even hold a sword to them without help.

But you can give him this.

"And then Roman," I start, taking a deep breath to prepare myself for what I have to say, "he was more than a best friend to me. He could have been a brother. We were inseparable from the time we met."

"It sounds like you had two really great friends in your corner, then. Where is Roman now?"

"Out in Oregon somewhere. Going to school. Business, I think."

"You *think*?"

I shrug, trying not to let my answer eat at me. "We don't keep in touch anymore. I haven't seen or spoken to him in years."

River rolls slightly, leaning up on his elbow to look at me. It's dark, only the faint glow of a crescent moon lighting his features, but I see the confusion on his face. "How does someone go from being like your brother to almost nonexistent in your life?"

I let out a huff of air, creating a small cloud in the frigid air between us. His eyes, imploring as ever, ask for only honesty in what I'm willing to share, and it's astounding how he knows when to push me for more and when he needs to let me come to him.

Tell. Him.

Rubbing my hand over my face, I groan.

"Roman…is bisexual."

At those three words, River's brows lift in the darkness, but he doesn't say anything, just waits for me to continue. "I knew the minute he figured it out for himself. We told each other everything, as best friends do, and it didn't change anything for us. It was something we never really talked about past the one time.

"But then the night before he left for college, we got drunk as hell while we were taking a late night dip in his pool. More drunk than normal because neither of us were ready for him to move across the country to Oregon, but it wasn't to the point where we were gonna do anything too stupid or reckless like drown, ya know? Or at least…*I wasn't.*"

Memories of that night flood me. Roman's dark hazel eyes staring into my soul from across the pool, drunken and full of lust, I thought I was just imagining. Because we were best friends, brothers, but never anything more than that.

"Everything was chill, we were doing our thing like we always did, but then Roman…he swam over to me from across the pool and he just…kissed me. He grabbed the back of my neck and he kissed me and I…and I kissed him back…and I didn't hate it. I didn't hate that he was a guy, or he was my best friend or that it was *wrong*. I…" I sigh, searching River's eyes. "I kissed him back."

River nods his head, his eyes dropping to my mouth before coming back to meet my gaze. "So, if you didn't hate it, what stopped you from being friends?"

And if that isn't the question of the fucking century.

My mind plays that night back, the softness of Roman's lips

on mine, the whiskey on his tongue as it slid into my mouth to tangle with my own.

"I've wanted to do this for so long," he murmurs, his voice husky against my mouth as he continues to lick and suck at my bottom lip like it's his God given right.

My fingers twist in his damp hair, bringing his entire body tighter against mine. I feel his erection against my thigh, long and thick, only being contained by his swim trunks. And I feel mine too. Desperate to break free from its confines, aching to be touched. Stroked.

"What took you so long?" I ask, sliding my hand between us to palm his cock through his trunks. "Why wait until the night before you leave?"

Because for the past year of my life, my thoughts about my best friend have been anything but friendly. *Hell, maybe longer than that. I've fought them, pushed them into the back of my brain and continued down the path of least destruction to my mental sanity.*

The straight *path.*

How long has he wanted this?

"Because, Rain," he says, uttering the nickname he coined for me against my mouth. "I had to know the taste of your lips, if only this once. I had to see if you felt it too."

I do. I feel it too.

His free hand snakes down, slipping into my trunks to grip my cock, giving it a long, slow tug that has me almost coming on the spot.

"Because I'm selfish, Rain," he tells me, his lips moving down my neck as he sucks and bites at the skin there. He continues to stroke me, and it's surreal that it's actually happening and not a figment of my drunken imagination.

Because this is something I've wanted, thought of, for far too long too.

Roman's body presses me back against the edge of the pool, the tile biting into the skin of my back as he continues to jack my cock. "And I have to have you this one time, even if it's the only time I can."

"Rain?" River asks, his voice bringing me back to the present.

"Yeah?" I ask, shaking my head clear of the memory fog that consumed it.

"I asked what happened to make you stop being friends."

I nod, flicking my gaze past his head to the stars above us.

"He kissed me knowing he was leaving. Knowing he wouldn't ever be coming back. Knowing he could never give me..." I trail off, not knowing where my thoughts were leading me. Or rather, not wanting to go there. "He kissed me, fully knowing it would only confuse me more. And I hated him for that."

Part of me still does.

Because Doctor Fulton was right the day in therapy when she called me out, telling me I was infatuated with Roman.

Though I couldn't accept myself as anything other than *straight*, I was dancing around the idea of him and I for years. Of what it would be like to be together as more than *Roman and Rain, best friends.* But he never so much as hinted he wanted something more than that until that night in the pool.

And by then, it was too late. Our time had run out.

So I turned to hatred, if only to mask the hurt.

But what I felt for Roman? It doesn't hold a candle to the way River consumes me entirely.

"And so he left the next day, not looking back? And your friendship was just over?"

I nod. "Pretty much, yeah."

River licks his lips and nods. I watch the gears turn in his mind, thinking of all the questions he's dying to ask. The apprehension is written all over his face, the open book he is. "And was he the only guy you've kissed?"

I nod again, my hand coming up to cup the back of his head. "He was the last *person* I kissed until *you*."

He smiles, big and brighter than the moon. "So, what you're telling me is I'm special?"

I roll my eyes and laugh because he most definitely *stole* that kiss, but I'm not about to remind him. It's not a lie, though. "Yeah, Abhainn. You're special."

His nose crinkles in amusement as he leans in to place a soft kiss on my mouth, short and sweet and leaving me wanting more.

"Is this your way of telling me because I kissed you, you're gonna ignore me again starting tomorrow?" he utters against my jaw. I hear the way he's trying to play it off in a joke, but it's not working.

I know him better than that, I can see past the jokester exterior to see the vulnerability.

"Never," I reply, fingers curling into the hair at the back of his head. "I just wanted you to know."

"Good, I'm glad. I don't want to lose you when we go back to school. When we leave this place," he whispers into my throat before kissing my Adam's apple. "I know it won't be like it is here, and I understand why. But I can't go back to enemies either."

"We won't," I say, swallowing gravel as the words come out. "I don't want to lose you either. Not when I know what it's like to have you."

River leans back and looks into my eyes, his own full of so

many emotions it would take me a thousand years to name them all. "You have me. *You will always have me.* Until every star in the night sky burns out. And maybe even then."

I smile sadly at him, knowing he means those words right now. Knowing *always* coincides with *forever* in his vocabulary. And he's anything but a liar.

But we live in a reality where lies spill from our lips disguised as the truth with our knowledge or not. "You don't need to say that, Abhainn. Not when we both know life is full of broken promises never meant to be kept."

"What do you mean?"

His fingers grip mine tighter, as if to ground himself to me. As if he knows the words about to leave my lips will be harder to hear than any insult I ever threw his way. "You'll meet someone. Someone who makes your heart pound in your chest, and whether it's a guy or a girl, if they're the right one for you, they won't force you to be someone you aren't. They won't attempt to shove you back into the closet. And when that happens, this will all become a distant memory." Rubbing my thumb against the backs of his knuckles softly, I sigh. "A happy one, I hope. But a memory nonetheless."

I can tell from his silence he's taking my words and letting them run rampant in his mind, trying to decode them and find hidden meaning where there is none.

"Hey," I whisper, catching his chin in my hand, his rough stubble scraping against my fingers, "I'm not saying that as a bad thing. We both know what we signed up for with this. It's run its course, but that's okay. Being stuck here with you has been the most enjoyable five weeks of misery I've ever had."

And if that ain't the irony of it all.

I thought coming to this cabin with River, being forced into cohabitating with him would be my own personal hell. And for a while, it was. But the day I thought he left me here, when I couldn't find him for hours, it was more than fear that clawed at my skin. The panic that set in also ground something into my soul when it came to him. And whatever the hell it was, it changed me, even if I didn't realize it at the time.

"Are you tired?" he whispers, craning his neck to look up at me with those eyes that twist my heart into knots every time I stare into their depths.

"No," I murmur. "Are you?"

He shakes his head before leaning up, searching for my mouth. "Do you want to go to bed?" he asks, his lips brushing faintly across my own.

I nod, wanting the chance to be with him one last time before this is over for good.

We move quickly to the bedroom, removing each other's clothing with lightning speed along the way. I don't know who ends up on the bed first or who is in charge right now. All I know is our bodies tangle together on the bed in frenzied passion while we touch and lick and bite at each other, desperate for time to slow down so this moment never has to end.

"What do you want, Riv?" I pant against his mouth, stroking his cock while his hand travels a lazy path down my chest.

"I want you inside me," he utters, his eyes lifting to mine. "I need it."

I bite my lip and smirk, not about to argue even though...I'd be lying if I said I wasn't hoping he wanted to take the lead tonight.

Something I never would have thought I'd desire even a few short weeks ago when we started sleeping together.

I don't waste time after that though, lubing my cock before sliding into him bare.

It's the best feeling I've ever experienced, being inside him with no barrier separating us. I became addicted to it that first morning in the shower, desperate for more of it. I don't know how I managed to ever hold out as long as I did.

Part of me hates myself for it. Knowing there could have been the extra days of this with him if I hadn't been such an asshat.

Sliding in and out slowly, I shift his hips to get the best angle to hit him deep. Thrust after long, leisurely thrust has River squirming beneath me, frantic for me to pick up my pace. I can see it in his eyes, his body language.

But I can't bring myself to do it. That will only make it end sooner when all I want is to stay buried inside him for the rest of my life.

Because this isn't just sex anymore. It's not the pure, unfiltered lust it was a few weeks ago.

No, what we're doing right now is nothing short of melding our bodies together at a slow, torturous simmer. Worshipping and adoring every single inch of each other in every way possible.

With lips. Tongues. Hands.

As our bodies move together, fused as close as humanly possible, we're also laying out the cards on the table for the other to see.

The vulnerability. The pain. The passion. The fear.

The love.

Rolling my hips, hitting the spot inside him that drives him mad with desire, I pull back to look down at him. His eyes are closed, lips parted slightly as soft pants slip through them with each thrust I make.

"Look at me, Abhainn," I whisper fiercely, my hand moving to cup the side of his face.

When his eyes open, they reveal the deepest shade of teal I've ever seen.

"Give me it all. Fucking everything."

And he does.

Grabbing my head with both hands, he pulls me down over him, his tongue lashing at mine inside my mouth before I can think. Melding with mine like it was created for that sole purpose.

We're a mess of tongues and teeth and sweat and love when we're both close to finishing. And when I stroke him through his climax, the way his ass clenches around my cock has me following right behind, spilling deep inside him.

I glance down at him, my chest heaving with effort as he wipes the glossy sheen of sweat on his forehead.

Fuck me, he's so goddamn sexy.

Sensual and perfect.

And he's mine.

My brain screeches to a halt at the thought.

No, he's not mine.

Not really. That's not part of our agreement.

Because it would never work out between us.

The pieces of who we are as people don't fit. It's more than a square peg and a round hole. Everything about who we are as people doesn't work. We're opposites in all ways that matter when it comes to forming lasting relationships.

The most important being he knows *how* to form them.

And me…?

I've never had anyone who wanted to stay long enough to try to make one.

Pulling from his body, I kiss him harshly before grabbing his hand and leading him to the shower, where I proceed to clean every inch of him.

Not with just the water, but with my lips and tongue.

Once we're clean, I drag him back into his bed, the bed we've made *ours* since the first night I slipped inside it to hide from my nightmares in the safety of his presence.

How the fuck I'm going to live without that again, I'm not sure.

River curls into my side, our legs tangled together beneath the sheets and soon enough, his breathing evens out into deep steady breaths. A sign sleep has overtaken him.

But I just lie here, not tired in the least.

How can I be when every second I spend asleep tonight is one less I'll have awake with him?

My want, my need for him, it's consumed all I am.

It has from the very moment he pulled me to the edge of the cliff and forced me over into a free-fall I never wanted to take. Even though it was the very thing I needed.

The thought brings me back to the last therapy session I had with Doctor Fulton. The words she spoke to me that set me off in a fiery rage.

He has this way of making you *lose the control of* yourself *that you're so desperate to cling to. And I think it could be good for you. I think you* need *it.*

He didn't just make me lose control, though.

He gave me new experiences, new insights. He showed me what it was like to have someone accept you for who you are without trying to change you.

He gave me every piece of himself and asked for nothing in return.

And she was fucking right.

I needed it.

Him.

Glancing down at his sleeping form, the way his hair flops down on his forehead, I feel it. For the first time in my life, I feel what it's like to need someone and to accept it isn't necessarily a bad thing.

Not when they have so much to teach you about yourself. About life.

About love.

That word, four little letters packed with a large meaning, rolls around in my brain. I'd be lying if I said it hasn't been for a while now. Ever since the night I told him about my stepfather, it's been in the back of my head.

And when it comes to River, that little word takes on a whole new meaning.

"Tá mé i ngrá leat, Abhainn," I murmur into his ear before gently kissing his temple.

They are words I had heard my father speak to my mother on countless occasions while he was still alive. Never in my life did I think I'd be saying them to anyone, let alone the guy who became my sworn enemy. But I took the easy way out, speaking them in my father's native tongue.

Even if he is awake, he won't know what I've said. What I've just declared.

But I do.

I am.

And I have no fucking clue what to do now that I've undoubtedly realized it.

I'm in love with him.

THIRTY-TWO
River

DAY THIRTY-FIVE

"**K**nock, knock. You boys still alive?" I hear Coach Scott call from my bedroom, where I'm triple-checking the space to make sure I'm not forgetting anything before we leave.

Fuck, I can't believe we're actually leaving this place after five weeks. Even more, I can't believe I don't *want* to leave.

Returning to our lives, to school, only signifies the end of this thing between Rain and me. At least, the end of how things are while we've been here.

And I don't want that. If I had my way, things would stay exactly the same once we are back to civilization. We'd kiss and hold hands in public, like we did at the resort in Vail. Lay in bed naked, talking about anything and everything under the sun, or I'd watch him paint while reading whatever captures my interest in that moment.

We'd be *together*, no timeline as to when we have to quit each other or to know when we've run our course.

No expiration date.

Scrubbing my hand over my face, I huff out a sigh.

How the hell did we end up here?

Backpack slung over my shoulder and duffle in hand, I pause in the doorway to give the room one last farewell glance. From behind me, I hear Coach call out again.

"Lennox? Grady? You two here?"

"Coming, Coach," I shout back, closing the bedroom door behind me. My head instinctively turns toward Rain's room, finding it open. It's still surprising to see because, even after the paint sex fiasco, he was hesitant to let me into his space.

Into his mind, and dare I say, his heart.

Just as I'm about to turn away, Rain appears through the doorway, gathering the few cases of his artwork and paints together on his desk. Heat rushes through me at the sight of him, dressed in a hoodie and pair of dark gray sweats.

Why do I have to feel this way?

I take a step toward his door with every intention of grabbing some of his supplies to carry out to the truck, but the squeak of my weight on the floorboards gives me away. His head snaps up, landing directly on me.

Stepping into his doorway, I give him a small smile. "Need some help?"

A mischievous smirk graces his face. "Abso-fucking-lutely."

But when I go to sling my duffle over my shoulder to free my hands, Rain tugs it from my hands and presses me into the wall with his entire body. His lips descend on mine in a searing kiss, devouring them as if he thinks kissing with this much passion and intensity will allow him to reach into my chest and claim my heart as his.

Little does he know, he already has.

The words, those three fucking words, eight letters long, sit on my tongue, begging to slip free. I've never said them in my life to anyone who isn't a blood relative, mostly because I've never felt them until Rain.

Before Rain, love was just a word to me. A theory without meaning, speaking of hearts and flowers and the simplicity of looking into the eyes of another person and feeling that spark.

But after Rain? My theory is decimated entirely.

Being in love is a daily battle, not only fighting for the other person, but for yourself. It's finding the common ground, the parts of your souls that speak to each other, strengthening them in ways no one else's ever could. It's knowing your worth and not only telling the other person you won't accept anything less than what you deserve, but trusting them to provide that for you.

It's giving the darkest parts of yourself to another human, saying *this is who I am in all my fucked up glory,* and not asking them to fix you, but to give you what you need to mend yourself.

Loving Rain, while it's been the challenge of a lifetime, it's also becoming addictive. Seeing, holding, owning the parts of himself he doesn't grant access to the rest of the world. It's an all-consuming high that feeds the deepest parts of my soul. A high, while I know I can survive without it, I don't fucking *want* to.

Then again, that would be the basis of addiction, right?

But even still, I swallow the words that would ruin absolutely everything that's transpired between us these last few weeks.

Because they would. Especially if he didn't return them.

Doesn't mean I don't find myself ready to shout them from the rooftops if I thought they'd make a difference in what happens after today. If we could make this — *us* — real.

"Can we stay here forever? I can't stand the thought of leaving," I groan against his mouth before nipping at his bottom lip, sucking it into my mouth.

A husky chuckle slips from deep within his chest as his tongue moves with mine. "Me either, babe. But we can't always get what we want." He bites and nibbles and sucks at my mouth to the point I'm certain my lips are swollen and bruised, but I don't care.

The second we move from this spot, the moment we break this connection, it's over. Only, neither of us has the power to stop.

Finally, yet all too soon, Rain wrenches his mouth from mine, leaving us both panting and breathless, only to plant one soft, final kiss to my lips.

"Let's go, Abhainn. Before Coach comes back here to find two of his football players balls deep inside each other."

Reluctantly, I back away from him, throwing my strap over my shoulder before snatching a few of Rain's art boxes away from him. He laughs and pats my ass, giving it a slight squeeze before the release, then grabs what is remaining and follows me out to the living room.

Coach is sitting at the kitchen island, coffee in hand, when we come walking into the open common space. His eyes snap to the crates in my hands, then over my shoulder at Rain who is directly behind me.

"Well? Did it do you two any good to be out here? Or did you lose your minds?"

Glancing over my shoulder at Rain, I give him a shit-eating grin, knowing the comment was one thousand percent aimed at him. "Did you lose your mind, Ciaráin Grady?"

He gives me a smirk before answering Coach, all the while holding my gaze.

"Sure did, Coach. I lost my mind and found my soul."

Dropping to my bed, which I haven't seen in over a month, I let out a low groan as my face burrows into the dark green comforter. As weird as it is to be back here and as much as I didn't want to leave the cabin, I have to admit it will be nice to sleep in my own bed again.

The drive back to Boulder was uneventful, despite the tension that filled the truck for most of the ride. Thankfully, Coach didn't comment on our silence, just took it in stride by turning up the radio, bopping his hands on the steering wheel to whatever country song was playing at the time.

Rolling to my back, I stare at the ceiling, replaying the last twenty-four hours in my mind, unable to halt the thoughts racing through my head.

Will last night be the last time? Will this morning be our last kiss?

As much as I hate to admit, they both felt like he was saying goodbye. In all honesty, it would probably be for the best if we quit this cold turkey and went back to hating each other. It might hurt less, at the end of the day.

But his words play on a repetitive loop in my brain.

You'll meet someone. Someone who makes your heart pound in your chest, and whether it's a guy or a girl, if they're the right one for you, they won't force you to be someone you aren't.

I know those words were meant as a reassurance, a confirmation he and I aren't endgame. He doesn't think he can be that person for me, and I commend him for being honest about how he feels. It's not something that comes easy to him.

But it's also a load of bullshit.

To my core, I feel it. My gut, my instincts, they're all pointing straight at him, like a beacon in the night, screaming *this is it. This is the one you're meant to keep.*

If he'd fucking let me.

Because I'm painfully aware my entire fucking world now revolves around Ciaráin Grady and the *someone* he speaks of is a fucking crock of shit.

I don't want *someone.* I want *him.*

And hell if I'm willing to sit here and even contemplate the idea of him being with someone else too.

A twinge pricks in the back of my mind when thoughts of Roman start stewing in my brain. The only other man Rain admitted to having an attraction toward.

Don't get me wrong, I'm not so self-important to think I'm the only man Rain has felt something for. That would be completely insane. Even if he was unaware of his sexuality, the straightest of arrows can admit another human of the same gender is attractive.

Still, Rain willingly revealing his past is groundbreaking, and the nosy, competitive part of me is dying to know more about the guy who caught his eye.

I fight the idea for an entire half-second before snatching my phone from the nightstand and pulling up my Facebook app.

Yep, I've resorted to cyber stalking. Fan-fucking-tastic.

It doesn't take long for me to dig up Rain's profile, which seems to be inactive for the most part, as his last post was before he even left Clemson to come to Colorado. Seeing as his privacy settings are basically non-existent, I'm able to scroll through his friends list until I stumble across one Roman *Mitchell*.

Strange. For some reason, I thought his last name would be Anders.

No, not *some reason.*

He's the son of a Pennsylvania Senator, according to Rain, and I'd have to live under a fucking rock to not know about *Pennsylvania Senator* Ted Anders and all the fucked-up allegations against him, that have been making the national news. Put two and two together, and I thought it would be him. Especially with how tense Rain got seeing the newscast while we were at the resort in Vail.

It would make a lot of sense for him to have such an adverse reaction to seeing the clip if his two best friends for most of his life had a molester for a father. Especially when Rain himself was a victim of sexual abuse as a kid.

Even still, Roman could have a different last name than his father, so it's not ruled out entirely.

Clicking on the profile, I'm once again in luck his profile is also public. Or, at least public enough to be able to click through his photo albums. Starting with profile photos, I'm annoyed the instant I pull it up, noting…of course he's really attractive.

Not my type at all, seeing as he's dressed in a well-tailored suit, leaning against a fucking matte *maroon* Lambroghini Aventador like the rich prick he is.

Okay, I might be harnessing my inner Judgy Judgerson right now, but it's not out of jealousy of his wealth or connection to Rain. I mean, come the fuck on. Your half a million dollar car in your profile photo? Are you trying to compensate for something, Roman?

See? Not jealous at all.

I quickly flip through the photos from the past four years, ones either of him alone or with the same group of four other guys. They're all good-looking, but again, all dressed in suits or expensive as fuck clothing with their fancy cars. One of them even looks a little like my friend Asher.

Overall, none of the images are of interest to me since he and Roman haven't spoken since Roman left for college in Portland, or at least somewhere close to there.

Wait.

My brain screeches to a halt.

Portland.

That night at the hotel in Portland comes rushing back. Jerking myself to images of him in the shower. Coming out to find him hard as a rock. One of my *many* proposals to get my mouth on that gorgeous cock of his.

But then…the sudden text message he received and his almost immediate departure from the room after.

He didn't come back for hours, keeping me up half the night worried out of my fucking mind that something had happened. And when he did finally stumble back into the room well after last call, he was drunk off his ass and completely sex-mussed.

At the time, I thought he hooked up with some random chick. But now…

Did he see Roman that night?

Unease bites at my stomach, causing it to roll, but I push it down.

No. Rain wouldn't lie to me when he said he hadn't seen Roman in years. He wouldn't lie to me anymore.

Shaking the thoughts running rampant through my overactive mind, I start looking through albums that are a bit older. High school aged ones. Ones I might find more insight into his relationship with Rain from.

Still, for a while, I find nothing except tons of photos of Roman and Siena.

Just as I'm starting to get discouraged, I find one.

I almost flip past it because it's a photo of a photo, and he's only tagged in it. It's some sort of magazine photo. In it, I see Roman. Dressed in a suit, *because of fucking course,* with his arms wrapped around a man who looks *very* much the older version of Roman. Same brown hair, just cropped closer to his head, and same dark greenish-hazel colored eyes. He must clearly be Roman's father. But here's the thing.

He's not Ted Anders.

Okay…so Roman isn't the son of that fucking rapist. Good to know. Guess I have that piece of the puzzle figured out.

But then, when I arrow over for the next photo, all the puzzle pieces start snapping into place like magic.

Because in the image, another photo of a photo, has four men in it. From left to right is Roman's father and then Roman himself. And beside Roman, it's him.

Rain.

Younger Rain, that is. But it's still Rain in, you guessed it, a suit.

I've seen Rain in a suit countless times, but I can tell this one is easily worth thousands of dollars more in comparison. And fuck, he looks sexy, even as teenager, probably about sixteen.

But the fourth man...the sight of him shoots ice through my veins.

Ted fucking Anders.

I feel my blood pressure rise as I take in the four of them, Roman and Rain between the two older men. If I didn't know Roman was next to his father, I'd think the two of them just happened upon the two Pennsylvania Senators at the same charity gala or whatthefuckever event function they were at.

But that *is* Roman's father.

So that begs the question...why are they taking a photo with Ted and not only the three of them? Why would Roman's father be introducing them to the other Senator, as if they would care who he is at sixteen years old?

And why the fuck is Ted fucking Anders slinging his arm over Rain's shoulder like it's his God given right?

My eyes scan the photo over and over again, searching for some kind of clue as to what the hell is going on inside of it, but I come up short. The photo itself is more grainy than the first of just Roman and his dad, and when I zoom in to check the caption, it's a blurred, pixelated mess. Looking at Facebook caption, I see it's a photo from an annual charity gala in Philadelphia.

Doing fast math in my head, I pull up Google and type in the name of the gala along with the estimated year and then Ted

Anders, hoping like hell to find a digital version of the magazine the image from Facebook was on.

And luck is on my side, because halfway down the page, I find the image again.

But my luck runs out when the caption stares me straight in the face.

Nausea rolls over me as I reread it ten, twenty, eighty fucking times, hoping to find a different result.

But it's still there in black and white.

Pulling up a new tab, I simply Google search *Ted Anders* and instantly news articles and video clips of broadcasts pop up in reference to his recent legal troubles. Thumbing over a video, I click play and listen to a broadcast from only a few hours ago.

I listen intently to the anchorwoman as she goes over every aspect of the case the FBI has released to the public, doing my very best not to lose my breakfast at the graphic picture she's depicting. Covering my mouth with my hand, I fight the overwhelming nausea.

Praying this is some kind of mistake.

But in my gut, I know.

This is really happening.

Oh, my fucking God.

THIRTY-THREE
Rain

Being back in Boulder means things are going back to normal. Well, at least as normal as they can be, now that River and I are…hell. I don't know.

I don't know where things between us stand. I don't know where I want them to go. I don't know if what I'm feeling for him is actually love, the real fucking thing, or something my mind has latched on to in some weird Stockholm syndrome type deal from being thrown together for over a month with no one else around.

I just don't know.

That's why my ass is walking into the waiting room to Dr. Fulton's office not more than an hour after Coach dropped me off at my apartment. This appointment was already set before I left for the cabin, but for the first time, I'm extremely glad to come in and have her help me unpack the shit that plagues my mind.

I walk up to the receptionist, Joan, to check in like normal, and her eyes snap up to me and widen before she scrambles out of her seat.

"Ciaráin, you're here. Perfect," she says quickly, "Doctor Fulton had a cancellation before you, so you're free to go back right away. I'll let her know you're on your way." Her tone is filled with anxiety and unease as she glances around the waiting room to the other patients waiting to see their own psychiatrist or therapist. No one seems to be paying us any attention, but her agitated state sets me on edge.

What the hell?

"Thanks, Joan," I remark, slipping through the door to the hallway holding each individual office. Nothing seems out of place, save for Joan's apprehension of…what, I'm not sure.

Stopping outside Doctor Fulton's door, I knock twice before twisting the handle and letting myself in. She's sitting in the same chair she always is when I come for my appointments, and when her head snaps up, she gives me the same warm and welcoming smile as always. The one that lets me know I can trust her.

And for some reason, as foolish as it might be, I do.

"Ciaráin, hi. Why don't you get seated so we can start right away?" she says in greeting. I fold myself onto the couch across from her, resting my arms on my knees and looking at her. She seems to be acting normal, unlike Joan, but it's the words that come next that set me on edge. "I'm so glad you decided to come in today with everything going on."

Immediately, I tense, my mind flying to everything that happened up in the cabin with River. *How does she know?*

"What do you mean?"

"Everything with your stepfather."

I roll my eyes, partially at the fact that she's bringing up my stepfather, but mostly at myself and my paranoia. Of course she was talking about him, not me and River. "What has he done now? Last I heard, they can't find a way to put him away for anything yet."

She gives me a puzzled look. "Have you not been keeping up with the news while you were on your trip?"

Nope, no news here. Just lots of very *dirty sex with my* very *male quarterback.*

I let out a dry laugh. "I was trapped in a cabin in the mountains for five weeks with the only form of television coming from Netflix and Hulu. Safe to say the nightly news wasn't on my list of activities."

Doctor Fulton visibly pales and she goes rigid in her seat, and instantly I know something is really fucking wrong. The way she's looking at me right now, the way Joan acted in the waiting area.

What have you done now, you bastard?

"Tell me," I demand, my fists clenching tight enough I feel my nails digging into my palms. She winces slightly at my tone, then meets my eyes, hers filled with understanding and maybe even fear. "Doctor Fulton—" I start again.

"Please, Ciaráin, call me Erica," she cuts me off, rising and grabbing the laptop from her desk. "Our relationship is about to become a lot less professional once I show you this." Returning to her seat, she opens it and starts typing.

What in the ever loving…?

Jesus, did he go and get himself killed? She should know from my file that his death would be the least of my concern and there's no way in hell I'll ever be caught mourning his depraved ass in my life.

So what could it be?

Not until she hands the laptop over to me, showing me a video news clip from a few hours ago of a woman anchor, the same I've seen covering my stepfather a thousand times, sitting at a news desk. Swallowing hard, I glimpse at the headline before hitting play and see…*my name.*

Oh. My. Fucking. God.

"New information has been brought to light in regards to the ongoing investigation into Senator Theodore Anders' child molestation allegations. It's been revealed by a credible source in contact with the FBI that the child in question, Ciaráin Patrick Grady, now age twenty-one, is none other than the stepson of the senator himself.

"Ciaráin's testimony against the horrid and appalling acts Senator Anders forced upon him for five years, starting at the age of nine, while not suitable to share on air, have strengthened the FBI's case against Anders. The recordings provided enough evidence for an arrest warrant, allowing Anders to be brought into custody for questioning. According to a spokesperson for the Bureau, the senator was formally accused with a third degree statutory rape charge, which can carry a prison sentence of up to seven years and up fifteen thousand dollars in fines, along with other minor charges. Anders' bail was set at one million dollars, which was posted, and he was released less than forty-eight hours later.

"In regards to the stepson, Ciaráin Grady has not been seen or heard from in over a month. He was last seen at his college campus in Boulder, Colorado on the eighth of December. There is cause for speculation amongst the Bureau that the circumstances behind his disappearance could

potentially be related to the charges brought against Senator Anders, stating kidnapping, foul play, or aggravated assault are not out of the question."

There's still easily another minute of the news clip, but my mind is spinning faster than a fucking tilt-a-whirl, so I snap the laptop shut. Not meeting her eyes, I hand back the device to Dr. Fulton.

"Ciaráin—" she starts after a drawn out silence, but I fucking snap.

"Who do you work for?"

She pauses, brows furrowing. "Excuse me?"

"You fucking heard me," I seethe, pushing off my knees into a standing position. My feet drag my body back and forth across the length of her office. "Who the fuck do you work for? I know it's my mother who pays you, so what? Do you feed all the information I've given you back to her and Senator *Ted fucking Anders?* Help them build a case against me, calling me mentally unstable or whatever else bullshit they'll try to use to sway a jury in his favor."

She winces at my words. "No, I can promise you I am not under your stepfather's employment. He has no idea you're even seeing another therapist. Your mother made sure of that." Erica's blue eyes rise to meet my manic ones, sorrow circling in them. "I work for your mother and *only* your mother."

My brows furrow. "What does that even *mean?*"

Sighing, she brushes back her hair, tucking it neatly behind her ear. As if it were even out of place in the first place. "It means you aren't completely off-base when you asked if I was relaying our sessions back to your mother. I absolutely am."

At those words, I see red. I'm in her face, my nose an inch from hers, when I spit the words out at her, "And you expect me to believe she didn't tell Ted *every. Goddamn. Word?* Are you fucking stupid?"

"No, she wouldn't—"

I let out a harsh laugh. "Of *course* she would. Or don't you know? I *told her* what he did to me. When I was *thirteen years old*, I told her how he would bend me over and shove his cock so far up my ass I thought it might rupture my spleen. I told her he would force me to my knees and stick his dick down my throat, making me choke on it until he came."

Stepping back, I scoff at the broken look on her face. She doesn't get to be broken, not when I'm the one who went through hell. Continuing through clenched teeth, I hiss the words out, "So I went to someone else, someone I thought I could trust. And told my story. All of it. How he would hurt me. Abuse me. Fucking *rape* me when she was sleeping right down the hall. How she refused to listen, to do anything about it."

Tears start streaming down her face, and bile rises in my throat. Fuck her.

"But then? When I thought I could trust that person, the one I spilled my damn guts to for years? I found out the piece of shit turned around and betrayed me. Every single word, every emotion, every inner thought I shared was recorded and taken back to my mother and Ted. They knew *everything* I had to say."

And it's true. Every fucking word I told my therapist was never kept private like it should have been. They never should have been recorded in the first place, but Ted has friends in high places.

Apparently high enough to bribe a fucking doctor who took a Hippocratic *oath* to break it for a sweet payout.

"And now? Those goddamn tapes have been leaked to the FBI. Hell, probably to the media too. Every word I said in private, every private thought and every *intimate detail* of what he did to me are all out there for the fucking *world* to hear. So, now when I walk onto the football field or into class or the grocery store, they'll see me. Recognize me as the kid who was raped and abused by his high-powered stepfather. And their reaction? It'll be disgust or fucking pity. And I don't have it in me to unpack which of those would be worse."

Honestly, I could handle the disgust. It's pity I can't stand. The look in their eyes that says *I'm so sorry* or *that poor guy* when all I fucking want is to move on, to find myself, to become something, *anything*, other than what Ted is.

But I am a product of my environment. I've proven as much.

"And the *worst* part of it all?" I shake my head, the irony knocking me on my ass. "The worst part is I'm just fucking like him. I took from someone what wasn't mine to take. I forced myself on someone who didn't deserve my anger and resentment simply because he was secure in who he is as a person. The only difference is instead of using and abusing him like he was a worthless piece of trash before shutting him up with a nice pay out for the *liability*, I fucking fell in love with him."

I fell in love with River in that cabin. It was never supposed to happen. Or maybe it was, and I was too blind or stupid or arrogant to see the immediate chemistry I felt with him was life slapping me in the face saying *get your head out of your ass, Rain. We made this one just for you.*

And he is. Made for me, that is.

I'm not certain of anything else in my life at the moment except for that. River Lennox was put on this Earth to be *mine* and mine alone. Once this shit with Ted is all sorted out, I'm going to make sure he damn well knows it.

"Listen to me, Ciaráin," Doctor Fulton breaks through my tangent. "You mother has no intention of letting your stepfather know about the things we have discussed. She was only hoping to get more insight seeing as..." She trails off, her throat visibly straining to swallow. "He is still doing it."

Ice licks at my flesh. *"What?"*

"Your mother. She...she walked in on the act. He had brought home another boy. A mere child. From her words, he couldn't have been more than thirteen. The same age as you when..."

She doesn't finish her thought. She doesn't need to, though. I know where it was going.

The same age I was when I tried to tell her what he was doing to me.

"So all those months ago, when everything started surfacing..."

"That was your mother's doing, Ciaráin. Well, partially." Doctor Fulton lets out a long sigh, rubbing her temple while I stand frozen in place, gaping at her.

I bite my tongue because *Jesus Christ,* I want to bite her head off some more, fully knowing it won't get me anywhere. "Start from the beginning. Leave nothing out," I demand, once I manage to reign in my temper...slightly.

Licking her lips twice, she inhales sharply before meeting my penetrating gaze. "A few months ago, when the news first got wind of a scandal with Ted, it wasn't because of the tapes." My brows shoot up in surprise, fingers gripping the back of the chair before me painfully hard. "There was an investigation into your old therapist. For bribery, breaking her Hippocratic oath, they were even looking into racketeering. When the FBI raided her office in search of information on someone they thought to be part of a drug and sex-trafficking ring, they confiscated all of her files. Including yours.

"Of course, you and I both know what the folder contains. More than enough to build a plausible case against Ted. The only thing they were missing were…"

"The tapes," I finish for her, remembering the day Ted had shown them to me in his office, locked in the safe while my mother stood idly by. Not doing a damn thing.

She nods. "Your file references them often enough that the FBI knew they were missing a key piece of the puzzle. But the issue was, they combed the office for *days* in search, thinking Ted was somehow involved in the ring they originally were trying to take down."

My head shakes of its own accord, disbelief flowing through me. "Okay, but that was months ago. Why is shit hitting the fan right now?"

"Because of those tapes. The FBI never actually had them until recently, only alluding to their importance to the case. It's why they hadn't given your name to the public, they weren't sure what evidence they contained against Ted, only that they could be the nail in his coffin. I don't know why they went that route, letting the public think they were in evidence, but I can guess it was to get whoever had them a reason to turn them over.

"All I know is your mother, she listened to them, once your file was taken in as evidence. All of them. When she found Ted in that…*precarious*…position with that boy, she couldn't turn a blind eye any longer. And so she turned them into the FBI. She realized she was wrong not to listen to you all those years ago when you came to her, speaking your truth, only to ignore it entirely."

My stomach flips when the realization hits me like a freight train.

All of this mess, me having to leave Clemson, the FBI, the arrest and trial, the newscasts…it's all because my mother, my fucking *mother* decided to finally be something other than a society slut hopped up on pills.

No, no, no.

Fuck, Mom, why did you have to get involved now? *Why couldn't you be a goddamn parent years ago when I needed one and told you what was happening with your husband directly under your roof?*

Why couldn't you love me more than your money and vices and take me at my word?

And why the fuck does my *therapist have such insight into the behaviors of my mother?*

I give her a hard stare. "Who *are* you? You speak about her as if you know her."

A grimace mars Erica's face. "Your mother and I…? We knew each other. Quite well at one point in our lives, until she married Ted, and I moved out here. When she found out you were coming to Colorado, she contacted me. Begged me to help you out, if only to give you someone to talk to once she heard your own voice recounting all the things he did to you on those tapes." She pauses, taking a deep breath. "Once she sent the tapes into the FBI, she called me and told me everything. She wanted to be sure you were okay, but no one had heard from you. The media doesn't know this, but Ted is missing. He fled Pennsylvania, maybe even the country. We don't know where he is."

My brain gets stuck on those last words. *We don't know where he is.*

Which means, he could be anywhere.

He could be *here.*

I clamp my hands behind my head and focus on inhaling deep, steady breaths like my first therapist taught me when panic starts to set in.

And that's what I'm doing. Full-blown fucking panicking.

The good doctor must notice my agitation rising again, because she watches me carefully as I work through my self-soothing methods. "That's it, Ciaráin," Doctor Fulton praises from her seat. "Keep breathing."

Her words are knives being driven through my eardrums, so I tell her just fucking that, all the while counting back from one hundred in my head.

Three times.

And I'm still not calm.

Five more minutes later and I'm *still* not.

My mind is running in circles, question after question forming before I can even think about how to answer the first.

Where is Ted? What is his next move? Is he going to out me for that night he erased from history like he threatened before I left for college? Does he plan to eliminate me entirely?

Does he know about River?

Fuck, River.

My brain latches onto thoughts of him again, using them as an anchor to hold me steady, keep me grounded.

His aqua eyes and chocolate hair. A sleepy smile, the kind he only gives me first thing in the morning when he wakes up. The weird musical tapping fixation of his I've grown to love, even pray to see at least once on the daily so I can ask him what song is in his brain.

Over the past few weeks, I've learned I can deduce his thoughts from them like a fun sort of detective game. Because they always give away more than the words he says aloud, and it's those thoughts I crave more than his body.

That's a lie. I crave everything about him.

His laugh, his smile. His steady heartbeat under my ear. His lightness seeps into my black soul, giving it life — *purpose* — for the first time in forever.

He's the calm in the storm.

And I fucking *need* him. I won't let Ted ruin the best thing to ever happen to me.

And Ted *can't* know about him. There's no way. We were stranded in that goddamn cabin away from the world for five weeks. The entire world thinks I'm *dead* for fuck's sake. Or kidnapped or whatever.

So he can't know about River. There's no way. It's impossible.

Except I know the power and reach Ted has. When he wants something, he gets it.

Ted wants to rape and molest his underage stepson? Done.

Ted wants to cover up someone's murder and use it as leverage? Easy peasy.

Ted wants to find something to use against me so this shitstorm blows over? You can bet your ass he will find it. Extort it. Grind it to dust in his efforts to get every inch of an advantage he can before tossing it to the wayside, labeling it as collateral.

And if he found out about River. About the power River holds over me, the lengths I would go to keep him safe?

River would become the perfect bargaining chip to get whatever he wants from me. Only I can't trust River would make it out of any scenario with Ted alive and well. Not in this case.

That alone tells me what I fear most.

In order to keep River safe, I have to let him go. I have to break off this…thing between us, whatever it is. Honestly, I don't know how to classify it anymore. What started as a clash of enemies became secret fuck buddies with no labels and an expiration date, then somehow turned into love.

Not puppy love or infatuation. The real fucking deal kind of love. I might have been questioning it when I walked into this office, but now I'm absolutely certain.

What I feel for him is nothing short of head-over-heels, I'd-do-anything-for-you love.

The love you move mountains for. Cross oceans for.

The love you *give up* to keep that person safe from the psychotic asshole who will take anything you care about and annihilate on a molecular level.

I can't, I fucking *can't* let him do that to River.

Leaving me with only one option to protect him from Ted. The only one that makes sense, at least.

I have to leave him.

Break this off for good, even if doing so will be as if I cut my own heart out of my chest in the process. No matter how much I don't want to.

A war wages within me at the thought of living for the

foreseeable future without River. Seeing him, but not having him. Feeling so strongly for him, but not being able to express it. It causes an ache in my chest so sharp I actually rub the spot above my heart in an effort to soothe the pain.

I can't do that to him. Cut him out like he meant nothing. Fuck, I can't do that to *myself* when he's become fucking everything to me.

Only a fool cuts the cord to his one lifeline.

But I have to do it; to protect him from being a casualty in a battle that isn't his to take part in.

I'll take down Ted, somehow, some way. And I'll get River back.

Jesus Christ, am I losing my mind right now?

My body quakes with untapped emotions as I sit on Doctor Fulton's couch, head in my hands, debating my next move. I'd never be able take on Ted on my own, in any way, shape, or form. Not when it comes to this.

The only problem is, the people I know who can help, he has his hand in with them too. My stepfather's hold over people is limitless, something I've known for a long time but seem to just now be realizing.

"Is there someone, *anyone*, you can call? Who can help you in a time like this?"

Glancing up at her, I see tears welling in her eyes and immediately feel like the biggest dick in the world for assuming she had anything to do with this. I give her a brief nod, even though I don't know if I have it in me to make the call.

"You can call whoever it is from here, if you'd like. Take as much time as you need, Ciaráin," she says, grasping one of my hands in both of her warm ones. "The situation you've been forced into…" She trails off, shaking her head in dismay. "I feel for you. In all my years in this field, I've never had to deal with this situation. I understand if you have no desire to continue your sessions. Just know I'm here in whatever capacity you need me to be."

She leans back when I give her a nod again.

At this point, I don't think I can open my mouth to speak without some semblance of a scream or wail breaking though. But I have to do *something*.

Anything, *anyone*, that could help is better than nothing.

Swallowing my pride, I steel myself for the move I have to make, even though I'm not sure it will do much good. His number could have changed in the last four years since I've spoken to him. And if by some miracle he does answer, will he even want to talk to me? To help me?

When did everything get so fucked up?

My hand still shakes as I pull my phone from my pocket. I stare the name on the screen, a name that has been on my mind more and more as of late.

Sending up a prayer to whatever divine being that might listen, I jam my finger on the call button and wait. It rings once. Twice. Three times.

And the second I hear the click of the line being picked up, the words rush out of my throat in a choked sob I didn't realize I was holding back.

"I need you."

THIRTY-FOUR
Rain

An hour and one agonizing phone call later with someone whose voice I never thought I'd hear again, I'm pulling back into my apartment, lost in a haze of…nothing.

I feel absolutely fucking nothing.

Numb. Alone.

Defeated.

For once in my miserable life, I'm grateful I'm in therapy. Lord only knows how I would have reacted finding out about Ted, seeing the news, having my life flipped upside down, in any other place than the safety of Doctor Fulton's office.

Still lost in thought, I don't even notice my door is unlocked when I walk through it. That being said, I'm startled to find a pacing River in the space between my kitchen and living room, moving back and forth across the vinyl floor fast enough it might ignite under his shoes. I want to ask how the hell he got in my apartment without a key, but I'm too drained to care.

"Abhainn," I breathe.

He halts on a dime at the sound of the door closing behind me and for a second, we just look at each other, taking in the appearance of the other.

River's hair is a disheveled mess, like he's been raking his fingers through it constantly. His eyes are a dark forest being consumed by wildfire, filled with terror, sorrow, and uncapped amounts of rage. He's a wreck, but I probably don't look much better with the shit I've dealt with over the past couple hours.

Before I've had a chance to take off my shoes, set down my keys, or even fucking think, River is on me, pressing me back into the door of my apartment and devouring my lips. His tongue is in my mouth, tangling with my own, needy and desperate, as if we're both drowning and this is the only way we can figure out how to float.

In my case, that isn't far off from the truth because *goddamn* I didn't even realize how bad I *needed* this right now.

Needed *him*.

My hands are in his hair while his are busy clawing at my clothes, attempting to get them on my skin.

"I saw the news," he murmurs against my lips after he whips my shirt over my head, moving his attention to my belt. I lift his shirt from his body and quickly slip out of my shoes, then my pants and boxers once he pushes them past my hips.

"I don't want to talk about the fucking news," I growl, ripping the remainder of his clothes from his body before dropping to my knees in front of him. Not wasting a minute, I take his dick, thick and ready for me, in my hand before running my tongue down the length of it. Lapping at his cock, paying special attention to the head and sensitive underside, I move my hands around to knead his ass cheeks in my palms.

"*Fuck*, Rain," he hisses when my tongue makes contact with the underside of his dick before taking him deeper into my mouth, then down my throat.

My finger glides down his crack in a teasing caress before I slip it in further, finding the tight puckered hole that has become my latest addiction.

No, that's a lie.

He has become my addiction. Even if sex was taken completely out of the equation, I would still want every piece of him for myself.

But realizing more than sex is about to be taken off the table when it comes to him hits me. Everything, friendship included, is about to go up in smoke once this is over, no matter how much my heart aches at the thought.

This is the last time, I tell myself, chanting the phrase over and over as I continue to work River's cock.

The last time I'll have him like this. The last time I'll allow myself to trust another person with my body, my soul.

It's the last time I can let myself be truly fucking happy.

As much as I don't want to say goodbye to this man, who has come to mean more to me than my own life, I have to do it. I told myself, over and over again on my way home, each and every reason why I had to distance myself from River with everything coming to light about my...*relationship* with *Senator Ted Anders*.

Ted's hold on me, it's fucking deep. And I know he will go to any length to make sure he keeps it. I've learned firsthand he isn't above covering up crimes for his own gain.

Even crimes not committed by himself.

So ending this thing with River, I have to do it. If only for his safety.

My mouth moves faster at that thought, tears pricking in my eyes. Whether it's from his length hitting the back of my throat or the regret and anguish coursing through my veins, I refuse to determine.

"Baby," he groans, his hips thrusting with each bob of my head on his cock. "*Baby*, you need to stop."

I don't stop.

His words might say that's what he wants me to do, but his body is telling me the exact opposite. A niggle of guilt taps at my skull, reminding me of that first time in the shower.

No. This is different. It's not a hate fuck. It's goodbye.

River grips my hair roughly with both of his hands, and I prepare myself for him to fuck my face in a way that turns me on like no other. But instead of shoving his cock deeper down my throat, he yanks my head up and away from him, effectively releasing himself from my mouth.

"What are you doing?" His brows are drawn, and he looks... almost pissed. "I asked you to stop."

My brows furrow as I push back to my feet, suddenly aware of the vulnerable position I'm in kneeling before him. "Your body was asking for something completely different. By now, I think I know when to listen to which head."

River reaches down and yanks his boxers and pants back up his legs, leaving them unbuttoned and unzipped in the most tantalizing way. Panic begins to rise in my throat as his shirt also is thrown back onto his body, leaving his hair a tousled mess atop his head.

Wait. Is he leaving?

Running his fingers through his hair in an attempt to manage the wild locks, he sighs and leans into me for a kiss. "Baby, I get you're upset, but I think we do need to talk about it."

Talk? No. I just need him one last time before I have to be a fucking martyr and give up the one good thing in my life.

My jaw ticks as I reach down and redress in my underwear and jeans. "And *I think* you need to shut up and let me fuck you."

A soft chuckle leaves him, oblivious to my rising frustration. "You can't fuck away your problems. It doesn't make them nonexistent."

I let out a low growl from my throat, tension forming in my forehead. "Jesus Christ, you're not a very good casual fuck if you refuse to put out, Lennox. At this rate, I'll have better luck getting laid at a fucking convent."

River steps away, his eyes wide, clearly taken aback by the bitterness of my voice. "What is going on with you? One minute you're on me like you're ready to consume my very being and now you're..." he gestures with his hand, up and down, in my direction, "...*this.*"

A scoff of disbelief slips out of me before I can even think to stop it. "*This* is who I am. The *real* me," I snarl, jamming my index finger into my chest. "The me you knew in the cabin is long gone now that I have access to a regular supply of pussy on the west side of campus."

His face contorts into a grimace as disgust flares in his eyes, along with another emotion. Something like hurt, I'd imagine.

"Where the fuck do you get off?"

I cross my arms over my chest, cocking my head at him and squinting as if thinking in depth about my answer. "Well, if you would have asked me last week, or even yesterday, the answer would have been inside of you. But now?" I shrug with indifference, "I honestly don't give a fuck where. In fact, maybe I *will* hit up Sorority Row once you leave here tonight."

I know it's not true, but that doesn't keep me from feeling guilty because of those words. His mouth drops open slightly in a way that is almost comical as he gapes at me. Blinking in rapid succession, attempting to process my vicious retort. Clearing his throat, he shakes his head in disbelief before speaking again.

"What is happening right now?" he asks slowly.

"I guess you could say I'm ending whatever this is between us."

"How can we end things when we've never even started?" he rumbles, a menacing tone to his voice. "You're keeping me at arm's length, and *for what?* Don't you see all I want is to be here for you? You just won't let me!"

"And don't *you* see I don't give a flying fuck about what you want? I shut *everyone* out! You're nothing special!" I roar, my temper finally getting the best of me. I regret the words instantly, because they are the furthest thing from the truth, but I keep digging myself a deeper hole to bury myself in once he walks out of my life for good. "I don't *need* you, River. I'm not some fucking pet project you can sit here and try to fix. A broken toy you can put back together, piece by piece."

"I don't want a goddamn project," River shouts as he throws his hands down, his voice booming through my tiny apartment.

He swallows roughly and shakes his head before speaking again in a gravel-filled voice. "Jesus Christ, Rain. I just want *you*."

My brain screeches to a halt as it processes his declaration.

I just want you.

Never in my life has anyone uttered those words to me, and I didn't realize until now how much I really needed them. How desperate I was to be desired, not sexually, but in general. As a whole person.

My body ignites in warmth at the recognition that *this* is what it feels like to be—fuck, loved. But the moment is short lived when the reality of my situation drenches me in despondence like a bucket of ice water, reminding me that River and I...we will never work.

And that thought? The sting of it might as well kill me.

"Well, I don't want you," I grind out, the words tasting bitter on my tongue, but I have to swallow down the poison I'm forcing down both our throats. It's for his own good.

If only he would take my words at face value.

"That's such horse shit, and you know it. You had my cock down your throat not ten minutes ago"—he glances to my crotch— "and you're harder than fucking steel as we stand here screaming at each other, yet you don't *want* me?"

My fingers on both hands latch onto the strands of my hair. Partly in irritation, but mostly so I don't do something insanely stupid, like touch him. Or fucking kill him.

Lowering my voice to a deathly soft level, I force myself to toss out insults. It's the only way I can think to get him to leave, to forget about me and what we had while up in the mountains.

"Here's the thing, Abhainn. My cock might want you, but he isn't the one in charge. Even if he was, all he wants is that tight ass and warm mouth. But the thing is, he can get that just about anywhere." Ripping my fingers from my hair, I press my palm to my chest. Speaking in staccato, slow and deliberate, I hope he gets the message. "*I*, on the other hand, *do not want you.*"

The lies keep piling up, but I hold my ground, daring him to challenge me again. Part of me, hell, *all of me* wants him to keep fighting, if only to keep him here in my apartment and in my *life* for a little while longer.

But I can't stand knowing I'm hurting him and inflicting damage to the bond we share with every word leaving my mouth.

River spins away from me, walking through the living room to the wall of windows. He leans his arms against the glass pane, resting his forehead against them, causing the muscles of his back and shoulders to ripple under his shirt. "You can sit there and pretend nothing happened in that fucking cabin, but we both know you'd be a fucking liar. So what? Now since we're back, you're done with me?" Turning back to face me, he slants his body back against the wall. The fire in his eyes is burning me from across the room as a bite is mixed in with his tone. "You told me you didn't want to lose me. But what you're doing right now is making sure you do just that."

Holding my arms out to the side, I let out a quick huff of agitation. "What did you think would happen? We'd come back from our fuck fest in the mountains and magically be a couple? Live happily ever after?"

Because yes, that is exactly what I thought.

I don't let my thoughts derail me. I advance on him, pinning him in place with a vicious stare as I release the most blasphemous words to ever leave my mouth. "You were nothing more to me than a place to stick my cock. That's all it ever was, and that's all it will ever be."

Nausea started overwhelming my senses a while ago with each and every lie I threw his way, but that one causes bile to rise in my throat. I think I might actually be sick.

I hate this. I hate myself for having to push him away. I hate River for not *letting* me. I hate these circumstances we've found ourselves in. I hate Ted motherfucking Anders, and the rest of the goddamn world.

I hate that I can't love him the way he deserves to be loved.

River winces, tears starting to well in his eyes as he searches mine. "Is that really how little you think of me?"

No, baby, I think the world of you. I'd give the whole damn thing to you, if only I knew how.

But instead, I go in for the kill. "And therein lies the problem." I smirk, my voice tainted with calamity. "Because I don't think of you at all."

River pushes me, spitting mad and boiling with rage. His hand comes to my throat, gripping me there firmly before spinning me so my back hits the wall.

I don't make any efforts to fight him off. Even *I* am self-aware enough to realize the shit I'm spewing is more than enough reason to be knocked the fuck out.

Only he doesn't deck me.

He slams his mouth to mine again, his soft and supple lips attempting to coax the truth from me, and it's physically painful not to cave and kiss him back. I know he's trying to pull some emotion from me, to get me to reveal my lies to him.

Which is why I don't kiss him back.

I let his lips mold against me, not giving an inch, even when his tongue slips along the seam of my lips before prying them apart. Something like a moan, or maybe a sigh of frustration, leaves him at my compliance. His teeth nip at my mouth and his hands roam my still naked chest. All of my willpower is being focused on the fact that Ted will kill him without batting an eye if he ever found out what River means to me, giving me the strength I need to resist his onslaught.

River breaks away after a moment, realizing I won't give him what he's seeking, before leaning his forehead against mine. My eyes slide closed at the contact and I simply breathe him in, filling with disappointment that our last kiss was an empty one.

"If you put half as much effort in trying to make us work as you are in trying to rip us apart right now, we could be fucking unstoppable," he mutters softly. "We'd be everything."

His words hit me like a bullet to the chest.

We already are, my love. You are everything. I only wish I could tell you that.

For a moment, the tiniest of a nanosecond, I debate giving in and telling him everything. Not just about Ted, but about every dark and depraved thing I've done, that has been done to me, that was beyond my control.

Not just the half-truths I've given him about the molestations, and the drug and alcohol use. There's also the full story of Deacon's death. The cover-up. The suicide attempt.

The flinch.

All the sources and subjects of my nightmares, laid on the table for him to see.

But instead, I simply sigh and forge down the road I've already paved for myself. "We don't fit, River." For once, the words leaving my lips are the cold, hard truth. "We're water and oil, and those two things never fucking mix. You have to accept that."

His eyes search mine, green as the tree we cut down for Christmas, and every part of me is breaking at the pain in them. "How can I accept something that isn't true?"

Goddamnit, mo grá. Please don't make this harder than it already is.

I lick my lips and sigh. "Just because you don't want to believe something doesn't mean it isn't true."

"But it's *not true*," he urges, pushing off my chest and putting space between us. "You and I both know it! And I can't sit here and let you lie to my fucking face anymore!"

My teeth sink into my tongue so hard the taste of copper fills my mouth. Tossing my hands, my exasperation back with a vengeance, I shout the words at the top of my lungs, "Then fucking *leave*, River! Get the fuck out of my apartment and my fucking *life!*"

River's teeth latch onto his bottom lip and he nods his head absently. When his eyes flash up to mine, they are brimming with resentment.

Good, Abhainn. Hold onto that.

"I swear to God, Rain. If I walk out that door, there's no coming back from this."

My jaw ticks at his threat because *fuck me,* that is the last thing I want, but the one thing I know has to happen. I clear my throat, forcing a bored expression to slip on my face. "Do I get bonus points if I act like I care?"

How can it be so easy for me to verbally abuse him like this? If I really love him, how can I treat him like this? When you love someone, aren't you supposed to fill them with that feeling, rather than force hate and disdain down their throat at every turn?

It's then when I remember what River once said to me in the cabin, before we agreed to our arrangement.

Better be careful, Rain. Love and hate are two sides of the same coin.

And while those words ring home, it was what he followed up with that is the real kick in the nuts.

You'll be falling in love with me before you know it.

Fuck. He made us a self-fulfilling prophecy, ensuring we really did blur the lines between love and hate after all.

His scoff brings me back from my reverie, forcing my eyes to rise and clash with his. Harsh and gruff, he spits his next words at me, seething. "Far be it for me to expect you to give a shit about anyone but yourself."

The words hit me like a freight train, and I almost laugh at the irony behind them.

I'm doing this because I care, mo grá. I care about you, about your safety, more than I do about my own happiness.

I only wish he could see that.

Tears prick behind my eyes, but I force them back, looking up at the ceiling.

I have to do this. There's no other option anymore.

No matter how much I want to drop to my knees and beg him to stay. Tell him I was lying before. None of it is true. Every word I've spoken, every look of disgust or indifference, was just another wall I know he's strong enough to break down or climb. He has to know I would gladly give my life if only to make sure nothing bad ever happens to him.

But. He. Can't. Know.

If he did, he'd only fight for us harder, demand more truths I'm not willing to give him. Pieces of myself I might never be able to reveal.

But even so, he has to be blind to not see I'm in love with him.

My eyes flick to his, and I bite back a sob when I see how fucking shattered his expression is right now. "Just go. Go, and don't come back." It's the last thing I want, the furthest thing from what I *need*. Which is why the next words leaving my mouth might be the most colossal lie of all. "I can't do this anymore. Not with you."

His eyes search mine, for what, I'm not sure, before running his tongue across his teeth. River scrubs his palm over his face, then through his hair, before gripping the back of his neck.

Over the course of knowing each other, I've seen him take hits on the field that would send lesser men packing. Watched him get harassed by his father because of his sexual orientation. *Personally* made him my very own punching back to use and fuck and fuck *with* whenever I deemed fitting.

But I've never seen him look this defeated.

Something inside me snaps, causing me to turn away like the coward I am. I can't do this.

I can't look at him as I break his fucking heart. Not when I want to be the one he trusts to hold onto it forever.

The tell-tale sound of the door opening signals he's finally learned to listen and is leaving, but the sound of his footsteps pause. His relenting sigh fills the room before he speaks, effectively cutting me with his words.

"I didn't want to fix you, only save you from your nightmares. Too bad I didn't realize the real nightmare is you."

And then he goes, like I fucking asked, the door slamming shut behind him. Leaving me in the empty space surrounding me like I once left him in that shower.

Bloody and fractured beyond repair.

THIRTY-FIVE
River

M y hands shake and my body ripples with rage as I storm down the stairs of Rain's apartment building, making a run for my car.

How fucking dare *he?*

Treating me like shit before, when we didn't know each other the way we do now, I can get over it. But tossing me to the side, insinuating all I was to him was a convenient way to pass time? Just another hole to get off in? That what happened up in the cabin was anything less than fucking *fate* intervening and handing us the person we're meant to be with...maybe even forever?

That's unforgivable.

How can he think we don't work, that we don't *fit?* Jesus Christ, what does that even *mean?*

He can compare us to water and oil until his dying breath, but it's not true.

He and I... hell, we're fluid in motion. Moving together in waves, synchronized at the molecular level, rising and falling as a single entity. Just like *any* body of water does.

It doesn't matter if it is from a mountain spring or the city gutters. Pure enough to drink or salty like the ocean. Clear and beautiful or dark and murky. A lake or a stream.

A river.

The rain.

When all's said and done, water is just that...water. It will always mix.

After a devastating flood. After brutal hurricanes.

After rain falls.

Water will always fuse, and you would never have known it was anything but one.

So I don't understand how he doesn't realize...we're one in the same.

Wrenching open the door to my Range Rover, I hop in and floor it back to campus and the parties on Sorority Row before classes resume tomorrow. I know full well I'm too pissed off to be driving right now, but it's only a five-minute drive, and I need to get somewhere with booze as fast as fucking possible.

Maybe find Abbi and see if she would be down for a quick...

Goddamn. I can't even finish the thought without my stomach threatening to revolt.

What have you done to me, baby? What the fuck have you done?

Pulling up to the Tri Delt house, I throw my car into park and sprint to the entrance where a red-haired girl I recognize from the cheer team is manning the door.

"Well, if it isn't our very own QB one." She smiles in a way of greeting before handing me a cup and ushering me with her hand to go inside. "Don't have too much fun in there while Abbi isn't around. You know how territorial she gets over you."

Well, shit. Abbi isn't even here.

I guess this is Jesus's way of keeping my dick in my pants, even if I could stomach the idea of fucking someone *other* than Rain at this point.

"Thanks," I tell the girl as I step through the threshold, popping my dimples with a smirk. It feels flat and wrong on my face.

Inside the house, I find a blur of bodies dancing and grinding to a cover of "Talking Body" by Five Hundredth Year as if they have no fucks to give about classes resuming tomorrow. I don't blame them, because I'm most definitely in the same boat at the moment.

Spotting a couple linemen from the team near the keg, I head over and start up conversation, pouring myself a beer. Then another. And another, before I realize cheap ass beer isn't going to give me what I need tonight.

Andrew notices me staring into the bottom of my third empty cup before pulling a handle of Jameson from a pantry cabinet. Uncapping it, he pours three fingers worth into my solo cup before discreetly returning the bottle to its rightful place.

"Bottom's up, Len. You look like you need it," he nods, motioning for me to take a swig of the amber liquid, a shade lighter than Rain's eyes.

Fuck me. Everything always comes back to him.

Tossing back the whiskey, I down the contents of my cup in two gulps, relishing the smooth liquid coating my throat before sending a warm burn into my stomach.

I gesture to Drew for a refill, to which he simply laughs and refills it yet again.

And soon, I'm surrounded by bodies on the couch, finally buzzed enough for my liking...or maybe I'm just drunk? I don't know anymore, nor do I care. I'm reveling in the freedom intoxication brings to my senses, loving that I can't see straight, let alone find it in me to give a flying fuck about Ciaráin motherfucking Grady and the vile shit he spews from his mouth.

No, no, no. Don't think about him, I chant internally, but it's too damn late. I should have known I'd never be able to escape him, even when I'm drunk.

My brain fixates on thoughts of him, especially his *damn mouth.* His mouth I can't seem to get enough of, no matter how fucking shitty he seems to make me feel every time he opens it.

I'm finally starting to realize everything about him is that way.

He tastes immaculate, like he came straight from heaven, yet all he ever does is try to send me to the deepest pits of hell. Like an addictive poison, he's in my blood and I'm hooked. I can't seem to quit, even though I know it will send me to an early grave.

Groaning, I rise from the sofa and amble my way to the bathroom, where I lock the door and lean against the wall in a drunken stupor. Loathing engulfs my senses as the room spins around me, and I find myself stewing in its toxicity—in hate. Hating Rain, hating myself, the entire goddamn world.

But the one thing I despise most of all?

Love.

Who the fuck needs that shit, anyway? Apparently not Rain,

because that's what I was ready to offer up to him. I was willing to put everything, my heart and fucking soul, on the line for him. To give us a chance and be with him through all the bad shit that's about to come hurling at him faster than a freight train.

Hell, I'd be lying if I said I didn't already give him those pieces of me. We both know I did. It was obvious, from the very beginning, I was *in this*. I gave him all of me, and instead of giving me all of himself in return, he just engraved his name on my heart, claiming it as his, but never truly wanting to *own* it.

And my soul? *Our* souls?

When they touched, it was nothing short of divine, and for a moment, I thought this is it. This is what it feels like to find your other half.

Your soulmate.

The person you're meant to belong to for as long as you walk this earth. The person who can mend the fractured portions of yourself with one look, one touch, one kiss. The being who holds the key to the parts of you that you never knew were missing.

But with us, that isn't what happened.

Our souls tore each other apart rather than healed the broken and battered pieces. But oh, how they loved the chance to dance together in a tangle of passion and destruction.

For the first time in the history of my academic career, I skipped class due to overindulging in alcohol. My body aches from sleeping on the bathroom floor, I'm hungover as fuck, sick to my stomach, and wishing, more than anything in the world, I could punch something.

Unfortunately for me, the university pays for my education on the contingency that my left hand be viable for four years of football.

Asshole higher ups and their fucking semantics.

I can't wait until after next season when I actually have the ability to toss a few punches into a bag. Or someone's face. Whichever at this point. But I suppose a workout in general is the next best thing, even if I'm literally sweating out Irish whiskey as I do it.

Irish. Goddamn it, Rain.

I shake my head, trying to clear my thoughts of him as music blares around me in the weight room, but instead of picking up the lyrics by The Word Alive, all I hear is Rain's voice, whispering *Abhainn* to me that last night at the cabin, over and over in my ear as he worshipped my body with his own.

The night before everything crumbled around us, leaving us in shambles, trying in vain to pick up the pieces.

"One more," a voice breaks through my thinking, finally pulling me from the haze that has clouded my mind.

My triceps and deltoids are on fire as well as my pecs when I press the bar for the final rep, loading it back onto the rack. I shake out my arms, shooting up on the bench into a sitting position and glance over at Garrett. As quarterback, I'm not supposed to bench press, which Garrett knows full well. Thankfully, he keeps his trap shut though, since right now, I need the burn it brings.

Pain cancels out pain, you can only feel one form of it at a time, and if I can make my body ache enough, maybe it will ease the one in my heart after all the bullshit with Rain.

That's exactly what it is too. A bunch of fucking bullshit.

Every single word out of his goddamn mouth was a goddamn lie, I'm almost positive. I'd be willing to bet my life on it.

The real question is...*why?*

Why did he lie? Why is he trying to push me away? Why is he hiding things from me? Why didn't he tell me Senator Anders was his stepfather?

Why? Why? *Why?*

All these damn questions have been searing in the back of my mind since I woke up this morning, with a headache to last the ages, and I had a chance to comprehend everything he said. No matter how many times I replay the conversation in my brain, I come up with the same conclusion.

It doesn't make sense.

Which, in all honesty, isn't much of a conclusion at all. *But,* because it doesn't make sense, I might be able to get some answers, so long as Rain will actually speak to me once I manage to track his ass down.

I tried calling him this morning, when I was *sober,* thank fuck, but he didn't answer. To be expected, since we were screaming at each other not even twelve hours prior. I could keep calling, hoping he will eventually pick up. Except he would probably end up blocking my number, if he hasn't already.

Maybe go to the registrar's office and get a copy of his schedule and switch into one of his classes, so he has to see me every day? No, that's a little too much.

There's always the option of staking out his apartment like a damn stalker and waiting to ambush him into a conversation.

Fuck me. I'm not proud of the fact that I'm seriously debating the last one, but clearly I'm getting desperate. It hasn't even been a full twenty-four hours since our…fight? Break up? Falling out?

Whatthefuckever.

The point is, I'm already going half insane and probably took ten years off the life of my liver last night alone. There's no way I can go through the rest of my damn life feeling the loss of him, knowing there were all these unanswered questions that might give me some form of closure.

I love him enough to let him go, if that's what has to happen. But I at least deserve a conversation not involving jabs and insults shot out like bullets aimed to kill.

"Ain't that Grady? I thought he lifted at a different time during the off season?" Garrett asks randomly, effectively pulling me from my newly formed stalkerish tendencies. I glance up at him to find him pointing out the large glass window separating the weight room from the hallway to Coach's office, the locker rooms, and other parts of the team's facilities.

Rolling my eyes, I attempt to refocus my thoughts when his words finally register.

Grady.

My head whips around, and my heart practically leaps out of my chest because, *holy shit,* God really does exist and performs miracles because Garrett is right. That's most definitely Rain walking down the hall, heading toward the exit. I'd recognize that ass anywhere.

Not wanting to waste a moment, I jump to my feet and bolt for the door, grabbing my duffle along the way. I glance at Garrett over my shoulder, calling out to him. "I need to talk to Grady for a minute, let's pick this up tomorrow!"

I don't even bother waiting for a response from the freshman, jogging down the corridor in the direction the man—who I'm positive is the love of my life—just disappeared down.

I run after him, surely looking like a lunatic, but when I burst through the doors leading to the quad, I don't see him right away.

Fuck, did I lose him?

I almost laugh at the irony of that thought, for more than one reason. Because, yeah, I did fucking lose him. I lost his overwhelming presence, his intoxicating laughter, his dirty smirk and flirtatious smiles. I lost all of him. Every fucking piece.

But in reality, I know that isn't right, because you can't lose something that was never truly yours to begin with.

Spinning in a circle, I frantically search for him, knowing he can't have gotten far. Deciding he's most likely heading to his car, I make a beeline for the parking lot the student athletes use across the open quad.

My palm slams against my driver's side door as I dig with my other in my duffle frantically looking for my keys. A flash of orange flies through my peripheral and I instantly recognize it as Rain's Jeep Wrangler.

Thank God for his ostentatious-colored vehicle.

I watch as he peels out of the parking lot and down the street away from campus. Clutching my keys in my fist, I scramble into the driver's seat, closing myself inside the car, starting the engine and throwing the Range Rover into reverse.

It doesn't take long to catch up to Rain's vehicle as he weaves his way through the busy traffic of Boulder on a weekday afternoon. I follow a few car lengths behind him, making sure I stay close enough to always beat a light if needed, but far enough away he wouldn't be able to recognize me through his rearview mirror.

It could be any Rover on the streets of Boulder, I tell myself, seeing as they aren't all that uncommon in the area. *He doesn't know you're tailing him like a fucking creep.*

Huh. Well, I guess I'm really not above stalking after all.

My fingers blanch against the wheel, my grip is that tight, as I continue to trail behind Rain, "in the dark" by Bring Me The Horizon filling the silence of the car. Even as he branches off onto less busy streets, heading in the direction of the Boulder Municipal Airport, I still feel my body on edge.

Why is he going to the airport?

Sweat breaks out on my forehead, or maybe it was already there from chasing after him, as we pass through a gate with ease leading to the tarmac.

He had to have noticed my car by now and realized I'm following him. Ours are the only two vehicles entering the airport, from the same place, at the same time.

He has to know, right?

I slow to a crawl, watching as Rain continues down the tarmac, passing multiple hangers before pulling to a stop a few yards from with what looks to be a private jet sitting idle just past the parking spots.

As discreetly as possible, I slip my car into a parking spot at the hanger directly next to the one Rain is at, about a hundred yards away.

A football field. That's what is separating me from the love of my life, the man I want to *fight* for, right now.

But not for long.

Opening my door and siding from the seat, leaving the engine still running, I head in the direction of Rain, who is standing with his back against the passenger door of his Jeep.

A twinge of unease pricks at my brain, causing the hairs on the back of my neck to stand on end. Who is on the plane?

It's not...Ted...is it?

There's no way Rain would be driving to the airport to pick up that fucking *molester* like he's dropping by for a fatherly visit.

No, that's not fucking possible. It would be a cold day in hell before that happened. Rain might not have given me all the details, but I saw the disdain in his eyes, heard the loathing laced with anguish in his husky voice when he spoke of his stepfather that night in our makeshift fort.

Hatred isn't a strong enough word to describe the way Ciaráin Grady feels about Senator Theodore Anders. If I can be one hundred percent positive about *anything* when it comes to Rain, it's that.

Speeding to a brisk walk, I close the distance between us. Distance I'm *never* going to allow to stay between us after this.

One way or a-fucking-nother, we're hashing our shit out, here and now.

Half a football field to go, the door to the plane begins lowering to the ground, revealing a set of stairs leading to the plane's interior.

Forty yards. Rain rises to his full height, taking a step toward the stairs.

Thirty yards. A form appears at the top of the stairs, clearly male, but hidden in the shadows still.

Twenty-five yards. *Please don't be that fucking bastard, or I swear to God, I won't be leaving here unless it's in a body bag or handcuffs.*

Twenty yards...

My eyes must be playing tricks on me...because *Roman fucking Mitchell* steps from the shadows of the plane.

And my entire world collapses, the sky slamming into the surface of the Earth, and nothing, not even a cockroach, could manage to survive this level of desolation.

I'm frozen in place as, to my horror, Roman begins descending the stairs, looking like the rich prick he is, dressed in a navy suit and a light blue dress shirt, the top button undone and a navy tie hung loosely around his neck. But it isn't his expensive look or his expertly styled hair that fracture my heart into thousands of pieces.

It's the smile on his face, bright and white and fucking perfect, when his arms wrap around Rain with familiarity. And, if that weren't bad enough, Rain returns the gesture, coiling his arms around Roman in return. As if they had just seen each other a couple days ago, rather than living the past four years in silence.

Four fucking years.

A hand punches through the flesh and bone of my chest, snatching my heart in its grip. Slowly, painfully fucking slow, the fist tugs and pulls and rips until my heart is yanked free from my chest. Because that's when I realize...this is it. The end of the line.

We're water and oil, and those two things never fucking mix. You have to accept that.

How could I have been so blind? Of course he was right.

We don't mesh.

From the very beginning, Rain fought this attraction between us, whereas I was open and accepting about it. Eventually he caved, succumbing to the lust and desire we felt for each other, but even when that happened, he didn't actually let me in enough for us to ever be considered anything more than fuck buddies.

It's a means to an end, that's it.

I never actually believed those words from him; I thought he was putting up a front, a wall aimed at keeping me out.

Except, as I watch Roman and Rain still locked in their embrace, it seems Rain really was keeping me at arm's length, all the while willingly using me as his guinea pig, his goddamn test dummy. And that is what he did. *Used* me to sort out his sexual preferences. He took hold of my mind, wormed his way into my heart, made me fall in-fucking-love with him. But like he said, only as a means to an end.

You were nothing more to me than a place to stick my cock. That's all it ever was, and that's all it will ever be.

My throat constricts, eyes blurring with unshed tears as I finally understand all I ever was...was a placeholder. Now that he has seemingly accepted himself, thanks to my help, why wouldn't he be with the man he wanted desperately, the guy who knows him better than I could ever dream? Though it wasn't for my lack of effort.

I shut everyone out! You're nothing special! I don't need you, River.

No, Rain, clearly you don't when you had someone else all along.

The gaping hole in my chest where my heart used to be aching, pleading for the piece of me that's now missing, I now know I'll never get it back. Not fully. Still, my hand flies to my chest, rubbing absently over the space where my heart once lived as if to ease the pain.

After what seems like a million years and thousands of unshed tears on my part, Roman pulls away from Rain, one hand still on his upper arm, giving him a warm smile. His mouth moves, the words unintelligible from this distance, and he bites his lip at Rain's response before letting out a throaty laugh.

My eyes fixate on the back of Rain's head and the silky dark brown hair as I try to regulate my breathing, but it's no use. I've never experienced a panic attack before in my life, but I think that is what this is.

Chest pain, labored breathing, nausea and dizziness.

Sure as hell sounds like a panic attack to me. That, or a heart attack.

Except I no longer have one of those.

Rain opens his body toward me, his hand motioning for Roman to hop into his Jeep, and it's in that moment I'm finally spotted.

Two pairs of eyes snap to me instinctively, one I know to be the color of golden whiskey I'd recognize as well as my own. The other, a dark hazel green, so dark they're almost black, as I learned from the images online that brought this whole mess upon us.

Roman glances between Rain and I before his eyes finally settle on Rain, and he speaks. What he says, I couldn't tell you, but whatever it is, Rain nods in response, his eyes never leaving me.

Tracking Roman's movements with my gaze, he opens the back door of the Jeep, tossing in a bag I didn't notice he was holding before climbing into the passenger side of the vehicle. Our stares lock once again through the windshield, and I hold his eyes, fighting to assert myself, even when it's pointless.

Clearly, the line has already been drawn and I'm on the wrong side of it.

I know I should leave, walk back to my car with my head held high, let him realize on his own what he is missing out on. Swear on my life, I try.

But *godfuckingdamnit*, why can't I make my feet move?

The minute Roman breaks our connection, my eyes slide closed in an effort to keep the tears at bay. He's not fucking worth them. Neither of them. At least, that's what I tell myself, when the truth is Rain is worth every goddamn hardship, every minute of walking through hell and battling his demons.

He. Is. Worth. It.

But apparently I'm not the only one who knows that, otherwise Roman wouldn't be here, after all this time, attempting to make things work between them. No matter the pain it might cause me, the tension that will break us once again, Rain chose him. But in doing so, he will also turn us back into the people we were before we went to that cabin.

That might be the worst part of this whole thing.

To think, after everything we went through—the hatred, the intoxicating desire, and the soul-consuming connection we formed—we're going back to what we were before. What we said we would never be again.

Enemies.

My eyes slowly open and make their way back up to Rain, and I find his amber stare is still locked on me. From a distance, I can't get a read on them, no matter the amount of effort I put into analyzing them.

My mind and my feet are at war with each other, one holding me firmly in place, but the other desperate to propel me forward in order to reach him. But, as if sensing my internal struggle, Rain spins around and climbs into his vehicle. As the door slams behind him, without a backward glance, and the roar of the engine starting drowns out the whimper that falls from my throat, I know.

I realize I was wrong.

We're not enemies anymore.

We're something much worse than that.

Strangers.

THE END...FOR NOW

A Note From the Author

I know you're probably feeling a lot right now.

Angry, hurt, betrayed. Empty, broken, confused.

Completely pissed off with that cliffhanger.

I wish I could tell you I'm sorry for that, but I'm not a liar. I'm *glad* you're feeling these things because that means you were able to connect with River and Rain on an emotional level and that is *exactly* what I wanted for this novel.

Just know that everything you've felt? I had to feel it multiplied by a thousand when I wrote down each and every word of this book. These two own such a large piece of my soul and I honestly don't know if I'll ever recover the part of myself I gave them in writing this book.

Now, don't fret. **This story is far from over.** All your questions, because I'm sure you have plenty, will be answered in the second half of this duet. After Rain Falls is coming and it will be the conclusion to River and Rain's story.

I hope you fell in love with River and Rain as they started this journey together. More so, I hope it was hard for you to choose which one you loved more. Pieces of who I am are inside each of them, and while their journey of self-discovery might not be one I've taken myself, it has been cathartic on a multitude of levels in working out my own issues.

I don't know exactly where I'm trying to go with this other than saying *thank you* for making it this far. For the kind words and reviews and messages and just *everything*. For loving them even a fraction of the amount I do.

Thank you, and all my love,

— CE Ricci

Acknowledgments

Wow, okay. So I wrote a book and actually published it. That's a little insane to me because it's been a dream of mine since I was in middle school and to see it come true is honestly the greatest feeling in the world. But I didn't take this journey alone, so I have plenty of people I need to thank for helping me reach this point.

First, thank you to Abby Capps. You know as well as I do that this book would never have happened if it wasn't for you pushing and pushing me to give M/M a chance. I fell in love with it because of you and that alone has me forever indebted to you. To be honest, River and Rain wouldn't exist in this capacity if we'd never met. You're the greatest friend, beta/alpha, and PA in the world and there will never be a day I won't be forever grateful to have you in my life. I value your friendship, opinion, and love so fucking much. Thank you for putting up with me and all my insanity. **I love you. River is yours.** (Except when he's mine, obviously).

To Jess, for sticking through this with me from the beginning when I started writing again over a year ago. For giving me a place to go write when I needed silence and letting me bounce ideas off you, and for not judging my overactive imagination when it comes up with dozens of new ideas before making it through the first one. And for being my damn soulmate, no matter what our husbands have to say about it. I love you long time, my little ENFP.

To my other alphas/betas, Pernilla, Rita, Haley, and Mickey. Thank you for sitting there and listening to me call this book trash probably a million times, helping me work through plot issues, dealing with my

ADD tendencies, hyping me up, and making me stick this journey out. Y'all are the real MVPs.

To my super mega early ARC readers, Taylor, Sam, and Yaneli, for letting me send you the most ridiculously cryptic message asking you to blindly look for something in this book with absolutely no other direction and just going with it. Your feedback was helpful times a million, so thank you!

To Elle, for bringing me into the bookstagram community, being a hella supportive friend to go to for help with literally any question I could have, and encouraging me to write when I was questioning myself. Thankful everyday that Vaughn brought us together, babe.

To Liza James and KV Rose for answering my numerous questions, holding my hand through this process, and mostly for letting me know I wasn't alone in every single thing I was thinking and feeling while trying to publish this book. Your friendship and guidance is invaluable to me and I'm thankful for both of you everyday. The love I have for the two of you is endless.

To Kate, for creating these stunning covers that help me redefine my brand and are true to River and Rain's stories.

To Amy Briggs for being a bomb editor and helping me perfect River and Rain into something that I can be proud of and in turn, making me a better writer. THANK YOU.

To Zainab for proofing these two and refusing to let them out into the wild without being in tip-top shape!

To anyone I've forgotten to thank so far. Just know that it wasn't intentional, but there are so many on this list I was bound to miss something or someone. Thank you for loving and supporting my forgetful ass.

Lastly, to all of you. The readers. For taking a chance on me and reading my debut novel. For hyping me up on IG and Facebook and anywhere else. For messaging me your kind words and sending me gorgeous edits. All of it gives me life and makes the struggle to get here all the more worthwhile.

Thank you, everyone. From the bottom of my heart.

About the Author

CE Ricci is an international best-selling author who enjoys plenty of things in her free time, but writing about herself in the third person isn't one of them. She believes home isn't a place, but a feeling, and it's one she gets when she's chilling lakeside or on hiking trails with her dogs, camera in hand. She's addicted to all things photography, plants, peaks, puppies, and paperbacks, though not necessarily in that order. Music is her love language, and traveling the country (and world) is the way she chooses to find most of her inspiration for whatever epic love story she will tell next!

CE Ricci is represented by Two Daisy Media.
For all subsidiary rights, please contact:
Savannah Greenwell — info@twodaisy.com

Printed in the USA
CPSIA information can be obtained
at www.ICGtesting.com
CBHW050028061024
15442CB00010B/723